OUT OF EXILE

OUT OF EXILE

THEIR ANCESTORS WERE EXILED.
THEIR CRIMES HAVE NOT
BEEN FORGOTTEN.

KATHERINE FRANKLIN

A CIP record for this book is available from the British Library.

ISBN 978-1-915007-08-7 (E-book edition)
ISBN 978-1-915007-09-4 (Paperback edition)
ISBN 978-1-915007-10-0 (Hardcover edition)

This is a work of fiction. Any similarities to real persons, living or dead, are coincidental and not intended by the author. Characters are the products of the author's imagination.

No content in this book or its cover was generated, to the author's knowledge, using machine-learning algorithms or artificial intelligence.

Cover design and formatting by Design for Writers.

First edition: 2024

Published in the United Kingdom.

Contact: katherine@FranklyWrites.com
Visit www.FranklyWrites.com

To mum,
For doing very many things that I am very bad at expressing thanks for,
but nonetheless very appreciative of.

And for enjoying these books. Hi, mum!

PREVIOUSLY, IN *BILE AND BLOOD*...

WHILE PALIA HAD LOST her memories of Ferrash, she was still dead set on finding him and trying to fix the mistakes she had made during her fight with the Magister. Still, she didn't know where he'd holed up and events had made it clear that she needed to learn how to handle the Empyrean with less accidental lethality. As the new magister, her old friend Fabien assigned the empyrric Archivist Lilesh to train and watch over her.

Ferrash had returned to the Protectorate world of Hesperex with revolution on his mind. For years, he had operated as the head of a mysterious secret police known as the Reiart, and had used his position to draw power away from the Protectorate's governing authorities. The crowning moment, now that he knew the old magister's plans, would be the destruction of the Empyrean.

Palia ended up following a false trail Ferrash had laid to Munab, where the civil war had gone hot. She made it off the planet alive, but Bek lost an arm after being crushed inside a mech, and they were no closer to finding Ferrash.

In a bizarre twist of fate, the two of them met at Fabien's wedding, the magister having ensured Rythe's support in the war by choosing to marry one of their nobility. Ferrash tried to slip away, but relented when Palia recognised him.

They returned to Hesperex together, but Ferrash's plans were all unravelling. The Keepers even sent his own empyrric daughter to kill him, and he was forced to kill her in self-defence.

Distraught, dying, with Bek imprisoned and with his long-brewing revolution erupting too early, Ferrash escaped Hesperex with Palia. Their goal – to use the prime nexus as a focal point for the Empyrean's destruction.

They succeeded in this goal, but they also destroyed much of the technology their galaxy relied upon. They couldn't even stay to fix their mistakes, as the prime nexus reformed into a gateway to an unknown region of space. Waiting on the other side was an unfamiliar ship, calling itself *Ammit* of the Allied Reach, and declaring the new arrivals under immediate arrest...

Have you forgotten what happened in *Bile and Blood* or want to find out more about the *Galaxy of Exiles*? Check out the wiki via Frankly-Writes.com/lore.

CHAPTER ONE

TWENTY SOLDIERS CAME TO escort them from the ship – or perhaps they were police, or guards. Ferrash couldn't tell. They wore sky-blue suits of powered armour, close-fitting compared to the bulk he might expect and like nothing he had seen before. Their boots made the telltale clanging of magnetic clamps as they shifted position in zero-G. Ferrash eyed them through a haze of pain. Even weightless, the wound his daughter had dealt him before he had escaped Hesperex made him want to curl in on himself. If anyone asked him to put his hands up, he might keel over.

Clustered around the bottom of the ramp, the guards' faceplates remained dark and unreadable; twenty rifle barrels pointed at him, Palia and Lilesh.

Three of them guards weren't human. They rested on short hind limbs and knuckles, their heads like armoured anvils, their faces hidden. One towered above everyone else, over three metres tall. While the other two still stood taller than the humans, they were at least a metre shorter than the big one.

Ferrash stared. He wondered, trembling from the pain of his recent injuries, if going through the Prime Nexus – or the gate, or whatever it had become – had actually killed him. Now his mind conjured armed guards and aliens like giant, hunched primates to give him an interesting afterlife. Except there was no afterlife, and everything hurt, and the guards wanted to arrest them.

'Well?' Palia asked from beside him. She had barely been able to keep still while the ship was being towed inside this space station, and tension strained her voice. 'Are you just going to stand there, or will you tell us why we're being arrested?'

Why wasn't she more interested in the aliens? She'd built a career around xenobiology and now several xeno somethings were staring her in the face, she... well, she had her priorities straight, that's what. Ferrash's grip on the ramp support was so weak he could barely keep from floating away. When Palia tried to slip an arm around his waist to steady him, all twenty rifles twitched. She stayed put.

After a pause that implied the guards were about as shocked as Palia should have been, one of the humans – or perhaps an alien of human shape, since he couldn't see beneath the armour – jerked their head towards the bottom of the ramp.

A woman's voice issued from the armour's speakers: 'Come with us.'

Ferrash nudged himself forwards and floated down the ramp, arms raised as high as he could manage without reopening the gash in his side. Palia floated faster and moved on ahead. A handful of the guards clunked up either side of the ramp to surround them.

'Move!' one of the guards behind him said.

Ferrash looked over his shoulder. Lilesh hovered in the ship's corridor, blank-faced, dull-eyed, unmoving. An empyrric from birth, she hadn't been the same since the Empyrean died. Since they had killed it.

Killing the Empyrean had killed a galaxy. Getting arrested was appropriate, all things considered.

Lilesh finally began moving after a guard prodded her in the back. They floated out past the end of the ramp. Something tugged at Ferrash's heart as he left the ship behind, in the hands of strangers. He might never see it again.

What he *did* see, very clearly now, were the three aliens. The tall one had shoulder-mounted cannons jutting out to either side of its massive head. Those were either overkill or it couldn't hold weapons any other way. The top section of its helmet, slightly domed, pulsed in pale yellows and reds.

Ferrash shuddered. Even if he had been in good condition, running wasn't an option.

Two guards took hold of each of them by the shoulders to move them through the air, which would have felt ridiculous if not needing to move himself hadn't been such a welcome relief. They led them across a metal-panelled floor through an empty hangar big enough to fit a dozen ships the size of theirs. The hangar didn't have any viewscreens, just muted red light from overhead strips. When they reached the exit, a circular panel slid out of the wall towards them. The guards took them around the other side of it then stepped onto the vertical panel itself, pulling their charges after them in a vertiginous change of orientation.

Ferrash closed his eyes to dismiss a sudden wave of nausea. His feet touched against the surface and when he next opened his eyes, they were moving... well, it felt like up. This was a lift. They were standing on the floor. They were going up. But telling himself that did little to convince his vertigo.

He risked a glance at Palia, but she seemed to be coping better. Looked pretty pissed, in fact. Maybe she'd done zero-G training as part of her mandatory service.

Lilesh, of course, remained vacant.

'Where are you taking us?' Palia asked.

No one replied.

'Fine. If you can't tell us that much, where are we? The Confederated Outer Reach? Somewhere even further that we haven't heard of?'

Two of the human guards shared a glance.

As they rose, Ferrash's weight began to return to him, settling onto all the aches and pains the lack of gravity had eased and intensifying them.

Ferrash cleared his throat. 'So you've probably been ordered not to talk to us, but can you at least tell us if we'll need to walk much further? Not sure how far I can manage.'

The dome on the big alien's head pulsed and a wave of trumpeting noise echoed around the lift shaft. Ferrash winced and took an involuntary step back into one of the guards. The translator in his implants did nothing.

'I don't understand,' he said, though couldn't hear himself past the ringing in his ears.

The alien swung its head round to another guard, who shrugged and said, 'Must not have rahtuan in their galaxy.' They nodded to Ferrash. 'You're injured?'

Palia answered for him. 'The wound's plugged but he's lost a lot of blood. It needs looking at.'

The guard looked him up and down, and Ferrash resisted the urge to stand straighter.

The guard said, 'It's not far to where we're going, and once things are done there, we can get you transported to the hospital.'

As they spoke, the lift reached the top of the shaft and emerged from the floor of a wide corridor with a curved floor that made Ferrash feel dizzy to look at. He stepped out onto a well-worn carpet that might once have been orange, supported by a guard to either side. Even Palia wobbled a bit as she took her first step. The sensation of falling pickled along his spine, but he had a floor beneath his feet and something like gravity held him to it. He knew it was because the station was spinning – he'd seen as much on the way in, when their armed escort ship *Ammit* hadn't been obstructing the view – but being inside it was altogether different. Even if he hadn't been arrested, it wasn't like he'd have many other options. He hadn't seen any planets in this system on the way in.

'It's just through there,' the female guard said, indicating a door amidst a wall of living greenery. This continued as far as he could see both ways down the corridor: two living walls, a faded orange ground, a light-blue ceiling, like someone had tried to emulate an avenue of hedges open to the sky. A few people peered out from rooms along the corridor, fearful expressions on their faces. One man, who had been walking their way, turned up his nose and spun around. Turning his nose up at them or those 'rahtuan' aliens? Ferrash didn't have the context to judge.

Someone prodded him in the small of his back, sending pain shooting through his left side where his daughter had burned a chunk of flesh away. He half hissed, half groaned, earning a worried look from Palia, and stumbled towards the door. It slid open. He filed through with Palia and Lilesh in tow. Before he could turn around, the door slid shut again and locked with a loud, final *clunk*.

He grimaced at Palia, then glanced about the room. 'Weird choice of cell.'

A semi-circular desk made of some pink-hued, crystalline substance took up most of the space. It had a flat diamond of many shifting colours set into the front. When Ferrash tried to make sense of the pattern in it, his vertigo returned in full force. He took a step forwards and thumped down onto a strange, cushioned lounger before he lost his balance completely and fell over. There were two of these facing the desk, and Palia took a seat on the edge of the other. She leant forwards with her elbows on her knees, her chin resting on bunched fists.

Ferrash tried to dredge up some reassuring words but found himself sinking into the lounger instead. He shuffled along to the section of lounger that had a backrest and settled against it, his eyes growing heavy.

Above him, in a ceiling-wide viewscreen, the stars beckoned. When you travelled as much as he did, you never really got used to a fixed canvas of stars. But there were usually bits you could recognise, no matter where you went. He always used Duenin, the binary star system in the Hegemony, as an indication of how far away from home he was. He recognised nothing here. Nothing but the circular gate hanging above him, bridging the familiar *there* to the alien *here*.

'Ash, look.'

He blinked awake at the sound of Palia's voice, unaware he had shut his eyes. 'What?'

Palia pointed to the stars, to the ring gate that used to be the prime nexus, and he squinted at it. The membrane that stretched across its interior flashed and a dark shape passed across it before becoming almost invisible against the void. Flashes of flame guttered along the ship's side. As the ship moved, it spun through a slow, uncontrolled arc.

'Someone else is through,' he said. But who? Who could have survived what they had done? By boarding the prime nexus and destroying the Empyrean in one swift blow, they had removed the tool the galaxy relied on for so many things. Inertial dampers were one of those things. They had turned their ship's off just in time. From the wreckage he'd seen when they'd emerged from the transformed nexus, no one else had managed. Acceleration suddenly unopposed, things inside ships would have found themselves outside pretty fast. He remembered the ice, glittering amidst debris, freshly flung from ships' stores. It would have gutted those ships in its exit.

Wherever they were now, the same hadn't happened. And those were survivors falling through the gate. The thought sobered him.

A few more ships passed through the gate, each at different angles and speeds. Two crashed into each other and a bright flare washed across the darkness. The explosion flung debris in every direction, knocking another ship off course as it passed through the gate. That ship crashed into the edge of the ring and began to spin nose over tail, its front end buckled. Ferrash wanted to feel something at the sight of it, but it was all so distant, so quiet. Just lights in the void.

Around them, despite the muffling of the living walls, the sounds of the station made themselves known. Several people ran down the corridor outside. Something *scuttled* past. Ferrash hoped it was something like the hauler robot he'd used to carry his mother's prison up the mountain on Hesperex, rather than a giant bug. He couldn't handle giant bugs right now. A few people shouted to each other. Somewhere further away, a resonant *clang* heralded a ship releasing from docking clamps.

He should stand up. This was his fault, all of it. He had picked up where the Magister had left off. He had planned to destroy the Empyrean. He had convinced Palia and the Hegemony to help him. He should stand up and face his deeds, but he figured he'd faint if he stood too long – not to mention get a crick in the neck staring up at the ceiling.

'We did that,' Palia said, her voice so quiet that he could have imagined it.

His guts twisted into a knot. 'I did. I shouldn't have talked you into it.' On the other side of that gate, everyone he knew could well be dead. Bek, poor Bek, who Ferrash had been forced to leave stuffed in a vat somewhere on Hesperex. Only a matter of time until the Protectorate chose to kill him, if Ferrash's mother hadn't fulfilled her promise and got to him first, if the Protectorate even still existed. And even then, Ferrash had left him in the middle of an uprising that would leave its food production capability in tatters, with no way to import food or receive aid. When he went back, if he was ever able to, would he just find a frozen ball of ice where his friend should live?

Palia began to pace a few moments later, forwards and back across the carpet, her face contorted with anger and grief. She even stopped and waved at a door on the other side of the desk, but it wouldn't budge.

Ferrash kept his eyes fixed on the ceiling, on the ships fleeing from the mess he had created, on the ships going towards them from the station. A ship like that had demanded Ferrash's arrest the moment he had arrived. Were they going to arrest all of these survivors, too?

A ball of dread settled into the pit of his stomach. Whoever these people were, they seemed well organised, and already had opinions about people from the other side of the gate. Whatever their plans, they couldn't be good.

CHAPTER TWO

SHAHIDA HADN'T EXPECTED TO be interrupted. It wasn't the done thing while conducting brain surgery, after all, even if the machinery did have enough failsafes built in that she couldn't knock anything in surprise.

The chime came at the door again, quiet, yet insistent. 'Doctor al-Shimaya,' said the rahtuan on the other side, her unfiltered trumpeting significantly less quiet than the door chime, 'the Speaker would like to see you.'

She frowned, made sure the operation was at a safe stage to hand over, and turned to her colleague. The man raised an eyebrow behind the bubble of his face plate.

'Take over from me,' Shahida said.

He nodded, not needing an explanation. While the Speaker sometimes invited her for a chat and a cup of coffee, she wouldn't interrupt surgery unless it were urgent. Shahida knew that. Her colleague knew it, too.

With a last glance over her shoulder at the patient in the theatre on the other side of the window, she left the control room. When the door opened, the bulky figure of the rahtuan, Pashena, stepped back on her knuckles to make room for her.

Shahida craned her neck to look up at Pashena. Her helmet had been shaped to leave the five inflatable sacs on her head exposed – two on her chin, two on her furred cheeks and one large sac on her forehead.

'Did the Speaker tell you what she wants?' Shahida asked.

Speaking with her mouth rather than the sacs now that Shahida wasn't behind a wall, Pashena shook her head and said, 'Not to me, not to anyone, only that it was urgent. Come.'

They started along the curved corridor of the ship's medical quarter together, gilded geometric patterns stretching up the walls to either side, the spray from a nearby fountain misting the skin of their environment suits. Pashena's red-and-white patterned fur flashed beneath transparent sections of her suit as she walked. Occasionally, they passed members of the three species that made up the ship's residents, but for the most part this area was quiet.

'Do you think her summons has anything to do with the news?' Pashena asked.

Shahida quirked an eyebrow. 'The news? I've been in surgery for a couple of hours. Enlighten me.'

Pashena regarded her for a few seconds, her sacs inflating and deflating, passing through a range of colours in excitement. She wanted to stay quiet for whatever she was about to say.

They passed out of the medical quarter onto one of the ship's main thoroughfares. The trees lining each side of the central transit rail looked like their fruit would be ripe soon, and Shahida's stomach growled at the thought.

Once they had settled into a clear transit capsule and begun down the rail, Pashena breathed out the excitement she had been holding.

'Warden Station,' she said. 'There's been activity at Warden Station.'

A tingle of excitement and fear wound through Shahida's body. She sat up straighter. If the gate at Warden Station opened now, in her lifetime...

She gathered her thoughts and asked, 'What kind of activity?'

'No one knows. They're not saying. But there's been increased movement today.'

Shahida forced herself to temper her expectations. 'They're probably just doing practice drills. You remember when they did a weapons test there a few years ago and everyone thought the gate had activated?'

Pashena hummed – a deep, reverberating noise that made Shahida's sternum ache. The weapons test hadn't been officially sanctioned – not by officials uninfluenced by the tuk-a-wa hive mind, anyway. They had wanted to see if they could destroy the gate, the only way the exiles could ever return to the galaxy they had once called home. The uproar that followed their attempt hadn't been loud enough. Shahida hoped they hadn't made another attempt.

At last, Pashena said, 'This feels different. And with the Speaker calling upon you...'

'I'll see what she has to say. Let's hope it's good news.'

A blurting laugh shook the capsule. 'What good could ever come out of Warden Station? Whoever comes out of that gate, if they ever do, they won't be prepared for the reception the tuk-a-wa want to give them.'

Shahida sighed. 'No. No, they won't.'

They disembarked the transit capsule by the entrance to the Speaker's chamber, where Pashena resumed her position guarding it and left Shahida to her business. The Speaker's guards had an easy job and mostly ended up running errands for the woman. No one in the fleet would ever harm the Speaker, and if some outsider who wanted to ever found out she existed, got aboard the *Inzekir* and reached this spot, many other precautions would have disastrously failed. Pashena had a prestigious role, nonetheless.

Shahida strode through the foyer, the painted history of the Speaker and her people looking down on her from either side amidst silken drapes. Behind the last of these drapes stood a wide door, also gilded, and it slid open to let her into the security airlock. She waited in the small room while it scanned her for tuk-a-wa parasites. About three minutes later, the system beeped from wherever it was installed in the ceiling and a green light came on above the plain door on the other side of the room. She retracted her faceplate, stepped across to the door and knocked once.

'Enter,' a deep voice called.

Taking hold of the handle, she waited a second for it to verify biometric information with her suit, then pulled it open and stepped inside. The Speaker sat illuminated by a yellow lamp across the other side of a polished wooden table, two cups of coffee steaming on its surface. But it wasn't her who had spoken, and in the dim light, it took Shahida a few seconds to make out the person who had. The Speaker's guard stood by the wall. He wore an all-black environment suit shaped as a robe, only a curved black surface showing beneath his hood. His hand rested, as ever, on the hilt of the curved blade at his hip.

'Leave us,' the Speaker said, her voice commanding despite its youth. The guard inclined his head and retreated to another room.

Shahida pulled out the chair opposite the Speaker and sat, feeling underdressed. She usually visited in her embellished purple robes, not her plain blue medical suit. At twelve years old, the current Speaker may have only come up to her chest, but she always dressed to impress. It was part of the job description when you housed millennia inside your head. Her robes were red and black, festooned with goldwork, her helmet topped with an elaborate headpiece that held loops of beads from the end of a thin nasal strip.

They might have been Shahida's robes, had the former Speaker died younger. The Speaker was a whole made of two halves: the host and the parasite; the mortal and the immortal. The Speaker's replacement host changed every ten years until their death, and Shahida had been the replacement until three years ago.

Once they had both sipped from their cups, the Speaker asked, 'Have you heard the rumours?'

'Of something happening at Warden Station? Yes, but no more than that.'

'Well,' – she placed her cup down and spun it idly by the handle – 'would it interest you to know I've received a message from the station commander?'

Excitement returned to Shahida in a rush. 'Kaktek? What did he say?'

The young Speaker fixed her with old eyes, shocking green against her dark skin. 'The gate has opened.'

Shahida exhaled and leaned back in her seat. She took another sip of coffee, hoping the bitterness would cut through one shock with another. 'So it's gone, then. The Empyrean.'

The Speaker snorted. 'It certainly took them long enough.'

'But you wouldn't have called me here if that was all Kaktek told you.' She narrowed her eyes, wishing the Speaker wasn't always so fond of games. 'And Kaktek wouldn't have contacted you unless there was more to it.'

Nodding, goldwork glittering in the half-light, the Speaker said, 'A ship came through the gate. They have been arrested, as per standing orders, but Kaktek hasn't had chance to speak with them yet. He sent me a message as soon as the ship arrived.'

'He's afraid the tuk-a-wa will claim them, isn't he?' The exiles had been banished for using the Empyrean against the tuk-a-wa millennia ago. Hive minds held long grudges. Making the exiles part of their mind – giving them all parasites, stripping them of all individuality – could be their preferred flavour of revenge.

'He fears a great many things, I imagine, and claiming them as hosts is perhaps the worst outcome. Death will be first on the tuk-a-wa's mind – a petty revenge borne from a mind that should no longer be able to feel such.' She pouted like the child she partly was, but her eyes sparked with the deep anger of a species the tuk-a-wa had driven to the brink of extinction. 'Kaktek wishes the Grey Sails to go to the station. I have told you of the resistance networks, have I not?'

Shahida nodded.

'So difficult to remember what I have told to whom, these days.' She sighed. 'Kaktek is an instrumental player, hence his contact with us. He expects trouble. This moment may prove pivotal. It may prove the moment we have been waiting for.' She eyed Shahida over the top of her beads.

For a moment, Shahida sat there, unable to find words. For such a moment to come in *her* lifetime... The Speaker had waited hundreds of lifetimes for this moment.

'It might be too late,' Shahida said. 'They may already have been infected. The tuk-a-wa's influence remains widespread, and it only takes one parasite.'

Without scanners, you couldn't even tell a host apart from an uninfected person. Here in the migratory Grey Sails' fleet, in the ships they all called home, they built scanners into every room. Perhaps living on ships meant they had always been more cautious than the planet-bound. In any case, the rest of the galaxy was not so cautious.

'You don't need to tell me that.' The Speaker smiled, but the humour didn't reach her eyes. 'In any case, the resistance leadership has agreed. We're making our way to Warden Station now, or so they tell me. We will be the first of the resistance to arrive. Of all our ships, the *Inzekir* was closest and best prepared. How fateful, that it should be my ship.'

Shahida nodded. She wasn't sure she would call it fate, but it was a stroke of luck.

'I just hope we arrive in time,' she said. How many people had been on that ship? Even if the tuk-a-wa infected one of them, there might be a chance to find someone uninfected. But even one infection would be a crime. The tuk-a-wa wasn't meant to take unwilling hosts. That's what had caused the first war.

Still, none of this explained why Shahida was here. This news would spread through the Grey Sails' fleet soon enough. 'What do you need me for?'

This time, the Speaker's smile did reach her eyes. 'It's likely we will need a representative on Warden Station. I trust everyone on this ship, but I know you well, and I know how you act. You have received the same knowledge and training as I did, before I Spoke. Will you do this? Will you represent the Sails? Will you be our voice?'

Struck by the importance of the occasion, Shahida bowed her head. 'I would be honoured.'

'It will be dangerous. You know this. Maintain your suit. Do not leave it under any circumstances. Don't trust anyone, even Kaktek, for anyone beyond our fleet could be tuk-a-wa. Trust yourself and your instincts only.'

'I understand.' But she had never left the fleet, and the thought of leaving it for the unfamiliar corridors of Warden Station made her throat dry up. She swallowed. If she took a wrong step, if she got infected, she had a husband and a son who would both miss her. So, she understood perfectly well. 'How would you like me to act?'

'I cannot dictate actions for you, child,' said the ancient in the body of a girl. 'Only observe at first, but act if you think there is a need to do so. Go armed, go protected, go aware.'

'I will.' Shahida dismissed worries that she wouldn't be ready. She had sparred only yesterday. Physical preparedness wouldn't be a concern, but she would be outnumbered. 'How long until we arrive?'

'Five days, give or take.' The Speaker drew a piece of candied fruit from a pocket and raised it to her lips before reconsidering. 'That's plenty of time for you to spend with your family, Shahida. I've already put the paperwork through with the hospital. You have time off, if you wish to use it.'

A small wave of relief washed through her, and she smiled. 'Thank you. I'll do that.'

As the Speaker popped the piece of fruit in her mouth, Shahida resealed her faceplate and saw herself out, already thinking of the safe where she kept her knife and gun, and trying to decide which of her suits would make the most imposing impression.

CHAPTER THREE

PALIA BEAT HER FISTS against the door. 'Hey!' she shouted. 'How long are you going to keep us here?'

She hated being cooped up in this tiny room, with its stupid eye-strain desk and its stupid ceiling viewscreen. The view pressed down on her, even when she wasn't looking at it. Space, dark and endless, weighed down on her shoulders, taunting her with all the destruction it contained. Here Palia was, a whole galaxy away from home and surrounded with aliens, but she was stuck in a tiny room and none of the aliens were *speaking* to her. She ground her teeth and sat down on the weird couch next to Ferrash, who startled out of a light sleep. The smart bandage he wore would be trying to keep him stable, but it couldn't work miracles – his skin had taken on a pallid tinge that she didn't much like the look of.

She frowned at the couch. This part of it had no back, only an extra section that jutted out in front and behind. If she had to hazard a guess, this part was designed for those big aliens, the rahtuan, they'd seen earlier. One limb either side of the spur, chest supported by the middle. Whatever language they spoke, they couldn't understand it. Was that why it was taking so long for someone to come and see them?

Lilesh hadn't sat down yet. Palia chewed at her lip. 'You okay?' No response. 'Lilesh? Archivist!'

The woman jolted at Palia's use of her title and stared at her, blinking. Palia had never seen her so at a loss.

'Sorry.' Lilesh put a hand on the back of the other couch and used it for support as she walked around it to sit down. Then she perched there, her back straight, her face pinched. The woman had only been Palia's teacher for a short time. Palia didn't know her well enough to say anything that might help.

Instead, she placed a hand on Ferrash's shoulder. 'Ash, can you find a way—?'

Before she could finish, the door behind the desk slid open and something scuttled in on eight legs. Palia bolted from the couch and backed away, her heart hammering. Ferrash tried to do the same but winced and sat back down.

It only came up to her waist, but that didn't stop the sheer alienness of its appearance giving her an instinctive urge to flee. Two large eyes peered at each of Palia's party in turn, swivelling independently from atop eyestalks on its head, multifaceted and shimmering in the light of the ceiling panels. In two long arms that sprouted from its upright torso and ended in pincers, it held the handles of a small box. Palia counted two tiny limbs tucked away under what might have been its mouth – or maybe they were part of its mouth – and four other limbs that ended in wide black paddles folded against its chest. Flashes of orange and blue formed opalescent patterns on its crystalline scarlet carapace.

It hesitated for a moment, then walked over to the desk with what seemed like exaggerated slowness compared to its entrance. It placed the box on the desk, then stepped back. Then, after unfolding the four paddles from its chest, it held them out to either side like flags.

Palia bit her lip, struggling to dismiss the image that the alien was shrugging and thinking, *How did these humans end up in my office?*

Iridescent colours began to flash across the surface of each paddle, much like the pattern of the diamond on the front of the desk, but always in motion. Every now and then the alien added a series of clicking noises.

A hurried masculine voice issued from the box in the centre of the room. 'I am Kaktek-ek-tsikik-tset, of the kluqetik species, in command of Warden Station. I apologise for my lateness. Your arrival came in the middle of mating season. Were you harmed or touched on your way to my office?'

Palia said, 'We got prodded by guns a bit and manhandled through zero-G, but not...' She trailed off, wondering why touch was so important and whether it had anything to do with the mating season the alien had just described.

'Manhandled? Was there skin-to-skin contact? Did anyone breathe out unobstructed in close proximity to your face?'

'What? No.' Screwing up her nose, she said, 'Look, Kaktek, uh...'

'Kaktek is fine. The translator is overzealous. Our names are never shortened in our language.'

'Okay. I get that we're not from around here and you probably want to quarantine us to make sure we haven't got any diseases you're not used to, but if that's what all this is about, you could have just left us on our ship for a while. The people who collected us were all wearing suits, but... well, now we're here, and we've gone through an open corridor, and you're here with us without a suit. What's going on?'

Kaktek settled onto the chair behind his desk and rested his torso on the frontrest. 'Ideally, yes, you would be quarantined. But it is more urgent that we understand the situation that brought you here. That's what I would like you to tell me.'

'The situation that...' Palia scoffed. 'How we came to be here is none of your business. You can't just arrest everyone that happens on by!'

Ferrash shifted on the couch beside her. 'Palia...'

She glared at him, then returned her gaze to Kaktek. 'No. Why are we here? Why couldn't you just talk to us while we were still on our ship?'

One of Kaktek's legs twitched up and down as he stared. A nervous tic, perhaps? 'This is Warden Station's job. Anyone who comes through that gate, we arrest. In an ideal situation, it's more of a formality.'

'A formality?' Her voice pitched up a fraction more than she had intended, straining at her throat. She took a breath and dialled it down a bit. 'How about explaining things first as a *formality*?'

Ferrash spoke up before the translator could begin on Kaktek's next sequence of colours, and Kaktek placed a pincer over it to stop it speaking over him.

'You said "in an ideal situation". If you always expected someone to come through, what's not ideal about this?'

'I will explain,' the box said for Kaktek. 'Just let me hear your story first.'

'Ours is probably longer.'

'There is plenty of time, and your story could help me understand how to organise those still coming through the gate.'

With a sigh, Ferrash said, 'Okay then,' but Palia cut him off before he could continue.

'No,' she said. 'We're not telling you anything until you tell us what's going on.' She pointed to Ferrash. 'He needs to go to the hospital as soon as possible.'

One eye swivelled to take in Ferrash. Palia found herself wondering what sort of vision Kaktek had, whether he could see Ferrash's injuries without having to be told.

'The brief version, then,' Kaktek said. 'Or as brief as I can make it. You claimed yours was probably longer, but unless you remember your society's origins, I doubt it.'

Colours only danced over Kaktek's paddles for about five seconds before going blank again. The translation from the box lasted much longer. Palia supposed the colours condensed more information into them that it was possible to convey with sound.

'There is another galaxy on the other side of the gate. Your galaxy. Or rather, the galaxy your ancestors were exiled to, long ago, for crimes committed in this one. I don't know what you believe about your origins, but humanity began on a planet in this galaxy. Around a quarter of a hundred thousand years ago, there was a war, and your ancestors were on the losing side. The exile followed that.'

Palia waited for Kaktek to say something else. Perhaps he had wanted to wait for the translation to finish so he could gauge everyone's reaction and continue. But he said nothing.

'That's too brief,' she said. 'What were we exiled for? Why are we only humans? It can't have been humanity versus everyone else if you exiled all the losers – there are still humans here.' At least the handful she had seen had *looked* human.

'Not all were exiled, only those directly involved, and it was a predominantly human faction. Most factions are – humanity is the most numerous species besides my own. I believe there were political reasons why they were so many of them and so few of us in that faction, but it was a long time ago and I, personally, don't have the details.'

'So it's well documented?'

Kaktek paused. 'To the extent that it may as well be living memory, yes.' He rose from his chair again and began to pace in fast, tight circles behind his desk. Palia had to close her eyes to stop her head spinning at the sight. The tapping of his legs died down a few moments later, and she tentatively opened her eyes to see him standing, vibrating with pent-up energy.

Nerves crept up from her stomach. Was he angry? Or just fidgeting because this communication was too slow for him?

'As for why you were exiled, I'm not sure if you still use the same name for it, but are you aware of a weapon by the name of the Empyrean?'

Her breath caught in her throat. 'Yes.'

Kaktek clacked their pincers. 'I wish you would have told me your experiences first so I could not pollute your knowledge with the truth. But as it is... Your ancestors wished to deal their enemy a blow so strong that the war would end. The Empyrean was the weapon they created to do so. They wove the weapon into their blood and used it against their enemies. The weapon succeeded. The damage to their enemy's species was irreparable. This is the crime they were exiled for, and the Empyrean was effectively exiled alongside the last of those who wielded it.'

Kaktek's words struck Palia even more than the view of the destruction she had recently caused. The Empyrean *had* been designed as a weapon. That cruellest of powers that stripped life and emotion from anything it touched, that had been used as a tool to suppress billions in the Protectorate... And if it was just that – just a weapon, just a tool – then Varna wasn't real. It was just a side-effect, or something more fundamental to the way the Empyrean worked. Varna, the afterlife people in the Hegemony had believed for so many millennia, was a lie.

How had they forgotten? Which of the many near-extinctions their galaxy had been through had been the one that lost this knowledge? Or had their ancestors covered it up out of guilt? Even Lilesh had the wherewithal to look stunned.

Ferrash drew a deep breath. 'So the gate let us back because the Empyrean's gone?'

An eye snapped back to regard him. 'Is it?'

'We destroyed it.' Weariness hung on Ferrash's words. 'Not without cost.'

'From the wreckage falling through the gate now, I take it you had to fight to do so?'

'That's not even half the problem.'

Now the eye shifted between him and Palia, with the other resting squarely on Lilesh. 'I don't understand. The gate was programmed to open when the Empyrean was gone. What problems could destroying the Empyrean possibly cause? The people who wielded it would simply not be able to do so anymore, surely?'

Palia frowned. 'Was it *only* used as a weapon, originally?'

'To my knowledge, yes. A particularly potent one, but that was all.'

'We used it for more than that,' Ferrash said. 'Transportation. Communication. Inertial damping.'

'Ah.' The word came as four concerned flashes of orange. 'It was used for these purposes everywhere?'

'Apart from Rythe, maybe, yeah.'

Kaktek sat down again. If he always moved this much, Palia would have expected the carpet to be more worn.

'Then you have left your galaxy in a state of chaos, I imagine.'

Ferrash leaned forwards, wincing as he lost the support of the backrest. 'If your technology doesn't rely on the Empyrean at all, you can help. Send ships through the gate. Find people. Help them. A lot of people would have died the second it went, but the rest of them... they need support. Very few planets are self-sufficient.'

Very few in the Protectorate, at least. Half in the Hegemony would comfortably manage... if nothing had crashed into them.

'Again,' Kaktek said, 'I find myself in a position where more information on your galaxy would be helpful. Unless you have jump stations your side of the gate, any aid we send through could take decades just to reach some planets. We have time, even if they don't. There's nothing we can do about that. So tell me your story.'

Palia glanced over to Ferrash, unsure how to start, unsure *whether* to start. Kaktek still hadn't elaborated on why their being touched would be a problem, unless it really was down to the mating season. She didn't know why, but she felt that unspoken concern was more important than most of what they'd just been told.

It was the archivist who spoke first. Lilesh looked Kaktek in one of his eyes, still sitting straight as a pole, and said, 'It began when a group that would come to be known as the Protectorate parted ways from the Hegemony...'

CHAPTER FOUR

FERRASH CAME TO CONSCIOUSNESS gradually, disorientated and confused. It took him a few moments of fuzzy-headed calm to realise he was horizontal, then a few more to remember where he was. At that point, Palia's distinct lack of calm brought him crashing back to the present.

'Ash? Ash, can you hear me?' She leaned over him, concern in her eyes.

Ferrash squinted under the bright lights that haloed her head and waved her off. 'Just thought I'd lie down.'

'You fainted.'

'No, no, just having a rest,' he said, despite ample evidence to the contrary. And because Lilesh wasn't reciting history anymore, and he was pretty sure his fainting was the cause, he added, 'Don't stop on my account. I'm comfortable here for a few more minutes.' The fuzz in his head dulled the pain in his side.

'You're going to hospital. Now,' said Palia, and Ferrash couldn't quite tell if her sternness was directed at him or Kaktek.

He didn't have time to complain that that was overkill. Bare seconds later, a scuttling sounded in the corridor outside, and the door opened, and the next thing he knew he had been strapped to a gurney. Two of Kaktek's species – kluqetik – lifted him in one smooth motion and carried him back through the entrance.

Palia tried to jog after them, but they whisked off down the leafy corridors faster than she could run. Soon, her footsteps faded in the distance.

Ferrash fidgeted under the straps. Those were also overkill. He felt better now – though a wooziness pervaded his head and his thoughts seemed to want to rocket all over the place.

His journey gave those thoughts plenty to work with. The two kluqetik carrying him were supervised by another two with rifles. They moved fast enough that he couldn't get a particularly clear impression of his surroundings, and he found it hard to focus regardless, but it was better than nothing. Greenery covered every surface but the floor, and furniture of the same crystalline substance as Kaktek's desk appeared every now and then in communal areas. Humans, rahtuan and kluqetik bustled through the corridors, all but the naked kluqetik in deep brown uniforms.

At one intersection, his escort had to slow to let a group of armoured guards past. They marched half a dozen vatborn prisoners between them, each wearing the deep red of Protectorate spacers, freshly fallen through the gate. Station personnel parted to let them pass, muttering amongst themselves and throwing dark looks their way.

How could one galaxy still hate another tens of thousands of years after losing contact? Their ancestors had 'permanently damaged' another species, though he didn't know the details. Were the people here really willing to carry blame across so many generations? Or did one of the species here have such a long lifespan that it was recent history to them? Ferrash shook his head. He'd leave that one to Palia to find out.

More important: escape routes. He might as well take advantage of this trip and try to identify some.

They couldn't chance the central dock they'd arrived in, which put their ship out of the question. The lift took ages. Even if he could open it on his own – and his upgraded implants had partially used nexite pathways to operate, which relied on the Empyrean, so were now limited – someone on the station would probably notice and stop them. Besides, there might be guards down there. *Should* be guards down there, if they were sensible. And if he could figure out a way past them in a zero-G environment, he'd still need to open the dock's airlock and get them outside. Too complicated. Too many steps. It wouldn't work.

The outer docks, though, they might work. He'd seen eight docking booms on one side of the station's rim on his way in, jutting out like the legs of a round table. Ships docked to either side of the booms with their bellies towards the centre of the wheel so they maintained the same semblance of gravity. If he could get them onboard one of *those*, they might be in business.

He kept an eye out for where the boom entrances might be. Hard, at this speed. More and more often, he caught sight of Protectorate and Hegemony uniforms. Relief and guilt mixed a painful concoction in his chest. At least some had survived.

They passed through a wide gathering space with a large viewscreen set into the ceiling. Another ship fell from the gate. They'd travelled quite a way across the station already – the viewscreens must all use one static viewpoint, or the gate would just rotate past all the time.

'How many people live here?' he asked his escorts. They replied with flashing colours, which of course he couldn't understand. He cursed silently. 'You can understand me, right?'

One of them bobbed its eyestalks, which might have been a nod, but could equally have been, 'Please shut up, you irritating human.'

'Reckon the hospital can fix me up with a translator or something?'

His escorts exchanged a glance and a few swift patterns on their paddles. Then the one that had nodded waved one of its eyestalks to a right-angle and back, and Ferrash was none the wiser.

So sudden that the glare left him blinking, the surrounding greenery gave way to pristine white surfaces. His escorts deposited him in a small room with a window along one wall. Instead of leaving, the two who had carried the gurney stepped back, retrieved rifles from holders on top of their carapace, and joined the other two in a protective square facing outwards. Interesting. What were they protecting him *from*?

A human doctor rushed in a few seconds later, red-faced and panting. She started towards him, but the nearest kluqetik barred her way. It clicked angrily – all clicking sounded angry, though – and pointed to the window. The woman huffed and went out again before reappearing in the room on the other side of the window. Something beeped, and her voice – accent unfamiliar – came through a moment later.

'Where are your injuries?' she asked.

Ferrash listed them off to her. Every now and then she cast a salty look at the kluqetik, but she nodded when he was done. Then a robotic arm swung down from a gimbal on the ceiling. Ferrash settled himself in for an uncomfortable few minutes.

Being drugged-up on anaesthetic meant Ferrash couldn't pay as much attention on the way back as he had going to the hospital. In fact, he must have fallen asleep, because one second he was being carried out of the operating room under the put-off gaze of the doctor, the next, greenery surrounded him. He blinked, rolled his dry tongue around his mouth and shifted uncomfortably on the gurney. The doctor had exchanged his wound's old dressing for some kind of healing gel – a scaffold, she called it. It felt cold and pulled at the nearby flesh. Apparently he was missing a chunk of kidney, and the only reason he hadn't died shortly after losing it was thanks to the Empyrean's tendency to cauterise the wounds it made.

The kluqetik slowed and Ferrash craned his neck to see their surroundings. A corridor passed by, devoid of plants, with what looked like an airlock door at the end. Darkness, stars, and a long tree of docked ships showed in a viewscreen above it. A docking boom. He ticked that off the list.

Cool air washed over him as they passed into the next room and vines waved in the path of an air conditioner. A door hissed closed behind them. The kluqetik put his gurney down, barely jostling him, and motioned for him to stand.

Ferrash swung his legs over the side of the gurney, wincing at the unusual sensation of gel compressing in the side of his torso. The room swam around him and he fought off an odd floating sensation. Before he could even think about hauling himself up, another door opened to his right and Palia rushed in, her eyes wide.

'Ash!' She took hold of his arm and helped him to his feet, then pulled him into a hug. Ferrash leaned into the embrace, eyes closed, drawing comfort from the proximity. She smelled of Hesperex, of snow and metal and blood.

He pulled back, but kept his hands on her arms and searched the worry on her face. 'I wasn't exactly gone long. What's wrong?'

'Nothing.' She shook her head, white hair whipping around her face. 'I just... I think it's best if we all stay together.' With that, she gave the kluqetik a pointed glance.

<The rules are there to keep you safe,> one of the kluqetik replied, in his head.

Ferrash whipped his head round and frowned at the alien. Were they telepathic? But no, that message had come through his implants' interface...

'They pushed a translation update out to our implants,' Palia explained.

'How? They won't be familiar with the interface.'

'One of the survivors they picked up was a software tech. He heard me asking about translators and offered to help.' She shrugged. 'Apparently it wasn't too difficult.'

'Right.' At least he'd be able to tell what was going on without the help of the box in Kaktek's office. Not that anyone would give them the whole picture. 'What's this about rules?'

Palia grimaced and led him over to a bench against a mossy wall. Three of the kluqetik chose that moment to leave, with the other remaining on watch.

'This station already has loads of prison areas,' she said. 'They're pretty nice. You get a private room but you can go out into the communal area and mingle.' The grimace returned. 'Only problem is, it's split by sex.'

Ferrash raised an eyebrow. 'They might wish they'd split by faction. I can't see keeping Protectorate and Hegemony in a room together going well.'

'You'd be surprised. They've grumbled a bit but they're keeping to themselves. Anyway, there'll be a forcefield between us. We can see each other, but it's soundproof.' A smile played around Palia's lips. 'Know any sign languages?'

He let out a small chuckle. 'One, but unless you ever worked for the Reiart without me knowing, I doubt you know it.'

'Well, I don't know any, so–'

'Wait a sec.' Ferrash concentrated on his implants and spent a few moments isolating whichever bits had stopped working. The fact that he couldn't run dozens of thought processes in parallel anymore made him feel like his thoughts were wading through sludge, but maybe a change of pace would be good for him. As it was, he managed to regain access to the most basic functions.

<Are you getting this?> he asked.

<Oh, yeah. Can't believe I didn't think of that. Right, well I guess we'd better get ourselves into prison before the guard gets twitchy.>

Sure enough, the guard stood up and began tapping three of their legs against the floor, shivering a little as they did. Ferrash felt a sudden pang of sympathy for them – having to watch and communicate with humans must be like Ferrash losing access to his implants' higher functions, forced to slow down.

It paused when the two of them stood, and Ferrash drew Palia into a quick kiss before it could take them away.

'I'll speak to you later,' he said, cupping her head in his hand.

She nodded. 'If you don't see me for a bit, it's because I'm in the shower. I haven't washed in... I can't remember.'

'Good call.' He gave her hand a last squeeze and watched her return through the far door. As she did, something wrenched inside him that had nothing to do with the gel or his injuries. He'd spent so much of his life alone, and he didn't want things to be that way. Not now, at least. In the past few days he'd lost a daughter he'd never known and a mother he'd always hated. He didn't even have Bek, and that thought gripped his heart with ice.

The kluqetik clicked and flashed a pattern at him from a paddle. <Your room is this way, if you will follow.>

Not having much of a choice, Ferrash followed it through yet another door, still a little unsteady on his feet. To his surprise, the plants continued on the other side. Surely they wouldn't continue when they reached the prison proper – you could do a lot with a little plant fibre, with sufficient motivation. He imagined that at least none of the plants would be poisonous, but with tens of thousands of years separating this galaxy from his, who knew?

At the end of a narrow corridor, they passed through a locked gate and into a wide, open space, blanketed by green walls and with a mock blue sky in place of a ceiling viewscreen. He wouldn't be able to see whatever was going on outside from in here. The thought made him grind his teeth. True to Palia's word, a forcefield ran clear across the centre of the room. It must have been an impromptu addition, otherwise it made a pretty weird design choice. Clusters of battered Protectorate spacers leered across the room at the Hegemites and Ferrash wondered if Palia had underestimated their hostility. He even spotted a few people from the void packs huddled in their own little group to one side. Everyone stared as he passed by.

The kluqetik pushed him onwards, towards one of many doors set around the perimeter of this half of the room. They leaned close and touched the door with one of their two smallest upper limbs, then stepped aside and flashed another pattern at him.

<Press your hand against the door for five seconds.>

Ferrash did so, and the door made a heavy *clunk* before swinging open. He glanced at the kluqetik for further instructions.

<You will find a desk with basic software installed inside, including a clock. Meals and medication will be delivered to your room through a hatch beside the desk at eight, thirteen and eighteen hours. Showers will be limited to five minutes every two days until we have a stable indication of the number of arrivals. Do you have any questions?>

The kluqetik fidgeted its arms as Ferrash processed the message, unused to so many words coming at him so fast. At last he shook his head. 'I'm good, thank you.'

Without further delay, the kluqetik bobbed its eyestalks and scurried back the way they had come.

Ferrash stepped into his room, the door automatically closing behind him. No plants in here besides a couple of leafy panels on the plain blue wall next to the bed. A cup of something steaming that smelled a whole lot better than Hesperex's brew called to him from the desk. He drew a deep breath, walked over to the desk and sat. A glimpse of a shower through a glass door at the end of the room had him longing for a wash, but first, he would drink.

He made a note of the date that shone from the corner of the desk. How many days would pass until they were free?

CHAPTER FIVE

SHAHIDA SPLASHED WATER ON her face and watched the news report she'd pinned to the corner of the mirror. Barely five hours after the Speaker's summons, news channels had caught onto the story: the infamous exiles, now returned, under arrest pending trial. The channel she had on was sympathetic to the tuk-a-wa. One of its usual hosts was, in fact, a host. Already, they spat out a narrative about dangerous ideologies and questioned whether the gate's conditions had been met or simply overridden. They took a brush and painted the exiles as irreparably damaged by the weapon in their blood.

That kind of polarising talk had been frowned upon for a long age now, but this new paradigm shift had brought it back into the mainstream.

The scanner beeped from the airlock that formed the entrance to their quarters. Shahida made her way out of the bathroom into the main room.

'Have you seen the poem Boan posted on the forum?' her husband Ruslan called from the open airlock, holding their son Spartak in one arm. Spartak was heavy enough at five years old that they wouldn't be able to carry him like that much longer. Shahida wasn't sure she enjoyed the thought.

Ruslan retracted the visor on his helmet and hung his satchel on one of the hooks by the door. Its reflection scattered across the metallic tiles that covered the wall in an abstract pattern of his devising.

'It's utter shit. It's only getting so much attention because he was quick with it.' He put Spartak down and began helping him out of his environment suit while she watched, a smile tugging at her lips. 'Honestly, the instant a galaxy-shaking event pops up, he tries to profit from it.'

As Ruslan talked, Shahida made her way to the kitchenette. Rich smells seeped out from the dish in the oven. Her mouth watered.

'Did you bring the fruit?' she asked.

Ruslan held a finger up, grinning. 'I did. As fresh as that bloody poem.' After going back to rummage in his satchel for them, he tossed her a cloth bag.

Shahida caught it with one hand, shot him a glare for not just passing them to her, and put them on the worksurface. 'You can chop them. I need to find the nuts.' She began searching through the cupboards for them.

'Top right, behind the spices.'

She waved a hand and switched to the cupboard he'd mentioned. 'What are they doing there?'

'A little monster I know broke in and tried to eat them all yesterday.' A giggle punctuated Ruslan's sentence and mischievous little footsteps rushed to the dining area behind her. A moment later, Ruslan snuck his arms around her waist and leaned against her, his moustache tickling the back of her neck.

Shahida grabbed the bag of nuts and turned in Ruslan's embrace to kiss him. When she drew away, she cocked an eyebrow at him. 'Does Boan even get paid for those poems?'

'No...' Ruslan spread his arms. 'But in acclaim, yes, he profits.' He stepped away from her to begin chopping the fruit, mumbling to himself all the while, and Shahida tried to still the pang of sadness at the thought of leaving for her trip on the station. In theory, it should be brief. Walk in, make sure everyone adhered to the 'Empyrean gone, no problem' policy and freed the exiles, then go home. It wouldn't be that simple, of course.

And the fact that the *Inzekir* would at least be floating in the same system as Warden Station during her trip didn't change the fact that only *she* would be leaving the ship. The fewer the visitors, the lower the risk.

A wave of scent washed over her when she brought the dish out of the oven. 'Fruit ready?' She closed the oven door with her foot.

'Fruit ready.' Ruslan brandished the chopping board as evidence.

She pulled the lid off the dish and wafted steam away as Ruslan scraped the fruit in, then poured the nuts on top before returning everything to the oven. 'Should be another half an hour,' she said, and a timer appeared on the splashback over the hob. 'Now, show me this poem you hate.'

Half an hour later and in more comfortable clothes, they all took a seat on pillows around the low table in the corner of the room. Shahida leaned against the wall, trying to think of the best way to break the news to her family while Ruslan ladled printed meat and real fruit into bowls. Every now and then, Spartak tried to pinch a piece of fruit from the dish and Ruslan gave him a joking tap with the ladle to stop him.

'Has the Speaker said anything to you?' Ruslan asked, putting the lid back on the dish.

Shahida blinked. 'Yes. Why?'

He picked up his bowl, waving the spoon in the air as he spoke. 'The gate, the exiles – it's all Speaker stuff. And it used to be your stuff, too, so it seems like something she'd talk to you about. Besides' – he jabbed the spoon at her – 'You haven't really spoken about it yet, which suggests you've already talked about it with someone, and I know you're all business at the hospital. So unless you met up with some friends on your way back home...'

'No, no. The Speaker broke the news to me just after lunch.' She spooned a chunk of fruit into her mouth and chewed, watching Spartak jab a hunk of flatbread into his meal.

Ruslan waved his hands at her. 'You found out before everyone else and didn't tell me? I could have got the scoop on Boan!'

'You don't write poetry.'

'I could have whipped up an impromptu art installation.'

'For profit?'

'Pah.'

Shahida smiled through the next few mouthfuls, then said, 'I have the next few days off work. Anything you want to do?'

'How come? You usually book weeks in advance.'

She poked at a piece of meat. 'You know we're heading for Warden Station, right?'

'Sure. They put an announcement out for it. We need to be there – that's sort of our job. To observe. To mediate.'

'Well, mission. If it were a job, someone would be paying us for it.' She stopped herself before she could get too pedantic, took a breath. 'Anyway, the whole ship may be sailing there, but we need someone to physically represent the Sails on the station. That's why the Speaker told me first. She wants me to go. In person. I said yes.'

'Cool.' Ruslan grinned at her, the tips of his moustache twitching upwards. 'Will you be taking a camera with you?'

'What? No. Why?'

'Why?' He slapped a hand to his head. 'It's *history*, Shahida. And you know as well as I do that *everything* once you get outside this ship is suspect. Anyone could be a tuk-a-wa host, with a parasite pulling all the strings in their brain. Anyone could be influenced by them. Except for us. We are the only people who can give an unbiased view of events and *you* are the only one of us who will be in a position to do so.'

Against all sense, embarrassment clutched at her chest. 'I'm not a journalist. And I wouldn't call us perfectly unbiased.'

'You love telling people the truth, though. Bluntly. So much so you make them cry.'

'That was one time!'

'But come on, though.' He reached forwards and put a hand on her knee. 'You don't even have to say anything. Just record the footage. Send it to someone on the fleet. As long as the footage gets out, that's all that matters.'

She patted his hand and leaned towards him. 'I think what matters more is making sure our least-beloved hive mind doesn't start infecting all of the exiles on sight, or shoving them out of airlocks.' She wouldn't put it past the tuk-a-wa to do something like that. 'It would be political suicide to do it openly, but I just *know* they'd jump on any opportunity that made it look an accident. *After* that, I'll worry about getting recordings to people.'

As she went back to her meal, Shahida let herself relax. She'd been expecting Ruslan to worry more. He probably was, inside, but at least he seemed enthusiastic about her involvement. Still, while Ruslan had the same view of history as everyone in the Grey Sails, he didn't have the depth of knowledge and training Shahida had been given when she had been the Speaker's replacement. The tuk-a-wa hive mind, the greatest enemy in all their minds, the greatest threat to galactic freedom, the greatest open secret beneath the surface of society, still didn't inspire the fear in him that it sometimes did in Shahida.

Caution, yes. Everyone was cautious where the hive mind was concerned. But making sure you wore an environment suit, checking its seals and filters, building airlocks and scanners into your homes... that was one thing. The fight against them was another.

Fights needed support, though. Ruslan had a point there. Unbiased footage might come out of Warden Station. Some media would spin it slightly one way, some slightly another. She imagined journalists were on their way to the station as she ate. But the *Inzekir* was close, and Shahida already had an all-access pass. If she could record her visit, send it to the right people, she might influence the discussion on what to do with the exiles even before having to participate in it herself. *Maybe* she could even interview some of them, get the personal angle.

In the meantime, she would spend as much time with her family as she could. She stared at Spartak, his chubby face smeared with sauce, humming a little tune to himself. Five years old, and not a day off the ship. Most people spent their whole lives that way, besides the change of ship that came when you left home as an adult. Even were you to find a green planet with a bright blue sky, you would have to go suited.

Shahida longed for a day when she would be able to set foot on a world and breathe clean air scented with the exhalation of a billion flowers, with the spray of an open ocean. And if not her, then her son, one day after she was gone. There had to be a future where that could be possible.

Releasing the tuk-a-wa's hold on the galaxy would ensure it.

Later that night, once they had put Spartak to sleep, Shahida sat on the armchair by her bedside and sharpened the knife she would be taking on board the station with her.

Reclining on the bed, Ruslan said, 'Why are you taking that old thing?'

She didn't look up from her work. Their dim night light reflected from the sheen of the metal blade. 'I'm not about to buck tradition. Not when what I'm about to get involved in is the reason those traditions exist. You'd take yours.'

'Of course, but...' He rolled over and rested his chin on his folded arms to regard her. 'Take a gun as well, will you? One of the sonic ones that don't punch holes in hulls.'

Testing the edge of the blade against her forefinger, Shahida said, 'They'd confiscate it. You know that. They won't confiscate the knife – first because that would be rude and second because they know we won't part from them. A gun would be new, and beyond the scope of the close-quarters self-defence we need to be armed for. Besides' – she waved the knife at him – 'this is personal.'

'I'd say shooting someone in the face is pretty personal, too.'

She shrugged, then softened. 'I probably won't have to find out either way. Don't worry about me.'

'Do you think the tuk-a-wa will make a move on the exiles?'

Chewing her lip, Shahida put the knife back in its sheath and went to lie next to her husband, who put an arm around her waist.

'They might,' she said. 'But if they did it straight away, they'd need to infect pretty much everyone on the station as well to make sure all the people in positions to conduct scans would ignore the results. Even then, people would find out eventually, and *we* would certainly find out when we arrived. But...'

Ruslan shifted closer to her. 'But?'

'The gate is *open*, Ruslan. Both ways.' She caught his gaze and watched the weight of her words sink into the depths of his brown eyes. 'The people on the other side of that gate might not remember the tuk-a-wa. Even if they do, they might not be prepared. If the tuk-a-wa just send one of their number through to the other side, the extent to which they would be able to propagate before anyone realised...'

'We don't know how many people are in that galaxy.' He shrugged. 'Maybe they only lost the Empyrean because most of them died out.'

'And if that's not the case? If there are trillions on the other side and suddenly they all become part of the hive mind?'

Ruslan let out a deep breath that tickled the hairs on her cheek. 'Then I guess we have another war on our hands.'

CHAPTER SIX

PALIA SAT BY THE forcefield towards the edge of the communal area, looking out across the prison. Three days had passed since being taken here, and there had already been a few incidents. One attempted drowning on the male side led to the guards draining the water from a decorative fountain, leaving a murky scum at the bottom of the basin. The Protectorate men responsible for the fight had been broken down into further groups and some shuffled off into other parts of the station. Thankfully, Ferrash wasn't one of them.

She counted them now. Around thirty prisoners from the Hegemony, three hundred outnumbering them from the Protectorate, as far as she could guess. A few might still be in their rooms, but most people were up. Harsh artificial sunlight beat down from overhead, forcing most people under the shade of broad, fungus-like projections growing from the walls. All in all, not bad for a prison, but not as cushy as the Hegemony prison world she had melted a few long weeks ago.

'Any news, Pestor Tennic?' a woman asked from behind her.

Palia groaned inwardly and tried to keep the emotion from her face. Even if she couldn't say she missed the Empyrean, she missed being able to better notice people sneaking up on her.

Too many people recognised Palia, this woman included. Palia turned to face her, keeping her voice calm. 'I know just as much as you do. That hasn't changed since yesterday.' She didn't even know the woman's name, hadn't bothered to learn it, wishing she would leave her alone. Yet every hour or two she returned, hunched and wringing her hands, begging for information she didn't have. She'd once had the nerve to accuse her, in a roundabout way, of lying about her ignorance.

This time, she didn't push further. She just scurried back to the group she'd been sitting with previously. Perhaps she was finally getting the hint.

<I'm back,> Ferrash sent her.

Palia perked up and scanned the male side again. Ferrash appeared by the prison entrance, still limping a fraction, his face paler than usual. She couldn't help imagining a ghost of what the Empyrean might have shown her – the spikes of pain, the compression of light as he suppressed it – but the image was a lie. Now she had to infer like everyone else.

Pockets of Protectorate prisoners glared at him as he passed, as they usually did, and whispered amongst themselves. One man near the exit got shoved by another after a particularly intense string of words.

<As popular as ever, I see,> Palia sent.

Ferrash picked his way around the other prisoners and came to sit against the wall on the other side of the glass, not facing her directly. She couldn't see the scars of his pain mesh from this angle, bar the faintest hint of a scratch on his forehead.

She sent, <You should ask the doctors to remove that next time you're in.>

One eyebrow raised, he tilted his head towards her, revealing the extent of the scarring on the left side of his face and the cybernetic tracery beneath. <Remove what?>

<That.> She pointed to the left side of her own face, and Ferrash twitched.

<Given they don't trust the doctors enough to be in the same room as me, do you really think letting them rummage around in my brain is wise?>

<Good point.> It just seemed to be a reminder. Of the Empyrean, of the Protectorate, of the pains of Ferrash's past. Maybe Ferrash wanted to keep it for that reason if nothing else, but it couldn't be comfortable. <Did you overhear anything while you were out?>

He shook his head. <No luck. I heard some shouting coming from Kaktek's office, or in that direction, but we moved away too fast to hear. And they have a whole corridor sealed off just for transporting people to and from the hospital. No one but prisoners and guards can get in. All the exits are guarded, and it goes under the main level in places so there's no access to any of the docking booms.>

Three days in prison and of course he was already looking for ways to escape. He probably had been since day one. Palia raised an eyebrow at him and he gave a small grin in return.

A loud trumpeting broke the quiet, followed by a series of fleshy popping noises. Palia flinched. Every head in the room turned towards the gap between the glasslike forcefields that separated the groups of prisoners. At the far end, where the door the guards used to enter for their patrols lay open, a blond-furred rahtuan rocketed back on its knuckles, hunched low to the ground.

He – the males, Palia had learned, were the smaller sex – halted and shook his head. The sac on top inflated a bright red and blared out another wall of noise that roughly translated as <Back!>.

A shadow fell over the doorway in front of him and a female stepped out, fangs bared. Her fur, a vivid magenta patterned with swirls of lime green, reflected crazily from the forcefield to either side. She towered over the male, and Palia didn't need to have studied their species to recognise his stance as submissive.

<Stand aside!> the female said, her blare echoing from the walls.

The male stamped his feet and recovered his posture, trembling. Both shoulder-mounted cannons aimed at the female. With a tap on the forcefield, it turned red, and the female snarled. At a guess, he'd triggered a mode that prevented her travelling through – the guards could usually walk through it at will.

<I have orders,> he said, and this time the words came as a quieter rumble from his chin and cheek sacs. <You are not permitted to be here, host. You should not have been granted entry to this room. Leave.>

The female rushed at him but skidded to a halt at the last moment when he wouldn't back down.

With a low growl, the male said. <You follow a rahtuan's actions without its mind. You have no sway over me, host. Leave.>

Everyone in the room held their breath, expecting to see the male rahtuan get beaten to death before them, or shoot both cannons into the female's face.

A couple of kluqetik burst out of the door between Palia and Ferrash at a breakneck pace, scrambling up the sheer sides of the force walls. The moment the female rahtuan saw them, she turned and lumbered back through the exit. The male sagged with relief, and one of the kluqetik passed him by to give chase.

Palia frowned, trying to make sense of the male rahtuan's words, but she couldn't unpick a meaning. Was following the actions without the mind an insult? Had he just been calling the female stupid? And how had she been trying to sway him?

The other kluqetik busied itself with a scanner and shoved the male rahtuan to make him stay still when he tried to move.

Scanning continued for what must have been ten full minutes, by which time most of the prisoners had gone back to whatever conversations they had been having before. Palia kept watching, intrigued by the interaction of these two aliens that no one in her galaxy had known about until recently. And there had to be some purpose to the scan, too. The female hadn't touched him, had only got very close. What had the male meant by calling her a host? Was she diseased? That might make sense of their treatment here on the station, but it wouldn't explain why no one wanted to talk to them about it.

<You've got that look on your face,> Ferrash sent.

When she turned to face him, the smile plastered across his face made her insides twist. <What look?>

<The thinking look.>

<I'm always thinking.>

That earned her another raised eyebrow.

Back by the far guard door, the kluqetik finished its scan and, apparently satisfied, removed itself to a position nearer to Ferrash and Palia's side of the room. The rahtuan sat on the ground, picking at his fur and grumbling to himself in a popping murmur that underscored conversations throughout the room.

<I'm thinking,> Palia sent, <it's been a long time since I asked anyone what's going on.>

<You think asking again will get any more results than last time?>

Her gaze still fixed on the rahtuan, Palia tilted her head. <I'll be subtle this time.>

After a pause of a few seconds, Ferrash sent, <You're about as subtle as a bullet, but at least you can't set things on fire anymore. Go for it.>

She shot him a glare, then stood up and began to make her way across the room. One of the Hegemony prisoners had managed to get a set of Hendat dice cleared past the guards, and she sat with a cluster of other women near the dried-up fountain. A few Protectorate women watched with interest but hadn't joined in. Palia circled around the group, taking note of Archivist Lilesh either meditating or asleep in the far corner by a rampant growth of wall flowers.

The rahtuan watched her from the corner of his eyes, and Palia noticed the conversation from the few groups of people around her had grown silent. She walked over to the wall and made it look like she was examining a particularly interesting plant instead, imagining Ferrash laughing at her from across the room.

When the conversation picked up again, Palia turned and sat on the floor near the rahtuan. She had thought about sitting a little further away to make things less obvious, but if the rahtuan always shouted the way they did to each other, perhaps their hearing wasn't that great.

With his attention still partly on her, Palia said, 'Hi. Are you okay?'

The rahtuan looked around, then settled into a more comfortable position. When he spoke, he used his mouth to speak rather than his sacs. <Do you need anything?>

41

'No, I just wanted to know if that...' Wait, she couldn't say 'woman'. That was a human term. 'If the other rahtuan hurt you.'

<She did not.>

'Then what was the scan for? It took ages.'

He shook his fur in a gesture that Palia took to be a shrug. <Those are standard procedure.>

'Standard procedure in event of what, people shouting at you?'

To this, the rahtuan said nothing, and Palia opted for a different approach. 'Look, I'm a xenobiologist, and back in our galaxy there aren't... *aliens*. Not that we can talk to. Not like you.' She pointed and let herself speak faster, excitement half genuine. 'I just... I have so many questions! And I don't mean to be rude, please tell me if I am, but I don't know what's normal and what's not. And the scans can't be unique to your species, right? Otherwise the kluqetik wouldn't have known to do it, unless you have a—'

A blast of noise interrupted her, and the rahtuan's forehead sac inflated purple. <They are standard procedure on this station, and elsewhere in the galaxy, for all species.>

'Is there a pandemic?'

His cheek and chin sacs inflated through a range of colours without making much noise beyond a hum. <Of a sort.>

Fear strummed a note in Palia's chest. 'Are we in danger?'

<You are safe where we have put you.>

Well, that was hardly reassuring. 'We'd be safer if you let us go back through the gate.'

He leaned forwards a fraction, and even though he stood much shorter than the females of his species, he still made Palia feel small. <And risk taking the illness back with you?>

A fair point, even if Palia didn't quite trust his answers. She played with a strand of her white hair, thinking. 'If you don't mind me asking, how long does your species live?'

<Depending upon location, around one hundred and thirty years.>

'And the kluqetik?'

He paused longer before answering. <Fifty, I think. Or forty, I can't remember. They go by fast.>

'And are there any other contacted species in the galaxy?'

The rahtuan had his head tilted to one side now. <Yes, but not compatible with the same environments.>

Palia leaned forwards and hugged her knees to her chest. 'Do any of those species live long enough that they'd remember a crime that our ancestors committed millennia ago?'

He froze, so still that Palia could believe that the forcefield had paused his image. Then he stood. Without another word, he walked out of the room, and the door slid shut behind him.

Frowning after him, Palia tried to piece together what, if anything, she had learned from that conversation. She had four unexplained facets to examine: another of his species that he called a 'host', a pandemic 'of a sort', a scan that had to take place after proximity with a host, and an unspoken entity that remembered events from aeons ago like they were yesterday.

She had a theory, but she did not like it.

CHAPTER SEVEN

Two days passed, and even though they didn't know the reasons behind it, the female rahtuan's attempt to get into the room had left its mark. People stayed in their rooms more often than they had before. Some of the Protectorate spacers, Ferrash noticed, had taken to posting watches on the forcefield, like they might on a secure part of their ships. In fact, they all seemed suspiciously organised and furtive. He wondered if stress was getting to some of them – Ferrash had spotted the spacers clawing bits of greenery from the wall where they thought no one would see last night. In that sort of environment, Ferrash kept as close to Palia as he could, feeling the need for someone to be close in a way he never had before. Before, he had always had a plan, or an escape route.

Or Bek.

He ground his nails into his palm and let out a slow breath, reluctant to leave his room but knowing Palia would be waiting for him. Across from where he sat on the edge of his bed, the desk displayed the words he had been putting together for the past couple of days: a list of everything that had to be done, and when, to save as many in the Protectorate as possible. It would be a lie to say any of it was accurate, but it was something.

Palia had mentioned they might have problems closer to home. Her talk with the rahtuan guard had left her suspicious of some kind of parasite running rampant on the ship. Yesterday, Ferrash had tried to weave his way into what he thought was the station's network to find out if those suspicions were true. All it had left him with was a headache that his hospital-issued painkillers wouldn't touch.

Groaning, he stood and made for the exit. His desk beeped to remind him he'd left his breakfast behind, but he ignored it. As nice as the food they gave them was, it made him queasy. He could just not take the painkillers, but that would earn him a telling off from the hospital staff behind the glass, and he didn't fancy pissing off people who could stab him with robot arms while he was unconscious.

Muted chatter greeted him when he stepped into the communal area. It all but stopped in the Protectorate huddles when they noticed him. A crawling sense of dread crept up from his gut and tingled along his spine. He pressed on towards his usual spot near Palia, the weight of dozens of eyes pressing against his skin. They settled on the left side of his face in particular, where the pain mesh lay. Even the Hegemony men gave him odd looks, picking up on everyone else's ill thoughts towards him.

<Are you okay?> Palia asked as he drew close.

He sat down slowly, stuck in the mode of wariness that had accompanied so many of his years working covert missions for the Protectorate – and covert missions against them.

<When the Empyrean died,> he sent, <anyone could attack the Keepers without fear of retribution. We saw the moment they realised that, back on Hesperex. People here might not have known at first. Now they've had chance to talk, word might have spread.>

Palia frowned at him, leaning right against the forcefield. <How is that a problem? I haven't seen any keepers here.>

<Besides the Empyrean, what sets a keeper apart from everyone else?>

She shrugged. <Green robes, bad attitude.>

He rolled his eyes. <Let's say they got changed and tried to blend in. What's left?>

It took Palia a few seconds to get it, and Ferrash watched her expression shift from amused confusion to concern over that time.

<White hair,> she sent, then flicked her gaze a fraction away from his, to the side of his face that everyone liked to stare at, <and a pain

mesh.> Then she shook her head, her lips pressed into a thin line. <But you're not a keeper, just hurt by them.>

Ferrash tilted his head and smiled at her, the determination of her statement making his stomach flutter. Not quite naive, not quite wise. <They don't know that. And they wouldn't believe me if I claimed otherwise. I look like the enemy.>

Palia huffed out a breath and looked away, shaking her head as if by denying their ignorance, she could make it unimportant. <But... I'm pretty sure you told me sannots get those, too. You're not the only non-keeper with a pain mesh. There are plenty of others, right?>

<Sannots work for keepers, unless they stay hidden, even if they don't want to. To anyone who doesn't know that, they're complicit. Keeper, sannot. Same thing to them.>

With a burst of urgency, Palia shuffled closer to the glass. <You shouldn't talk to me,> she sent. <If they already think you're their enemy, they'll hate you for talking to the Hegemony even more. And I'm white haired, so they'll be suspicious. Stop talking to me and talk to them. Let them know who you are. Let them know they don't need to hate you!>

He chuckled under his breath, but the sound drew attention from one of the nearer groups of prisoners. At least the guards would be quick to intervene if any of them tried anything – they had a male and a female rahtuan on guard today.

Ferrash sent, <Am I just supposed to go up to them and say 'Hi, I'm the Reiart, nice to meet you. You're welcome for the revolution, by the way. Sorry about the galactic disaster.'?>

She glowered at him. <You're meant to just talk to them.> Her face softened. <Like Bek would.>

A lump formed in his throat. He swallowed. Before he could respond, a bellow split the air. The same female rahtuan that had tried to enter the room the other day charged into the patrol gap, forcing the male to scramble back in alarm. The new female guard, black and yellow, roared in response. Ferrash winced and covered his ears. She flung herself along the partition, sailed clear over the cowering male and tackled the invading female.

And left Ferrash's side of the room unwatched.

He caught movement in the corner of one eye. In the other, Palia's mouth had just enough time to form an alarmed 'O'. Before he could react, someone slipped a piece of fibrous rope around his neck and yanked back hard. Ferrash choked out a garbled swearword. He clawed for the rope at the same time as jerking his head backwards. He smashed the back of his skull against his attacker's knee. Pain shot through him. His teeth ached. He gasped for air that wouldn't come.

On a panicked hunch, he stiffened the muscles in his neck and threw all his weight forwards. The rope tore at his neck and the gel in his torso pulled so hard that his left leg spasmed beneath him. With a snap, the plant-fibre rope broke and he collapsed to the ground in front of him. Warm blood clung to his neck where the thin fibres had cut into it. He drew in a deep lungful of air that burned in his throat.

Through pain-blurred vision, he saw Palia, hammering on the glass partition, her face red. She screamed, but he couldn't hear her. *I used to be better than this.* He hauled himself off the ground, blinking clear of the pain. A foot crashed into his ribs, flipping him against the wall. Ferrash wheezed and tried to push off it to break away, but someone grabbed him – a vatter, eyes full of fury, hands burned by the rope. Ferrash flailed more than parried the vatter's first punch, but his ribs screamed at him. Pain stabbed through his chest and constricted it. He couldn't breathe. He staggered back, landing an uppercut on the vatter's jaw that annoyed more than hurt them.

A fist connected with the side of his face and the impact cracked his head against the wall. Bright light shot across Ferrash's vision. The world spun around him. Everything was noise and light and screaming, paralysing pain. He fell with just enough sense to curl into a foetal position, his arms around his head, his back tensing beneath a flurry of kicks and punches. Threats and curses rained down on him, but even they were smothered by the noise that splintered through his eardrums, making the floor vibrate beneath him.

Ferrash opened his eyes, hoping for a last glimpse of Palia before he lost consciousness, feeling the need to make sure she was okay despite knowing she was safe on the other side of the forcefield. Instead, a wall of black and yellow fur flashed past his eyes. A clawed foot dug into the ground a short distance from his face and someone just above him screamed, the cry tailing off with distance and ending with a meaty *thud*.

A trumpet sounded so loud that the knife through his skull made him lose consciousness for a second. When he rose through the fug, he saw the forcefield approaching, panicked, and squirmed in the arms of whatever now held him. They passed through it. The field slipped over his skin like a frozen wave, warm and only slightly yielding. His squirming had reignited pain all across his body. It blazed, bringing bile to his throat, making the whole room spin around him.

Within the never-ending motion, Palia spun past. She ran alongside him, above, below.

Then, when he was on the verge of throwing up from dizziness, unconscious swept up over him, swift and silent, and the whole world went mercifully black.

CHAPTER EIGHT

WHEREVER HER CURRENT LEVEL of calmness came from, Shahida wasn't sure. She stood in the airlock, her favourite robed environment suit draping her in deep purples and greens. The weight of her hammer-headed headdress felt unfamiliar after the brief spell of zero-G before the *Inzekir*'s shuttle had matched Warden Station's rotation. Gold panels engraved with Ruslan's artwork clinked against each other as they settled into place.

She rested her left hand on the hilt of her knife, watching the light over the door. The airlock scanned her, but more importantly, it scanned the area immediately on the other side of the door. While unlikely, there would be nothing more embarrassing than taking one step outside Grey Sails territory and being infected by a tuk-a-wa.

They would have to get past the suit, first. And her knife.

The light blinked green, and the shuttle door rolled open with a muted rumble. Shahida took a step out, scanning the interior of this level of the docking boom, its muted red floor and cream walls making the place appear saturated with dirty yellow light.

No one was there to greet her.

Shoulders slumping a fraction, Shahida strode towards the central lift that would take her into the station proper. A series of rapid clicks approached from the same direction, and she paused. A kluqetik – which could probably move faster than the lift – scurried out of a covered maintenance shaft beside the lift. It paused upon catching sight of her, then flashed a series of patterns at her.

<My apologies for not being here to greet you,> the kluqetik said. He – it must be mating season, for his carapace glimmered with facets of purple and pink, and those who became female for mating became a solid white – wasn't Kaktek. The identifier her translator supplied to his words indicated as much. He could be a host, for all she knew, though kluqetik hosts tended to come in batches. If just one host won mating rights during a season, it would pass its infection to thousands. She was sure Kaktek would have taken steps to limit their participation.

'Is something wrong?' she asked, moving to follow when he beckoned her towards the lift.

The two whiskers sprouting from the back of his carapace curled at the tips. <The exiles have returned.>

As they passed into the lift, Shahida rolled her eyes to the ceiling. 'I know that part. Everyone knows that part. Where is the station commander?'

The lift dropped, and her stomach jolted. The kluqetik replied, <Dealing with an emergent incident. I'm not certain of the details myself. I'm sure it is nothing to worry about. We just have many prisoners, and dealing with them has presented interesting challenges.>

'Tell me about the exiles.'

He fidgeted his arms, one eye twitching to examine the various pieces of goldwork on her robes. <I believe only the commander knows the full picture, as he interviewed the first to fall.>

'Fall?'

<From the gate. The first ones came through undamaged, but the others all came through in flames or pieces, like they were falling.>

She quirked her head to one side. 'So the gate damaged them?'

<No. We suspect there was a battle. That would tally with the fact that we've had to split up the prisoners to stop them fighting each other.>

Shahida's heart sank. That would make it difficult to advocate for these exiles being different to their warring ancestors. Difficult to find a way to free them without the tuk-a-wa exacting its pound of flesh.

<We haven't sent anything through to the other side, so we can't know what happened for sure, besides whatever they told the commander in their interview.> And here the translator added some subtext that had been woven into the complex pattern of his words: <And the commander doesn't want to risk the tuk-a-wa inserting themselves into another galaxy.>

'Rightly so,' she said, as the lift came to a smooth halt.

The doors opened onto a vision of commotion. Guards rushed this way and that. A few rahtuan staffed checkpoints with handheld scanners and snarled at anyone trying to pass without their permission. Good to see that they were scanning at all, worrying to see that in all the millennia of Warden Station's existence, they hadn't built scanners into its design. But then few did, outside the Grey Sails, where all were hopelessly enmeshed within the desires of the tuk-a-wa.

<This way.>

The kluqetik turned down the leafy corridor and scuttled away, one eye facing backwards so he could maintain Shahida's pace. Shouting echoed from further down the station, a hubbub of enraged voices. Did Kaktek really have a handle on the situation?

They broke away from the main thoroughfare and down a ramp to a plain-walled lower level, where they stopped at a checkpoint to be scanned. Impatient to get to Kaktek and find out what was going on, Shahida rubbed her thumb along the hilt of her knife, unable to feel the engravings through her suit glove but knowing, at some level, that they were there. These handheld scanners were much slower than those built into the Grey Sails' ships, and she had to wait a full twenty minutes before they were allowed to continue. Twenty minutes that the tuk-a-wa could use to take advantage of the chaos, if now was when they planned to play their hand.

Finally, they continued their journey across the station. The distinct smell and bustle of a hospital began to make themselves known. They passed by a few storerooms and a staff room. As they rounded the next corner, the kluqetik said, <Commander!> and hurried on ahead.

Another kluqetik, red carapaced, turned to face him. He flashed a greeting, dismissed his subordinate, and turned his attention to Shahida.

<You have good timing,> Kaktek said.

Shahida inclined her head and peered through the door to Kaktek's right. It led to a room with pale blue walls, devoid of furniture but for a long chair. A man lay strapped to it, shirtless and unconscious, his long brown hair spilling over the side of the headrest. A strange, puckered gash ate into the flesh just about his hip. His face, lolling in her direction, bore a terrible network of scars along one side. Dark bruises covered his torso, and a thin line of blood marked his throat. Robotic arms worked around him, controlled by someone she couldn't see. They placed a curved scaffold around the gash in his side and poured a gel solution in.

'What happened to him?' Shahida asked. 'Did the tuk-a-wa do this?'

<No.> Her translator did a good job conveying the grumble in Kaktek's voice. <Although I suspect they aren't entirely innocent in this. He was attacked by some of the other prisoners.>

She eyed the extent of his injuries. 'The guards didn't intervene?'

<They were distracted. A rahtuan host tried to enter the room with the prisoners. This was the second time she had tried.>

Breath catching at the thought she might have been too late, she asked, 'Did they succeed?'

<Only in distracting the guards long enough for the attack. On the surface of it, that was the prisoners' doing alone.>

'But only on the surface?'

Kaktek's mouthparts moved without making a noise, and his tendrils twitched. <I believe one of the hosts may have been messaging the prisoners who attacked him, turning them against him, encouraging them to attack. I assume it was their backup plan to get a prisoner out when they couldn't get a host in. I have people working to break the encryption on those messages now. No one should have been able to message them, but... You know how well the tuk-a-wa can pull

strings. Of all the hosts on this station, one called Ilhan acts as their mouthpiece. His influence is too strong for my liking.>

They could pull almost every string in the galaxy if they needed to. That's what made them so dangerous. 'Do you think they might have infected any of the prisoners?'

<No. I ordered all hosts clear of the prison areas and I have a constant feed from the cameras.> Shahida thought she saw it, playing on the inner surface of the thin bubble that encased one of Kaktek's eyes. <I would have noticed.>

'So why this man?'

<I'm uncertain.> As Kaktek replied, the robotic arms appeared to approach the end of their task. They removed the scaffold, revealing set gel, then covered the area with a swathe of artificial skin. <It's possible they already hated him for some reason, and Ilhan took advantage of this. But he and two others were also the first through the gate. The tuk-a-wa may consider him to be symbolic. He already had injuries from before, which we were treating, but every time he is removed to hospital, he is vulnerable. I worry that they intend to infect him in particular.>

'Have the council been in touch about arranging a trial yet?' That should be the process. The exiles, when they appeared, should be held, subject to a trial to ensure the Empyrean was gone, then set free. That was all there was to it. Except it wasn't. Not with the tuk-a-wa involved.

If only the ancient exiles had gone one step further during their war with the tuk-a-wa and ended them for good.

With the man freshly bandaged and a monitor wrapped around his arm, two other kluqetik appeared from inside the room and took hold of his chair. Kaktek stepped back to let them pass, then fell into step behind them. Ahead, another three kluqetik made ready to clear the way, and she suspected from the sound of clicking that there might be others behind her. Kaktek wasn't taking any chances. She felt a little guilty for slowing them down.

<They haven't. From what I gather, the council have been arguing amongst themselves.> Kaktek's subtext read, <It's not like we've all had millennia to prepare for this.>

Shahida didn't have to check her translator's notes to detect the tight anger running beneath his words. Have enough conversations with kluqetik and you could sense these things within the vibrancy of their patterns. Slashes of black, stabs of red washing across the canvas of their paddles, electric blue threads crackling through it all.

'Then we need to contact the council and get them to pull their act together. This needs resolving as soon as possible.'

<Resolve things too fast and they may not resolve to our liking.>

They emerged into the upper corridors, and the kluqetik who weren't carrying the chair cleared the way around them of people for as far as the eye could see. At length they came to a residential area, long unused from the coat of dust on the floor. They deposited the man on a bed in one of the rooms, rolled him gently – if a little too fast – onto his side, then left the room again. The kluqetik took up positions to either end of the corridor to keep watch, and Kaktek beckoned her inside.

Shahida eyed the unconscious man. 'What are you thinking?' she asked Kaktek. He couldn't be planning on staying here and keeping watch himself, although if anyone could be in many places at once, it was a kluqetik.

<I think it is about time we explained the full situation to them.>

'You haven't already?'

Kaktek clattered his arms in a way reminiscent of laughter. <For one thing I didn't wish to overload them. For another, I was worried it would cause panic. Besides which, I imagine the council might complain I had biased the exiles if I was the one to tell them.>

The man groaned in his sleep. Shahida inclined her head to him. 'But what are your plans beyond that? There's a credible threat to the exiles and the galaxy they came from. Our ancestors didn't even know if there was life in that galaxy when they sent them through. If the tuk-a-wa slip through after them, it might not just be exiles at risk – if you can call such long-removed descendants exiles at all.'

<The tuk-a-wa can and do call them such, and therein lies the problem.> Kaktek sat down, then immediately got back up and began to pace. <No, there is only one way to ensure their safety, and that is a two-fold plan: One, to remove them as far from any hosts as possible. Two, to prevent the tuk-a-wa from travelling through the gate.>

'The gate can't be destroyed, or closed.'

Kaktek paused in his pacing. The colours that played out across his paddles were analogous to a smile. <I am still the commander of this station, and if I order that all hosts be imprisoned as well, it is within my power to do so.>

Shahida crossed her arms, trying to work out if his smile had hidden a note of rashness behind it. 'How many hosts are in this system? How many on the way?'

<Twenty on the station. And Ilhan has diplomatic immunity, so he could prove difficult. But I can close the system's jump stations if needed.>

'The tuk-a-wa will call it an act of war.'

<They can call it what they like. I signed up to stop them. That is what I intend to do.>

CHAPTER NINE

PALIA BARRELLED THROUGH THE station corridors after the kluqetik guard, the memory of Ferrash's beating playing over and over in her mind. Rage boiled through her blood. She had tried to draw upon the Empyrean to help him, but of course that hadn't worked. Now it felt like she had no way to dispose of excess emotions anymore, no way to keep them in check, no way to transform them into something useful and violent.

Instead, she had had to watch and scream at the guards to help. Then they had taken him away faster than she could follow.

Her breath rasped through her throat and her legs burned, but she kept running. Greenery whipped past to either side. They rounded a corner and came to an abrupt halt where some other kluqetik and a man blocked the way. The man had sickly yellow skin and a balding pate, and the kluqetik guards he faced had their guns aimed at his chest.

'What's... going on?' she asked, gasping in between words.

Her escort turned a paddle her way and flashed, <Stay back.>

She gritted her teeth. 'But I need to see Ash! You said—'

'Then we are both here for the same purpose.' The man turned to regard Palia briefly, then raised his hands towards the kluqetik. 'Let us in to see him. We do not mean him harm, we promise. We only wish to occupy our rightful place in negotiations. We should have been invited to the initial debrief, but we were not, and this has been noted.'

'Which "we" are you talking about? What negotiations?' Palia took a step towards the man but her escort blocked the way with one of its pincers. Her heart flipped in her chest. If her theory was right... could this man be part of the hive mind? The reason why all prisoners had been so thoroughly quarantined from the rest of the station? How did it propagate? She resisted the urge to back away – if the kluqetik could be this close to him without concern, surely she would be okay.

She tried sending Ferrash a message, but he didn't reply. Maybe his injuries were too great. Maybe he was just recovering from treatment. Maybe both. She wouldn't find out until she got past this man.

No one had answered her question, either. 'Is there another way?' she asked her escort.

It pointed to a door half-hidden by the other kluqetik. <That's where we need to go.>

All she wanted to do was barge past, but the arm wouldn't budge. She bunched her hands into fists, digging her nails into her palms, wishing she could use the Empyrean to push everyone away or just *see* what was going on in their psyches.

Then the door her escort had pointed to opened and Kaktek stepped out, paddles flashing with restrained anger. A tall figure emerged beside him, human as far as she could tell but covered by green and purple robes from head to toe. They wore a seamless golden helmet that completely covered their face and flared out into a thick strip at the top.

The man stiffened. 'What are the Grey Sails doing here?'

A woman's voice rang out from the helmet with a buzzing undertone. 'Ensuring no foul play. Your presence here goes against orders and suggests ill intent. Leave.' As she spoke, her hand tightened around a knife at her hip.

'We have diplomatic–'

'Your rights,' she interrupted, 'are as defined in the ancient agreements. You may sit on the panel of judges at the exiles' trial, whenever that may be, but your involvement is not required before that point. Leave, or at the very least step aside so you are not *in the way*.' Her last words snapped out, cold and harsh.

After a moment's red-faced hesitation, the man turned towards Palia. The woman grabbed hold of his arm. 'The *other* way.'

He turned and stormed off down the corridor. When he approached the kluqetik and Kaktek, they backed up against the corridor walls. Only the woman stood her ground, bumping shoulders with the man as he passed.

'Stay still,' the woman said. She produced a handheld scanner and aimed it and Palia's face.

One of the guards clicked at her. <This isn't necessary. She wasn't close enough.>

Unwilling to wait the long minutes she knew the scan would take, Palia ducked around the woman's arm and made for the door. She expected someone to stop her, but no one did. Footsteps followed behind her. When she glanced over her shoulder, the woman had followed with her scanner.

'Who are you?' Palia asked.

'Shahida al-Shimaya, representing the Grey Sails.' She inclined her head in greeting, making little panels and beads tinkle against each other.

That meant nothing to Palia, but at least she had a name. She turned back to the door and opened it.

Ferrash lay facing away from her on a wide bed against the leafy wall to her left, lit by a sun-bright panel that covered the entire ceiling, the same brightness as lights throughout the station had been on the way here. She rushed to the far side of the bed and knelt, taking Ferrash's outstretched hand in her own. A frown creased his brows, and the skin of his cheek twitched at Palia's touch. A skin-coloured bandage wrapped around his throat where the other prisoners had tried to garotte him, but she could just make out the dark edges of a bruise around it.

'Oh, Ash,' she whispered, then touched his fingers to her lips.

A heavy *clunk* sounded from the direction of the door, and Palia looked up to see Kaktek and Shahida standing by it.

'That man outside,' Palia asked. 'He's a host, isn't he? For a hive mind? That's what all this fuss is about. That's who really wants us imprisoned.'

A pattern of muted whites and yellows curled across Kaktek's paddles. <I was about to explain as much. It appears you have beaten me to it. Perhaps I should wait to elaborate further until your friend has woken up.>

Palia's heartbeat quickened, a heavy pulse pounding in her chest, tightening her throat. She nodded. 'Will he be okay?'

<He has some broken ribs and other injuries that will take time to heal, but he is alive.>

'I want to stay here. With him. Don't put me back with the other prisoners, please.'

<We'll check with him once he's awake, but if he agrees, I see no reason why we can't allow that. For security reasons, however, neither of you will be able to leave this room. Not until the trial is—>

Raised voices sounded just beyond the door. Ferrash's fingers twitched in Palia's hand, and she snapped her gaze back to him. He shuffled on the bed, wincing, and opened his eyes a few seconds later.

'Palia?' he croaked.

Palia smiled, something catching in her chest at the evidence of his pain. 'Hey. Good job getting beaten up – apparently that's all it took for them to decide to tell us what's really going on.' With her last comment, she shot a pointed look at Kaktek.

Ferrash let out a laugh that broke into rasping coughs, then tried to prop himself up on one elbow to follow Palia's gaze. He didn't get far before falling with his face contorted in pain.

He peered at Palia. 'Help me up?'

With some reluctance, Palia took hold of his shoulder, but Kaktek clicked to get her attention.

<The bed folds.>

Using the control panel he indicated, Palia helped Ferrash roll onto his back, then raised the head of the bed so he sat at least a little upright. He looked paler for the attempt. Yet as much as Palia wanted some time alone with Ferrash to make certain he was okay, she also wanted answers. They both did.

'So,' Palia said when they were ready, 'Tell us about the hive mind.'

This time, it was the woman who spoke. 'They are called the tuk-a-wa, although you may hear them refer to themselves as The Great Convergence, should you ever speak with them.'

Kaktek's next words were so fast they barely interrupted Shahida's. <My species was the first to encounter them.>

'Each organism they are made of is a parasite,' Shahida continued. 'They seeded themselves through much of the contacted galaxy before anyone noticed. After a brief period of conflict, they made contact through their hosts and eventually became ambassadors for their species, which was relegated to its own territories. This didn't last. Many hosts were discovered in positions of galactic power. That sparked a war of its own. Your ancestors' side, the Free Colonies, fought against the tuk-a-wa and their sympathisers. They developed the Empyrean, stripped the tuk-a-wa of their fastest mode of internal communication, and were exiled for their troubles. Would that they had finished the job.'

Palia blinked at the influx of information. Beside her, Ferrash frowned.

'Finished the job?' he asked.

Shahida inclined her head, and Palia imagined a growl in her voice. 'No matter what anyone says, the tuk-a-wa will never obey limits. Your ancestors should have wiped them out while they had the chance.'

Kaktek shifted on his legs in a fluid motion that was oddly slow compared to his usual stuttering movements. <In any case, they retain prominent positions to this day. In theory, hosts are a matter of public record. In practice...>

'No one can be trusted,' Shahida said.

Palia felt her resolve falling away from her. All they wanted to do was go home. Now here they were, trapped in another galaxy with

history's sword hanging over their heads, surrounded by hidden enemies whose weakness was a weapon they had just destroyed.

Thinking of the man outside, she asked, 'How do they propagate?
Spores?'

'No. A host contains many parasites and can transfer one or more via
bodily fluid. It's best to remain at least a metre away from a host at all
times, though. First, so they aren't close enough to touch you. Second,
so they can't breathe near you. They can sometimes pass a parasite
short distances that way. This is why I wear an environment suit.'

It didn't look much like an environment suit on the surface. Palia
would have thanked her luck that she hadn't been close enough to
the man outside, but then a knock came at the door.

Shahida and Kaktek exchanged a glance, then Kaktek let out a
series of loud clicks that echoed around the room. 'What is it?'

The man from earlier said, 'Please let us in. Commander, you will
find we *do* have permission to be present.'

'Would you like me to get rid of him?' Shahida's hand drifted closer
to her knife.

A rapid series of patterns that Palia couldn't follow flickered across
Kaktek's paddles, which he hadn't even held up fully for people to see.
Her translator caught enough of it to get, <...good-for-nothing child
of one father entranced by all their shifting wavelengths. The hive
dances and you comply. Empty, good-for-nothing puppet brain...>

No one broke the silence following his outburst. It only lasted a
second or two, but Palia had learned that was a long time by kluqetik
standards.

<My superiors have granted him permission to enter. He must have
swayed them. I cannot refuse without losing my post,> he said, then
added in audible clicks, <Enter, but keep your distance.>

The door slid open and the balding man stepped in, his expression an unmoving picture of amused politeness. Something about it,
about how still it was, sent a shiver of unease into Palia's stomach. She
tightened her grip on Ferrash's hand without really meaning to. The

man didn't move beyond the open door, and he cast a quick glance towards Shahida. Whoever she was, whatever her presence meant, Palia was glad she was here.

'Fill me in here,' Ferrash said, his voice a low, hoarse warning. 'Why exactly do you want permission to come in here in the first place? I'm resting. Or trying to. Not exactly an interesting conversationalist. And if you're here to talk to those two' – he inclined his head, wincing, towards Kaktek and Shahida – 'I'm sure you can do that anywhere else but here. Who are you, anyway? Besides a... *host*.'

The man's lips curled into a smile that didn't fit his face, like how Palia imagined a snake would look if it smiled. 'This host is Ilhan Urzdmir. And we wanted to come here because we have a proposition that you will all be interested in.'

'I doubt that,' Shahida said. Trusting her judgment, Palia quelled the little rush of optimism that the hive mind was considering forgiveness.

'Humour us. We only seek a means to unify both our galaxies, after all.' Ilhan made a sweeping gesture that took in both Palia and Ferrash. 'We have no connections inside your galaxy. No knowledge. No insight into what you people have become since we exiled you.'

'Our ancestors,' Palia said. 'You exiled our ancestors, a long time ago.'

'What is time,' said Ilhan, 'but a convenient place to hide events you would rather everyone forget. This is beside the point. No, we are willing to forgive. We will happily let all aboard this station go free without trial, on one condition. We want to *know*. We want to explore the consequences of your exile, to see what you have become, how your weapon shaped you. All we require is one host. We understand that you were the ones to destroy the weapon, so you are the perfect candidates. And your people' – he turned his sickening smile onto Ferrash – 'yours, I hear, were most affected by its existence. So it is simple.'

Ilhan unfurled a hand with his offering. 'Join with us.'

CHAPTER TEN

ILHAN'S PROPOSAL HIT FERRASH harder than any of the attacks his fellow prisoners had landed on him earlier. He sat in his bed, chest screaming with pain, while the room erupted around him.

'Absolutely not!' Shahida took two paces forwards. Given her hand's tightness on her knife, he was certain she only resisted attacking Ilhan through monumental effort.

Beside her, Kaktek stood stiff and unmoving. Patterns raced across his paddles. <Regardless of whatever agreement you have struck with my superiors, you are still bound by the agreement that governs your movements. You may not take a host without their permission. Nor may you wrest all autonomy from them.> And the subtext he failed to hide said, <And we know you never abide by that aspect of the law.>

That false smile spread impossibly wider, like the hive mind had sampled all of humanity's faces and averaged them into something didn't fit. 'I've always been free within the Convergence. You confuse your understanding of the law with your misunderstanding of my experience.'

Kaktek let out two angry taps with one foot. Palia had such a tight grip on Ferrash's hand that it began to ache above the pain in his ribs.

'I don't agree,' Ferrash said, and let out a rush of air alongside it. 'There. I've said it, and with witnesses, too. You can't take me.'

Ilhan raised an eyebrow. 'On the contrary. The council have the power to make an exception, and the matter of a trial is still in question. Past crimes require punishment—'

<Which is precisely what the exile was.>

'—and if we can save the hassle of a public trial simply by taking one host, we are sure the council would be amenable to this solution. We only need ask.'

Shahida gave a tense laugh. 'If the council agree to this, they are fools. That or they are entirely under your influence.'

'Not at all. Just pragmatic.'

However preposterous the idea seemed – and Ferrash didn't know enough about this galaxy to judge – Ilhan glowed with self-assurance. The smug curl of his lips seemed unrelated to any overextension of an ordinary smile. For a moment, light-headedness overcame Ferrash. When Palia's grip brought him back into full awareness, it was to a hot churning in his gut that had nothing to do with his injuries. Fear. He couldn't let this happen. He had to escape. He hadn't destroyed one way in which his emotions could be laid bare to others only to become hopelessly enmeshed in another.

Every nerve in his body screamed at him to leap from the bed and run. His brain raced through routes he'd pieced together in his trips to and from hospital, pointing a way to the closest docking boom. But it didn't matter what he could think up – he couldn't even get off the bed in his condition.

<Until the council says otherwise, the law applies.> Kaktek followed this with a couple of red flashes that translated to a phrase Ferrash didn't recognise but was pretty sure was a strong insult.

If Ilhan had been smug before, he oozed the feeling now. 'Perhaps you ought to check your messages, then, commander. You might find the council has already spoken.'

After a brief pause in which Ferrash's stomach seemed to drop clear through the bed, Kaktek burst into motion. He scurried away from the door, to the wall and up its side until he reached the ceiling. Then he dropped back down and paced the room with rapid, frustrated steps.

'What is it?' Palia asked before Ferrash could muster any words. 'What did they say?'

Kaktek reigned his movements in and eventually came to a halt by the end of the bed. One eye regarded Ferrash. The other remained fixed on Ilhan. <I am sorry. They have agreed.>

Palia's hand slipped from his. She stood up, every muscle quivering like she would launch herself across the room at Ilhan. Her fingers curled the way they had when she had wielded the Empyrean.

'They can't,' she said. 'This is ridiculous. What kind of galaxy is this? And it's meant to be the place we're all *zashen* from? To *Varna* with this galaxy. Send us all back and forget we ever came here. We'll find a way to destroy the gate and you won't ever have to worry about us again.' Her chest rose and fell, and her eyes flashed with wild anger.

'And who would help your people, hmm?' Ilhan's voice became as smooth as glass. 'As we understand it, in destroying your own weapon you risked the lives of everyone in your galaxy. Is anyone back home equipped to deal with that? Who will save all those poor souls stuck with the consequences of your actions? Comply with this and we will send aid through to them.'

Anger flared in Ferrash's chest at how much the hive mind had been able to learn in only a few days. 'That'd be aid with complementary indoctrination, I take it?'

'We won't touch an unwilling soul. Have no fear – the exception applies only to you.'

Palia rounded on Kaktek and Shahida. 'We can appeal this, right? We have time, surely.'

Ilhan shrugged, and again the gesture seemed too big on him. 'Permission has been granted. We see no reason to delay.'

'Of course *you* don't.' Palia bared her teeth, her voice a gritty hiss.

'If I may,' said Shahida. 'While it is certainly easy for you to take a new host, if this must be done, it would be best done supervised by a neutral party. Preferably administered, too. If you want this to be seen as an act of union, putting your own hands to the task will simply make it seem an act of revenge in the eyes of others.'

With a wave of her hands, Palia cried, 'Now you're trying to legitimise him?'

Shahida ignored her. 'Let the Grey Sails oversee this. You send us one of your para– One of your *individual units*. We'll prepare a suitable location. You can watch to make sure we administer the unit correctly. In this way we ensure that no one else is contaminated in the process and the dignity of the host is assured.'

'Whose side are you—?'

Ilhan cut Palia off, nodding. 'This is acceptable to us. How long will you need?'

'The procedure can take place tomorrow.'

'Good. We trust we will see you there.' He lifted his chin a fraction. 'If we don't, we assure you that you will have the council to answer to.'

<I'm sure we will.> The colours on Kaktek's paddles were laced with displeasure. <In the meantime, you can leave us. You seem to know as much as I would be able to brief you on what I have learned so far anyway.>

This time, Ilhan gave a short bow. He backpedalled out of the room a moment later.

Ferrash tried to project every ounce of anger and discomfort he possessed into his expression, but in truth he just felt tired. Even Kaktek seemed to sag.

'You're really not going to fight this, are you?' he asked.

<No. I truly am sorry.>

Air rushed from his lungs. 'Get out.'

A quizzical pattern played across Kaktek's paddles.

'Get out. Both of you.' Ferrash's lip curled, and the pain as it tugged at his bruises added an involuntary growl to his words. 'If this is the last day I'm going to spend as my own person, I'd like to spend it with who I choose. And that certainly isn't either of you. Get out.'

With a last shared glance, Kaktek and Shahida followed Ilhan out of the door, leaving Ferrash and Palia alone.

Palia leaned against the bed, took his hand in both of hers and held it to her forehead. 'I almost miss being able to set stuff on fire just by being pissed off.'

Ferrash chuckled. 'I don't.' Then he sighed. 'If this hive mind's as good at infecting people as they say it is, life's going to be pretty weird for us going forwards. At least a metre's distance between us at all times.' He raised an eyebrow. 'You feeling inventive?'

Palia's laughter filled the room, but it still couldn't cut through the dread. By this time tomorrow, Ferrash as an individual with full autonomy would, in essence, be dead.

CHAPTER ELEVEN

<We must destroy this station,> Kaktek said.

Shahida had never seen a kluqetik so angry. He stood stock still, legs raising him to his full height of almost a metre, paddles splayed wide. Vivid reds and blacks splashed across them, entirely static, a solid punch of information. *'This is my statement,'* it said, *'immutable and vehemently held'.*

She wished she could display her own anger as vividly as Kaktek – she had never met a host before today, and Ilhan's presence had made her itch all over.

For now, at least, she was free of him. They had retreated to Shahida's shuttle, ostensibly to make sure the place was suitable to transport the exile and Ilhan without unplanned contamination.

In reality, they prepared for war. Shahida held no illusions about that. Going directly against a council mandate would put them against the government, though if the truth about *why* came to light, they might at least have a lot of people on their side. Voluntary hosting was enshrined in the galaxy's collective consciousness. Everyone outside the hive mind held a deep-rooted, suppressed fear that the tuk-a-wa wouldn't honour it. They believed, on the surface, that they would. They must. The rules said so, and no one ever broke rules, did they?

Well, the council had made the rules several hundred thousand years ago. By all accounts, their enforcement had slipped since then. The presence of hosts had been normalised as ambassadors to the wider mind, their treatment by the exiles showered with sympathy, the old fear largely forgotten.

And who knew how wide the wider mind had really become?

We must destroy this station. Shahida rubbed at the surface of her mask, wishing she could scratch the skin beneath. 'That's a little over-kill, commander. If you destroy—'

<I know.> Kaktek sagged a fraction. <I don't mean to destroy in the complete sense. But the tuk-a-wa cannot cross over to the other galaxy with any of their hosts. And we can't... We mustn't let them claim this man as their own. I don't care what the council has demanded. We must do something before that happens.>

'I agree.' Shahida took a seat on one of the comfortable gel chairs lining the walls. 'All we need to do is work out exactly how we're going to stop all of that happening. You knew this day might come. Do you have a plan?'

<Sabotage. Escape. Regroup. Gain support. Force the council to reconsider.> The words came as a burst of rapid colours, there and gone in the blink of an eye.

Shahida had been thinking more about specifics, but if there was anyone she trusted to make plans on the spur of the moment, it was a kluqetik. Kaktek could process all the relevant information and make decisions faster than she could even put words to a problem.

<You also have a plan? If I am to set this in motion, I cannot be at the procedure. The exile's fate rests in your hands. Will you be able to keep him safe?>

She tightened her grip on her knife. 'I won't let any part of the tuk-a-wa near him. Not alive, that's for certain.'

<Then I leave you to make preparations,> Kaktek said, and then he was gone.

Despite her suit, Shahida's heart beat a nervous tattoo against her ribs as she waited for the *Inzekir*'s airlock to finish scanning her. The memory of Ilhan's slimy presence still crawled over her skin. She wanted nothing more than to run back to her rooms, strip naked and shower until the feeling subsided. But she couldn't. She had to see the Speaker.

When the scan completed, she breathed a sigh of relief and took the nearest lift to the habitation cylinder. From there, she boarded a capsule along the tree-lined central avenue towards the Speaker's chambers. Shahida found herself angling her head towards the road to her family's residential quarters as it passed by. The pale blue flowers by the archway didn't grow anywhere else on the ship. The species had been created by combining genomes for wisteria and some gloom-loving flowers favoured by the kluqetik. They shone gently with their own light. When she saw them, she never failed to think of home.

Still, she sailed along, and soon she had to pass through the airlock into the Speaker's chamber. Her heart raced again, but for a different reason. What they were about to do would throw the galaxy into chaos. The extent of that chaos depended on how deep the tuk-a-wa's infiltration of the galaxy went beyond their official limits.

Shahida found the Speaker in a side room adjoining where she had last spoken with her. All she had to do was follow the sounds of knives slicing through air. Shahida stood in the doorway and went no further. The Speaker danced within the bare room wearing a simple gi, a knife in each hand, graceful and deadly in equal measure. Shahida had never quite got used to how surreal it looked to see such learned motions and mannerisms on a girl so physically young. When she had been younger and new to the role, it hadn't come so naturally – thousands of years of memorised techniques still had to work their way into muscle memory. Now, she embodied each of those years.

After a few more seconds, the Speaker sheathed her knives in one fluid motion and cocked her head to one side. 'How are our exiles?'

'Under threat.' Shahida filled the Speaker in with what she had seen on the station and the tuk-a-wa's proposal to turn the injured exile into a host. As she did, the Speaker prepared a cup of tea for them both.

By the time she finished explaining, a cup sat on the table in front of her, steaming its aroma into the still air. Shahida had also backed up the camera footage from her helmet while she spoke. The Speaker would know where best to send it.

Eyeing Shahida over her tea, the Speaker said, 'You must go through with the procedure.'

Shahida blinked. 'Well of course, I'll pretend to go through with it. I need to lull Ilhan into a false sense of security while Kaktek puts his plan into action.'

'In doing so, you will be bringing Ilhan onto this ship, and they will still expect you to make their prisoner a host no matter what Kaktek achieves.'

'Well of course, but...' The words died in Shahida's throat. 'We can just lock Ilhan up, or jettison him in an escape pod.' Or kill him, preferably. 'We're not agreeing to this, are we?'

'We are. We have to. Their demand is law.'

The scent of the tea seemed to curdle. Shahida's gut churned. This went against everything they stood for. If she didn't know better, she would accuse the Speaker of being influenced by the tuk-a-wa. And yet... the political situation around the tuk-a-wa was delicate. The earlier war had been put down to the misunderstandings of first contact, the exiles' use of the Empyrean labelled an act of xenocide. The council had adopted certain resolutions against similar acts that also restricted what people could do to limit the tuk-a-wa's spread. For millennia until the gate opened, the tuk-a-wa had been worming their way into the public's and politicians' hearts. Only now were they showing their true stripes. Now could be too late.

At length, Shahida licked her lips. 'What's the plan here? I don't understand.'

'It is simple, and close to your proposal.' The Speaker took a sip of her tea. 'Go through with the procedure. Take the parasite. Go to inject the boy. If Kaktek executes his plan, you will be interrupted and will not need to follow through.'

'What if Ilhan insists? The tuk-a-wa is everywhere. Other hands will be dealing with Kaktek's sabotage while Ilhan stands with me.'

'Delay as long as possible. See if his impatience provokes him. If it doesn't, you may have no choice but to follow their demands for our cause to remain in political favour.'

'No choice?' Shahida drew in a breath. 'I can't—'

'Trust me. Trust my judgement. The worst-case scenario may not be as bad as you foresee. I have had a long time to think of this scenario, among many. All has been accounted for.'

No reassurances could completely halt the way Shahida's certainty floundered in that moment. Every moment you lived amongst the Grey Sails, it was beaten into you: Know the tuk-a-wa as your enemy. Never trust them. Take every possible precaution to ensure they never infected you, nor your friends, nor any uninfected individual. To allow an infection, to even come close to purposefully facilitating it... Shahida had been stalling for time when she made the suggestion. She hadn't meant to go through with it. The thought of it being *her* fault was almost as bad as the thought of it happening at all.

'I can't do this,' she said.

'Do you recall my just telling you to trust me?' The Speaker's face broke into a bright smile. 'Really, I remember so many millennia, but I could have sworn your memories stretched longer than this.'

Shahida breathed out half a laugh. 'I remember. But what you're asking me to do—'

'Is difficult.' The girl nodded. 'That's how you know it's worth doing. Now' – she took another sip of her tea – 'let me tell you what you are going to do next.'

Absorbing the Speaker's instructions, Shahida finished her tea more out of politeness than enjoyment. The curdling sensation never vanished. It rose and fell with the strength of her disquiet. The task was simple: isolate Ilhan and the prisoners; retrieve a sample of the parasite from storage; pretend to go through with the injection but pull out at the last moment when Kaktek did his bit.

Still, as she left the chambers behind a few minutes later, nerves tingled in her gut. She found herself clenching and unclenching her hands. So much could still go wrong.

Policy usually had ships dock in the zero-G hangar in the centre of the habitation cylinder, where she had left her shuttle. With Ilhan and the exile, they had more considerations. That a tuk-a-wa host was being allowed aboard the ship at all was tantamount to sacrilege. As it was, Ilhan's journey from shuttle to operating theatre and back had to be as short as possible. No telling what kind of mischief he could achieve in the lifts or any of the corridors en route. He could somehow lay a trap that would infect the next person who passed, and no one would know until that person next tripped a scanner. By then, any number of others could also have been infected.

No, the best way to keep him away from anywhere he could do harm was to carry out the procedure in an airlock adjacent to where the shuttle landed. That ruled out the central hangar. The Speaker had instead suggested the emergency shuttle bay by the hospital. It was there that Shahida headed now.

A couple of technicians had begun setting the room up by the time she arrived. The airlock door lay open. A glossy membrane covered the gap in the ceiling that normally opened onto the same artificial sky as the rest of the habitation cylinder, sealing it off from the potential of infecting everyone's air.

She squinted up at it. 'That's a bit premature, isn't it?'

One of the technicians paused from clamping an operating chair to the airlock floor and followed her gaze. 'Oh, we were just testing it. Wanted to see how fast it could make a seal.'

The phrase gave Shahida pause. Had the Speaker let these technicians in on what would be taking place here when she asked for their help? They both worked with fastidious precision, fingers working rapidly at buckles and straps, a slight tremble in their hands when they moved between tasks.

'It's looking good,' Shahida said.

She decided to stay out of the technicians' way and instead paced to the centre of the landing bay. Taking one deep breath, she narrowed her eyes at the scene where tomorrow's events would play out.

She would land the shuttle here, doors locked until the overhead membrane had engaged. No, scratch that, the first step needed to come earlier. They had to get Ilhan into an environment suit, one he couldn't subtly get any of his breath or fluids out of. That should happen on the station. If they couldn't manage it there, she'd have to get people to help her force him into it here. She hoped it wouldn't come to that. It would likely lead to a diplomatic incident before they were ready to react to one.

Kneading a knot of muscle in her shoulder, Shahida tried to quell a sudden flush of worry. Why had she suggested this ship? This ship, with all her friends, her husband, her son. This ship, with thousands of people living aboard beyond the reach of the tuk-a-wa. She closed her eyes and took a few slow breaths. Tomorrow, at least something would happen, and they'd have a direction to strike out in.

Until then, this was what she had to work with. One hastily prepared airlock for her operating room. No one else from the Grey Sails would be there but her. She made a note to ask the Speaker to assign a guard or two in case things got ugly.

She watched the technicians work for a while, then they left. Besides the chair, they had installed and stocked a tall, glass-fronted cabinet. Shahida walked up to it, chills marching up and down her arms. Inside the cabinet, beyond the usual tools and material she would need for the procedure, on a shelf roughly at her eye level, sat a small sample tube. It gleamed, dark red and malevolent in its potential. An isolated parasite in a tablet containing a nutrient solution would have been cleaner, but she supposed there hadn't been time for that. The tuk-a-wa must have prepared this as soon as they had decided on the procedure for it to have arrived so quickly.

No, it was blood, so she would have to inject it after making sure it matched his group. Far more personal than asking a patient to swallow a tablet, even if both would end their independence.

She contemplated reaching in and crushing the tube in her gloved hand. It wouldn't be satisfying. She'd want to watch the thing die, squirming, gasping for its last breath. And even then, the greater hive mind wouldn't care, so what would be the point?

Instead, she glared at it, and curled her hands into fists, and hoped she'd get to crush it in front of Ilhan later.

CHAPTER TWELVE

No matter how often Ferrash tried to persuade Palia to pretend tomorrow wasn't going to happen, she wouldn't stop moving. When she didn't pace, she wrung her hands. When she wasn't wringing her hands, she was scratching her arms. In the brief moments when he got her to pause, her eyes flicked to every corner: searching for exits that wouldn't materialise.

At last, she came to the side of the bed and sank to her knees. 'There has to be some way to get you out of here,' she said.

Ferrash shrugged. 'Unless it's in a body bag, I don't see that happening. Not in time.' Then he patted the bed beside him. 'Now come on, get up here.'

'Ash...'

He raised an eyebrow at her, figuring this was something Bek would no doubt be better at, then feeling a little weird for thinking it. 'This is the last night I'll be able to spend anywhere near you. Get up here. We've already wasted what, twenty minutes of it?'

'We should be finding a way to escape. Ash, I won't let this happen to you.'

'I don't think it will. And if you get up here, I'll tell you why.'

Though her eyes narrowed in doubt, Palia clambered onto the bed. She kicked off her shoes before burrowing under the blanket and wrapping her arms around him. Her hand settled against the gel patch and Ferrash stifled a sudden intake of breath at the touch. With a mumbled apology, she moved it to his chest instead. It nestled there, a little piece of warmth just above his heart.

'Go on, then,' she said. 'How do you think you're getting out of this one?'

Ferrash smiled and played with the strands of her white hair where they splayed out across the bedding. 'What do you think of the situation on the station?'

'I thought I was the one asking the questions?' Palia pursed her lips, annoyed, and the sight made him grin. Feelings fluttered beneath the band of pain that wrapped his ribs.

Eventually, he realised he still hadn't answered her. He cleared his throat, embarrassed. 'Fine, okay. There's clearly a rift. On one side, you have the hive mind – and presumably a handful of people who support them, though I can't figure why they would. One the other, you have Kaktek and Shahida and all the people who oppose the hive mind.'

'And everyone who falls in the middle.'

In his current position, Ferrash found it hard to imagine who would stand between 'let the hive mind take control of people's brains' and 'don't let them do that'. Of course, there was more nuance to it than that, but the nuance was *scatz*. At least, it was to him.

Palia brushed her lips against his fingers, bringing him back into the moment.

'My point is,' he continued, 'that the two people who just agreed to carry out an action on behalf of one side are really on the other. Not the same side, not the middle. You saw how angry Kaktek was about it. It drove him up the wall. Literally.'

Frowning, Palia wriggled further up the bed until she could rest her head on the pillow beside his. 'But they have orders,' she said.

His voice barely above a whisper, Ferrash said, 'So did I.'

Palia regarded him for several seconds, her vivid green eyes and bright shock of hair the only reminders of her time with the Empyrean. Ferrash wondered for a moment if he'd thrown all his caution aside. This place had to be bugged. If the hive mind had its hosts in as many positions as it seemed, any conversation they had here would make it back to them eventually. Or perhaps that was his Protectorate-induced paranoia speaking.

'So if you were them,' Palia said at last, 'what would you do?'

Ferrash took his time to think of an answer. In the meantime, Palia slipped through his arm, nuzzled her face against his neck and curled up beside him, which made thinking more difficult. More than just the pain ached, now. He absent-mindedly ran his fingers along her spine and the small of her back, finding calm in the sensation of smoothness. Or... well, not calm, exactly.

Focus. The situation's urgency called for a fast response. Ferrash's fondness for complicated plans that took years to come to fruition wouldn't be the way to go here. He knew enough about Kaktek to guess at what he could do, but Shahida... Beyond that she was in the Grey Sails, he knew nothing. Who the Grey Sails even *were* was another question. When asked, one of the guards had said they lived in a fleet of ships and had done for thousands of years, but that hardly explained anything.

'You can think out loud, you know.' Palia's breath tickled his neck.

'Sorry,' he said, and kissed her forehead. The fluttering sensation tightened around his stomach, and he remained there, breathing in the citrus scent of the prison's shower gel in her hair before pulling back. 'Kaktek's in charge of the station, so I can only assume he has a lot of resources at his disposal. If I were him, I...' He frowned. The fluttering solidified and turned to lead. 'What if the hive mind sent someone through to our galaxy?'

Palia stiffened. 'What?'

'Our galaxy. The gate. No one on the other side knows the hive mind exists.' He felt his panic rising as he said it. 'How many people could they infect before anyone noticed?' Maybe it had already begin. Maybe they had already sent someone.

A couple of inches from his face, Palia's gaze unfocused. 'Have you seen the other gates in this system? There are three, not just the one we came through.'

Ferrash tried to think back to their journey into through the Prime-Nexus-turned-gate. 'I'll be honest, I was focusing more on the ships.' And half dead from the hole in his side.

'Well, there are two more gates for incoming and outgoing traffic. They call them jump stations. Now, when we came through the Prime Nexus, it didn't accelerate us or anything. Not like it used to do with the Empyrean. So unless their ships do something weird with physics, they don't have FTL.'

'And?' That wouldn't stop them going through the gate. It would just make everything slower. For a functionally immortal hive mind, 'slow' was a matter of perspective.

Palia trailed her fingers up his stomach – mercifully going nowhere near his ribs, or he'd have had to object. 'It means they have plenty of time to work things out.'

'I don't see why they can't work things out while they're over there.'

She fixed him with her gaze. 'How much more efficient would an invasion be with local knowledge compared to without? They want one of the exiles as a host so all that knowledge becomes theirs. And think: we were first through the gate. They probably think we're important to the galaxy.'

Ferrash raised an eyebrow. 'Aren't we? Depending on how many people died when the Empyrean did, I figure we're on a bunch of hit lists. Makes us pretty popular.'

Palia narrowed her eyes and nudged him in the ribs. Pain shot through him, and he let out an involuntary scream, muffled only a fraction through his clenched teeth.

'*Zash*, sorry.' She drew her hands back and grimaced, then suppressed a chuckle. 'I guess we're not getting up to much tonight, huh?'

Wheezing, he said, 'We really going to let a handful of broken ribs stand in the way of a good time?'

'Yes,' she said. 'Yes, we definitely should.'

He laughed. The motion hurt his ribs and set him wincing, but he didn't care. After tomorrow, he wouldn't be able to do this. Wouldn't be able to share a bed with anyone, let alone Palia. The hive mind might make him do it anyway, if that's how it wanted to spread itself. He hoped he would be able to resist.

He took in the sight of Palia on the bed beside him, the way the light fell across the smooth warmth of her brown skin, how shadows gathered in the crinkles at the corners of her eyes. Bringing his other arm around, he tucked a strand of hair behind her ear and drew her into a kiss. She pressed against him, her fingers trailing over his neck, his chin, his ear.

A moment later, she pulled back, her lips still close enough that they brushed against his when she spoke. 'You still haven't told me what you think Kaktek and Shahida are up to.'

Ferrash played his hand around the neckline of her shirt, brushing the skin beneath it, trying to remember where the damn thing fastened. 'It doesn't matter. It's out of our hands. All we can do now is wait and see.' And it wouldn't be long to wait, after all.

When he still hadn't found the fastener a couple of seconds later, Palia took hold of his wrist and led him down to a tie at her waist. She pressed her lips against his while he set about undoing it, her lips warm and urgent, her hands roaming across the uninjured portions of his abdomen. He felt a sudden urge to tell her he loved her, that he always would, somewhere deep inside, no matter what happened tomorrow, no matter what controlled his actions. But he couldn't know that, and he didn't know if telling her would be cruel, somehow. Or if saying it now, just because it was the last day they had together, would somehow cheapen it.

An ache of fear took hold of his stomach, and he drew a deep breath in, his forehead pressed against Palia's.

'You okay?' Palia asked.

He nodded, then shook his head a moment later, a shudder passing through him. 'Scared,' he said. Releasing the last of the knot, he slipped his hand beneath the fabric of Palia's shirt and rested it on the curve of her hip.

'I know.' Palia's hand drifted lower, following the furrow where his leg met his abdomen. 'I'll be with you. Every step of the way, I'll be there.'

Don't be, he wanted to say, but he couldn't. His guts clenched with a visceral need not to be alone, not again. To stay by her for however long he happened to live, no matter the circumstances. He kissed her again, longer than before, harder. As if by impressing his will on this one moment it could stay with him forever. He mirrored the motions of her hands, heart racing at the change in her breathing when he slipped a hand inside her trousers.

She kicked them off a moment later, then slipped on top of him, taking care to avoid his ribs. Still, he grunted at the weight on the hip that had had a little chunk taken out of it.

Palia paused, concern carving a little furrow in her brow. 'You good?'

He nodded, drawing one of his hands up her torso to cup at her breast. She sighed, stroked her thumb across his cheek, and said, 'Just try not to move too much, okay? Doctor's orders.'

He *tried*.

Not long afterwards, Ferrash lay on his back, feeling like someone had taken half a dozen knives and shoved them into every angle of his chest cavity. It had been worth it, he thought, in the brief gaps where he could think through the pain.

Palia's face rested somewhere between disapproval and amusement, and had maintained that expression since the first time he had tried to roll over and screamed in her ear. At least next time could only be an improvement. Except, of course, there wouldn't be a next time. Not unless he wanted Palia to lose her autonomy in the same way he was about to.

He tilted his head towards her and licked his lips, chest tightening with what he was about to ask of her. 'Palia.'

She flashed him a toothy smile. 'That's me.'

'I want you to promise me something.'

Her expression turned serious. Maybe it was the seriousness of the statement, or perhaps she'd picked up on his change in mood.

'What is it?' she asked.

'After tomorrow, if nobody intervenes and they really do turn me into a host...' His stomach flipped at the thought, as if it was only just now sinking in. 'I don't want to get you infected too. But I don't know what the hive mind might try, if it might use me to get close to you.'

'Yeah, okay. I'll just stay far enough away from you.' Though she tried to dismiss it, he could tell from the pain in her eyes that she knew it wouldn't be that simple. That Palia would be in danger every moment they were close. If it weren't for his injuries – and they would eventually heal – he doubted she would be able to keep him, or a thing using his body, away.

'Palia, I need you to promise me. If it looks like I'm getting close and you can't get away, or if they try to send me back home after they've infected me...' He swallowed, tongue suddenly heavy in his mouth. 'Then kill me.'

She recoiled as if struck, letting cool air rush into the new gap between them. 'What? No! That's...' She shook her head. 'I'll just knock you out or something.'

'But if you *can't* just knock me out. If the only thing you can do to stop me is kill me, then do it. Please. Promise me.' Ferrash held her gaze, staring into the pained clarity of her expression.

Palia closed her eyes, let out a shuddering breath, then buried her face in his neck. Her voice came out muffled. 'Only if there's no other way.'

'You promise?'

'I promise.'

With that, Ferrash looped his arm around her and drew her close, hoping beyond all else that Palia would be able to keep her promise if circumstances demanded it.

CHAPTER THIRTEEN

FERRASH WOKE SOME TIME early in the morning and listened to the background murmur of the station, muffled by its many leafy walls. His arm had gone numb beneath Palia's weight, but he didn't want to wake her. Warmth solidified into a tight ball in his chest. He drew her a little closer.

When the lights bloomed into dawn-brightness a few hours later, they took it as a sign that they should prepare. They got out of bed and dressed in silence, tension straining the air between them. Palia began investigating each of the room's walls, peeling back vines, peering behind flowers, opening every drawer she could find in the few pieces of furniture.

'What are you doing?' Ferrash asked, struggling with a boot.

Palia glanced back at him, her face pale, her eyes filled with urgency. 'Just looking for anything that could help.' She came over to examine the bed, running her hands all over the frame and under the mattress.

He tried to bend to tie his boot again, but pain sliced through him and he rocked back, grimacing. 'Found anything to help me with this?'

With a sigh, Palia came to help him. 'I was more hoping for something sharp.'

'Don't reckon they hid a knife under the mattress for us while we weren't looking.'

While she didn't reply, Palia did have another quick look under the mattress after finishing his boot.

'Leave it, Palia. There's nothing we can do.' At least the search might keep her occupied until someone came for them, though. The phrase 'hurry up and wait' came to Ferrash's mind. So wait they did. In her investigation of the room, Palia had discovered a little meal dispenser. By the time Shahida arrived to collect them at the full brightness of the lights, they had each finished their second hot drink of the morning.

Shahida checked they were decent before entering the room. She wore the same robes as yesterday, the gold panels catching the morning light.

'Come with me,' she said.

They followed.

Ferrash turned down the wheelchair that waited in the corridor for him.

'Playing for time?' Shahida asked, no hint of a joke in her tone.

He shook his head. 'Might be the last chance I get to walk of my own volition.'

Shahida inclined her head, then turned and led them away. Palia slipped an arm around his waist to support him and he hobbled forwards, his ribs and abdomen an agony of pain, but at least the agony was his. Behind them, many scuttling legs indicated the presence of a kluqetik escort, but he didn't try to seek them out. Kaktek wasn't one of them, he was sure, and he desperately hoped his theory about this all being a ruse would turn out to be correct.

At length, they came to the corridors nearest the docking boom. A crowd had gathered, completely silent, held back by some of the station's guards. Ferrash paused, chest heaving, half wishing he'd been less stubborn and accepted the wheelchair. His right knee kept buckling every few paces, and he couldn't even remember injuring that one. He didn't like how loud his breath sounded in the eerie quiet. He remembered the dark looks the station's inhabitants had given them when they first arrived. Now they just stared. Their unfamiliar faces looked drawn, where their faces were human enough to tell. Light glinted from a camera somewhere to his right, and he spotted a man subvocalising with a camera perched on his shoulder.

Great. He was a news item.

If only they weren't so quiet. A good riot would have been the perfect opportunity for Kaktek and Shahida to pull off whatever escape plan they'd thought up. If they had. Ferrash shoved the thought to the back of his mind. He had to believe they would do something.

As Shahida beckoned them onwards, Ferrash wracked his brain for something he could say to the crowd. If they had free media, and that man was a journalist, his words would surely get out to regular people. But he couldn't think of anything that worked, couldn't put words to the fear that had gnawed an aching hole through his insides over the course of the last day.

His last day.

He shuddered, and closed his eyes, and they passed through to the empty length of the docking boom. To his relief, a conveyor in the floor took them where they needed to go without his needing to move a muscle. Much of his weight fell on Palia now. She kept shifting beside him, trying to find the best way to relieve the effort.

So many ships. He could see them all through the viewscreens lining the boom. Big, hulking things at first, but not too many of them. The further out the conveyor took them, the smaller and more recognisable the ships became. Most were Protectorate vessels, ramshackle even before they'd taken damage, ugly cuboids of nondescript grey. Any Hegemony ships stood out in stark contrast with their sleek curves and bright colours.

They passed the wreck of a Hegemony ship that would have been crewed by hundreds. Thousands of glittering icicles pierced its hull alongside a spear of ice the length of a smaller ship, jutting from its midsection. Ferrash had, in the course of his career as a spy, become familiar with most Hegemony ships. In all likelihood this ship's crew had been in a reinforced central control room when the ice hit, but even so... Hard to imagine anyone surviving that.

'Step off here,' Shahida said.

They followed her off the conveyor, though Ferrash stumbled at the sudden change in velocity and Palia had to catch him. The fall sent pain shooting across his ribs. He hissed in shock.

Shahida's head snapped towards him, goldwork jangling. 'If you're too injured for this, I can try to have the procedure delayed.'

'You could?' Ferrash asked. She wouldn't say that if she had an escape planned, would she? Panic rose burbling from the pit of his stomach to his throat, and he swallowed to hold it back. Palia's arm tightened around his waist.

'I could try,' Shahida said, but her shoulders sagged. 'I doubt it would work, though, and it would only be delaying the inevitable. Come on, let's get this over and done with.'

Despair dropped onto his shoulders. With nothing else to do, he struggled on, Palia at his side.

Soon enough, they approached the side of the boom. Ilhan stood there, bolt upright, his scalp reflecting the light of the viewscreen's stars. For how still he was, he could have been standing there forever. Ferrash's feet grew heavier with each step they took towards him until it felt like Palia was pushing him along rather than just holding him upright.

Ilhan smiled his too-big smile. 'Welcome.'

Ferrash grunted. He could think of a few choice responses, but couldn't summon the effort to say them. Palia's hand gripped his waist so hard that it tugged at the sore muscles of his ribs, causing an underlying sensation of constant pain so like the experience of using a pain mesh that it felt almost nostalgic. It made him feel, even if just for a moment, that everything was normal and he could fix things with one of a half dozen different plans up his sleeves. He had none, of course, and his mind stumbled over that fact whenever it encountered it.

Shahida came to a halt three metres from Ilhan, her grip tight around the knife at her belt. 'You're not in an environment suit.'

Raising an eyebrow, Ilhan asked, 'Were we meant to be?'

'You know full—' Shahida cut her own statement off with something half growl, half sigh. 'Yes, you were meant to. You're not boarding that shuttle without one.'

'This is unnecessary. We will not seek to join with your people.'

'Say whatever you like.' She shrugged and practically spat out her next words. 'This is final. No suit, no entry. Be thankful we're allowing you to board at all. The suit in the cabinet to the right has already been inspected and prepared for you.'

'And trapped?' Ilhan asked, moving across to the cabinet she had indicated.

'If killing one hurt the whole, I assure you, we wouldn't be speaking.'

Ilhan donned the suit in silence. As he did, Palia's grip on Ferrash's waist loosened. Turning to check that she was okay, Ferrash found her gaze fixed on Shahida's knife. Her muscles had tensed, and she stood poised to leap for it while both Ilhan and Shahida were distracted. Except Shahida still had hold of the knife, and Ilhan was connected to a hive mind that could presumably bring chaos raining down on them in an instant.

Before she could try anything, Ferrash let the last dregs of strength drain from his legs. He crumpled sideways against Palia, crushing his side against her so heavily that an undignified wheeze squeaked out of his lungs.

Palia yelped and took his weight, taking a wider stance to brace against the floor. '*Zash*, what have you been eating?' she muttered. 'Are you okay?'

'I'm fine,' he said. And just in case she took him too literally, he added, 'Thanks for keeping me upright. Not sure I could manage this on my own.'

Palia made no further moves for the knife, though she kept glancing at it. When Ilhan finished donning the suit, Shahida ran some kind of scan from a panel on her wrist. Only then did she nod her assent. She made Palia get into a suit as well – presumably making her change after Ilhan so the two didn't come too close using the same locker. Then the four of them passed through a hatch in the wall and into the hold of a shuttle, where they took seats as far away from each other as they could.

A thud rang through the hull as the docking clamps detached. Then the downwards pull of the station's spin slipped away and a gentle thrust pressed Ferrash back into his seat, building the further from the station they travelled.

He closed his eyes, but he could still see Ilhan's too-wide smile printed inside the lids. He couldn't get away from him.

Soon enough, with their minds part of the same whole, that feeling would be all too literal.

CHAPTER FOURTEEN

SHAHIDA IMAGINED SHE MIGHT have worn the engravings off her knife's handles by the time they reached the *Inzekir*, so hard had she gripped and fidgeted with it during the flight there. The *Inzekir* had been forced to dock at a refuelling buoy near the station, clamped there by demand of the tuk-a-wa and the council so they couldn't just leave without conducting the operation. Shahida had wanted to fight it, but on the Speaker's advice, the Grey Sails complied. That made their new position more vulnerable that Shahida would like. They touched down with barely a whisper from the engine, settling into a stillness broken only by Shahida's doubts and the exile man waking from sleep.

She still hadn't learned his name, she realised. Here she was about to hand him body and mind to the tuk-a-wa, and she didn't even know the name of the person he would no longer be.

With her eyes closed, she counted to ten and breathed slow breaths. On the edge of her hearing, something rumbled, came to a halt. A notification told her the shutter had rolled closed. So far, so good. And when she opened her eyes again, Ilhan hadn't moved from his position opposite her. The perfect picture of compliance.

Well, of course he would be compliant. She was giving him exactly what he wanted.

You'd better get this right, Kaktek. She still wished she knew more of his plan, but it was likely too flexible for the kluqetik to cement in words.

Unstrapping herself from her harness, she said, 'Come on. It's just outside.'

With guilt rumbling in her chest, Shahida helped the exile to his feet and, along with the suited female exile, walked him through the open shuttle door onto the floor of the landing bay. Ilhan's footsteps sounded a short distance behind them, but she had brought up a rear view in her helmet's interface to keep an eye on him anyway. She wasn't about to let the first host to ever board a Grey Sails ship go unwatched.

Shahida kept her voice quiet and asked, 'What's your name?'

'Ferrash', the man answered, his voice hard-edged with pain. He stared straight ahead, jaw set in a hard line, no doubt fearful of the transformation to come. As anyone should be in his position.

The woman answered a moment later. 'I'm Palia.'

Shahida nodded, glad to have asked but unable to think of anything she could say to them. She had no reassurances, only a dull hope that Kaktek would pull through before anything could happen.

With one command, she closed the shuttle door and started opening the airlock to the impromptu operation room. Ilhan came to stand beside them, though still maintained a respectful distance of a couple of metres.

'Is this all?' he asked.

'We hardly need much equipment for this.' Shahida began leading Ferrash and Palia towards the operation room, nodding to the two guards in the far corners. 'What did you expect? An audience? You have enough eyes in your head to count as one, I should think.'

In the spite-loaded silence that followed, Shahida and Palia helped Ferrash onto the operating chair. He had his eyes closed. A vein pulsed in his temple on the unscarred side. Whatever he had beneath the scarred side looked cybernetic. Shahida hoped for his sake that it was some kind of health mod that would be able to isolate and destroy the tuk-a-wa parasite, but she didn't hold out much hope. If it was meant to heal him, it wouldn't have scarred him.

When they had finished, Shahida took a step back. Palia stood holding Ferrash's hand and shoulder, her face tight with worry beneath her suit's clear visor, and Shahida gulped at the guilt the sight sent rushing through her. If Ruslan had been strapped to that chair, no power in any galaxy would have stopped her fighting back.

She turned away from the scene and opened the cabinet. Her fingers shook as she withdrew the tube of blood and inserted it into a syringe. So small a thing with so high a cost. And by her hand. She almost considered asking one of the guards to do it for her, but they might not know the whole plan.

Ilhan had entered the room behind them. He stood at the edge of it now, staring around him, eyebrows forming angry daggers. 'Where is Commander Kaktek?'

Shahida shrugged, her heart beating a fraction faster. 'He had other matters to attend to.'

'But this is a moment of historical importance!' he cried. She noticed the flash of a button camera pressed to the interior of his helmet just above the seal. 'It is the commander's duty to oversee the fate of the exiles. He has to be here.'

What goodwill the tuk-a-wa could hope to gain from publicising this footage, Shahida wasn't certain, but the thought of him recording without her permission set her teeth on edge. She forced herself to loosen her grip on the syringe in case she broke it. A response began to form on her tongue, but Ilhan had already opened a call to the station – on loudspeaker, presumably to rub it in.

A connecting tone rang out from the speaker, and Shahida said, 'You—'

Ilhan held up a hand to silence her. An artificial male voice sounded from the speaker. 'Station commander's office. How may I be of assistance?'

'Where is the station commander?' Ilhan asked.

'At present, there is no station commander. I can pass a message to the acting station commander if you would like?'

Dread struck Shahida. 'What?' What had happened to Kaktek?

Ilhan asked as much, and the voice replied, 'Station Commander Kaktek resigned his commission precisely twenty-three minutes ago in a public notice denouncing the council's complicity in acts of psychecide against the exiles' descendants. Would you like me to read the contents of the letter?'

'This is unacceptable!' Ilhan snapped.

'I take that as a no. If you have any further enquiries, please get in touch,' the voice said, in a tone that sounded almost gleeful, and ended the call.

Shahida drew a quick breath in through her nose. This was it. Whatever Kaktek had planned, he was doing it now. The syringe weighted her hand like lead.

A snort from Ilhan made her jump. 'While Kaktek's behaviour is inexcusable, it doesn't affect our agreement.' He gestured to her, then to Ferrash. 'You may proceed.'

Come on, Kaktek. She took a step forwards. The chair was too close. She should have had them move the cabinet further away. One step more and she was by his side. He had his eyes open now, glistening, his head tilted away from Shahida, his gaze fixed on Palia's face.

'This might sting a little.' Shahida's voice seemed to come from someone else, outside her helmet. Her heart flipped in her chest.

Then a hollow *boom* rang through the structure of the ship. The floor tilted underneath her and Shahida fell sideways. She let go of the syringe as she flung her arms out to catch herself on the chair. It bounced, clinking, from the floor several times before rolling away. Metallic groans reverberated in the aftermath. A slight pull tugged her at an angle against the *Inzekir's* spin.

Palia stared at her wide-eyed from across the chair. 'What was that?'

Shahida staggered to her feet, not quite sure of her balance with the strange new forces acting on her. Logging into the ship feeds through her helmet, she watched the refuelling buoy creeping away from them through the dark. One of its docking booms hung loose, the ragged midsection that they should have been clamped to marred by scorch marks.

This was Kaktek's sabotage. He had blown the docking boom. He had freed them.

With newfound determination singing in her veins, Shahida turned to Ilhan, only he wasn't where she had left him. He crouched at the far side of the room, hunched over the ground, searching for...

Shit. The syringe. Shahida shouted, 'Stay where you are! Guards!'

Ilhan lunged up from the floor before the guards could catch him, syringe in hand, straight for where Ferrash lay in the chair. Shahida's vision narrowed to Ilhan's movements. She rushed towards him and the chair and drew her knife from its sheath in one smooth motion. It flashed as she sliced across his throat, lightning fast. Arterial blood sprayed crimson through the air. Palia yelled in surprise, the blood spattering her visor, and Ilhan wobbled on his feet.

Then he fell, and his hand slipped from the syringe embedded in Ferrash's thigh.

CHAPTER FIFTEEN

CONGEALING BLOOD FORMED A pink-ish smear on the side of Palia's visor. She willed herself to move. She couldn't take her eyes from the syringe. She hadn't even seen Ilhan stick it in Ferrash's leg. Fury boiled within her. She could have *stopped* this, dammit.

Ferrash bent double with a cry of dismay and yanked the syringe from his flesh, throwing it across the room before collapsing back against the chair.

Teeth bared, he turned his head to face Shahida. 'Please tell me that was just normal blood. Please.'

A part of Palia quailed at the crack in his face. She wanted to do something, anything, but she didn't know what. On a whim, and with her heart hammering in her chest, she said, 'Tourniquet. We need a tourniquet.'

Before anyone could say anything, she launched herself towards the cabinet so she could search it, but the ship jolted beneath her feet. She sprawled on the floor, jarring her elbow against the metal panels. She gritted her teeth to stifle a cry of pain.

'Get him into a suit,' Shahida snapped at the two guards in the corners of the room.

Palia hauled herself up onto one elbow. 'What are you doing?'

'He's been infected. He needs to be contained.'

'He needs to be *cured*.' With her anger solidifying into a constant pulse, Palia stood and threw herself between Ferrash and the guards. 'Get a tourniquet. We'll stop the infection tra—'

'It's too late. It can't be stopped.' Shahida's helmet stripped her voice of any humanity. Without any warning, she dropped her knife and pushed Palia out of the way of the guards.

Palia tripped over her own feet and fell sideways. Pain lanced through her hip when she hit the ground. Another jolt sent her skidding to the far wall. She screamed and called on the Empyrean, but nothing answered. She stretched her useless fingers out towards Shahida, longing with every fibre of her being for some green spark of flame to take hold and set the woman alight.

As the guards approached, Ferrash rolled off the chair and landed on unsteady feet. Sweat beaded his brow. He snarled, chest heaving. Then he glanced towards Palia, pain writ deep into his eyes.

'Give me the suit,' he said.

The two guards glanced at each other, then one of them retrieved an environment suit from the cabinet and threw it at him.

'Put it on,' the guard said. 'Quickly.'

Shahida walked to the wall beside Palia, ignoring her outstretched hand, and pressed her hand against a panel. The airlock door slammed shut and a fine vapour hissed from overhead vents. Then she offered her hand to Palia.

Palia eyed it, tension spiking across her back, trying to find some way she could turn the situation to her and Ferrash's advantage. But Ferrash had complied. Maybe as long as they could keep him contained, they could find a way to save him. She didn't even know how long it took for the parasite to take root. It could take weeks. It could be reversible. *Zash*, they must have medicine for it, surely?

She took Shahida's hand and let herself be hauled upright. Ferrash struggled his way into the suit, coughing at the vapour. Palia moved to help him, but Shahida held her arm across her chest.

'Stay away from him,' she said. The woman didn't trust her not to interfere.

Ferrash tilted his head to give Palia a small smile. 'It's okay,' he said, and repeated, 'It's okay.'

A lump rose to Palia's throat. She wanted to go to him, comfort him, help him – not stand here at a distance treating him like a piece of dirt.

'It's okay,' she found herself whispering to keep up the lie. But Ferrash fumbled at the straps, and by the time he had the suit fully closed, he couldn't stop tremors running all the way up his left side.

The door panel beeped. Shahida said, 'All clear!' and pressed her hand against it, reopening the door. 'Take him to one of the pods.'

Each guard took hold of one of Ferrash's arms and frogmarched him from the room. His head lolled like he was struggling not to fall asleep.

Shahida moved towards a small door on the other side of the shuttle, Palia trotting to keep up. Gravity kept changing around her, and she wobbled from side to side in an attempt to compensate for it. Nausea clung to her stomach.

'What's happening?' Palia asked. 'Why's the ship moving?'

Shahida answered without looking behind her. 'We're heading out.'

Palia's steps faltered. 'Back through our gate?' Speeding after Shahida again, she asked, 'Did the hive mind do this? Are they flying the ship through to infect our galaxy?'

'No. The tuk-a-wa have no hold over the *Inzekir*. We're not heading for your gate – we're going for the jump station, getting out of this system before anyone can stop us.'

The relief that gave Palia wasn't much, but it was something. 'But our gate's closer.'

'We don't know anyone on your side of the gate,' Shahida said, opening the door. 'And with what we've just done, we need all the allies we can get. Besides, from what I hear, there might not be much left on your side.'

They bundled into a wide corridor together. Tall hatches lined the wall.

'"What we've just done?"' Palia scoffed and gestured behind her at Ferrash. He sagged between the two guards, one of his legs twitching arrhythmically against the floor, a tic passing through the muscles of his face every couple of seconds. 'If you were trying to stop him getting infected, you failed. You've done nothing!'

Shahida rounded on Palia. 'We've shown our hand.' Her voice softened a fraction for her next words. 'I am truly sorry I couldn't stop Ilhan. I– I never wanted this to happen. We didn't plan to go through with it. I'm sorry. But it's too late now.'

The guards passed behind her and halted beside one of the hatches. Dread clamped a cold hand around Palia's gut and her insides constricted.

'Too late?' Palia asked, her voice hitching. 'What are you doing?' She pushed Shahida aside and jumped between the guards and the hatch. Her mind supplied a thousand nightmares that could lie behind it – a furnace, an abattoir, the cold void of space.

'It's just to keep him contained.' Shahida hauled at her elbow but Palia wriggled from her grip. Ferrash watched the scuffle, helpless, his brows drawn low over his eyes.

Palia bared her teeth, assuming a fighting stance, but she wasn't fooling anyone. One of the guards let go of Ferrash and lunged for her, but Shahida stopped them and held a calming hand out to Palia.

'It's an escape pod,' Shahida said, her words coming in a hurried flood. 'It'll keep him contained while we work out what to do, we can separate it from the *Inzekir*'s air supply and it'll be easy to move him to somewhere better later.'

Palia trembled with sick adrenaline, not wanting to place Ferrash's life in the hands of the woman who had just so badly failed to safeguard it, not knowing who to trust. She couldn't even trust Ferrash. Not for long. Not anymore.

Through eyes blurring with hot tears, she saw the hatch swing open. She screamed inside her head, the sound wanting so desperately to escape that it made a hissing whine at the back of her throat. She yearned for the Empyrean to be hers again, to be able to slash and burn and *win* when everything she loved was at stake. But she didn't even have an enemy in front of her to fight. Not this time.

Ferrash gave her one last look as they bundled him through the hatch, and though his eyes rolled up into his sockets, a message from him appeared in her implants.

<It's okay. I'll be fine. I love you.>

'Wait!' Possessed by a sudden sense of dread, Palia threw all of her weight towards the hatch. She would go with him. They couldn't deny her that. But Shahida held her in a grip like iron.

The hatch slammed shut. The tension fell from Shahida's shoulders. On the other side of the hatch, Ferrash examined his surroundings, his face devoid of emotion.

'We should contact the captain,' Shahida said, 'and the Speaker, and—'

Before she could say any more, a mechanism *thunked* and something hissed in the space behind the hatch.

Palia jerked forwards again. This time, no one stopped her. She pressed her visor against a porthole on the hatch, but all she saw behind it was a white cross painted against a red swatch on the opposite wall. The pod was gone.

'Did he just...?' Shahida put a hold over where her mouth would be and turned away from the hatch. 'There's a manual release inside the pod. He activated it himself. Shit. *Shit.*'

Palia's legs failed her. She slid to the floor with her helmet resting against the cool metal. A hole carved itself into her guts in Ferrash's absence, and a tear rolled down her right cheek to drip from the tip of her nose.

'The station will pick him up if we can't get to him first,' Shahida said, her voice coming as if from a great distance. She started rattling off orders and hypothetical solutions, but dismay laced her every word. She had no hope of getting him back.

Maybe Shahida trailed off herself, or maybe Palia had shut the words out, she didn't know. All she knew was that Ferrash was gone, both physically and spiritually, and everyone else she knew besides Lilesh was a galaxy away. A galaxy away and dying.

The tears came in force, then. She curled into herself, right there in the corridor, and let them come.

CHAPTER SIXTEEN

THE SIMPLE SET OF rules that the Grey Sails followed to keep themselves free of the tuk-a-wa's influence had existed for millennia. Shahida agreed with them. Who couldn't? They made complete sense, and she had never once considered breaking them. Earlier, she would have been completely within her rights to vent that man to space, but that hadn't been the path she had chosen. She shouldn't feel sorry about the fact he had done it himself. She shouldn't regret that she had put him in a position to do so. But she did.

Palia's pleas still echoed in her ears. A peculiar numbness had settled over Shahida since, but her brain kept replaying Ilhan's attack and the way Palia's hand had clawed at her through the air, as if she could eat up the essence of her soul.

Since Shahida's presence was only making things worse, she had apologised profusely and left Palia with the guards. They would see her settled into temporary accommodation for as long as she flew with the Grey Sails. They had only recently added another ring to the habitation cylinder, so they had room to spare. Shahida could only hope she didn't go stir crazy up there. The woman had no friends here, no frame of reference, no familiarity with Sails society. Perhaps Shahida would have to find her a peer to keep her company. Or a therapist.

In the meantime, she made the journey to the Speaker's chambers once again. When asked what was going on, the Speaker's response had simply been, 'Come and see, when you're ready. Take some time to calm yourself if you need to.' That was when Shahida had left Palia and boarded the nearest transport capsule to the Speaker's chambers.

She stepped out of the capsule now, blinking. Flowers glowed in the recesses of an arch.

This wasn't her stop. This was home. She'd stepped off here out of habit, completing her workday route of hospital to home without even realising. Shahida stood staring at the flowers, at the arch, at the familiar faces chatting in the shade of the trees around it.

She would take this time, she decided. News wouldn't reach the rest of the galaxy for a good while. Their acceleration had stabilised. There wasn't much a ship their size could do in terms of manoeuvring if it came under attack – the most warning Shahida might get is the jolt when something hit them. For all she knew, Warden Station could have launched its entire arsenal of missiles their way and she could be dead in a matter of minutes. Even more reason to see her family.

For the first time, having to wait for her airlock to cycle through its scan felt like an eternity. She paced the whole time, preoccupied with the thought of a solitary escape pod racing across the void behind them. What horrors had she allowed to be unleashed upon Ferrash? The tuk-a-wa didn't take long to claim a host, but it couldn't be painless. Every instinct in her shuddered at the thought of having her control over herself gradually stripped away.

The airlock beeped and Shahida rushed through.

'Shahi?' Ruslan looked up from where he sat with Spartak on the cushions in the dining area. A dark bruise spread across Spartak's cheek, and his eyes were red from crying.

'What happened?' she asked, taking a couple of steps towards them.

Ruslan tickled Spartak's chin. '*Someone* took a little tumble when the ship had a bump, didn't he?'

Spartak sniffled. 'I'm fine.'

'Right you are.' Ruslan winked at him, then stood up. 'Now go on, get ready for school.'

Once Spartak had left the room, Ruslan turned to face Shahida, his face drawn, a trace of panic flashing in his eyes. 'I heard we blew the docking boom on the refuelling buoy. What happened?'

Shahida wondered if Ilhan's camera had been transmitting back to the station, whether the footage even now was circulating throughout the tuk-a-wa-controlled sections of the media, whether it showed her face, her blade, his blood. She shook the image free of her head, spoke the words that she never thought she would hear in her lifetime. 'We've triggered the resistance.'

Ruslan took hold of both her arms and pecked her on the cheek. 'Shahi, I love you, but you must get better at telling stories. Is your job done?'

She opened her mouth. Closed it again. Her job had been to represent them on Warden Station, and she'd done that, but the Speaker still wanted to speak with her, and she needed to find out what would happen next.

Sensing unfinished business, Ruslan patted her on the arm and gestured back at the airlock. 'Go. Go on, go do whatever it is you need to do. Unless you stopped by for food and forgot as soon as you walked through the door?' He spread his arms wide in an admission of guilt. 'I have done that *so* many times.'

She hadn't, but she kissed him goodbye and took an apricot with her anyway. She ate it on the way to the Speaker's chambers, and the tang of the ripe flesh brought her mind back into focus. By the time she stepped out of the capsule – in the right place, this time – it was racing ahead of her, trying to predict what the tuk-a-wa's next moves might be.

The Speaker greeted her with a nod when Shahida found her in a meeting room in her chambers. A ball of scintillating colours hung in the air before her, fading to a dull grey globe just as Shahida entered.

'I couldn't stop them,' Shahida blurted out. 'I couldn't stop them infecting the exile.'

The Speaker tilted her head to one side. 'I reassured you that that wouldn't be a problem, did I not?'

'Yes, but...' Her words hadn't exactly reassured her at the time. Since Kaktek's sabotage, she'd hoped it had just been a little lie to make

Shahida worry less about any delays, that the Speaker had arranged for Kaktek to strike at the exact moment he had. But that would be assigning too much credit to chance – such a sequence of events had too many variables to be certain of.

'Come,' the Speaker said, and patted at a cushioned chair beside her. 'Sit. Commander Kaktek is here with us now. I'm sure you'll want to speak with him.'

Eyeing the inert ball of light, Shahida took the offered seat and tried to get comfortable.

The light pulsed, and patterns splashed through it like paint through water. <I saw you launched an escape pod,> Kaktek said. <Was that Ilhan? It was a good idea to send him back alive as a good-will gesture, if so.>

Shahida pulled a face. 'That wasn't Ilhan, and it wasn't me that launched it.' And she related the events of that morning, of Ilhan's attack on the exile just after the clamps blew, of the infected exile launching his own escape pod that she'd been fool enough to put him in.

<That is unfortunate.> The light spun slowly on its axis. Shahida had always found kluqetik virtual communications entrancing and she had to reign her focus in to concentrate on the translation, fast and condensed as it was. <I received a request to pick him up, but he was already too far gone. Had I received the message sooner, I would have been happy to accommodate him. ...Although I suspect you might not have permitted us to fly with you, then.>

'Your suspicion would be correct,' the Speaker said.

<I worry about the cost of this error. What if the first thing they do is send him through the gate, back to his galaxy? I activated enough traps to keep them wary of going through, but it won't take them that long to realise I didn't trap the gate itself.>

'Don't worry about it for now.' Calmness reigned over the Speaker's young face and ancient eyes. 'I know much of the behaviour of the tuk-a-wa. I evolved to live alongside them, to hide within their hosts, to go unnoticed. This and the Sails' charity is the only reason I survive today. Unless they have altered the habits of millions of years of existence, they will behave the same here. Once they have physical control, they like to take their time to incorporate a new host into their consciousness before giving it an active task. They will spend the next few weeks or months scouring that boy's memories, familiarising themselves with his galaxy through his eyes. Knowledge will aid their eventual invasion, should that be the path they choose. How long the process takes depends upon his ability to resist.'

The thought of another mind peeling apart the layers of her own made Shahida shudder. 'Whatever we do, we need to do it before it reaches that point. We can't let them send him through.'

A mischievous spark danced through the Speaker's eyes. 'Actually, now that they have him, his passing through may be the best way to save him.'

Shahida stared at her, trying to match her knowledge to the Speaker's motivations and failing for the second time that week. 'You want to use it as a symbol? Spark protests off its back? But the cost...'

The Speaker shook her head. 'That would perhaps be a side effect, but it is not my intent.' After a pause, she added, 'I would like to speak with the other exile. I will outline my reasoning when she is present. It may be that she needs to know, and in any case she deserves to.'

That the Speaker hadn't told her of her reasoning before and wouldn't even give a hint of it now chafed at Shahida. Even though the Speaker was by her nature paranoid – and understandably so – Shahida had thought she trusted her. How much else had she held back over the course of their friendship?

Kaktek had begun speaking during the Speaker's statement, the light from his message washing patches of colour across her face. <If we can't stop them infecting it, we can at least use the situation to our advantage. If it creates enough of an uproar, we could demand that the tuk-a-wa send all their hosts there and leave this galaxy alone at last.>

With a snort, Shahdia said, 'Because shifting the problem onto someone else's back is a lovely sentiment.' Her words provoked a flash of apology. 'Besides, would you trust them to send all their hosts through?'

<We can detect them.>

'Not if they go on the offensive and infect as many as they can. You won't be able to trust whoever maintains the scanners. You won't be able to trust anyone. We'd be setting ourselves up for a worse situation than we're in now if we went down that route. No, we need it to be a public revolution. We need to convince people to distance themselves if they haven't already, take matters into their own hands if they have to.' She made a sweeping gesture. 'That's what our resistance is *for*. How many ships do you have, Kaktek?'

<Currently? One. I might have been able to bring more from the station if I'd had time, but I was only able to make sure this one was clear of hosts. We're holding the others off your rear.>

Shahida's skin prickled at the revelation that they were under attack. Warden Station had something like fifteen warships at its disposal, and they could all accelerate much faster than the *Inzekir*. 'Will you be able to hold them off long enough for us to leave the system?'

<I pushed a few of the exiles' ships free of their docking clamps at the same time I blew yours. It took the station some time to clear the mess and come after us. Not all of the staff helped, for which I'm sure the acting commander will receive a lecture from the council.>

Amidst the next set of colourful patterns, Shahida thought she could make out the shapes of stars and ships. <Only two station ships are following, possibly one for each of the other hosts on the station. They've sent a few long-range missiles, but nothing we can't handle.> With a note of pride, he added, <They'll get close by the jump station, but they can't outfly me.>

'And then it's to Sol,' Shahida murmured. The exclusion zone around humanity's homeworld was the resistance's designated meeting place. She had been there once before, when her birth ship the *Yuldzar* had passed through, but the thought of returning still prompted a little wave of awe. 'Won't they track us there?'

<The measures the resistance prepared for this eventuality include a network attack that will trigger when we begin our approach to the jump station. It should prevent anyone gleaning our destination from its logs. Sol's jump station could be trickier to obfuscate, but with any luck, someone's working on it.>

The Speaker cleared her throat. 'We have a couple of hours until we reach it, in any case. The remaining exile – what does she call herself?'

'Palia,' Shahida said.

'Then bring this Palia to me. There is much I still need to tell you all.'

CHAPTER SEVENTEEN

PALIA'S GUARDS CRAMMED HER into some kind of transport pod to get her to her new rooms, and she couldn't help finding it too alike to Ferrash's escape pod for comfort. She kept imagining him alone in there, slowly losing his mind to a parasite he couldn't fight back against. Or trying to fight back and going mad in the attempt. Would it hurt? The xenobiologist in her presented scenarios: a thorny worm wrapped tight around his brain stem, something with pincers latched onto his spine, a thousand tiny ants burrowing into every part of him like fire.

The pod's walls felt too close. The guards pressed in to either side of her. Her suit clung to her skin. They'd washed the blood off it, but the surface of her helmet was still blurry, a long smear hovering irritatingly close to her eyes. She couldn't breathe properly. Her eyes were gummy with half-dried tears. When at last they arrived at her new rooms, everything they explained to her went in one ear and out the other. Before they had even finished, she walked in, shut the door behind her, took her helmet off and flopped down onto a floor cushion, exhausted.

How long had it been? Two hours? Three? She had woken up in Ferrash's arms this morning knowing he wouldn't be himself for much longer, but not really believing they would be separated, or that any of it would really happen. The promise she had made to him buzzed around her skull. *Sorry, Ash. Looks like I'll be too far away to keep that one.* Not that she had wanted to, of course. That was another situation she'd known could happen but hadn't really believed. It had made promising easier. Hypothetical.

She rubbed at her eyes. They stung, tender from tears that had since dried.

Okay, think. She wasn't about to sit around and be useless. She'd killed the Magister, fought in wars, destroyed the Empyrean. And how *did* that work, anyway? What made an empyrric empyrric? Their blood? The nexus network? The Empyrean had been created in this galaxy, before that network existed. As far as she knew, they had only destroyed the network, which meant... She shook her head. Sitting and speculating was just as useless. Even before she'd had the Empyrean, if she looked before her time on Everatus IV, she'd never been one to sit idle. But her mind ached, and tiredness clung to her bones, and nothing about this galaxy was familiar.

The least she could do for now was eat. Neither she nor Ferrash had had breakfast – a looming brainwash didn't exactly do any favours to your appetite.

A search of the cupboards revealed a tin of some crisp mix of starchy fried vegetables and dried fruit. Palia sat crunching them on the pillow, deliberately clearing her mind of thoughts in an attempt to achieve a sense of calm. The weight of her body dragged down on her, but it felt like she had her head in a vice, squeezing her mind, refusing to let it rest. All her attempts got her was a headache, and if the guards had told her where to get painkillers, she hadn't listened.

Some time later, a knock came at the door. Palia hesitated, but chose to ignore it. Instead, she examined her room. The floor and ceiling curved in odd places like they had been carved by scooping hemispherical chunks out of them. Coloured lights formed odd shadows in their pits and curves. The effect was alien and unfamiliar.

The knocking came again, this time followed by Shahida's voice. 'Palia, are you in there?'

Anger bubbled to the surface of Palia's mind and she scowled. It was Shahida's fault Ferrash had been infected. Her fault he was gone.

'Palia, I know you must be upset. I understand. But there's someone who wants to speak with you.'

Palia bit back a retort and considered just leaving her out there. She hadn't been paying attention to the guards' instructions, but she was pretty sure you couldn't unlock the airlock from the outside if someone had locked it on the inside. And she probably had enough food in here to last her several days. But...

'Who wants to talk?' Palia asked.

'The Speaker.'

'I don't know who that is.'

'She's...' A long silence stretched outside. 'It's probably better if she explains herself.'

Well, it wasn't like she had anything better to do. And maybe, she thought, not getting her hopes up, they had a way to save Ferrash. Her insides twisted just thinking about him again. Palia stood up, put the snacks away and stepped into the airlock as she refastened her helmet. When the airlock opened, Shahida stood there, still in her gold and green environment suit. Palia still didn't know who these people were, besides people who hated the hive mind. She didn't know who Shahida was supposed to be, besides someone who made terrible suggestions.

'Come on,' Shahida said. 'It's not far.'

Time-wise, she was right, but their trip in the transport pod blurred by so fast that they must have covered quite some distance by the time they reached their destination. Arriving meant passing through yet another airlock in a ship that seemed to be made of them. This one opened onto what appeared at first glance to be a throne room. Cushions lay scattered about on a thick carpet leading up to a short dais. A young girl sat in a nest of cushions on top of the dais, her robes even more heavily embellished than Shahida's, her face partially obscured by beadwork that fell from her headdress.

Palia glanced at Shahida, confused. 'I thought—'

'That I would be older?' The young girl's voice rang high and clear across the room, not quite imperious, but certainly full of confidence.

'Are you the Speaker?' Palia asked, taking a step forwards. 'I... I don't know what I was expecting. I don't know who you are. Or what.' The sight of the girl confused and disturbed her in a way she couldn't place. A bright intelligence played behind her eyes. Palia had met some clever children, but this felt different.

'Poor girl,' said the child who wasn't a child. 'Out here in the unfamiliar dark with so little to go on. Let us enlighten you. Sit! Would you like coffee?'

Palia set her jaw, an angry retort on the tip of her tongue. She hadn't come here to sit and chat. But she lowered herself to a cluster of cushions on the floor. 'What's coffee?'

The girl – the Speaker – jerked her chin at Shahida and the woman disappeared into another room, leaving the two of them alone. Palia's sense of unease strengthened.

'Your fellow exile. What relation is he to you?'

Palia blinked. A knot of pain twisted inside her. She opened her mouth, but couldn't find words to fill it.

'As yet uncategorised, I see. A lover of some variety, then, in which case I'm sure recent events have been hard for you.'

'You people haven't exactly helped,' Palia said, but she was so taken aback by such an old voice coming from someone so young that her words didn't have the force she'd intended.

'We did our best in a difficult situation. What was his name?'

'Ferrash.'

The Speaker gave a short nod and Shahida returned carrying three steaming mugs that filled the room with a strong, earthy aroma. Palia accepted her mug, took one sip and gagged at the bitter taste.

'It takes some getting used to,' the Speaker said with a brief chuckle. Then her face grew serious. 'Now then, the parasite that as we speak is rooting through your Ferrash's brain: that is part of a hive mind called tuk-a-wa, which calls itself the Great Convergence. You know this much, yes?'

Palia nodded, gritting her teeth at the Speaker's callous description. Palia had forgotten the names she mentioned, but they sounded familiar. 'Is there a way we can get it out of him?' She shot Shahida a hard glance. 'If we can find him again, that is.'

Shahida had removed the front section of her helmet to drink her coffee, revealing a round face with smooth copper skin and green-gold eyes. She had the grace to blanch at Palia's comment.

The Speaker made a dismissive gesture. 'We'll get to that. A little background first will go some way to explaining who I am, also. The tuk-a-wa, after all, originated many millions of years ago on the planet that was my home.'

More than *ten* years would be a stretch for the figure before Palia, let alone tens of *millions*. She narrowed her eyes, confused and suspicious. The xenobiologist in her jumped at the thought of learning the tuk-a-wa's origins, but the cynic in her had doubts.

'Don't look so bemused, Palia. Allay your curiosity with this: there was not one hive mind evolving on my world, but two, and I am the host for the other.'

The coffee curdled in her stomach. Palia straightened in shock. She cast a glance to Shahida, the woman who had had Ferrash thrown into an escape pod for becoming a host, but she looked awed, if anything. She noticed Palia's gaze and gave her a small nod and smile. *It's okay*, she meant.

It was anything but.

'If you're a host,' Palia said, the words snapping from her tongue, 'then why are you breathing the same air as us? It's been made abundantly clear that that isn't allowed. Or are the rules different for you?' With a jolt of panic, she jerked her gaze back to Shahida. 'Are all of you hosts? Is this some stupid war between the two of you that I've got stuck in the middle of?'

'I am the only host of my kind.' The Speaker's words rang out with unexpected depth and echoed around the room before being absorbed by the cushions. A small smile twisted her lips. 'I suppose that makes me a rather small hive, doesn't it? The difference between myself and the tuk-a-wa, child, is that I choose voluntary hosts. The connection is a relationship. Personal. Intimate. The tuk-a-wa don't rise to such morality, as you have seen. They take whomsoever they wish, whenever they think they will get away with it, and such a strategy has afforded them unmerited success in their evolution.

'In a way, you are correct that we are at war, but the tuk-a-wa think our war ended long ago. They think I am dead, and so I live here, in hiding.'

Palia shook her head, part in disbelief, part to clear her mind of how crazy this all seemed. 'You could just be one of them trying to trick me. You all could be. Why should I believe you?'

'Every soul in this galaxy could be tuk-a-wa as far as you're concerned. If that were so, there is little you could do to protect yourself. That you are still yourself and that the tuk-a-wa had such trouble infecting Ferrash is proof enough that that isn't the case. But there is a better way to impart this information to you.' Saying this, the Speaker unsheathed a knife from her belt and strode towards Palia.

At the sight of it, Palia leapt to her feet and backed away, heart gripped with sudden fear.

The Speaker stopped. She held the blade of her knife against the flesh of her palm. 'I can share the memory with you through blood.'

'No,' Palia breathed. Then she said it again, louder. 'No. I won't. I won't be infected like Ash was.'

With a small shrug, the Speaker sheathed the knife again. 'As I said, I only choose voluntary hosts, but I can't blame you for your caution. Still, I have no better way to convince you.'

Palia let out a heavy sigh and rubbed at her temples. 'No need.' She had no reason to trust them, but where else could she go? It was a cold, airless walk to distance yourself from people in space.

The Speaker sat down on one of the nearby cushions rather than returning to her dais. 'I imagine you're in the mood for good news now?'

Eyeing the girl with suspicion, Palia took a seat.

'The first part of this won't sound like good news, or news that will make you like me.' The Speaker took a sip of her coffee, one eyebrow raised. 'We didn't plan to go through with the procedure on Ferrash.

Ilhan, of course, interfered with that plan. But I imagined such a thing might happen and I planned for its eventuality.'

Palia bit her lip, waiting for the good part of the news. Hoping for it.

'My apologies here extend to Shahida as well. I told no one of the contingency. For in that vial of blood, there was not only a part of the tuk-a-wa, but a part of myself, as well. The *seylenon*.' She spoke the name of her species with a languid delectation, as if she didn't get to speak it often and wanted to savour the effect on her tongue.

The world dropped out from Palia's stomach. So Ferrash had been infected with not one, but *two* parasites. And this woman, girl, whatever she was, claimed she only took *willing* hosts? Well that was a load of *zash*. She curled the fingers of her right hand, willing there to be flames, knowing there would be none.

The Speaker grinned. 'If you could still wield the Empyrean, you would not be in this galaxy to be having this conversation.'

Palia jerked back, surprised. 'You know about it?'

'I was there when it was made, but that is an entirely different story. Let us first get some colour back into your face. The part of me Ferrash carries is dormant. He won't know it's there at all, and nor will the tuk-a-wa. That grants us an opportunity.' The deck beneath them shuddered. 'If the tuk-a-wa do send him through to the other galaxy – your galaxy – he will be disconnected from all tuk-a-wa in this galaxy. Likewise, the seylenon will be disconnected from me, but it will be able to attempt to kill the tuk-a-wa infecting Ferrash.'

'Then...' Palia screwed up her face, thinking through the implications. 'Then we went the wrong way!' She flung her arms out to either side. 'We could have picked him up and gone through the gate with him on board. *Zash*, you could have just fired his escape pod at the gate yourself and crossed your fingers!'

It was Shahida who answered, her expression dark. 'There are three problems with that. First, I hadn't been made aware of the arrangements, or I might have acted differently.' With that, she shot a wounded glance at the Speaker. 'Second, had we launched his pod ourselves and he had made it through to the other side, he'd have probably died of thirst or asphyxiation unless anyone happened to be near enough to rescue him which, hearing about the destruction in your galaxy, I think is unlikely. Third, there's a heavy guard on the gate, so anything we attempted in that direction would have been intercepted.'

Deflating a little, Palia asked, 'So what can we do?'

'We gather our allies at Sol,' Shahida said, lingering on the unfamiliar name, 'then we attack.'

The Speaker added, 'It is unlikely that we will be able to defeat the station's forces in an attack, and defeating them wouldn't get us anywhere. But if we can get through the gate, we can blockade it and negotiate, which will at least protect your galaxy for the foreseeable. With luck, doing so might lure your friend after us so we can rid him of the tuk-a-wa. If not, well, we can add that to our bargains.'

Scratching at her smooth skin, the Speaker gazed off into the distance. After a moment, she flicked her gaze back to Palia and Shahida. 'In the meantime, Shahida, I want you to familiarise our guest with the *Inzekir*. We can't very well leave her wandering this ship alone and confused, now, can we?'

At first it seemed like Shahida might protest, but then she nodded with her lips set into a thin line. Apparently the dislike was mutual, or perhaps Shahida just thought it an inconvenience. Resentment coiled in Palia's gut, and she ground her teeth in frustration. Not long ago, she would have been able to *see* what Shahdia thought. And it might have been open to misinterpretation, but at least it was something.

They finished their coffee – Palia more out of politeness than any love for the drink – and then Shahida left with Palia in tow.

As she left, Palia clung to the one little spark of hope that the second parasite represented. Ferrash had a chance. It was just a matter of time. And yet... the months she might spend on this voyage stretched out ahead of her, a yawning chasm of inactivity. She left the Speaker behind with that unasked question ricocheting around her brain: *But what can I do?*

CHAPTER EIGHTEEN

FERRASH LAY IN A heap on the floor of the escape pod, panting. He clenched and unclenched his right hand because he still could. Tears stung his eyes and pain screamed in his ribs from where he'd fallen to the floor after unbuckling his straps. If the escape pod's manoeuvring took him out of action by battering him around the inside, that would frustrate the hive mind's plans. At least for a while. Either that or it would take over completely while Ferrash was unconscious, but there was nothing else he could do. He cursed himself for not being able to stop it launching the thing.

His left hand clawed for the edge of the bucket seat and he grabbed at it with his right, heart pounding. Odd sensations danced across his senses. For a moment he could have sworn he smelled toast, and then a clean salt breeze. Swatches of colours flickered across his eyes.

'No you don't,' he growled. He could feel the muscles in one of his cheeks spasming, but he still had control over the rest of his face. His legs kicked out against the deck, but that wasn't him. That was the parasite.

With a roar, the escape pod's engine kicked in and force slammed against Ferrash. He crashed against one end, his head smashing back into the wall. His vision blurred. He tasted blood. When the fingers of his right hand flexed without his asking them to, he tried with all his might to stay awake. The gorge rose in his throat. He couldn't even hear the engine anymore past the ringing in his ears.

He must have blacked out for a couple of seconds, because the next thing he knew, he was back in his seat, doing up his harness straps.

Blood dripped onto the back of his hands from somewhere on his face. Maybe his nose.

He couldn't stop his hands.

A wave of fear so massive that it brought a scream trailing on the back of it washed up from the pit of his stomach to his chest and hung there, a stabbing pain beyond all his others. He screamed a long stream of incoherent words, railing against the newfound prison of his own body. He could imagine himself moving, but he couldn't do it. He could only beat his head back against the headrest, but after the first couple of hits, his hands came up to keep it still.

Another presence swam like oil in the back of his subconscious. Had this been how Bek felt when the Protectorate had stuck him in a vat and dredged his memories? A sudden pang of homesickness shot through him.

The force pressing Ferrash to the chair gradually increased until it felt about the same as it had on the station, then a light above the hatch shone green. Then came a thud. It must have docked. Unbidden, his hands undid his harness straps and he walked out into the interior of the docking boom.

The parasite didn't seem to care for his pain. It walked normally – or perhaps a little off, like its strides were the average of many human strides – when Ferrash's injuries would have had him hobbling. He could just about feel it controlling his actions, he thought. The sensation of moving his limbs ghosted a fraction of a second before they actually moved. If it weren't for being barely able to keep hold of his own head right then, he might have tried to disrupt each command with one of his own. As it was, his body began a leisurely stroll towards the station proper, and Ferrash couldn't do anything about it.

A kluqetik scuttled towards him holding what looked like a bulky repair kit.

'Hey!' Ferrash called. The sound almost surprised him, and he felt a thrill of pride at still having control of his own voice.

The kluqetik slowed, curious, but Ferrash's legs sped up, and a weight seemed to press on his brain.

Ferrash spoke as fast as he could. 'You have to get help. The...' *Scatz.* He couldn't remember what they were called. 'The hive mind are trying to take me over. Please—' But the instant Ferrash had mentioned the hive mind, the kluqetik had launched back into a run and disappeared along the boom.

Ferrash swore. His insides burned with the urge to *do* something, but all he could do was try to keep hold of the parts of his body he had left and shout at people. He hated having to talk to people. Fighting people to get stuff done? Yes. Sneaking around and manipulating everything from the shadows? Yes. Although of course he hadn't turned out to be as good at that as he thought, had he? He wished Palia was here to do the shouting for him, and then he was glad she was nowhere near him.

Alien thoughts oozed at the back of his mind, reshaped, solidified. He got the wordless impression of power and numbers and hopeless futility. *Do not resist,* he expected it meant.

In response, Ferrash targeted a clipped string of thoughts towards the sense of the parasite in his mind. *Screw you,* it said, with imagery a little more pointed and graphic than the words could convey.

For his efforts, a splitting headache stabbed through Ferrash's eye socket. He groaned, and they – the parasite and Ferrash – kept walking out of the docking boom into the leafy corridors of the station.

Ferrash shouted at everyone he passed, hating the way they looked at him, hating that he had to beg, hating that this was the only thing he could do. And why would they help him, anyway? They knew he'd been chosen to become a host. They knew their council – bunch of *ostat* sannots – had commanded it. Or given permission, whatever. The point was, they'd made it legal, so why would anyone help him? He clearly didn't get a say in it. He clearly didn't matter.

Still, he swallowed back the bitterness of that thought and kept pleading. In his mind, the parasite grew more and more annoyed, in its slippery alien way. It sent stabs of pain shooting through every part of his mind. He could have sworn it started walking funny, too, twisting his hips in a way that pulled at his ribs and the wound in his torso. The pain sickened him, and it was all he could do to hold onto his speech in those moments. He couldn't tell where they were in the station now. Faces swam in his vision.

What if it took control of his breathing? What if it stopped and let him suffocate until it could wrest full control? Adrenaline kept Ferrash's consciousness fastened tight to the last of itself. He'd lost control of some of his neck muscles, and he could only move his head in a tight arc now.

Find someone else, he tried to tell it. And like a coward, he added, *There's hundreds of people in the prison. Take one of them. Don't take me. You don't want me. Please.*

All that came from the parasite was the sense of callous disregard.

At the very least, Ferrash noticed as his vision cleared, his shouting had drawn a crowd. People watched on from doorways and side corridors. They pressed themselves against the walls as he passed. He redoubled his efforts, pretty sure he was crying, terrified that with its disregard of pain and its control over his body, the parasite could do whatever it liked to him. Put out his eyes, clamp hold of his tongue, gag him with his own body. The *indignity* of it, as much as the possibility, frightened him.

'Hey!' someone in the crowd shouted. Ferrash's hopes soared. 'Hey, stop!'

A man jumped out in front of Ferrash, a small drone hovering by his shoulder, a red light shining from beside a camera lens. He held his hands out before him. One of them held a microphone. 'Johannes Enries from Petrik Pangalactic. Can you fill us in on the situation?'

The parasite shoved the man aside, but he trotted after them. Ferrash wanted to scream again. Having spent his life in the Protectorate, where broadcast journalism was either state controlled or had a life expectancy measured in minutes, he failed to see how this man would break through any walls in a galaxy whose government had just sentenced him to this fate.

Ferrash growled his response. 'I've got a damned bug in my head and I don't want it there. Is that filling you in enough?'

The man hopped over a bench to keep up with him. 'But the council announced this was a diplomatic gesture between the tuk-a-wa and the exiles. Is that not the case? You didn't volunteer?'

'I didn't—' Ferrash began, but then his mouth clamped shut. He made a strangled noise in the back of his throat as his mouth filled with blood from where his teeth had clipped the edge of his tongue. Bursts of pain bombarded his mind and spots gathered in his vision. He blinked them back, not sure if it was him blinking or the parasite.

A bright cavalcade of colours rushed past him and a rahtuan scooped the journalist up and away. Spurred on by the shock of its appearance, Ferrash wrenched back control of his mouth, cranked his door open and yelled, 'They didn't even ask me!'

And then his face was moving without his input, and the oily weight of the parasite pushed him back into the darkest recesses of his mind, and after a fearful few moments of dislocated isolation, Ferrash ceased to be.

CHAPTER NINETEEN

ALL SHAHIDA WANTED TO do was go back to her job, to her family, to the status quo that would have only been improved upon by being able to go about it all in fresh air on an uninfested world. But the Speaker, through her wide influence within the Grey Sails, had seen Shahida placed on indefinite leave and assigned her to watch Palia. Or make friends with Palia – she wasn't exactly sure. It felt a little like the aeons-old mind had suddenly picked up a dollhouse and started throwing tea parties.

Palia hated her, anyway, so the Speaker wasn't going to get what she wanted. Shahida couldn't blame her. She just wished she didn't have to be there to remind her about it all the time, rubbing Palia's face in the fact she'd let her... whatever he was to her... get infected and catapult himself out into space.

At least she hadn't done it on purpose. That had to count for something, right? Someone else might have spaced him as a matter of principle.

'You're seething,' Ruslan called out from the small study that led off from the lounge area.

She came back to herself and made an annoyed noise in the back of her throat, putting aside the tablet with the book she'd meant to be reading. 'I'm not seething, just annoyed.'

'Same noises, Shahi.'

Rolling her eyes, she levered herself up from the nest of pillows and wandered over to lean against the study's doorframe. Ruslan had configured the chair in there to have him leaning back with his feet up and he waved when he saw her, his moustache quirking upwards.

'And *you're* meant to be at work,' she said.

Ruslan waved a hand. 'You always say I'm meant to be at work when you find me at home during the day. Just because *some* of us have fixed work hours. Besides, it's nearly dinner time, and I am working.' He flicked his fingers and a projection of a new piece of art hung rotating in the air by his head. 'See?'

She grunted. 'I wish I was working, too. Those brains don't fix themselves.'

'No, but your colleagues do, and you have some extra paid time off. You can hardly complain. *Unless*, of course,' he held a finger up in the air and smiled that frustrating moustachioed smile of his, 'you're actually just nervous about Palia coming round.'

Shahida gave him her best glare, even though none of them ever succeeded in flustering him. 'You didn't have to invite her to dinner.' In the two days since leaving Warden Station, the woman hadn't engaged with anyone Shahida had sent to check on her. She clearly didn't want company.

'Well I had to invite *someone*. I was terribly careless shopping and bought more than enough for four.' His lips twitched up further into a grin. 'Speaking of which, I think the potatoes need turning over. Could you?'

Grumbling all the way, Shahida followed his request, turned the potatoes, and prepared for the most awkward dinner since meeting her in-laws.

Shahida was tending to a small row of orange flowers in the hydroponic tray in their bedroom when the door chimed. Before she could move, Ruslan swept through from the study and unlocked the airlock. He whistled as he went, choosing a particularly lively tune that he was well aware annoyed Shahida every time she heard it.

Putting aside the plant cuttings, Shahida stepped back into the lounge, eyeing Spartak where he sat by the dinner table. He was engrossed in an evolution simulation, the same as he had been for the past few weeks. She wondered if the obsession would slip away once he finished the homework it was attached to. He did look up when the airlock finished its cycle, though. They didn't often get guests in the home. Home guests were family. For everyone else, they had outdoor spaces. Ruslan enjoyed bucking convention.

'Welcome, welcome,' Ruslan said as Palia stepped through the door, her arms hugged tight around her. He made a sweeping gesture, inviting her in before returning to the kitchen and calling, 'How's the room they've given you?'

'It's... not what I'm used to. Nice, though. I've been stuck with a bunk for the last while.' As she spoke, Palia glanced about the space. Her face grew a fraction paler when she spotted Spartak.

Not a fan of kids, then, Shahida thought.

Palia asked, 'So I take it the suits are only mandatory in communal areas?'

'Oh yeah, it's house rules in here. You know, the one we've given you is horribly generic. We like to customise ours, make them show a little of ourselves. Shahi adores me, of course, so she has my art all over hers.'

Rolling her eyes, Shahida said, 'And you never returned the favour.'

'Well what am I meant to do? Stick brains on my suit?'

'I take it you all wear the suits to protect against...' Palia began after removing her helmet, then trailed off with a glance at Spartak, who had stood up from the table to watch her with interest.

Shahida rubbed her hands free of any residual dirt and took a step forwards. 'You don't have to watch your words around Spartak. He knows about the tuk-a-wa. We all do, from the moment we're old enough to understand. We wear the suits even when there are no hosts on board. And the fact that we let a host on board at all was... an exception.'

'Yes.' Palia's lip curled, but it was a sad motion, not an angry one, Shahida thought. 'One regret in a string of regrettable events.'

Ruslan chose that moment to breeze through from the kitchen carrying the starters. 'Come on, sit. Eat.' He placed the dish of stuffed leaves, steamed dumplings, bread and dips in the centre of the table then paused, hovering over it. 'You're not allergic to anything, are you?'

'Not that I know of.' Palia shook her head and lowered herself onto a cushion. 'But if there are tens of thousands of years between your galaxy and mine, no doubt there'll be some things in your food I'm not used to. Then again, if we came from this galaxy to begin with...' She shrugged.

Barely had Palia finished talking when Spartak bounced over to her side. 'You're from a whole other galaxy?' he asked, eyes bulging.

'I uh...' Palia shifted where she sat, her face set in a fixed half-smile. 'Yes?'

'Cool!' Spartak's face split into a wide grin. He ignored the food Ruslan was serving onto his plate. 'What's it like being exiles? Do you do pirate stuff? Do you still have the Emp... the Empur... the thing that muted the tuk-a-wa?'

'Spartak,' said Ruslan. 'One question at a time.'

'Well' – Palia busied herself with her plate to recover some composure – 'Until a few days ago, I didn't know we had been exiled. None of us did. The first we knew was when we got arrested coming through the gate. And we're not pirates.' She chewed at a leaf parcel, then swallowed and corrected herself. 'I mean, there are pirates in my galaxy, but there are probably pirates in yours, too. It's just the same.'

After millennia with the Empyrean in their midst, Shahida doubted their galaxies shared many similarities beyond the basic template of humanity. Especially if they had forgotten about their own exile. It must be hard to forget the defining point of your society's existence unless you actively suppressed it or some calamity set back your knowledge a few thousand years. If only they had spent those millennia refining the weapon against the remaining tuk-a-wa.

Shahida dunked some bread in a tangy dip and took a bite. Spartak was quiet for now, but she could tell from the way he jiggled in his seat that he was bursting with questions, probably just trying to work out which to ask first.

'So,' Shahida asked before he could, 'the Speaker seemed to think you were one of those who wielded the Empyrean. Was she correct?'

The question curdled Palia's expression, and she put her stuffed leaf down. 'She was. I was.'

'Were you the last?' For the gate's open condition of the Empyrean no longer existing to be met, all those who wielded it must have died out, or somehow given up their power. But Shahida didn't think that was possible, so how could Palia and the rest of the exiles be here?

'No, but I was one of the ones who destroyed it.' She frowned down at her plate. 'Me, Ash and Lilesh. The Empyrean was so horrible we all thought it would be a good idea. But... there were a few problems we would have noticed if we hadn't been so pressed for time.'

'Wossit—' Spartak began to ask, then swallowed when he realised he still had half a dumpling in his mouth. 'Wossit like to use?'

Palia looked his way, her expression conflicted, hesitating on an answer.

Ruslan answered for her. 'Not pleasant, I imagine. Spartak, why don't you help your mum with the main course?'

Their son grumbled, but dutifully followed Shahida when she left the dining area behind for the kitchen. She ruffled Spartak's hair as they walked.

Palia's presence nestled like a foreign object in her mental image of her home, a threat and a guest and a stranger, all in one. She seemed normal enough, though – just tired and awkward around kids. And she only felt threatening because of her justified anger at... well, everything that had happened.

When Shahida returned with the main course, they mostly ate in silence. Ruslan punctuated it with snippets of life with the Grey Sails – the names of all their ships, stories from when they'd all last convened in the same location, a lengthy diatribe about that one piece of fruit that the newest ship grew that no one else had figured out how to grow yet. Half of his stories probably made no sense to Palia, but they filled the silence.

For her part, Shahida just ate. Ruslan was a lot better at filling silence than she was, and Ruslan hadn't got Palia's lover jettisoned out in an escape pod with a parasite in his head.

Halfway through his portion, Spartak broke his silence and started pestering Palia with questions again.

'So did you live on a planet?' he asked, eyes wide, after a couple of questions about what animals she'd seen.

Palia chewed the rest of her mouthful slowly, then said, 'I was born on one. Have you ever seen one?'

'No! It would be so weird. The sky bends the wrong way.'

'I get you can't go to planets where people live in case the hive mind's there,' she said, glancing at Shahida and Ruslan to include them in the question, 'but can't you visit planets where there are no people? There must be some that are breathable. Conservation worlds and the like.'

They had one conservation world, if Palia meant what Shahida thought she meant, but no one was technically allowed to visit it. But mentioning that wouldn't answer her question. Instead, Shahida said, 'The tuk-a-wa aren't just limited to sapient species. As far as we know, they can infect virtually anything living. Nowhere outside the fleet is safe. Some do choose to go on holiday, but it's a risk. Not everyone takes it.'

Palia nodded in understanding, and for the rest of the dinner, tried to answer Spartak's questions about living on a planet as thoroughly as possible.

Eventually, when they had finished pudding, Ruslan went to tuck a reluctant Spartak into bed and Shahida prepared cups of sweet tea for the three of them.

'So,' she said while it stewed, 'I take it you're not a fan of kids?'

Palia said nothing. When Shahida turned to regard her, she had tucked her knees close to her chest and rested her chin on top of them. Her gaze lay somewhere beyond the floor. Her eyes watered a fraction, glinting in the soft light.

Shahida felt a sudden weight in her stomach. *Shit. There* had *to be a tragedy behind it. Well done, Shahi.*

'Do you grow your kids in vats here?' Palia asked.

'Sort of.' Shahida cocked her head to one side then, no longer able to watch Palia's expression, turned to begin straining the tea. 'We have little pods that you can plug in at home, watch them grow, occasionally give a bio sample for antibodies and the like.'

'Huh. Sounds a lot better than our vats. Ours are... you go to a special building and they lead you to a room, and there's a baby growing in the tube.'

'That doesn't sound so bad.'

'Well I guess it's not, for most people.' She sighed. 'It's a stupid story. Kind of long, too. The short version is that I got led to one of those rooms and the baby in there was mine, but that was the first I knew he existed.'

Shahida couldn't help wincing. What exactly happened on the other side of the gate that led to stuff like that? She imagined some horribly dystopian society that spawned children without their mothers' consent – it was some small kindness that they had vats, at least, but it was oddly impersonal. Maybe just a bureaucratic slip? Whatever the root cause, Shahida wasn't about to go digging... Not in that direction, at least. There was still one question hanging poised over the chasm of a tragedy.

'What happened to him?' Shahida asked.

Palia stayed silent for perhaps a full minute, spinning her tea around in its cup, a reflection occasionally glancing off the surface onto her face. Then she said, 'You all hate the hive mind, and it was the Empyrean that... what, drove them back?... before our ancestors were exiled. What do you think of it?'

Taken aback by the change of topic, Shahida thought for a moment. She had, in fact, thought about it many times before, but the question had thrown her. 'The idea is abhorrent,' she said at last, 'but if it hurt them once, and it still existed, then it could hurt them again. We could use that. Why?'

Palia grunted. 'All the Empyrean ever did is hurt. Derren and I used to live in orbit above a planet. I loved that world. Beautiful. Untouched.

Full of alien life. The Empyrean destroyed it, and my son, and forced me to see it. I wasn't empyrric before then. I hadn't seen it used before then – who had? Then suddenly I couldn't get away from it.' She stared at the tea, her jaw set in a hard line. 'A lot of people died because of me.'

Her words reframed her presence in the room. The shadows around her became deeper, the lines on her face more stark. Here was a woman with blood on her hands, and she couldn't wash it off.

Palia looked up at her then, as if sensing Shahida's thoughts. 'Do you still think you would use it?'

'No,' Shahida said, quiet. But she would have used it against the tuk-a-wa in a heartbeat, if it meant her son could spend the rest of his life beneath a real sun and sky. Perhaps that was what had made the exiles so dangerous – the will to take a weapon and run with it, no matter the moral cost.

How many morals will we have to sacrifice to win this time? She wondered.

CHAPTER TWENTY

AFTER THE MEAL WITH Shahida's family, Palia had been trying to keep to herself as much as possible. So for now, she was holed up in her rooms. It wasn't that she didn't like them, she just couldn't tell if Shahida pitied her or couldn't stand her, and she didn't like either option all too much.

Palia almost wished they had been able to bring Lilesh from Warden Station so she wasn't the only one from her galaxy here. Not that Lilesh had spoken much since the Empyrean died. The most formidable empyrric Palia had ever seen, perhaps excepting the magister, reduced to a husk.

So, here she was, keeping to herself.

The fact that their journey to Sol would take several weeks wouldn't make avoiding people easy. Palia had heard the name a few times since Shahida had first mentioned in in their meeting with the Speaker, but she still hadn't figured out why people spoke the system's name with so much reverence. She pondered it as she took a shower. What was it? A place of religious significance? The galactic capital? The latter wouldn't make sense to gather at, given the council who governed the galaxy were the same council whose orders they were rebelling against. Maybe it just looked pretty. She'd have to ask someone.

First, though, she needed to think like Ferrash. Intel. She needed to familiarise herself with this galaxy and its denizens as much as possible to stand any hope of being useful. And, as a somewhat unwillingly retired xenobiologist, if not a very good one, she knew exactly where to start.

Towelling herself off from her morning shower, still energised from the hot water, Palia left her strange bedroom behind and began to walk. From her journey through the ship the other day, she figured most of the ship's area was connected by those long, straight corridors with transport rails down the centre. It surprised her that none of the ship's interior opened onto artificial skies – perhaps that was another case of technology her galaxy had and theirs didn't. Maybe if Palia was an engineer, she'd know whether her galaxy used the Empyrean to make things like that possible.

If she was an engineer, she would have known destroying the Empyrean would come at a cost, too.

When she'd walked along the corridor for a good twenty minutes, she emerged into a thick copse of trees with coloured pennants hanging between the branches. She hadn't seen anyone on her way there, probably because this section was so new that no one else lived in it yet. Or maybe they reserved it for guests. Did they even have guests that often? She couldn't imagine they did, not with their justified paranoia surrounding the hive mind.

At least the direction she should walk next was obvious. To her right, the avenue ended in a dull grey wall. Compared to the rest of the ship, its walls either alive or embellished, it seemed unfinished. Ready for whenever they needed to add the next section of ship. So she went left, down the massive corridor that she presumed ran the length of the whole ship.

It took five minutes for her to notice signs of life beyond the leaves and trees. She had been squinting ahead, trying to work out if those were people she could see far in the distance, when movement in the corner of her eye caught her attention. Turning, she found a kluqetik pruning bad growth from the wall with their pincers. Their carapace was the same shade of green as the leaves, almost invisible until they moved. At first she thought they didn't have a suit on, but then she caught the way light glinted from the edges of some transparent covering a centimetre or so from their skin.

Palia stopped and scanned the immediate area for any more kluqetik, but this was the only one.

'Hi,' she said.

The kluqetik clattered its mouthparts. <Greetings, exile. Are you
lost?>

'No.' Palia's translator had assigned a note of friendly helpfulness to
the muted colours that slid across what she could see of their paddles,
and she was grateful for the emotional indicator. She hadn't wielded
the Empyrean for long, all things considered, but she had still grown
to depend on the awareness it granted her. 'I was wondering if I could
ask some questions?'

The kluqetik kept snipping, but angled two of their paddles her
way to talk. <Ask away. I can answer many questions in half the time
you take to ask them.>

It didn't come across as a boast, but it did carry a note of understate-
ment. Palia resisted the urge to ask how fast they could communicate
with each other – it would be too difficult to get a meaningful measure.
Instead, she asked, 'How many different sentient species are in this
galaxy?'

<Unknown. This galaxy is vast, and sentience is contested,> the
kluqetik replied. <There are five communicative species within the
Allied Reach, which the council controls. Two more species exist
independent of the Reach, that we know of, one residing far from
all other inhabited space, one that used to be part of the Reach. But
these are majorities, in some cases. Some members of each species
may exist within or without.>

'I've seen humans, kluqetik and rahtuan. How come I haven't seen
the other two?'

<Incompatible environments. When we reach Sol and meet the
rest of the Grey Sails, you may see some of their ships. They can't live
with us and they can't live with each other, but they sail alongside.>

'And you can all be host to the hive mind?' Shahida had said as
much, but Palia wanted to make sure.

The kluqetik drew a scanner out from a utility belt and took readings of the area they had just pruned, but they continued the conversation uninterrupted. Discomfort coloured their patterns now she had mentioned the hive mind. <For all we know, the tuk-a-wa can infest all that is living. No one has seen otherwise. My kind were the first among the Reach to encounter them. It was not a good time.>

'How many did it infect before you noticed?' Palia asked, thinking of her galaxy, sat unaware on the other side of a hive-mind-controlled gate.

The pictorial equivalent of a shrug flashed across the kluqetik's paddles. <This was countless spawnings ago. I know it was many of us. From one may spawn hundreds.>

Palia blinked and the question, 'You reproduce asexually?' rolled off her tongue before she could wonder if it was impolite to ask.

<No.> They clattered their mouthparts and rattled their limbs in what might have been a laugh. The question didn't seem to embarrass them, though a note of warning appeared in their colours, faint and orange. <One to spawn the eggs, hundreds to compete, five to fertilise and raise. Such it has always been.>

'That's a lot under threat.' Palia could see why being exposed to the hive mind would have been catastrophic. The vectors it could spread through just from one female... In a curious tangent, Palia asked how to tell kluqetik sexes apart, since she hadn't seen any obvious differences yet. She'd guessed colour might be something to do with it, but the kluqetik said they had no sex. Given the translation seemed a little iffy, Palia asked for clarification, and found kluqetik only produced reproductive organs during the mating season, remaining sexless the rest of their lives. Beyond that, the kluqetik wasn't comfortable to explain.

Then the kluqetik, apparently finished with their work, started down the avenue at a sprint. About fifty metres away they slowed and waited for Palia to catch up, as if they had forgotten she couldn't move so fast.

Bringing her questions back on track, Palia asked, 'And there are no species that can resist the hive mind better than others?'

<Beyond the seylenon, the Speaker's species, no. And another hive mind doesn't count.>

Her heart sank, and her motivation to continue the conversation sank with it. The kluqetik took the opportunity to go about their business undisturbed.

For some time, she wandered the avenue, a deep and aching loneliness lodged in her chest. Here and there she paused to examine an interesting plant, making a half-hearted attempt to decide what sort of planet they might have originated on. She only found herself drawn to the question because it was easier to answer than the one she really needed an answer to.

How do you defeat a hive mind?

Perhaps she had the terminology wrong. People called the tuk-a-wa a hive mind but to her, a hive had to have a queen, or at least some controlling consciousness. So what would you call the tuk-a-wa? A collective? A shared consciousness? A group mind? Its base form was small enough to go unseen in a vial of blood, so she didn't know what it looked like. She didn't know anything about their biochemistry, but they could adapt across a wide range of species.

How could you do it? With a species so adaptable, if you wanted to kill it or even just isolate all its hosts, you would have to turn over every rock, find every lifeform, ensure it wasn't a host. What was the smallest thing it could infect? Insects? Single cells? Probably not the latter, but even at the insect level, that was more than you could deal with. On a ship or a station, perhaps, with as many scanners as the Grey Sails had, you might be okay. But on a planet? All it would take was one biology-laden meteorite striking near some form of life, and there would be nothing you could do.

And they planned to rebel against it, somehow. Palia tried to picture how that wouldn't end in the hive mind just spreading as far as it could, as fast as it could, both in this galaxy and hers.

The question dogged her journey, and several hours of walking passed before hunger brought her back to the present. She blinked and stared about herself, not quite sure where she had ended up, then followed her nose to the nearest place serving food. She entered through the airlock, bought some glazed artificial meat wrapped in soft bread with the allowance her hosts had given her, settled herself down at one of the nearby tables and removed her helmet.

As she came to the last few bites, a man's voice called, 'Hey, Palia. How are you doing?'

Palia frowned, trying to place the voice, and looked up to see Shahida's husband walking towards her from the airlock. What was his name again? *Scatz*, she couldn't remember. Usman? Rusman? No, Ruslan, that was it.

She smiled, mostly with relief. 'Still finding my way around.'

Ruslan sat across from her, lounging in an easy manner that reminded Palia of Bek. A frown threatened to pull at her face, but she maintained a strained smile.

He made a back-and-forth gesture above his head. 'We've got things laid out so you can access every kind of thing you could need in either direction. Along the shaft, round the perimeter, whichever way you fancy. Whatever you're after? Ten minutes away by shuttle.'

'You kind of need to know where you're going, first.'

He shrugged. 'The beauty of not knowing is you're always finding something new.'

Palia laughed, not because he'd said anything funny, but because all this was new to her. This whole *zashen* galaxy, the hive minds, the species they threatened. This time, she couldn't stop the frown. She needed to do something. They needed something that would fight the tuk-a-wa with the same degree of virulence as they could propagate. They needed a virus, a pandemic custom-made for parasites. And if the Empyrean had hurt them before, then maybe she could look at the problem in a way no one in this galaxy could. If the Empyrean had been *engineered* to hurt them, there must have been a reason. It must have been tied to their nature, to the method of communication it had destroyed. Perhaps the Empyrean and the hive mind were two sides of the same coin.

She stared across the table at Ruslan, who had a faint look of concern plastered across his face and was opening his mouth to speak.

'Kaktek's ship is flying with us, isn't it?' she asked.

His mouth still part open, Ruslan frowned. 'It is for now. Why?'

'I'd like to visit it.' Palia considered saying why, but her own idea disturbed her, and she imagined it would disturb the people living in awe of a second hive mind even more. 'We don't have aliens in my galaxy. Not any we can speak to and expect an answer from. And I didn't exactly get chance to explore when I was in prison.'

'No, I don't imagine you did.' He raised an eyebrow and gestured at the occupants of the nearby tables. 'But plenty of kluqetik and rahtuan call this ship home. Why go to another?'

'A different perspective.' It was the first excuse that came to her head, and true enough, so she rolled with it. 'There's more to this galaxy than...' She couldn't remember the name of their group, or even if they'd given her one, so she waved around her head and said, 'This. Isn't there? I want to hear what everyone else thinks of the hive minds.'

'Don't trust our thoughts?' he asked.

She gave him a sardonic smile. 'It's been hard to trust anyone since I came through into this galaxy, but that's not the reason.' Not that she *did* trust the Speaker.

Ruslan shrugged. 'Okay, well, I'll ask about it and see.' He rapped his fingers against the table and blew air through his teeth, clearly thinking. 'They won't have gone through the scanner yet, and we'll have to visit before they split off for scanning. Will you want to wear a suit over there? I'd recommend it.'

Palia hesitated with 'no' on the tip of her tongue. She thought of Ferrash, lost in the depths of his own mind to an alien parasite. She thought of all those stupid horror holos where the scientists got complacent and took off their suits. She nodded.

'Well then.' Ruslan waved a hand at the suit she was currently wearing. 'We can at least get you something better than that thing first.'

CHAPTER TWENTY-ONE

WHILE THEY WAITED FOR permission to come through for their trip to Kaktek's ship, Ruslan took Palia to a suitmaker to put together a custom suit for her. She didn't really see the need for it. Her current suit was functional enough, and it wasn't like she knew what aesthetic the kluqetik liked even if she had been going out of her way to make an impression. She couldn't help remembering her brief shopping excursion with Bek, either, just before they visited Austela's party on Sirat. He would have come up with an utterly crazy suit if he were here.

Palia opted for something more sensible: a black jumpsuit with flaring trousers and rectangular green patches marching along the seams. She paired it with the plainest helmet she could find, with a smooth, clear visor over the face and a sort of flexible, segmented metal crest on its rear. Ruslan insisted on adding a lurid yellow half cape of tiny holographic panels that shimmered in the light as she pulled it on. It made her cringe at first, but on the way back to her rooms, plenty of brighter colours shouted out at her from the people she passed. And soon she would be visiting the kluqetik, whose very communication was colour. Maybe her suit translated into 'please forgive the foreigner in your midst'.

Maybe it just made it easier for Ruslan to keep an eye on her.

Permission came the next day: because the kluqetik ship didn't have in-built scanners, they had to leave to visit a dedicated scanning ship soon, so Palia and Ruslan would be staying with them as long as the scanning took, reuniting with the Grey Sails at Sol. Ruslan chattered away the whole journey from the Grey Sail's ship to the kluqetik's. Palia tried to focus on the strange light distortions of whatever medium they travelled through between jump gates – so like Varna, yet so different. Soulless, almost. She shivered.

'You okay there?' he asked with the same genuine concern under-scored by a note of enthusiasm that Bek would have had.

She nodded. 'Fine. Thanks. Just wondering how your jump stations work.'

Ruslan shrugged. 'Wormholes, I think? My physics teacher liked to explain things too technically for anyone to understand. Aaand I might have doodled through her classes. In any case, the jump stations are the only way we can travel between systems.'

'So you probably should have paid more attention, then.'

'Eh. You know what you use. I'm not a pilot and I don't build jump stations.'

As he spoke, the bulk of the kluqetik's ship came into view, blocking the light of the surrounding medium. Palia pressed her face against the wall where its image was displayed to get a better look at it. She felt a bit stupid when she realised it was of course just a wall display and getting closer didn't change the angle. The image did change a second later, though, presumably by Ruslan's doing.

Unless the kluqetik had evolved on a planet with exceptionally low gravity – which Palia doubted, given their physiology – they had definitely built this ship in orbit. Long spurs jutted out from a central mass, giving it the appearance of a sea urchin. Crystalline. A nod to their natural environment, perhaps, and a good way to radiate heat. Colours danced and shifted along each of the spurs, translating via her implants to a stream of information she couldn't even begin to parse.

Senses overwhelmed, she blinked and drew back from the wall.

'Beautiful, isn't it?' Ruslan said, then shot her a sympathetic smile. 'Don't go trying to read it all.'

'Don't know how I can avoid it.' Palia rubbed a thumb along her brow, where the first stabbings of a headache had begun to spring up. 'All I did was look at it.'

He laughed and leaned back in his seat, his faintly embellished brown suit at odds with the colours she would have imagined he'd choose. 'You know, I tried to learn it once. Learn it properly, that is. No translators. I knew it was a stupid idea, but I just couldn't help myself. All those *patterns*. I'd still be at it now and a hundred years from now. All because I wanted to make some art that spoke to them.'

'How far did you get?'

'I lasted about one day with a kluqetik teaching me before I felt like my head was going to fall off. Then a particularly humourless linguist came and boxed me round the ears for even trying it. It took us centuries to get to where we are now, humans and kluqetik. And humans aren't built for it. We needed tools and screens and machines that could perceive a lot faster than we could. Definitely not an artist with a stupid idea and no grasp for language.'

Palia stared out at the approaching ship. The blunt tip of the nearest spur split open as it grew closer. 'Then I'm glad we fell into this galaxy when we did.' If she'd arrived unable to understand anything or be understood... Well, she'd probably still be in prison. Or worse. The fact that her translators had been able to work from such a distant common root was a small miracle in itself.

She suppressed a shiver as they passed into the shadowed interior of the spur. In that darkness, they pulled themselves floating out of the shuttle. It was only when its door closed behind them that the hull panels began to shimmer with darting lines of a thousand different colours.

Grunting at the wall of information that flooded her brain, Palia asked, 'Can't the translator filter all this out?'

'No such luck.' Ruslan floated ahead of her and grabbed the handholds of a pole attached to a plate in the centre of the space, indicating that she should do the same. 'Kluqetik communication is all contextual. Their language is modified by environmental light. Filter it out and you get a whole bunch of little mistranslations.'

For a few seconds, bombarded by constant information, with a queasy feeling rising behind her nascent headache, Palia considered asking to go back the way they'd come and leave all this confusion behind. But she'd never get anywhere with that attitude.

At least she could close her eyes through the next bit. She followed Ruslan's lead, positioning herself on a plate slightly further down the pole that she assumed must be a lift travelling the length of the spur to the central section. After a moment, a slight pressure through the soles of her feet suggested movement. She glanced down at the shuttle, receding with increasing rapidity, then clamped her eyes tight shut.

They began to slow a little while later. When Palia felt the change, she opened her eyes again. The end of the spur came to a dead end in front of them and colour spiralled into the centre of a circular hatch before washing out again, pulsating, like ocean waves drawn to one spot. The hatch opened to let them pass, and they halted in a mercifully dim chamber while mechanisms ground around outside and an artificial gravity asserted itself. Palia was a bit slow to predict what would end up as the floor, so ended up in an awkward heap by the time it finished and the other hatch – on what was now the ceiling, opposite the hatch they had come through – hissed open. A ladder dropped down from it.

Ruslan held out a hand to help her up. 'Are you okay?'

She nodded, then asked, 'How come they didn't send anyone to fetch us?' as Ruslan started up the ladder.

'You've seen how fast kluqetik do everything. They'd only get bored keeping pace with us.'

That certainly tracked with what she'd seen so far, but Kaktek... Well, no. Kaktek had made an effort to stay around them, but he'd been fidgety. Hoping he would still be willing to dedicate some time to talk with her, Palia climbed the ladder behind Ruslan.

They emerged onto an inwards-curving patch of ground that she guessed curved all the way around the near-spherical interior of the ship like a flat ring and rotated to emulate gravity. If that was true, it should stretch all the way over their heads, but Palia could only make out patches of the other side through a crystalline lattice that filled the space within like honeycomb. Its material, too, was crystal – or something that looked indistinguishable to Palia's eyes. The lattice didn't move, rotating with them. It filled the rotating ring like marrow in a bone, forming strange pillars and bubbles where it met the floor. Kluqetik scurried to and fro through the hollows of this lattice, even near the centre where artificial gravity failed them and they had to rely on their own momentum.

And even in the faceted depths of the crystals themselves, colours flickered and darted.

Palia gaped at the sight. Her head swam. When she tried to shake it clear, lowering her eyes, she saw all the kluqetik around her. They passed in clattering blurs, the colours on their paddles moving too fast for Palia to make out, but fast enough for her implants to make a go of translating them.

<—third communication from Warden Station—>

<— lattices on sea-green-blueward spur are exhibiting slow repair—>

<—shows swirling binary. Did you see?>

<—anyone seen my bow harp? It's been moved.>

This last message flashed along from kluqetik to kluqetik until Palia couldn't see the front of their paddles anymore, then at some point an answering, <Here!> returned along the same path. All this happened physically in the space of half a second. Palia blinked and was surrounded by entirely new conversations before she had even finished processing the old ones.

Closing her eyes, she searched about in her implants and found a setting to turn visual translation off entirely. When she opened her eyes again, all was quiet, bar the constant clicking susurrus of kluqetik feet upon the ground.

She drew in a deep breath. 'What now?' She didn't know the details of what, if anything, Ruslan had organised with the kluqetik, besides general permission to board.

'I think they have quarters set aside for us,' Ruslan said.

Glancing around, Palia tried to locate anything that might be a building. Did kluqetik sleep and work all out in the open? Kaktek had had his own office, but that had been on a joint station, and presumably someone from another species might have worked there before him. The latticework seemed filled in in some of the bubbles near the ground, so perhaps they had some room inside there.

That still begged the questions: Where were they supposed to go? Who was supposed to meet them? And how was she meant to find Kaktek in all this?

Palia cleared her throat. 'Excuse me.'

There was a shift in the colours of the paddles passing by. One of the kluqetik drew to a stop in front of her. Palia remembered to turn her visual translator back on just in time to catch their sentence,

<The greeter bids you welcome, has been informed of your arrival, and is on her way.>

It scurried off before Palia could ask more. Then, before she could even turn to talk to Ruslan, another kluqetik appeared. This one's carapace was a milky white, it walked with a regular stride, and the other kluqetik gave them a wider berth than they did each other. From the droop in its forelimbs, Palia imagined it as sluggish. An older kluqetik, perhaps? But surely she would have seen more by now.

<Greetings, visitors,> the kluqetik said. Even the colours on their paddles appeared dull. <Kaktek is currently busy, but I can show you to your rooms.>

Palia's translator gave the translated voice a slight feminine note that she hadn't heard on any other kluqetik. So if she'd been right in her earlier guess, maybe this was a female kluqetik, temporarily possessing of sex for the breeding season. It would be rude to ask, as much as she itched to know. She'd have to ask Ruslan for access to whatever passed for feeds or libraries around here.

At least focusing on the plainness of her carapace gave Palia's mind some rest from the colours racing past, and she managed to reach their accommodation without her headache making too grand a reappearance. When they stopped, she looked up to see her earlier guess confirmed. Here, the lattice closed in on itself to create a domed structure on the inner curve of the ring. Its walls stood just thick enough that she couldn't see anything behind the translucent, faintly purple material. A door was the only thing that marred its surface, and it opened as they approached.

<We will deliver food here thrice daily until you decide to leave. We have had human visitors before, so you will find the accommodation suits. Kaktek will send for you when he's ready.>

'Are the rooms sealed?' Palia asked. 'Against the... the hive mind?'

The pause before the kluqetik replied felt intentional, like a level stare, and her muted colours gave off a humoured irritation. <If the hive mind were present on this ship, we would all know it by now. Yes, the rooms are sealed.>

The kluqetik left them, then, and Palia cast a curious glance at Ruslan. 'What do they *do* all day?'

'Hmm?' Ruslan turned back from the entrance to another room within the accommodation block.

She gestured outside. 'All of them, running around like there's an emergency. But we're just floating. What are they running to?'

'You've never met a fast walker, have you?'

'What?'

Ruslan shrugged. 'People have a default walking speed. For some people, it's close enough to a jog. And people *hate* going slower than their default. This is just that. They walk faster. They think faster. They do everything fast, to our minds. And they like to have multiple careers on the go at once, so they always have places to be.

'Also' – and now he nodded in the direction the kluqetik had left – 'if she's like that, it means they're just coming out of mating season. All those careers won't have been touched in a while for a good portion of the population here. They'll have plenty of stuff to catch up on, and... well, I don't know much about it, but maybe they're still a little high from whatever biology's been doing to them for the past while.'

She guessed that made sense, and she took Ruslan's lead in examining her own room. It wasn't anything special. Just an odd shape, strange material, glinting colours. A cushioned hammock hung from the ceiling.

Though their escort had said the rooms were sealed, they didn't have separate airlocks or scanners like the Grey Sails' rooms, and even having not stayed in them for long, Palia's back itched at their absence. Multitudes called this ship home, and their constant scurrying put them in contact with a constant stream of fresh faces.

All it would take was one parasite. One microscopic parasite like the thing currently controlling Ferrash's body.

Palia bit her lip, curled her hands into fists, and considered the biological warfare she had come here to suggest to Kaktek.

CHAPTER TWENTY-TWO

Two days later, Kaktek still hadn't become available. Given how fast he could process tasks, the fact that he couldn't spare a few minutes to talk to them worried Palia. In her time aboard his ship, she'd pieced together enough information from passing kluqetik to understand everyone was trying to coordinate support in the wider galaxy. Kaktek and a good number of kluqetik had apparently always been part of the resistance alongside the Grey Sails, but they weren't enough. If Kaktek was having a hard time of it, that didn't paint the wider galaxy in a good light.

She knew nothing about this galaxy. All she knew was it housed a bunch of people who wanted to treat the hive mind as an equal with equal access, and others who wanted the hive mind either banished or killed. And somewhere in there was a middle ground, but it was a thin dividing line indeed.

It hadn't all been a blur of carapaces, although she had spent a good part of the last two days nursing a headache while she acclimatised to all the noise. She had taken a tour of an area used as an artists' workshop, marvelling at the myriad patterns she could find in their abstract designs and the million translations her implants provided her. She had accidentally stumbled into a room full of theoretical physicists whose rapid and complicated messages had made her head spin. Last night, one young kluqetik who was pursuing a career as a multi-species masseur had harangued her until she gave in and let him practice.

This morning, as their ship made its approach to the dedicated scanner ship, Palia sat in a larger lattice room with a sore back alongside

Ruslan, on a bench grown from the crystal. The room stretched out ahead of her, part cave, part amphitheatre, all grown from the same translucent purple crystal. Most of the kluqetik had carapaces that same shade of purple, but many – all beginning the process of reverting from male – clashed in vivid greens and yellows, fresh from the throes of the mating season.

One kluqetik, a deep orange, sat on a saddle couch in the centre of the amphitheatre. A complex web of strings surrounded him. In contrast to his fidgeting fellows, he held a prolonged, meditative stillness.

Palia leaned towards Ruslan. 'This is the fifth art event we've been to. I'm beginning to suspect this was your real reason for accompanying me.'

'Well, one can never pass up an opportunity to broaden your cultural horizons, can you?'

She snorted. Then the air above the kluqetik filled with a projection of the space outside – void so black it obscured the seats behind him, stars so real she could reach out and grab them. Her brain grasped at a memory with a chunk in its centre: the flagship, the projection of Hesperex in its sights, her fight with the Magister. Only the shape of an approaching ship differed from her recollection, thereby calming it.

The ship, so large she wanted to call it a station, was one giant tube, like a nexus with only one entry and exit. It had one purpose: to scan the ships that passed through it, to make sure no trace of the hive mind existed anywhere within. It had been built, Ruslan told her, in millennia past when the galaxy had been at war with the hive mind and her ancestors had still been there to fight alongside everyone else. The Grey Sails owned the scanner now, as a neutral third party. Anyone travelling to Sol had to be scanned by it and registered before their arrival, with no detours between it and Sol's jump station. The Grey Sails, with their own scanners, were the exception. Maybe they were already at Sol.

She was about to ask Ruslan what was so special about Sol, but then the Kluqetik flourished its limbs and, with fluid grace, began to play the web of strings.

The concert was a live event – a commentary, in music and colour, of their approach to the scanner. From a brief attempt to search through their library between headaches on the first day, Palia knew kluqetik liked to view events this way, even the most banal, and had filled their records with millions of such vivid displays. It had made finding anything important difficult, and they didn't even organise their records in any fashion she could recognise. She suspected searching with colours and patterns instead of words would have met with more success.

Towards the middle of this event – or some way through, since Palia didn't know when it would end – a new note slipped into the performance. The scanner's great maw loomed as a halo around the kluqetik's head then, with a tinkle of soft notes on the strings, a colour-spoken message shifted through the visible latticework.

<Kaktek is available for guests,> it read.

Palia stood at once, then blushed in case the concert-goers thought her rude. Ruslan gave her such a pitiful look that she had to bite back a laugh.

<It's fine,> she sent. <I'll go alone.>

<Are you sure?>

She had already started picking her way through the crowd on her way to the exit. <Of course. Enjoy the show.>

A line of colour in the latticework, tagged <Palia, here>, led her through several rooms to Kaktek. He stood examining a rock in the middle of a verdant garden full of what might have been lichen. These plants filled every surface, growing from the floors and ceiling, clinging to the walls and the rocks of an ornamental pond refilled by water dripping from the ceiling. A deep, musty smell struck Palia through her filters.

Kaktek made a short collection of clicks and paddle flashes without turning her way. <My apologies for taking so long to see you.>

Palia tilted her head. His red colour had muted since she'd last seen him, and only his forelimbs moved against the rock. Was he gardening? She marvelled that he had patience for the speed of plants.

'That's okay,' she said. 'It'll be ages before we reach Sol anyway. I've heard you've been busy getting support for us.'

A dismissive grey-yellow flashed on his paddles. <Everyone has. We need help, and we need everyone to be aware why.> He sent a second flash on the tail of the first. <What was it you wanted to talk to me about?>

Palia searched about for a bench. Not finding one, she stayed standing. 'The hive mind. The tuk... whatever they are. The strategy for beating it seems to just be fighting it, with or without the help of the rest of the galaxy, and perhaps luring Ash through the gate to my galaxy and then... reproducing that result somehow for however many of them there are?'

<We are limited in our options,> Kaktek said before she had even drawn breath to carry on. <With enough support from the rest of the galaxy and provided they haven't infiltrated too far, it would in theory not be too difficult to scan, isolate and exile.>

'Exile where? Were you just going to pop open another galaxy?'

One eyestalk turned to regard her. <We lack the knowledge to repeat that feat of engineering. And they would be exiled to their home system, from which they first began to spread.>

Palia figured the Grey Sails' pet hive mind had an equal claim to that planet, but she didn't know if Kaktek knew – or was meant to know – about it and the Speaker.

'What if there were a more efficient way? Faster?' she asked.

A second eyestalk turned to join the other. <You have something in mind?>

'Well. It depends if you've already tried it or not. Have you ever examined them? The parasites. On a cellular level.'

<If by 'you', you mean me personally, no. If you speak generically> – and here Kaktek's colours professed a disappointment at human languages' inability to convey such things simply – <then yes. They were examined during the war following our first encounter with them. Since the war ended and they became part of the Allied Reach, there has been no examination. Any research the creators of the Empyrean conducted was exiled along with them, and scant little record remains here. Much of that can't be reproduced or tested. The tuk-a-wa appear to suffer no medical ailments, or if they do, they hide the fact, so no treatment has required examination. But generally speaking, we understand their physiology. Why do you ask?>

A strand of trepidation wove through his colours. Palia wondered how much of her wanting to visit the kluqetik had been a subconscious desire to recapture the ease of the Empyrean. The kluqetik wore their emotions on their sleeves. Or paddles, rather.

'It's... not something I want to suggest.' Her own trepidation churned around her gut. 'I wouldn't suggest it if the situation wasn't what it is, or if they could be reasoned with. But has anyone ever tried to develop a contagion to drive them out of a host?'

Ripples of almost-disappointed blue-grey sadness rippled across Kaktek's paddles. <Not that I am aware of. The development of such weapons is highly illegal and condemned.>

'But what if they're the ones making the laws?' It was a stupid statement. Any decent person would make a law like that. 'And what if this is the only thing that works? If we manage to find a way to just force them out...'

<The tuk-a-wa cannot survive outside their host body. Except, presumably, if they emerged into conditions similar to those they first evolved within, which are unknown to us.>

'Then' – Palia felt like she was grasping at straws, but she had to grasp at something – 'if the contagion put them into a hibernating state...'

<You don't even know if such a thing is possible, and even then, what happens to the hosts? How can you guarantee the contagion causes no

harm to them? Those parasites have adapted to the physiology of many species throughout the galaxy. Any contagion aimed at them would have to be guaranteed safe for those species. And understand> – the colours on Kaktek's paddles became more difficult for her translator to parse, speaking of grand scales and things beyond comprehension – <that the species it inhabits are not just those sentient members of the Reach. There are species we have never encountered, from the simplest to the most intelligent creatures, whose biochemistry we know nothing about.>

'Then we piggyback the way the parasites themselves adapt.'

Kaktek skittered back and forth, relinquishing the calm of gardening. <Are you even proficient in the creation of contagions?>

'No,' Palia said. Her shoulders sagged. The last dregs of actionable hope were escaping before her eyes. 'But it was the Empyrean that hurt them last time, and I have more experience with that than any of you here. Maybe—'

<The Empyrean is gone.>

Palia blinked. Her heart clenched, and the colours of Kaktek's carapace swam in her vision. 'Yes. Yes, of course. I did that. And maybe I could *undo* it somehow, just for...'

Alarmed red and orange flashes bloomed on Kaktek's paddles. Before she could ask what was wrong, he darted away, out of the garden, leaving her alone. Had she done that? Her tongue felt thick with the ideas she had suggested, and she swallowed hard. But if Kaktek had left out of disgust with her, surely she would have seen some indication of that pass across his paddles? All her translator had picked up was alarm and perhaps a little anger.

With a sinking feeling in the pit of her stomach, Palia turned and walked back the way she had come. But as she left the garden behind and saw bare lattice again, the colours racing through its structure flooded into bright shades of red with messages too numerous for her to parse beyond a general sentiment of danger. She broke into a run.

Perhaps a minute later, she burst back into the concert room to a rolling crescendo of strings and drums. Above the audience's head, within the dark ring of space visible from their position inside the scanner, bright dots approached.

Clambering over to Ruslan, Palia took in his pale face and asked, 'What's happening?'

'Someone's shown up to crash the show,' he said. 'Ships. From Warden Station.'

'How did they find us?'

'The scanner's location is a matter of public record. They knew we'd come through it.'

Palia stared at the dots, thankful they at least hadn't been found because of any parasite aboard the ship. The confines of the scanner tube hazed around her, pressing down, offering no escape. If this were the Hegemony, a ship the size of the scanner would have weapons just as big. She just had to hope this galaxy had the same design philosophy.

She gripped the bench, tension rising with the strains of the strings, and settled in for the fight.

CHAPTER TWENTY-THREE

<Prepare for thrust.> The message flared as one great swathe of bright yellow through the crystal lattice.

Palia stared wide-eyed at Ruslan, gripping the bench tight, heart hammering. All around them, kluqetik hunkered down in place and began sinking into the crystal.

'What do we do?' she asked.

Ruslan looked around them, stared at a string of rapid colours on the wall that Palia missed, then hopped off the bench. He grabbed her arm and gestured to the floor. 'Lie down. Quick. On your back.'

Palia jumped down onto the floor beside him and lay back on the hard surface of the crystal. When she stopped moving, the floor became soft underneath her. It oozed around her arms and legs, and she was once more reminded how much it looked like honeycomb. In a panic, she tried to jerk one of her hands free, but only succeeded in moving it a couple of inches.

'Relax,' Ruslan said. 'It's just their version of a gel couch.'

'A what?' The crystal started to creep up the side of her helmet, and she couldn't keep a squeak out of her voice.

'Don't tell me you don't have gel couches in your galaxy. What do you do at high gees?'

'High gees? If you have those, your iner- Hey, if this covers our filters, how long will our air last?' The crystal covered her entire body now, and the thin layer between her face and the amphitheatre cast a purple sheen over everything.

'Don't worry about it. My suit's still getting air from somewhere, so there must be air channels or something. After all, everyone else is fully submerged, and it wouldn't do to cover their breathing holes. They can't hold their breath that long. I think.'

Palia didn't know how he could tell what his suit was getting, but just then the crystal began to shift again, moving her body with it. Through her blurred vision, she could make out the shapes of kluqetik rotating around her. The crystal turned them all to face the same way, as if lying on their sides, giving the impression of rows upon rows of solar panels turned to face the sun. A snort of laughter burst from her lips unbidden.

A moment later, the artificial gravity of the belt's rotation slipped away, though the pressure of the crystal around her still held her in place. She battled a rising tide of nausea, closed her eyes, and eventually won.

Then her sensation of gravity shifted again, and she threw up inside her helmet.

Some fans started whirring inside her suit, but thrust kicked in, pressing her back into the gel and splattering some of the vomit on her face. The sensation of it, burning against her skin, made her heave again. She panicked, terrified she'd choke on her own sick under such high acceleration, but she hadn't eaten much recently, so all she did was gag. When she managed to heave in a lungful of air, it came bitter and acrid.

From somewhere in the amphitheatre, the strains of kluqetik music continued to play. Had the musician brought his strings into the gel? Was he producing the sound via implants? Or had the whole thing been a recording all along?

The circle of the scanner's mouth exploded outwards in the holographic projection in the chamber as their ship burst from it. Stars spilled across the purple-tinted void. Then their ship turned, and the view shifted to look back along the length of the scanner, the enormity of which shrunk with increasing rapidity.

Palia wrested her breathing back under control. Sun-bright flashes punched across the scanner's hull from missile impacts. Colours shot out from where the kluqetik lay in their crystal cushions, data pouring from one node to the next, a constant roar of information that overloaded her translator. In the projection, other ships that had been undergoing scans scattered from the maw of the scanner. One, a boxy ship made of multiple compartments, burst apart in a flash of light and scattered its parts to the void.

<Do they not have shields?> she sent to Ruslan.

<Shields? No one has shields.>

Ancestors. The frailty of the structure surrounding Palia hit her like a physical blow, driving the air from her lungs. No shields? What was this mad galaxy doing? Why would anyone ever choose to fight in space? Any scrap of metal could be as deadly as a railgun round or an empyrric lance.

Something flickered briefly beside the scanner, then a chain of explosions burst in the void, *away* from the scanner's surface. Well, at least they knew about flak screens.

The next moment, the kluqetik ship lurched, and they began to accelerate in another direction, away from the scanner. Palia gagged a little at her shifting balance. Bursts of fire blossomed into life in the projection, obscuring all but the smallest patches of darkness for a few seconds.

We're under fire.

As soon as the view cleared, something punched the ship backwards. A ship she hadn't even noticed in the projection jetted a trail of gas and debris. The kluqetik must have railguns. Palia wondered how many of the ship's spurs contained them. If she strained her ears, she could make out a low grinding noise that started, stopped, gave way to an almost imperceptible *whoosh*. Force punched into her again. They were spinning. Each time they fired a railgun, they spun the outer hull and fired another.

The ship across from them limped away before they could destroy it and Kaktek's ship began to accelerate along the outside of the scanner's hull.

A message from Ruslan jarred her attention. <The council surely won't be happy about this.>

Palia tried to look over at him, but only succeeded in pressing her face against her vomit-smeared helmet. <Won't be happy about what?>

<The scanner. The tuk-a-wa can't just up and destroy the scanner. It's... It's unthinkable.>

<How can you tell it's them?> The scanner's hull raced past in the projection, cocooned in a flaming blanket of flak. Every few seconds, a distant patter of debris sounded from parts of the ship.

<Who else would it be?>

The projection jerked, and they swung away from the side of the scanner. A ship blurred past in front of them. <Aren't we technically outlaws now?>

<They're not attacking us. Or they are, but they're attacking the scanner as well. If the council turned a blind eye to this, they would be taking the tuk-a-wa's side in all things, for all times. There is no greater scanning capacity. There is no faster way to filter this galaxy into those who are compromised and those who are not.>

As Ruslan's message filtered through Palia's brain, the ship jolted. A shudder ran through the projection. A horrible grinding noise burrowed through the structure of the lattice and set Palia's teeth on edge. She struggled to free herself from the crystal, straining her limbs, her heart hammering. Had they been hit? She couldn't tell, couldn't read the myriad colours that exploded through the structure of the lattice and flashed inches from her eyes. All the translator could throw her was a jumbled mess.

<Impact on— curving lines of motion– yellow-redward spur broken off— blue-greenward sensor segment— orange concerto in deepest dark— lattice repair systems— manual tenders en route—>

She screwed her eyes shut. When she opened them again, they had reached the jump station. They were travelling so fast that it expanded from a tiny dot to a great ring and swallowed them whole almost before she could register the movement.

The weight on her chest eased off. The crystal retreated in a gelatinous wave over her body. She gasped, even though it hadn't stopped her breathing, and itched to open her helmet and clean her face, but restrained herself. All around her, kluqetik rose from the ground and darted to their various tasks. The strings, which had been so consistent throughout the attack that they had sunk into the awareness of Palia's subconscious until now, lapsed into more gentle strains.

Pushing herself upright, Palia turned to Ruslan. 'What about the scanner?' And realising she was shaking, she wrapped her arms around herself.

Ruslan itched at his helmet, whether by instinct or through some mechanism that translated into a good interior scratch, Palia didn't know. When he had finished, he said, 'We wouldn't have been much help to it. Not with just one ship and taken by surprise like that.'

She shook her head. She didn't like to think of that massive ship being picked off by parasites. 'How did they surprise us? We were hours from the jump station.'

That earned her a chuckle. 'Hours from the jump station if you travel through it under the legal speed limit. They broke it, like we just had to. So, either the rules don't apply to them anymore, or they just don't care how the council will react. And to not care how the council will react, well, they must be fairly confident that the reaction won't go beyond a slap on the wrist.'

Nodding, half lost in thought, Palia said, 'Hive mind has a lot of wrists.'

Just then, a cacophony of gunfire echoed through the lattice. Palia jumped, whipping her head around to find the source of it, but the shape of the lattice had scattered it so it seemed to come from almost every direction. If she took an average... it came out as the same direction that the grinding noise had come from before.

The musician, who had resumed his place in the centre of the amphitheatre, turned his eyestalks in the same direction with almost comic slowness for a kluqetik, as if coming to the same conclusion in the same slow-sensed way. Then his friend let loose a rattle of drums that seemed to bounce off every bone in Palia's body. A second later, he began a series of jagged, jerking notes on the strings.

In all that warlike symphony of rhythm and gunfire, Palia caught one consistent message racing through the crystal:

<Boarders.>

CHAPTER TWENTY-FOUR

FERRASH FLOATED AS A speck of dust in an infinite ocean, the scope of his consciousness the only sense of his existence. The ocean compressed him into that single point. He should have been able to swim, to navigate the vast expanse of nothingness, but he couldn't move. He had nothing with which to do so. He grasped at the concept of limbs and failed to comprehend them.

Only a fire in the back of his mind kept him from sinking forever. A constant scream. A rising torrent of rage.

He raged against this half-death. This suffocation of his self. This absorption of his body by some nameless parasite into a small part of its greater mind. He'd tried to reason with it, in the fragments of consciousness he had snatched over the past few... however long it had been. He'd tried to communicate. It never answered. Whatever the parasite was, wherever it had taken up residence inside him, Ferrash couldn't sense it. But then how could he, when he'd lost all connection to himself?

He lost hope, but still some ember raged. And just when he had resigned himself to the realisation that he must be in eternal oblivion, his mind caught on something.

Sensation. Pain, dull and distant, but so tangible in his sensory deprivation that he leapt upon it like a drop of water in a desert. The pain expanded. Light appeared as if through a camera feed, removed, but present. A noise, a high-pitched whir, spiralled around the emptiness of Ferrash's prison until stabilising in one general direction.

Ferrash held back. He kept the light, the sound, the pain, all tantalisingly out of reach. He recognised the presence of the parasite now as the weight that had been pressing against his mind. It still was, and he didn't want it to recognise him. He didn't want it to push him back down there for another eternity. The scream died into a whisper on his metaphorical lips.

After a few quiet moments, he edged towards the light.

The view resolved into the inside of the same hospital room Ferrash had been admitted to shortly after his arrival on the station. Robot arms retracted into the ceiling with the whirring noise he had been able to make out. A panel clicked shut behind them. Muscle and flesh returned to his awareness, and he ached to move them. He knew he wouldn't be able to. He knew all that would do was announce his presence.

A dull throb ached through his side. They must have brought him in for a check-up. When he looked down, fresh bandages lay across his chest.

So, at least they were taking care of his body. That was more than he could say about himself these past few weeks... or this past lifetime, even.

The parasite swung his legs over the side of the bed and stood up, glancing at a doctor on the other side of a window. It tapped his head, and Ferrash felt the reverberations of that ripple through him.

'Will this cause any problems?' it asked. It must have been asking about the pain mesh. Ferrash could almost feel those wires snaking beneath his skin better than he could feel his skin itself.

The doctor shook her head. 'It seems to be made of some sort of crystal. I'm not sure what purpose it serves. But I couldn't see it doing anything.'

A pressure wave washed over Ferrash's mind, probing for information, and he retreated. His view faded. For a moment he became disorientated, a distinct, dissociated headache that he could barely feel conflicting with a second ache that filled the infinite ocean.

After a moment, his voice came as if through wool. 'It needed the Empyrean to work. It's just a useless hunk of scrap now.'

'That's good, then,' the doctor said, and Ferrash drew closer again to that voice. She hadn't sounded convinced. 'You're free to go. Or... well, the station commander has summoned you. So you're free to go to her, I guess.'

A sensation of eagerness fizzed at the surface of the ocean and, with a nod, Ferrash's body turned and left under the parasite's control.

Ferrash resisted a wave of mental exhaustion by focusing on the four armed guards that met him outside the door. Three of them were human. One was the giant rahtuan who had come storming into the exiles' prison the other day... or week, or whatever it was now. A chill gripped his mind. How many of his fellow prisoners were now in the same situation as him? Not that there'd been any fellowship in the ones who'd beaten him up, but he couldn't find it in himself to blame them for that.

As they began walking down the corridor, Ferrash became aware of the presence of the other guards in the same ocean his parasite reigned over. The minds of these hosts' parasites hung like clouds over the surface. A constant cycle of precipitation, evaporation and condensation formed between them and the parasite. Ferrash couldn't access that information. It was too far beyond his reach, flickering too fast. He could just feel information passing from mind to mind at lightning speed.

I should try. What else could he do? If Palia were in this situation, she'd be trying to learn everything she could about how the parasites worked. He had to do the same if he were to have any hope of fighting against them. If there was any hope to be had.

So, bit by bit, he drew closer to the cycle. He drifted in the currents of the ocean, trying to stay hidden, a drop of water that the parasite couldn't hope to uncover. Fragments of the cycle revealed themselves. They flew at him without context or emotion, slabs of solid data, mostly visual. An image of shipwrecks being hauled to an impromptu salvage station flashed past, accompanied by details of the measurements separating it from Warden Station. Fragments of in-depth analysis splashed across his awareness. He couldn't make anything of them. They mentioned exotic minerals and a gate, so maybe they were talking about the remnants of the prime nexus.

Ferrash tried to pin down the relationships between the fragments, but couldn't. He couldn't match the clouds – the parasites creating the cycles – to their hosts, even with species separating some of them. They were homogenous. Every parasite was identical, forming a network, like communications buoys.

He set himself beneath one of the clouds, data washing over him like rain. If only he could have accessed his implants to make sense of it all. If he stretched his awareness far enough, pulled himself closer towards consciousness and discovery, he could sense his auxiliary AI sitting there, dormant. He wouldn't try to touch it now. He might need it later.

So he dropped back down and looked through his own eyes again. The clouds and their rain faded into the background and tugged a little part of his soul with them, with their constant and close voices. He couldn't focus on both at once, though. He had to see what the parasite would make him do.

Greenery passed by on either side. Ferrash recognised the corridors leading up to Kaktek's office. Of course, it wasn't Kaktek's office anymore. The doctor had mentioned the station commander and called her a her, so... But Ferrash knew next to nothing about these aliens, so who was he to assume he'd be able to tell one from another? Everything about them could change and be normal for all he knew.

The door opened. Ferrash recoiled at the disconnect between whatever was left of his mind and his body. He fixed his attention on the facets of the crystalline desk in front of him. If he could keep one point of reference, perhaps he could stop his mind drifting and pay attention long enough to get something useful out of this.

The station commander was another kluqetik – as far as Ferrash could tell. She stood there, milky white, all legs and paddles and bulging eyes and... she stood *too still*. A whisper from the cycles furnished her sex. Ferrash's memory furnished the oddity of her stillness. He'd rarely seen a kluqetik stand still. He'd never seen a white one either, but this felt wrong. Unnatural.

Then he felt her presence.

Information began to evaporate in a rush from the ocean around him, but she cast it down. She sent no information of her own, only one word: *Practice*. Little bursts of affirmation passed from Ferrash's parasite to hers.

'What did you call me here for?' Ferrash's voice came again. Having risen too far, sickened by the sensation of his own mouth and tongue moving under alien influence, Ferrash let himself slip back a fraction. He had an instinctual urge to vomit but no body with which to do so.

Still, when the station commander spoke, Ferrash had to draw closer again just so he could catch the translation of her words. He only got the tail end of it. <In Convergence, we have decided this.>

'Why this body? It is suboptimal' – Ferrash bridled at that – 'and not yet fully integrated. Others would be more...' There the parasite let his voice trail off, in fresh receipt of a wave of information from the commander. Clearly she didn't need as much practice.

Ferrash dipped down again, immersed himself in the new information. He saw a fleet assembled by the gate, stacks of food and equipment, doctors and engineers in crisp uniforms. The fleet slipped through, and Ferrash stood at its head. *Why this body?* Because they would recognise him. Back in his galaxy, they would recognise him, and see he came with help, and they would trust him. By the time anyone realised something was wrong, it would be too late. They would have been there too long. He would have served his purpose.

And then he would help infect that galaxy.

Ferrash baulked at the scope of their plan. The commander's message was more coordinated than the escort's information transfer had been. This seemed to come from both her and his parasite, strengthened by multiplicity. Her host contained many more parasites than Ferrash's one, and they joined their voices with his parasite's to communicate more effectively. She transmitted their plan in its entirety in a heartbeat, and it settled as a weight of understanding in the ocean around Ferrash.

To infect his galaxy would take centuries, maybe millennia. Without the nexuses, without near-instantaneous travel between one solar system and the next, they would have to go the old-fashioned way. They couldn't just create more of their jump stations – or not at first, anyway. Unlike a nexus, they couldn't just create one and send a second through it to get back. A jump station needed an end point, which meant they had to travel all the way there below the speed of light before they could properly bridge the gap. Even to get to the first infectable planet would take months.

But the hive mind had months. It had years. It had millennia. As long as it had one living host, it would survive. As long as it encountered new life, it would spread. And some day in the far future, with the advantage of technology they had lacked in their first expansion, they would come to encompass all life, and all life would be enslaved to its consciousness.

They didn't stand a chance. Not unless he could find a way to stop them.

CHAPTER TWENTY-FIVE

PALIA COULDN'T GET THE stench of vomit out of her nostrils and she couldn't get the sound of gunfire out of her ears. It echoed around the honeycomb lattice, mingling with the constant tapping of thousands of kluqetik footsteps.

She turned to Ruslan. 'Who boarded us? What's happening?'

His mask obscured his expression, but he held his head still, tilted to one side. His stance had the same feel to it as it would on a kluqetik – too still, too tense.

'We need to get to our rooms,' he said and, bursting back into motion, began to move away.

'What?' Palia grabbed his wrist. 'No one else on this ship is in suits. If that's the hive mind boarding us, we're the best equipped to fight them. Aren't we?'

Ruslan let out a huff of laughter. 'You're not even armed.'

'I—' But no, she didn't have the Empyrean anymore. 'I could be.'

'Do you know how fast the tuk-a-wa can spread? You see how fast the kluqetik are? By the time we reach whatever's going on, they could have taken the whole ship. We're better off holing ourselves up in our rooms where they can't get to us.'

Palia narrowed her eyes and gestured at their suits. 'They can't get to us anyway. And if you're talking about physical violence, how's locking ourselves away going to help? Where will we get food? What will we do when there are a thousand mind-controlled kluqetik trying to break down the door?'

A hiss came through the filters of his helmet. 'Okay, fine.' With a lighter hiss of metal on fabric, he drew a long knife from the folds of his robe. 'Come on, then.'

Eyeing the knife, Palia said, 'You're planning to run around with that thing?'

His shoulders sagged. 'I may have neglected my practice compared to Shahi, but—'

Something *thunked* further towards the sound of fighting and a strange sucking noise filtered through to them. The gunfire stopped a moment later. The kluqetik's normal susurration formed an eery silence after it.

'What was that?' Palia asked.

A kluqetik appeared at the entrance to the amphitheatre, then stood and flashed a message at them. <Come.>

Kaktek? It was hard to tell who was who when their colours changed a little each day. Then she noticed her translator had tagged them as Kaktek. She'd guessed right. But why had he come for them?

They followed him out of the amphitheatre, then out into the open space of the habitation cylinder beneath the arching maze of domes the honeycomb lattice created. A solid bubble of crystal that hadn't been there before bulged out of the floor in the distance.

Kaktek pointed to it and relayed what had happened with a shifting three-second burst of colour. <The tuk-a-wa boarded us there. We held them back to let as many as possible escape the section, until we were no longer able to. Then we sealed them in. The section has since been vented.>

'So they're all gone?' Some of Palia's tension drained from her.

<We cannot be certain.> This response came with an angry grinding noise from... Palia couldn't quite tell what he used to make the noise. He began moving towards the bubble again. <This is where we hope you will help. You have scanners, yes?>

'Of course,' said Ruslan. 'Don't you?'

<We have one static scanner. Nothing handheld. We have been over-reliant on external scanners like your ship, so haven't needed our own until now.>

'Even you, Kaktek? I would have thought you would be better prepared.'

Kaktek gave two sharp clicks. <Let us not speak of my lack of preparedness. Let us instead ensure there are no more of them on my ship.>

Ruslan came to an abrupt halt. 'We're still en route to Sol. We can't still go to Sol. We have to stop.'

One of Kaktek's eyes swivelled to face Ruslan. <You know as well as I that a ship cannot stop in the space between jump stations.>

'But—'

<They already know our destination. We have to assume that. If they infected a single one of us, they will know.>

Palia frowned. 'You told everyone about the really special secret place we're headed to?'

<There are no secrets among the kluqetik, and Sol's existence is no secret. Now will you help us scan this ship or not?>

A thick crowd of kluqetik had clustered around the bubble's exterior, never quite still, always full of fresh faces. As she watched, they scattered away from it like blown seeds, heading for the rest of the lattice. Palia pictured the rate of spread through that congregation.

'What do we do if we find one?' she asked.

<Kill it. Or trap it in a room for us to seal and vent.>

Palia took an involuntary step back. 'Those are your own people.' Ferrash was his own person, taken over by a parasite, and if the rest of the galaxy's strategy was to kill on sight...

<There is nothing we can do for them. If they had wanted to live, they would have run faster,> Kaktek displayed, a strobing flicker of impatience lacing his imagery. <There is no extracting the tuk-a-wa once it has taken root.>

Then, eyes flicking to the knife Ruslan held, Kaktek added, <We will assign a few drones to you, in case you meet more resistance than you can handle. Tag any hosts you find and they'll do the rest.>

'Of course.' Ruslan's voice had hardened.

A mild flash of thanks and Kaktek was gone. Palia stared after him before jogging to catch up with Ruslan, who had already started towards the bubble. He had spent his whole life in the shadow of the hive mind, shielding himself from them, scanning his guests, learning what he could of them. If he was going along with this, it had to be the only way. Distaste and guilt wormed through Palia's guts.

'So,' she asked, 'where are these scanners?'

As he walked, Ruslan opened a pouch on his belt and drew out a folded metal contraption. When he tugged at it, it reshaped itself into a squat box on a stick with three stubby antennae protruding in a triangle from the other side. It didn't have a screen – or any obvious buttons, for that matter.

'You should have one as well,' he said.

Sure enough, she managed to extract an identical – if less scuffed – scanner from a pocket on her belt. She managed to catch her finger in it when unfolding it, and the brief pinch of pain distracted her for about half a second from the fact she might be about to sentence a bunch of helpless hosts to death. At least it hadn't punctured her suit.

She needn't have worried. By the time they reached the bubble, Ruslan had explained how to use the scanner. It was pretty much a point-and-see operation with the results, in theory, displaying as an overlay on her implants. Different galaxies, different implants – all she managed to get out of it was a text readout. When she pointed it at the opaque crystalline wall of the bubble, nothing happened. No overlay, no text alert, nothing.

'It's empty.' Ruslan turned to regard her. She wished she could see his face.

'Looks like they definitely can't survive a vacuum, then.' Even if they could, they would have been sucked out into space when the bubble was vented. Had the kluqetik had to open a section of the outer hull to do that, or had they somehow shot their infected out along a spur? Palia placed a hand against the side of the bubble, expecting to feel the cold of space on her palm, but it all felt normal. 'If any escaped getting sealed in here... I guess we start here and scan outwards. But they're all so fast. They'll have moved by the time we scan them. Why couldn't we have just handed the scanners to Kaktek?'

'Look.' Ruslan gestured around and above them, and Palia reluctantly drew her gaze from the bubble. Sections of the honeycomb lattice that had been open before were now bubbles like this one. 'The rest of the lattice has sealed up as well. I think they've been told to stay in place.'

A voice by her ear said, 'That is correct.'

Palia jumped. Behind her hovered a pill-shaped, pearly white drone with a halo of spindly limbs and attachments. 'Kaktek?' she asked.

'No.' Whoever was operating the drone didn't furnish a name. Another moved in to join it from the left. 'Hurry to scan, please. We have much time before we reach Sol, but we cannot risk contagion by delay.'

Ruslan devised the route. With the range of the scanners and the extent of the lattice, it would take them over a day to cover the whole ship – and they'd need to, given how far any hosts might have run before the lattice sealed up. Kaktek had some engineers working on some drone-mounted scanners to help them, but until then, they were in for a long walk. Palia wondered if the kluqetik would be averse to giving lifts.

They ended up zig-zagging from one edge of the inner ring to the other and back again, in as much of a straight line as they could, going from bubble to bubble. The drones formed a constant presence behind them. Ruslan kept glancing back over his shoulder at them, at their many limbs. They could have covered the ground faster if they split up, but two things had stopped him doing so: first, that Palia's implants couldn't link to her scanner correctly; second, that if one of the drone operators got infected, they'd need to have each other's backs.

Half a day later, fresh from a hasty lunch, they'd only managed to cover two thirds of the ring and hadn't touched the lower-gravity inner lattice. One of the new scanner drones had taken on that job. Relieved that she wouldn't have to worry about the shifting gravity,

Palia looked forwards to finishing their sweep without event. The hive mind clearly hadn't reached beyond the bulge.

She trudged now on aching feet across a floor of a similar moss-like material to the one Kaktek had been tending in the garden. Obedient to their stay-in-place commandment, kluqetik sat embedded in the ground like peculiar shrubs, only their torsos sticking above the moss. Their gaze crawled across her skin, and she shivered. The extent of their attention surprised her. With their bodies embedded, they couldn't fidget. Maybe in this environment, that was a comfort?

'Shit,' Ruslan said.

Palia blinked. That hadn't translated. 'What's shit?'

Before anyone could reply, several things happened at once. Their drone escorts rose, one to either side, limbs spread wide. Three of the kluqetik erupted from the ground. Moss, dirt, and little fragments of crystal sprayed across their neighbours. Ruslan took half a step back, drew his knife and was halfway through saying 'Shit' again before the three kluqetik sprinted in different directions.

Two loud *booms* splintered the air. Shotgun blasts tore apart the ground where the kluqetik had been resting, tearing the back legs and tendrils off one but missing the others. The drones whirred back from their recoil and gave chase. Bright cutting lasers shone from their limbs, tracking at kluqetik pace.

One of the kluqetik – *hosts, they must be* – barrelled towards her. Palia reacted without thinking. She sidestepped and kicked out at the host as it passed, but their legs got tangled. Its momentum flung her to the ground and flipped her over. She rolled, head ringing, expecting sharp limbs to come stabbing down at her any moment.

When she looked up, the host was two hundred metres away, staggering on two legs, a trail of ichor glimmering on the moss behind it. *Not fighting. Maximising potential spread.* Someone would have a lot of cleaning to do after this.

'Don't touch the blood!' she shouted.

A drone hovering behind the host's unsteady form fired its shotgun again. The shot ripped through the host's body, sending fragments of its carapace flying in every direction as shrapnel, leaving the back of its torso and top of its abdomen a meaty mess.

Palia picked herself up from the floor and, nerves dancing through her chest, aimed her scanner at the kluqetik along the host's path.

One of them shuddered. She focused on the readout sent to her implants.

<POSITIVE. POSITIVE. POSITIVE.>

'Shit, shit, shit,' Ruslan hissed.

CHAPTER TWENTY-SIX

ADRENALINE FLOODED PALIA'S SYSTEM. Her heart hammered in her chest. Her throat tightened. She reached for the Empyrean, but it wasn't there, and it wasn't there because she'd killed it.

The kluqetik that had begun to twitch in front of her flashed out an urgent message. <Help me. Help me. Siblings, I am losing control of myself. Please help. Run. Run. Stay. Stay close to me.> The colours of its message shifted to a warm, welcoming green.

Stillness stretched around her, the drones seeming to hang motionless in the air even as they turned to face their next target, the kluqetik's muted twitches a focal point on the mossy floor. Palia patted at her waist. There, at the small of her back – the grip of a knife.

She tugged it free. At the slight noise, the kluqetik that hadn't already burst from the ground exploded into motion – all of them, all at once.

Run, the kluqetik had begged. And if there was one thing the kluqetik were certainly good at, it was running.

<POSITIVE. POSITIVE. POSITIVE.> She had no idea which of them her scanner was screaming about. Ruslan lunged and stabbed at something. The drones burst into slicing motion. She just stood there, knife in hand, teeth clamped tight shut.

'Kaktek!' she shouted. 'Someone get a message to Kaktek. We need those scanner drones down here, now!' They'd never catch them all, otherwise. Ruslan wouldn't be able to keep up to scan them and Palia wouldn't be able to isolate individuals unless they stood completely still.

They couldn't even go anywhere. The room was sealed. All the newly closed bubbles in the habitation cylinder only opened to let Ruslan, Palia and the drones through. But that would change if the hive mind took control of whoever managed the bubbles, unless that was an AI, and even then it had to take orders from *someone*.

That gave her an idea.

'Hey, Ruslan!' she called.

Ruslan glanced over to her from where he was having a standoff with a three-legged kluqetik, his arms spread wide, the knife glinting. 'What?'

'What's the best way to get a message to Kaktek?'

'Go—' The kluqetik lunged to one side and Ruslan threw himself on its back, sending them both to the floor in a messy heap. He drove his knife through a gap in the carapace between the kluqetik's abdomen and torso. 'Go through the suit interface and find the ship network.'

Easier said than done. Palia rushed over to Ruslan in case he needed a hand with the thrashing kluqetik. She wished Ferrash were here. He'd once mentioned the auxiliary AI in his implants – multiple programmatic replicas of his own consciousness, running in parallel to his usual thought processes. Never mind how fast he would have been able to communicate – he probably would have managed to hack the whole ship by now and control the lattice himself. Or perhaps she was overestimating his abilities, the same way Bek had been prone to do. The same way, she supposed, that Ferrash had before they'd messed everything up.

It took her five seconds to figure out how to send a message. In that time, the scrambling kluqetik had fetched up against the exterior walls, realised how little space was between them and their potentially infected neighbours, and begun either racing back for a clear space or climbing up the walls. Far above them, the crystalline ceiling deformed into two holes and the scanner drones came speeding through.

At least he got that message.

<Kaktek,> she sent, and gave Ruslan a hand up from the floor. On the ceiling, the two holes closed back up. <You know how you can reshape the crystal?>

<Yes.>

<Can you change its structure so it holds people in place? Like during the attack when we needed to accelerate?>

There was a fractional pause before Kaktek's next message. <Structure outside a burn is usually controlled by individuals via colour code, but I can override that. Done. Although this means no one can climb into it, either.>

<Can't you make it... I don't know, grab them or something?>

This time, she received no reply. Ruslan stood beside her, panting. The drones had paired up, one scanner to one shooter – though the scanners had plenty firepower themselves.

Then the floor shifted underneath her. She staggered and clutched onto Ruslan for balance. *Please don't make me throw up again.* She closed her eyes against the rising tide of nausea. When she opened them again, the floor beneath her feet was solid. It began to ripple and bulge, spreading out from her in every direction,.

One of the kluqetik that had been climbing the wall lost its footing and fell. It landed with an indignant chatter and was halfway to righting itself when the floor beneath it rose like gel squeezed from a tube, encasing its legs in an iron grip. All around them, tendrils and nodules of crystal broke free from beneath the moss and took hold of whoever stood above. It acted fast – so fast that with a sickening *crack*, one of the nearby kluqetik, moving too fast to stop, snapped its leg clean in two.

Palia winced at the high-pitched noises it made, like a knife on glass, and turned to Ruslan. 'It should be easier to scan now.'

He let out a rush of breath. 'Let's get started, then.'

* * *

Three hours later and Palia was more exhausted than she cared to admit. They'd had to pause for a few minutes when the ship exited the jump station at Sol and started its deceleration burn, but it hadn't been enough time to rest, and certainly not enough time to eat. Now she stood beside Ruslan, her stomach pulling at her insides, her scanner pointed at the final lattice bubble.

<POSITIVE,> it read, so many times that it formed a constant refrain. They hadn't even gone in there yet.

She sucked air between her teeth. 'I was hoping the ones we found earlier were the last of them. What can you see?'

Even the drones seemed to be unsure of themselves, hovering by the border like them.

Ruslan stared straight ahead. 'I... It's all over the place. Everything in there is infected. That's a few kluqetik and... lots of little shivery things. I think they're swimming?'

'Are they food?' Palia didn't know what the kluqetik ate. In actual fact, she couldn't remember ever seeing them do so.

The chittering of mouthparts behind her made her whirl around.

<They are hatchlings,> Kaktek said. With his colours fading, he looked weary. <They were spawned during this last cycle.>

A shudder ran through Ruslan. 'They're all infected,' he said. 'I'm sorry.'

Kaktek picked at his mandibles for a few moments before flashing a colourful reply. <Their loss will be regrettable, but hatchlings matter little. This batch is slow and has not yet become intelligent, and most would not survive to become shiverlings anyway. Kluqetik lives are not as long nor as precious as yours, human.>

Palia looked between the two of them and asked, her voice low, 'How many of them are there?'

<This was a good spawning. There were just over four thousand. I'm not sure how many currently survive. It doesn't matter. Were they shiverlings or adults, their deaths would still be a necessary sacrifice to ensure our survival. I'll have the ship eject them.>

'Wait.' Palia's throat tightened. 'This room is completely sealed, right? They can't get in or out, they can't somehow send parasites through the air vents?'

<That is besides the point. They are lost. Yes, they are isolated, but they are lost.>

'And they can't communicate with the rest of the hive mind, right? They're too far away.'

<Since the Empyrean stripped them of their long-range connections, yes. Why are you asking all this? Is such counterproductive pity common in your galaxy?>

Even without the words to back it up, Palia could tell she'd worn through Kaktek's patience. A frustrated yellow-brown pulsed on the surface of his paddles.

'I suggested experimenting earlier,' she said. 'We need to find something we can use against the hive mind. To do that, we need a sample.' She gestured to the wall. 'There are a few thousand potential samples in there, and you want to vent them into space.'

Kaktek stared at her, one foot tapping the ground, then said, <They can't stay on the ship. We won't stay in Sol forever.>

'Then send them somewhere else. Maroon them on a planet or something. Or sure, vent them, just let us go in and grab a few for research first. Do you have any sealed containers we can use that would keep them alive?'

<We can make one. And then we vent them.>

<Commander.> The surface of one of the drones pulsed with colour. <You might want to put that to vote, first. Word got out that the spawn is contaminated and opinions are... mixed. Venting them without discussion would set a course for discord.>

Kaktek sunk lower on his legs and dipped one of his eyestalks. A sigh? A gesture of acceptance? Who knew. <Very well. I'll head to the central chamber. Send these two what they need.>

<Thank you, commander.>

Without another word, Kaktek sped off, leaving them alone and exhausted by the wall separating the kluqetik from their infected young.

'It's working, I think,' Palia said. While they had waited, Ruslan had helped her hook her implants up to the scan properly – with a lot of cross-referencing of both their software manuals. Now when she peered at the wall, the red-lit shapes of creatures superimposed themselves on her vision, simultaneously projected behind the wall and visible in front of it. The contradiction made her head hurt, but at least she could see.

She made out two adult kluqetik in there, each standing opposite each other by the edge of the biggest mass of red. That mass swirled in one unified pattern, thousands of little shrimp-like shapes never once bumping into each other. She wondered if their coordination stemmed from their innate speed of thought or from their being part of one mind now.

How would being part of something like that from infancy affect a developing mind? Even if she did find a way to remove the parasites, how fast did kluqetik grow? Would they have any sense of self to return to?

'You're giving that wall the same look Shahi gives to x-rays,' Ruslan said.

Blinking, Palia took a step back, unaware that she'd been leaning forwards so far she'd almost set her forehead against the crystal. She couldn't tell what Ruslan was thinking behind his inscrutable mask. 'I, uh... I'm a xenobiologist. Or was. I was just thinking about what this means for the hatchlings. Do you know much about them?'

Ruslan shrugged. 'There are some spawning chambers on our – the Grey Sails' – ships, but they don't let anyone in them, and they don't really talk about it. At some point you just notice they've all picked up a bunch of beautiful colours, then they disappear for a while, then there are a few hundred little ones getting under everyone's feet.'

'Hmm.' She wished he had more answers. Not to worry. She wouldn't be staying in this galaxy long, if she had anything to do with it.

As if thoughts of escape had summoned them, a kluqetik appeared pushing a trolley full of equipment. <For the samples.>

'Thank you.' Palia bent to examined the trolley as it left. They'd given her four sample tubes the size of her torso, a water pump and a big net on a pole.

Taking hold of the net, she turned to Ruslan. 'Time to catch ourselves a parasite.'

'I don't care for your phrasing, but sure.'

CHAPTER TWENTY-SEVEN

SHAHIDA HAD NEVER HAD cause to go to the bridge of the Inzekir. So when she received an invitation from the Speaker – who had her own invitation from the captain – she at once knew something had gone wrong. She hadn't been able to pace in the small capsule that had brought them to the bridge, so she paced now, much to the annoyance of the bridge staff and the amusement of the Speaker, who stood chewing some sweets. She must have had them in a dispenser inside her suit.

The reinforced blast door separating the bridge from the rest of the ship slid open and the captain entered with members of his council close behind. He wore black robes that shimmered purple where they caught the light, and a silver-studded mesh glittered like stars where it fell from his upturned pyramidal headpiece.

'Thank you for coming, Speaker,' he said, and tilted his head towards the stairs further along the wall from the entrance. 'This way, please.'

The Speaker swallowed her sweet, licked her lips, and fell into step beside the captain. Shahida followed with the council. The stairs, like their twin on the other side of the door, curved upwards to an elevated level overlooking the main work area of the bridge. Glass separated the two rooms. Both were bare of ornament, stark whites and greys in contrast to the rest of the ship. Almost like her hospital, in fact.

When the door at the top of the stairs slid closed behind them, it did so with a solid *thunk*. Locked. Shahida surveyed the room.

An oval standing table stretched out before her, made from some kind of highly polished wood with a holoprojector jutting from the centre. The captain took his place at the far end and waited for the rest of them. Shahida stayed close to the Speaker, who settled onto a tall chair opposite the captain. Overhead, a light strobed. Orange, orange, blue. It only went blue instead of green because the Speaker was present.

'Scan clear.' The captain reached up and detached his helmet from his suit with a series of clicks, then pulled it off and laid it on the table. Around him, the others did the same.

Shahida hesitated, but removed hers as well. This room might not have an airlock, but the bridge itself did. Everyone in it would have had to pass through the scanners first – not to mention all the other scanners on the ship.

'So, Sato,' the Speaker began, 'what is it you've brought us here for? We haven't arrived in Sol yet, I know that much.'

The captain stroked at his wispy grey beard and moustache, the lines of his face creasing into a grimace. 'The tuk-a-wa have struck their first blow against us. There could be a positive element in the precise action they have chosen to take, but... we'll see.' His lips twitched, and a hard light came into his eyes. 'We just received word that they attacked the scanner.'

The scanner. No! Ruslan should have been travelling through that ship with the kluqetik some time in the last few days. Curse that exile and all the calamity she had drawn here. *No, curse the tuk-a-wa.*

'When?' Shahida asked.

'Four days ago. The message only just reached us. Don't worry, I'm aware your husband is travelling with Kaktek. It was Kaktek who let us know about the attack – they're still on their way to Sol.'

A weight lifted from Shahida's chest and she drew in a breath she hadn't realised she'd been holding.

The Speaker took her chance to speak. 'Then this is a war council, yes?'

'A... *partial* war council. We can't convene a full council until we meet with the rest of the Sails in Sol, but we can use the time we have now to come up with a plan.' His lips curled up into a playful smirk.

'Given how much faster our council can make decisions compared to the Reach, if we send out our idea as soon as we arrive, it might just get actioned the same day.'

'As I would expect.' The Speaker splayed her fingers out across the desk. 'Does the wider galaxy know of this yet?'

The captain shook his head. 'I don't know. We won't be able to tell until we finish our transit. But I can't imagine they would be blind to it unless the Reach committed to a massive cover-up. The scanner's location is public knowledge, and anyone can subscribe to its update feed. If anything happened to it—'

'Wait, "if"?' Shahida said. 'Do we know the scanner's status beyond that it was attacked? Did they destroy it completely? Does it just need repairs?'

'We don't know that either. Kaktek left the system before the situation resolved.'

And that was for the best, otherwise the captain wouldn't have had any good news to give her about Ruslan.

'In any case,' the Speaker said, 'once the public find out about this – and if they don't find out themselves, we should announce the loss in a way they can't decry as a hoax – there will be an outcry. We'll have some of that public support we so desperately need to turn events in our favour.'

Shahida made an involuntary tutting noise. 'No amount of public support will win us the council's favour if the tuk-a-wa has them wrapped around its little finger.'

'Do you have a better idea?' This came from the administrator, the woman who managed all lives aboard the *Inzekir* and whose stern voice contrasted her kindly features.

Glancing out of the window at the sterile environment of the bridge, Shahida cast her mind back. What did they have to fall back upon that was inarguable? What could the council not deny?

The opportunity jumped into her mind a moment later. 'Modjo's Law.' They had covered it in their history classes longer ago than she cared to remember. She couldn't remember if it had been part of the syllabus or some extra work, but it had been in school. 'We should invoke Modjo's Law.' She wracked her brain for the exact words, but settled on paraphrasing. 'Should the Sails have any reason to suspect foul play from the tuk-a-wa such that the integrity of the council of the Allied Reach might be called into question, each member of the council and their staff must submit to scanning. The host representing the tuk-a-wa amongst the council must go into voluntary isolation or be considered hostile. That's what we do. They destroy one scanner, we bring our scanners to them.'

Around the table, the captain's staff nodded and made murmurs of approval. The captain himself just looked thoughtful.

The weight of the Speaker's gaze nagged at Shahida's peripheral, so she turned to face her.

The woman's eyes regarded her from the girl's face. 'Invoking Modjo's Law is an easy-enough route to take, but of the options we can choose, it is the most likely to cause widespread conflict.'

Shahida cocked an eyebrow. 'More likely than the direct conflict of the tuk-a-wa attacking the scanner?'

'What's done is done. Don't pick bones with me, dear. We need to resolve this through diplomatic channels wherever possible, not by provoking war. Consider the possibilities: We publicly invoke the law and the council refuses. There would be revolution. There would be fights between the ordinary people of this galaxy and those the tuk-a-wa have inevitably infected over the millennia. That's if the council didn't try to claim they had been scanned and we just didn't like the results, or carry out some other manipulation.

'Say the council don't refuse. Say they accept, and they all test positive. We have the same result. If only some of them test positive, those may be successfully stripped of their positions, but how much trust would the public lose in their leadership having allowed that to come to pass? The way forwards would become difficult. And say they all test negative. Then all the public sees is us crying at the wind and everything being fine. They will become complacent. They won't believe us when we tell them about the threat that has long ago passed their doorsteps.'

'That's every scenario,' Shahida said. The room had closed in around them. 'You're saying there's no good way to win through the process enshrined in law.'

The Speaker smiled. 'There are rarely good ways to win in politics. When there are, you can count on a thousand obstinate individuals to stand in your way with their own interests, let alone the unified front of a galactic hive mind.'

'But what's the alternative?' Shahida looked to each of the faces around the table in turn, challenging them to think of something. 'If we just make the attack public – if it isn't already – we'll have an outcry. If the council is uninfected, they might actually be forced to do something about it. It'll take them months to muster any kind of response, even if they opt for the harshest approach. The tuk-a-wa will move faster. If the council is infected, or if the host on the council reacts to the outcry by infecting them, we might not know until it's too late. We need to invoke Modjo's Law now, before they have any chance to react.'

After considering it for a few moments, the captain nodded. 'I have to say, Speaker, I agree. We can't just rely on the public for this. From my perspective, every second we act against the council's will, even being who we are, is another second they might send warships after our home. I cannot countenance that possibility. Can we agree to invoke this law?'

Nods again, and the Speaker inclined her head. Technically speaking, she didn't get a vote in these affairs. She was a respected guest, here in partnership with the girl whose body she inhabited. Shahida didn't get a vote either, and she wasn't an expert, but somehow she had managed to get herself into a position where she could consult.

'Okay,' the captain said. 'The moment we reach Sol, we're refuelling and heading straight back out for Tilukettia. Shahida, if you and your son want to jump ship to wait for your husband, feel free to do so. I can't imagine you intended to be separated like this.'

The thought tugged at Shahida's heart. For a moment, she considered taking the captain up on his offer. How bad had the attack on the scanner been? She didn't know. None of them did. Ruslan could be injured – if he had died, Kaktek surely would have mentioned it – and at the very least he would be shaken. The rest of the galaxy liked to think of the Grey Sails as militant for no other reason than the knives they carried and the fact they knew how to use them. But that was it. They trained to fight the tuk-a-wa hand-to-hand, wherever they might meet them. They weren't a fleet of battleships. They had never been to war.

She had a son on this ship. If she stayed aboard with him, their visit to the capital world of Tilukettia would put him in the firing line of a compromised council. But Sol wouldn't be any safer, not if the resistance's stronghold in the heart of the exclusion zone was discovered.

Besides, she thought, Spartak was the reason she needed to get this right. Go to the council, force them to separate their interests from the tuk-a-wa's, get the public to pressure them to isolate the hive mind completely. It might take a decade to pull their tendrils from every crack. It might take longer. But at the end of that long fight, her son would be able to sink his toes into the soil of a free planet and feel the heat of its sun on his bare face.

So Shahida shook her head. 'I'm staying to see this through. Whatever it takes.'

CHAPTER TWENTY-EIGHT

SEVERAL DAYS LATER, SHAHIDA sat once more in the meeting room above the bridge, cradling a mug of coffee as they waited to arrive in Tilukettia.

'Do you think,' she said, 'that if we succeed here and force the tuk-a-wa to focus on either appeasing the council or fighting a war, they'll forget about the other galaxy?' It would be nice to give them a fighting chance to survive, and perhaps they could send a warning through, given enough time.

The captain took a sip of hot chocolate. No one had pointed out the thin skin of cream that clung to his moustache. 'They would certainly have bigger concerns. With their timescale, dealing with us first would be like having starters before moving onto the main course.'

'We just have to hope they *can't* deal with us so effectively,' the administrator said.

At the end of the table, the Speaker smiled. She had leaned across the desk, her head supported on one hand, toying with her empty coffee mug with the other. 'You know, I remember, before the tuk-a-wa forced me into hiding, when I was a mind of a million nodes.'

Her words made everyone around the table shift, unsure how the tale this ancient was about to tell would relate to their situation. The captain licked his lips, leaving a gap in his cream moustache. Shahida glanced towards the bridge, anxious for their arrival.

'Do you have any idea what that's like? Millions of nodes in a network, each of them a unique mind, each of them with a unique experience, all feeding into the whole. I say this, and you will imagine your machines. Your imagination is limited. Your machines cannot approach one such node, let alone several acting in concert. Your machines can access databases with thousands of years of history, but that is no memory. The machines have not lived it. They can only recall that which is given to them. They have no inkling of the years you have lost. We shared a living, beating history, a packaging of sensation and emotion, fact and pattern. If one node died and their mind could not be recovered, we still remembered.

'The tuk-a-wa were not like us in many ways. They saw the unique and made it identical. They were more of a machine at scale. But still, the experience of one becomes the experience of the whole. And if you think for one moment that a mind with millions of nodes, even cut off from fast communication, can't keep track of two active goals, you are very mistaken.'

Shahida kept quiet, but the captain made an expansive gesture with his hands. 'They are as bound by resources as the rest of us.'

This time, Shahida did speak. 'And how many resources would they need to infect that galaxy? One host, one ship, enough material to keep them alive until they made contact. They have everything they need at Warden Station. The only reason they're not sending every exile back home with a parasite in their head is because they want to keep the council's favour as long as possible.'

The Speaker smiled again, and Shahida couldn't help reading a little sadistic glee in the expression. 'You had better hope they keep that opinion after you pull this law on them, hadn't you?'

No one had time to say more. An alert tone sounded on the bridge, followed a short while later by the calm voice of the *Inzekir*'s autonomous address system.

'Transit will complete in five minutes. Please locate a burn pad and prepare for post-transit burn.'

Shahida leapt to her feet and began collecting everyone's mugs, needing an outlet for her pent-up energy, hoping the Speaker's apparent cynicism wasn't as accurate as she suspected it to be.

They came out of transit with the tri-mooned world of Tilukettia a bright dot in the distance, the gel-like structure of their chairs wrapped around them in supportive hugs. All around them, in a hug with more bite to it, the might of the coreworld fleet lay in wait.

An insistent orange warning indicator flashed in Shahida's suit display, pulsing with the beat of her heart. It was trying to beat out of her ribcage, a living thing frightened and racing for freedom. *Don't fire on this ship.* She willed the message to them. *Don't fire on my son. We're a civilian ship, you brainwashed bastards.*

They didn't fire. Not in the first second, nor the next ten. After thirty seconds, she let out a shaky breath. This jump station came out facing the system's star, so all she could see of the fleet was light glinting around their edges. A fleet of silhouettes, ghostly shadows in the dark.

Tinny voices chattered somewhere nearby. After searching the room with her eyes, head held immobile in the gel, Shahida figured it was probably coming from the captain – or more precisely, from his earpiece.

'What are they saying?' she asked.

The captain shook his head, which was angled to listen to the chatter even though it wouldn't get him any closer to the earpiece.

Shahida half wished they could have broken the jump station's speed limit and darted through before anyone could stop them, but that just brought her back to the fact they were a civilian ship: heavy, slow to accelerate, slow to manoeuvre, unarmed but for a few defensive emplacements in case they ever encountered pirates who thought they could take on a big target. Piracy hadn't ended up as common as the ship's designers expected, but it paid to be prepared.

In any case, such a move would still have seen them apprehended. Just with more force.

Again, the captain shook his head, but this time frustration clamped his jaw tight. 'They want us to hold,' he said. 'They see us as hostile after Warden Station, and they want us to hold to submit to an investigation.'

'An investigation?' the administrator clicked her tongue. 'That's less "hold", more "live here for a few years while we make a media circus of you".'

'Can they even impound a generation ship?' asked the community liaison, a short man in his late twenties with already balding hair. 'That's like impounding a planet. If they have a problem with us, they should be dealing with individuals.'

Shahida ground her teeth, flexing her muscles in the gel. 'Leave that for the lawyers.' She itched to get to her feet, but they had to stay in the gel in case they needed to make any fast moves. 'The important question is how specific they've been. They've told us to hold, so we stay still. Have they said anything explicitly forbidding broadcasts?'

Glancing to the ceiling, the captain pondered the question, then said, 'No. Not that I've heard. I'll check with the bridge crew.'

As he began to subvocalise, Shahida turned to the others. 'The longer we stay here, the less we can do. We don't know what they'll do next. We need to invoke Modjo's Law as soon as possible, and as publicly as possible. Agreed?'

All but the Speaker and the captain nodded – the captain because of his preoccupation with the bridge crew, the Speaker because she appeared to be asleep.

'Would you like to do the honours?' the administrator asked.

Before Shahida could reply, the captain refocused on the room. 'No, the lawyers should do that. If we want to ensure we have credibility, we have to get it right. No offense, Shahida – I'm sure you remember the Law as well as any of us do, but the rest of the galaxy probably neglects that particular aspect of history in their education.'

Raising an eyebrow, Shahida said, 'You'll need one of the versors, or they'll spend all day looking up the text.'

'Already done.' The captain's lips twitched upwards. 'Let's hope this isn't the last law they ever recite.'

Ten minutes later, after a quick explanation, a strong dose of coffee and a hasty change of clothes, the captain's chosen versor emerged in their ceremonial robes. A specialist in the memorisation of subsets of law, he should be able to recite what they needed at a moment's notice.

A shuttle had already begun making its way from Tilukettia to the *Inzekir*. They might not have long.

'Are you ready?' the captain asked.

'Yes.' The versor nodded. The silk-shrouded spikes on his headdress didn't quite fit within the field of the hologram. 'Were you planning to broadcast this live?'

After a moment's pause, the captain said, 'Probably best to record it and send that out.' A dark note in his words underlined the reason: a recording couldn't be interrupted by getting shot down. 'And don't react if you feel a bump. We'll be separating the bridge before we send it.'

As the hologram vanished, Shahida frowned. 'You can do that? What if they view it as a hostile action? They've told us not to move.'

'I am sure I can give them a convincing reason in advance.'

'Hmm.' She went to drum her fingers against the gel, but of course she couldn't move them. The *Inzekir*, like all ships of the Sails, seldom accelerated fast enough to feel. The sails that gave the fleet its name weren't meant to work that way. Shahida couldn't remember a time they'd had to use the gel couches. She only ever went under thrust in smaller shuttles. A tight ball had been building in the pit of her stomach at the thought of her home needing to go anywhere fast. It just wasn't built for that.

She chewed at her lip, then said, 'I collected a load of suit footage when I was on Warden Station. Do you mind if I leave the bridge and see what our media team can do with it?'

'Of course, but go quickly, and run any output past us first. Speaker, I suggest you leave as well.'

Shahida's gel couch began to reform around her before she had chance to check the Speaker's reaction, but when she managed to find her feet, the girl was already waiting by the door. Shahida let her go first, as was proper.

When they had their feet planted firmly on the floor of the corridor on the other side of the airlock, Shahida let out a sigh of relief.

'Let's go and find our media team,' she told the Speaker.

With time against them, they found the nearest room with a holoprojector, sequestered themselves inside and called the first three people listed in the *Inzekir*'s media guild. Two answered, both still in their gel couches, one with hair still wet from an earlier shower.

Shahida outlined the situation before either of them could start asking questions. 'I have a set of recordings from my suit cameras. They include everything I saw on Warden Station and afterwards. We may shortly need to highlight the tuk-a-wa's behaviour, and how far they have been allowed to act as they have, to the general public. Could you piece the footage together into something useable?'

The recently showered guild member squinted through a stray droplet. 'What reaction are you aiming for? And who's the target audience?'

Setting her jaw, Shahida said, 'Everyone's the target. We don't have time to worry about customising this. We're aiming for everyone who's not already a host, and we need them to kick up a fuss. To their neighbours, to their representatives, to the council. Whoever they can.'

'Okay.' They nodded, nonplussed. 'So we're not looking at hosts or Sails. We'll make a few audience splits between us so the tweaker doesn't take too long to churn out targeted variants.'

'How fast can you have it ready?' Shahida had never really paid much attention to media – certainly not to how it was made.

'Half an hour, depending on how long it takes you to put some words together.'

The Speaker leaned towards the holoprojector. 'I would like to contribute a message, too, if you could work it in. '

'That might take longer, then.' The guild member blinked, eyes widening. 'Wait, but you... Speaker, the rest of the galaxy doesn't know you exist. It can't find—'

'I decide the course of my existence, child, and who knows of it.' She waved a jewelled hand. 'And that is the kind of decision making we're trying to help people keep, isn't it? Let them know who I am.'

Her eyes flashed. 'Let them see the tuk-a-wa's first victim.'

CHAPTER TWENTY-NINE

SHAHIDA RECORDED HER MESSAGE first, giving context to her suit footage for the media team to stitch together. She knew her words couldn't possibly live up to whatever the Speaker was about to impart to the galaxy. Her helmet weighed heavy on her shoulders. Had the versor broadcast Modjo's Law yet? Surely they would be fired upon as soon as he did. The *Inzekir*'s hull felt closer than it should have been, more fragile, more obviously the destructible barrier between her and the gaping void.

Belatedly, Shahida realised that she and the Speaker could have recorded at the same time in separate rooms to get the message done faster, but the Speaker hadn't suggested it. Shahida had been too reassured by her company to even think up the idea until now, the moment she finished recording.

A nod was all the Speaker gave her when she was done. As the girl stepped up to the holoprojector to take Shahida's place, Shahida went to lean against a wall. She resisted sliding down it. Mixed emotions had sloshed into a churning nausea in her stomach – jubilant pride at taking the fight to the enemy after so many millennia, incomprehensible fear at the thought of what might happen to her family now she'd dragged them into this. The temptation to blame everything on Palia hovered on the edge of her mind. She ignored it.

The Speaker did not speak. Instead, she reached out with a hand and laid it against the control panel.

Frowning, Shahida asked, 'What are you doing? Do you have footage as well?' What could she have recorded, ensconced in her chambers on the ship?

'Something like that, yes.' She pulled her hand back. 'That's the important bit done. Quiet while I record, now.'

An urgent news alert flashed up in Shahida's helmet display – the versor's recitation of Modjo's Law was about to go live. Not wanting to interrupt the Speaker's recording, she turned on noise cancelling and listened to the broadcast. The versor's warm tone rolled around the inside of her helmet. Their words set an extra note of tension into her heart.

It was happening. The *Inzekir* would see the recitation before anyone else, but the capital fleet would be next, then the capital itself, then all the worlds of the Reach – if they didn't find a way to block the message first.

The Speaker finished her recording far before the recitation had ended. Shahida made sure to let the guild members know they had all the material once she noticed.

When the words came to a stop, silence hung in the air – even after she turned her noise cancellation off.

'We await their response, then,' the Speaker said at last.

Shahida nodded and was about to suggest returning to the bridge before she remembered it had detached to keep them safe.

Instead, she said, 'Do you want to wait for it in my quarters with me? There's no point us sitting here, twiddling our thumbs. The bridge isn't reattaching any time soon, and I have leftovers in the freezer.'

The Speaker smiled, her words contrasting with the childlike glow on her face. 'Lead with the food, next time. Yes.'

The council took their time replying. So long, in fact, that the guild members finished assembling the second broadcast and accepted an invitation to take advantage of any spare leftovers while they waited for the captain to review it. Shahida sat on a cushion, scrunching her fingers into another cushion beside her. Spartak hovered around the guild members' legs, barraging them with questions. He kept their legs between him and the Speaker at all times – Spartak had met her before, but hadn't been old enough to remember. Now, so much maturity in the face of someone not much older than him was more alien to him than any actual aliens in their galaxy.

The Speaker scared him. If Shahida hadn't been groomed for the role herself, hadn't spent so much time around her... she could easily see herself being scared as well.

On one wall of Shahida's chambers, a membranous smart screen displayed the Reach's most respected news channel: Suffurenu. More commonly known as Sulphur News by humans, its pebble-coated anchor floated in the murky yellow liquid of its natural environment and rattled off a constant stream of fact and bias checking. It all centred around the invocation of Modjo's Law. The word was out. No one could talk of anything else.

As Shahida chewed on a piece of dried fruit, the narrative stopped. A section of the screen switched to the council.

Shahida bit down hard. *Get this right.* The columns of the Alliance Dome shone tall and bright behind the council members' lecterns – a different shape for every species on the council. Standing lecterns, symbolic lecterns embedded in the walls of environmental tanks, nothing remote. Members had to be present so they could be certified as themselves.

Ironic. A council member in complete isolation was less likely to be corrupted.

A hush settled over the room. The council felt a hundred metres distant. A cough from the human tuk-a-wa representative – the only host officially allowed on the council – made Shahida flinch.

<This council,> the giant white-and-pink-striped rahtuan representative trumpeted, <has received a commandment to submit to Modjo's Law. For those unaware,> she said, as if everyone hadn't just heard the versor recite it, <Modjo's Law is an archaic stipulation of the Grey Sails upon members of the Allied Reach following the ancient war between the Great Convergence and the exiles.>

'It's not good that they're using words like "ancient",' said one of the guild members.

Shahida grunted. 'Or skewing the basic facts.' The Great Convergence, as the tuk-a-wa liked to call themselves, had fought the whole galaxy at first – not just those who would later be known as the exiles.

<The council in those ancient times agreed to respect the law in good faith and as a show of trust. In many millennia, that trust has continued, and there has never been reason for the law's invocation. However—>

'Here it is,' the Speaker muttered.

<—we are now dismayed to see the law invoked in such poor faith. It is obvious that the Sails see this momentous year as an opportune moment to sow discord and break apart the friendships we have built up over so much time. The exiles arrived, and were rightly arrested for investigation of their crimes, and the Sails saw this reasonable action as an invitation. While we do, of course, respect the laws that bind us, we are not the same society that we were when this law was created. We, today, are the Allied Reach. The Reach that agreed to Modjo's Law was the Reach of Allied and Sympathetic Species. The agreement that that Reach made does not bind us, and in light of the Sails' behaviour, we reject it wholeheartedly. The Grey Sails must now hand themselves over for arrest for their actions in aiding the exiles.>

No journalists had been allowed into the Alliance Dome. No one on the council would have to face a flood of questions, and they left their lecterns via the doors behind them unimpeded. Society would have to take their message and interpret it as it saw fit.

At the council's departure, the view of the Dome disappeared, replaced with live infographics of sentiments around the galaxy. The anchor rolled back on with their commentary.

Nobody spoke. A chill hung in the air, and it clutched at Shahida's insides with a cruel fist. Her whole life seemed so vulnerable, travelling around in a cluster of fragile ships full of life, surrounded by zombies – slaves to a hive mind. It could be all of them. In that moment, it felt like it was.

'Has the captain approved our footage?' Shahida asked.

The guild members nodded as one, mute.

'Send it.'

Their broadcast went out via the still-separated, still-intact bridge less than ten minutes after the council's denouncement. Shahida stared at the wall throughout her part of it. Spartak had huddled tight against her side as if sensing her distress, and he flinched when the footage of her tussle with Ilhan played. She pushed aside her instinctual regret that she hadn't put him in another room – he needed to see this.

When the Speaker appeared on the broadcast, Shahida straightened. The girl's face took up the centre of the screen, bold against a deep-black backdrop. Her beaded headdress shimmered.

'Appearances can be deceptive,' she began. 'You know this. A host can hide in plain sight. For millennia, you have trusted their promise of honesty to counter that, but you still know the truth. I know, too, and I have known it for millennia more, since I evolved alongside the tuk-a-wa in the seas of our homeworld. Like them, I am a hive mind. Thanks to them, I am a hive of one, fortunate enough to survive thanks to the hospitality of the Sails.

'If you don't believe me, or the footage you have seen, believe this: on each of the worlds of the Allied Reach, there is a protected store of encrypted data. This will now be made available to you. It contains all my memory of the tuk-a-wa, from the first moments to the latest, from multiple views of their conflict with the galaxy to this last remaining view. Experience these memories. Spread the word. Then decide if you wish to stand in support of the tuk-a-wa or not – if you wish to see the exiles assimilated for the crimes of their distant ancestors or free to live their own lives.

'The Sails know their stance. They have always done so. They will be waiting to hear yours.'

The Speaker on the screen disappeared, and the Speaker in the room wore a gloating smile.

Shahida turned to the Speaker, ignoring the continuation of her own message on the broadcast. 'Those memories – how did you get them all where they needed to be, and how long have they been there?'

'Oh, millennia. Everything is millennia, and money is no object when that's the case. The biggest problem will be seeing if they can still read the data at all.' She laughed softly. 'I forget very little, and I am always amazed by how often your species' efforts to preserve memories for future generations fall short.'

Hoping the Speaker's message would hit its mark – whether the data was readable or not – Shahida pulled up a display from the *Inzekir*'s external cameras. The bridge module hung out in the black, the dark shapes of the coreworld fleet forming a halo around it.

'You've hidden for millennia, and now the tuk-a-wa know you're still alive,' she said. 'A second ago the council wanted us to hand ourselves in for arrest. What do you think the tuk-a-wa will have them do now?'

The Speaker shrugged. 'If they fired upon us, it would only fuel that uprising you were so keen on instigating.'

Throat clenching, Shahida glared at the Speaker. Then she glanced at Spartak to make sure he hadn't heard – he was happily glued to the sight of his mum on the news. Before she could summon a reply, though, a message arrived from the captain.

<Some messages have come through for you, Shahida. I'll forward them now.>

For me? A worm of fear coiled around her stomach, and she tried to push aside the realisation that most of the galaxy had just *seen* her. She wished the captain had defined how many 'some' was. On the screen, the bridge's manoeuvring thrusters fired, and the fear coiled tighter. Any second now, one of those ships could shoot it out of the sky. The closer it came to redocking, the closer the threat came to her and Spartak. *Why redock now?*

She opened the first message. She didn't need to read the others.

This one read, <This is Councillor Rusuressen.> Shahida pictured the figure in the sulphurous tank in Alliance Dome. <My thanks for speaking truth to the galaxy. My clarifications for our actions: I was given no choice. The hive controls the council. It has the controlling vote. It knows how to threaten for silence. I don't know how many of the council are compromised. I have gone into hiding. My apologies: this does not help you. My promise: the fleet will not harm you for now. Escape while you can. Continue the fight. I will do what I can here.>

A heady mix of hope, fear and adrenaline rushed to Shahida's head. She grinned, leaned over to wrap Spartak in a one-armed hug, and said, 'We're getting out of here.'

CHAPTER THIRTY

It BEGAN WITH A whisper. Ferrash didn't know when the whisper itself began, but it permeated the space around his awareness, at once like a breeze across the surface of the ocean and a current in the deeps. He was meant to be finding something, wasn't he? The details slipped his mind. Something about information, but he couldn't remember what he needed it for.

The tension that held what was left of him together screamed for him to fix his mistakes. It showed him the ghosts of destroyed ships, scattered debris, lost expressions. It showed him Bek, hunched in the vat, and if he had been able to feel his heart just then, it might have been enough.

The whisper was kind, though. It suffused him with softness, and he opened himself to it.

Welcome, it seemed to say. Ferrash reeled, his reality becoming disjointed. It *was* speaking to him.

The whisper opened into a cloud, or a network of clouds. Ferrash struggled to place himself within it. Just as the hosts who had escorted him to the station commander's office had felt like clouds over the ocean, so did this, but on a much grander scale, much harder to comprehend. The ocean Ferrash's mind rested within had folded in on itself and become a droplet within it.

All in this cloud were rain, and all the little droplets spoke.

This is the Convergence, they said. *The Great Convergence. You are part of it, and you are welcome.*

He tried to reply, but he didn't know how. The voice had felt like his own, but also not – a thousand voices of which he was part. Something

196

kicked and screamed at the back of his consciousness, but he ignored it and drew the voice close to him.

You will get used to it. This came from a droplet close to him. He approached it from all angles, trying to get a sense of its shape, of who it was. An impression of fur and powerful muscles hung around it, so he guessed it must be a rahtuan. Another one of the hosts, in here with him.

A surge of love rushed through the fabric of the cloud, so strong it almost overwhelmed him. Ferrash reached for it blindly, on animal instinct, needing its touch in a way he had never even needed air to breathe. But as soon as he tried, the part of himself he had ignored leapt forwards and clawed him back. He withdrew without intending to, a cold distance growing between him and the warmth of the Convergence.

The whisper washed into a hiss. *Your guilt holds you back, but you have nothing to feel guilty for. We all make mistakes. We do not owe them anything. Stay close to us, brother.*

Brother. The word brought Bek's face flashing to his mind again. A shock ran through him. Ferrash examined each of the droplets again, picking out nothing to differentiate them but the vague impressions of their physical selves. He reached further and further, out beyond the first few droplets, and the remainder were static and grey.

The whisper sounded mournful this time. *We would feel them again, if not for the poison of the Empyrean.* He couldn't help but react to the name – all the hate of what it had done to him, to everyone he knew, bubbling to the surface. *You were the one who broke it for us. You destroyed that ancient weapon. We did not fear it, for its damage is long done, but we are glad it is gone. Glad to the extent that it left us able to feel so. Before the exile, when we were stripped and they remained, we could sense the presence of those who wielded it, supplanting the old network – the curse in their blood, piggybacking on our neurology. A cruel joke we could feel no true anger at.*

It was only then that Ferrash realised how devoid of sentiment the cloud had become. No gladness lay behind its words. Where was the love that had suffused him just moments before? Had that come from him? Had the convergence just manipulated sensations that only he could bring to the table?

He gathered his thoughts as best he could and tried to send them a message, half words, half sensation: that he knew what it was like to be devoid of emotion; that he knew what the Empyrean could do. *All those millennia ago... what terrible thing did you do that someone thought making it was the only choice they had?*

Despite the damage the Empyrean had done to them, despite the scarcity of their sentiment, a wordless rage broke as thunderheads on the horizon.

You can hardly criticise us, child. Thunder rolled. *You disagreed with your enemies and sought ways to destroy them. You struck at the weapon they used against you, and in so doing killed countless of your kind. Our enemies disagreed with us and sought ways to destroy us. They struck at the sense that let us act instantaneously as one body across distances those outside our Convergence could only dream of. In so doing, they took what made us great, what made us unified.*

Imagine, human, if there were only one of your kind, immortal, and we carved half the brain from your skull. That is barely comparable to the indignity we have suffered at your hands.

Ferrash stood firm against the pressure of their wrath. *My hands? My ancestors' hands, lost to time.*

All life builds upon itself. The state of the present is determined by the actions of the past. The unremembering are doomed to repeat it.

With the mental equivalent of a shrug, feeling more himself than he had in a long time, Ferrash thought, *Sounds like you've been repeating the old 'see it, assimilate it' routine ever since you crawled out of... I don't know, a swamp, probably. Do you remember the first body you stole?*

Thunder crashed. It dashed all sensation away from him for a moment, and when it returned, it wasn't the ocean anymore. He sat on a chair in a dim-lit room, his fingers twitching with impulses only half his own. Becoming aware of his own body again so suddenly came as such a shock that he couldn't see beyond it for a few seconds, but when he did, he noticed the sight beyond the window.

Over at one of the docking booms, a bulky warship wallowed. Blue light spilled in a rough cone from a tiny crack in its engine cowling and red lights flashed along its stern.

The parasite forced him to stand. Then he pressed a button on the desk and called the station commander. Could the hive mind not even communicate internally on the same station? Did they have to be right next to each other to talk mind to mind?

'Someone's sabotaged the drives,' came his too-familiar voice.

Drives? Ferrash examined the picture again. Sure enough, another three ships had red lights strobing along their hulls.

If someone had sabotaged them, that meant resistance – more than just the resistance Kaktek had put up in the attempt to stop his infection. That meant someone on this station was fighting on his side. Whoever it was, the thought of their existence sent a shiver of hope through him. He suppressed it as soon as he felt it, sensing the lurking threat of the parasite's attention nearby. But it was distracted, and it was all too easy for Ferrash to fall back on his old emotional habits.

The next time the parasite moved his head, Ferrash's attention lit upon a smaller ship nestled amongst all the others: his ship. They must have moved it from the internal hangar. Suppressing his annoyance at someone else touching his ship was harder than ignoring his hope, but he managed.

When the station commander finally gave a terse reply to its message, the parasite exited the room and began down the corridor.

Ferrash sank purposefully below the layer of consciousness where he could access his body's senses. He worried that perhaps he was being too compliant and the parasite would find his slipping away suspicious, but he didn't want to put up a fake struggle that might draw attention.

When he was sure the parasite hadn't cast any attention his way, Ferrash began picking his way around his own brain. The parasite had been getting his body enough medical attention that it must have recovered by now, surely? The process of finding out made his awareness spin. Every move felt like he was reaching forwards and poking himself in the back of his head. He reached for pathways that had once been as familiar to him as... well, as the ability to control his muscles, which was something else he couldn't do anymore.

There: a measure of acceptance. He grasped onto the interface of his implants like a lifeline. The fact the parasite had needed to use an external communication device to contact the station commander not only indicated that the hive mind couldn't communicate by itself at that range, but that Ferrash's parasite hadn't yet worked out how to use his implants. Or couldn't. The specifics didn't matter.

He couldn't interact with it the way he used to, as simple as thinking. That threw him for a while. Which bits of his brain did the parasite control and which bit was he left with? If it was just motor control, fine, but if the thing kept on taking over more and more of the rest, if it eventually took over all of it...

Ferrash pushed past the thought. He assembled the command himself, bit by bit, picturing his ship where it had been moored beside the bulkier vessel with a sabotaged engine. He pushed past the memories of his ship, too. The parasite would definitely notice if he let himself get melancholy about what he was about to do.

He had the command complete and ready, along with a chain of follow-up actions in case he didn't get chance to push any more. This was it. With a tremor of trepidation he couldn't control, Ferrash pushed it to his implants.

An explosion rocked the floor beneath him. Ferrash felt it even from where he slumbered beneath the surface of physical awareness. The parasite's attention thrashed in alarm, buffeting his consciousness in its wake. He flashed between access to different senses. In one moment, blood pulsing through a narrow section of his femoral artery became the whole scope of his existence, then muscles bunching, relaxing, warming. The parasite had pushed him into a run. His foot hit the ground, and the shock of that as his only sensation sent him spiralling away from it.

He saw through his own eyes, felt air on his face. In the viewscreen above him, a section of docking boom was gone. So was his ship. A snaking tendril of cable whipped in an endless spin. His heart clenched, but he didn't know if it was a physical sensation he'd just happened upon or the wrenching thought that he had just blown up his own ship.

As his vision wavered, his next action slipped the net.

<Lilesh,> his message read. <I don't know how much you've been told, if anything. They'd better be treating the rest of you better than me. Palia was with Kaktek and a group called the Grey Sails the last I saw her, working against the hive mind. It's them who hate us. Not the rest of the galaxy, just them, and they have everyone else under their thumb. They stuck a parasite in my head.> They'd injected it in his leg, really, but who knew where it had gone after that. <If you see me, don't trust me. If you see a chance to escape, take it.>

The message sent in an instant. In the next, pressure slammed down on Ferrash's awareness. He plunged back into the senseless ocean, propelled by the weight of the parasite's control, struck by a cold rage that defied emotion.

Before he slipped back into timelessness, he understood one last thing: his final action had worked. His auxiliary AI had come back online, keeping a low profile on a solitary thread.

Even if this was the end, even if he never returned from the pit the parasite was sending him to, a copy of him was lying in wait to fight.

CHAPTER THIRTY-ONE

PALIA WAS GLAD TO finally be leaving Kaktek's ship behind, even if there were a million more things she could have learned about the kluqetik. It had taken them over a week to reach the system of Sol, and it turned out the *Inzekir* had already left. Now, she sat in a shuttle with Ruslan and the samples she had collected, staring at the view.

'That's a pretty planet,' she said. 'Is that where the research station is?'

Ruslan turned to face her from his seat, a peculiar expression on his face. Blue-white light washed over the side of his helmet from the planet displayed on their shuttle's viewscreen. A lot of it was blue ocean, but green and sandy landmasses dotted its surface. Sunlight glared from white bands of cloud and two small ice caps. It looked peaceful, besides a cyclone forming over the ocean, and she couldn't see any signs of human habitation. Maybe another species lived here, or they kept an exceptionally low profile, or they were on the other side of the planet.

'Your galaxy doesn't know about Sol?' Ruslan asked.

'No.' Palia tilted her head, her curiosity building. 'Why should it?'

He laughed, placed a hand on the back of his helmet and stared out of the window. The planet mirrored itself in miniature on the curve of his faceplate. 'And you've not heard of Earth either?'

'No.' But even as she said it, she tried to unpick the mess her translator had made of the word. It had thrown up about a dozen different options, including 'soil' and 'planet'. Maybe it was just picking apart a particularly unimaginative etymology.

'Well, where do I start?' He let out a long sigh. 'The tuk-a-wa had you arrested for the crimes of your distant ancestors, because despite professing not to have emotions anymore, they can still manage to hold a grudge. But forget them. Go even more distant. Strip away most of our technology and dream of a species confined to a single world. That was us. My ancestors. Yours. Humanity evolved on that pretty little rock down there.'

Palia stared at him, then at the viewscreen. Wonder began to uncurl in her chest. They'd never known where they'd come from, in her galaxy. They had Origin, of course, but they knew that wasn't the origin of their species. Well, most archaeologists agreed that humanity must have arrived from elsewhere, given the lack of evidence beneath Origin's soil. The few who disagreed rarely had credible arguments. Looking at it now, she realised Origin, where the Prime Nexus had first been located before the Protectorate stole it, must have been the first planet her ancestors settled after being exiled.

For a moment she got sidetracked, wondering if the reason she found it pretty at all was thanks to some genetic memory of what home should be, but then she shook her head.

'So the Grey Sails own it now?' she asked.

'Huh? Oh, oh no, no one owns it.' He tilted his head. 'Well, in a sense they do, but the reason *we're* here and the reason we can take sanctuary here is because there's an exclusion zone. No one's meant to be here. It's the perfect place to hide.'

The planet – Earth – seemed perfectly harmless. Nothing had attacked or otherwise harmed them while they were here. 'Why *is* there an exclusion zone? Is it so the parasites can't get to it? And if it's that important, why didn't travelling through the jump station let people know we were here?'

'Well, easiest question first.' The shuttle fired its thrusters, jerking them in their harnesses. 'The station would normally give transit reports, but the resistance found a way to get around that. I don't know the specifics.'

A pale moon swung into view at the edge of the viewscreen. On the globe below, a bright stretch of desert rolled over the horizon.

Ruslan cleared his throat. 'The exclusion zone is purely for conservation. If you can trust a fledgling civilisation – a human one, at least – to do anything, it's to consume everything around it to advance. We've lost most of the details, of course, which for a crying shame includes most art from some time after they began to heavily industrialise onwards. I've seen—' He stopped himself and waved a hand. 'Anyway, we only know Earth wasn't in a great state when we left it.

'We weren't in a great state, either, for that matter. I've seen the population records, and... There have been a few points before and since when we've nearly lost it all, and this was close.'

Palia nodded, her wonder turning to sadness. 'So the exclusion zone protects the planet from us.'

'Correct. The whole system's out of bounds, just to be on the safe side.' He shrugged. 'It's been rolling along perfectly well since long before I was born, now. They did a good job restoring it. But everyone had already left by the time they finished, and guilt keeps us from moving back in. Besides, I've heard some of the animals we left behind have got quite big and scarily intelligent.'

It made sense that something would fill the gap. Palia couldn't draw her gaze away from Earth, from the promise of all that... ingrained *familiarity* lying in wait. She yearned to catalogue the life down there, to compare it to the species in her own galaxy. How many of those had they imported from here? How had time and separation changed them compared to their ancestors?

If only arriving in this galaxy hadn't caused such a mess, she might have known some of those answers by now.

Given the taboo on touching Earth, Palia wasn't surprised when the shuttle took them to the moon. They skimmed over the barren and pockmarked surface until they came to a set of hangar doors embedded in the ground. These opened as they approached, and the pilot took them down beneath the surface, kicking up fine dust in their engine wake.

As Palia stepped out of the shuttle behind Ruslan, she struggled to make out the corners of the room. It all looked run-down and abandoned, with dim lighting, dull grey walls and a worrying network of cracks on the surface of the landing pad.

Next to that, the simple flatbed hauler robot that came to take the sample tubes might well have come from the future. They followed it through empty corridors into a lead-lined lab, where it left them alone with the storage tubes. Palia didn't recognise half of the equipment, and her heart sank. Unfamiliar technology, unfamiliar species, a whole new galaxy and a task almost entirely outside her skillset – what was she thinking?

She was thinking of Ferrash, of course. She always was, in the back of her mind. Ferrash, Bek, Derren, Fabien – they would always exist, parts of her like ghosts, only whole when present. *Present and themselves*. That's what she had to ensure. Get the parasite out of Ferrash. Stop it reaching anyone else.

Easier said than done.

'So...' Ruslan's voice broke her out of her thoughts. 'Judging by the silence, I'm guessing you'll work best at this alone. And if I can be perfectly blunt, I don't want to stay in the same room as those things' – he pointed at the tubes – 'once you break them out. I'm sure you'll be careful, of course.' A warning note slipped into his tone.

'I will.'

'Good. The staff here said this room was built ages ago with the tuk-a-wa in mind. So, good news and bad news. You have plenty of monitoring in here, so you'll be able to tell where the parasites are at all times, and anyone checking on you will be able to see if you're alright. *But* the equipment might not be particularly recent. So, experimentation could prove difficult.' He turned to leave, then hesitated with one foot over the threshold. 'Are you sure you want to bother with this?'

'Yes,' Palia said almost before he finished speaking. She couldn't just *not* bother.

'Okay, well, call me if you need anything. I'll be injecting myself with some fine Earth culture in the museum. At least, I think they have a museum...' He continued talking to himself as he left, and the sound of his chattering eventually faded down the corridor.

I bet he and Bek would get along well. With a sad smile, Palia shut both of the airlock doors, checked the seal, and turned to the tubes.

'Right. Let's see what you're made of.'

At the very least, Palia had data on the parasites' physiology. She spent a good couple of hours reading through that before she even considered taking one of them out of the tube. Then she spent another four hours leafing through the lab equipment's manuals, hoping an easy first step would jump out at her. It didn't, so she left the question until after lunch.

When she returned, she woke up the lab's AI assistant to have someone to bounce ideas off, then picked the simple option of sticking the sample under a microscope to start off. Her curiosity suffocated any disgust she felt for the hive mind. She'd never asked if the hive mind had a queen, but she supposed the existing notes would have mentioned it if they did. And if no one knew of it by now, if it *did* exist, they had no hope of finding it.

No, she had to work with what she had in front of her. Under the microscope, the parasites turned out to be tangly little things with thousands of arms that liked to latch onto anything resembling a living brain. She knew this because she had printed an artificial patch of brain tissue and let a parasite loose on it to see what it would do. The sight of its arms wrapping and stabbing and burrowing had sent a tingling itch across the back of her skull that she hadn't been able to shift for ages.

She burned the brain rather than feed it to the recycler.

She hashed out the basics with more experiments: they didn't like getting dried out, they didn't like certain wavelengths of light, and they could withstand quite low or high temperatures as long as they were attached to (and encased by) healthy tissue. When she hurt one of them, the others became agitated, even in confinement. Palia hesitated halfway through that test, weighted with the knowledge she was torturing sentient creatures for science. It was so hard to see something microscopic as intelligent, and her brain kept slipping off the concept. She supposed that made her a terrible xenobiologist. And you could make enough arguments for and against the individual units (or small groups of them) being sentient that she imagined that kind of debate could last years.

None of this helped her.

A day passed. She ate, she barely slept, and she tried to think of ways to kill the grasping little parasites without killing their hosts.

Returning to the lab the next day, she enlisted the AI's help again, getting it to spit out suggestions and iterate on viruses that might affect the parasites. After four hours, she had something that simulations predicted would take five weeks to kill a host, but would kill rahtuan and humans within five days. She had plenty of samples, so she infected a batch to see what happened and had the AI work on some vaccines anyway, because something was better than nothing. As a last experiment before leaving that day, she tried nanobots. The parasites caused so much damage to tissue in their attempts to escape that they would have mashed their host's brain. No option there, then.

Picking at her dinner that evening, she wished it could be as simple as zapping the things with a localised blast of radiation.

With a new day came a new idea. Excited, she spent the whole morning remembering and reproducing the spectroscopic signature of nexite – a conductor of empyrric energy and a signature this galaxy had doubtless forgotten since the exile. Maybe the events on Everatus IV would at least be good for something.

She could get the signature for empyrric absorption working fine, but it took her another two hours to get emission sorted. When she did, she set up the apparatus near the sample and turned it on. The response was instant: they danced in the presence of emission for about four seconds before growing despondent. Or... well, she couldn't tell how they felt. If they felt.

If only she *could* tell.

Palia placed her hands on the side of a desk and arched her back, working out the kinks in her spine. If they wanted to get the parasite out of a host, they needed to see what it did in situ. Nothing in the existing data recorded what happened when they infected someone, or how they manipulated their actions.

She eyed the all-purpose medical scanner in the back corner of the lab, still covered by a protective sheet.

'Hey,' she said to the AI assistant, knowing this was her most stupid plan yet, 'I have an idea.'

CHAPTER THIRTY-TWO

'YOU CANNOT INJECT YOURSELF with the sample,' the AI assistant told Palia, visible only as a head and shoulders on the wall screen. Whatever personality had been loaded into it gave it a long-suffering air. 'That contravenes safe handling guidelines.'

'I know how to remove the parasite after injection, though.' Palia hoped the half-lie would satisfy it. The Grey Sails were relying on the same trick to rid Ferrash of his uninvited guest – but they were also relying on transit through the gate to isolate it, and the Speaker had only said her parasite would *attempt* to kill the other.

The AI shook its head. 'Injecting it in the first place is the problem. I can't let you do it.'

Two responses warred in Palia's head: *How do you think you're going to stop me?* and *Who do you think you are to stifle the fine tradition of self-experimentation?* She dismissed them both.

Instead, she took a deep breath and – having realised over the past few days that this wasn't as sophisticated as the AI in her galaxy – approached from a different angle. 'The galaxy is at war. The only way to save it is to find a way to stop the hive mind, and the only way to do that is for me to inject myself with the sample.'

'Injecting yourself with the sample won't provide any useful information.'

Palia rolled her eyes. 'I'll inject it during a medical scan. We'll record the whole thing. No one's ever collected that data before.' The closest she'd found was a scan two hours after the time of infection.

A few moments passed without any comment. An exaggerated

furrow appeared on the AI's brow. Then it said, 'An alert will sound the moment the parasite enters your bloodstream.'

'That's fine.' It wasn't like they could get there in time to stop her, and they'd know not to get close. No point warning them in advance – they'd never let her do it. She'd need to leave a note with the AI explaining what she'd done and why, and she'd need the AI to send the data somewhere safe and undeletable so she couldn't get rid of it under the parasite's influence.

Fear bristled along her spine. Palia swallowed an acidic rush of nausea. She took an uncharacteristic step back to examine her motivations – she *wasn't* doing this out of some misplaced, masochistic need to do to herself what they'd done to Ferrash, was she? No, she didn't think so. And she wasn't doing this just so she could stop feeling so powerless. That wasn't the *whole* reason, in any case. They really were missing this data.

With a sigh, she rubbed the bridge of her nose. 'Okay, let's get this thing started.'

Lying under the dim, rotating lights of the medical scanner, Palia's heart beat so hard she could almost feel it vibrating through the bed. She'd had the AI – in the robot body that had been on standby in a cupboard – strap her to it. Even locked in the room without permission to delete any files, once the parasite controlled Palia's body, it could smash the place up. She was going to be in enough trouble as it was. She didn't need to add to it.

'Are you ready?' the AI asked.

Palia licked her lips. The memory of Ferrash injecting her with inhibitors jumped to the front of her mind unbidden. On the scale of things she could get injected with, this came close to topping the list.

I'm going to get you out of this, Ash, she thought, then said, 'I'm ready.'

Something scratched the flesh of her left arm and pushed. She clenched her right hand tight and stared at the inside of the scanner, nerves jumping across her skin, heart rate climbing.

When would it begin? What if it figured out what she was up to and just... refused to take control? What if it just sat dormant in her bloodstream until she got untied and left the room? No, the scanners would pick that up, or...?

Her left pinkie twitched, tapping out a broken rhythm. Nerves? Palia tried to move it herself, and could, but it twitched again a moment later. *She* hadn't done that. A shiver passed along her arm. Then the muscles in it spasmed, and a wave of pins and needles passed through her legs in a seemingly random pattern.

'Is the scanner recording this?' Palia's voice came out squeaky.

'It is.'

Finding small comfort in the AI's voice, Palia tried to relax. And maybe knowing about the experiment would affect the results in some way, but it must be better than nothing. It had to be.

The scanner's lights dimmed, or became distant. For a moment, Palia couldn't tell which. Confusion clouded her brain.

Somewhere, a cluster of lights glowed, each distinct, each reacting to the others' presence in some subtle way that filled Palia with yearning. Exultation flooded through her veins, so sharp and overwhelming that tears sprung to her eyes. She couldn't keep track of her thoughts anymore. Pure emotion mixed with memories of parties and prisons and... and the Empyrean.

Dread crashed down on her. A weight she hadn't even noticed lifted from her mind and distanced itself. Hate radiated from within her – from the *parasite* within her – and suddenly it appeared before her, distinct in her mind, a thundercloud holding itself at arm's length from her psyche.

Nemesis. Its hatred clapped like thunder. *Destroyer. Exile.*

Palia gasped. They could communicate. It was in her head. She could just show it her memories and they could resolve all their misunderstandings. If it saw the narrow scope of a human memory...

I will not have my existence tainted by you. The parasite turned dark. The sharp edges of its mood stabbed out at her. In the Empyrean – and oh, how Palia hated how she hungered for the sight – the tenuous cloud of its psyche formed an arcing cloud of light. She could see it all again: the emotions, the life. The parasite's light spasmed and pulsed, and began to condense.

Wait, Palia thought. *Wait, don't go.* At the edge of her awareness, more clouds of light jostled in shining columns. The samples – she could see the other samples. If she reached out far enough...

Before she could try, the parasite in her bloodstream flared into blinding incandescence in the landscape of the Empyrean, then went dark. Palia held her breath, feeling as if her heart had stopped. Where had it gone? Could it hide itself from her? She couldn't sense its hatred anymore, couldn't feel it boiling over her skin. Chills marched across it instead. Her unease made itself visible to her for the first time since she and Ferrash had destroyed the Empyrean – dim waves with stuttering edges washing up and down her body. Even outside the Empyrean, with her unaided sight, the green light coming from her skin coloured the inside of the scanner.

'What did you do?' the AI asked.

Palia jumped at its voice. The restraints dug into her wrists and ankles, and her heart beat against her ribs.

'I didn't do anything,' she said.

'The sample you injected is dead. It had made its way to your brain, but then it died.' An element of surprise laced the AI's words. 'I thought you said the Grey Sails' solution could only be applied after you injected it?'

She had. What's more, she assumed whatever the Grey Sails had injected into Ferrash was something only their Speaker could provide, and the Speaker wasn't even in the same system as Palia.

'I think...' Hesitating in disbelief, Palia shook her head. 'I think it killed itself.'

The AI paused. 'Why?'

'I...' She stopped herself. If she told the AI that the Empyrean had returned to her, that she was empyrric again, who would it pass that information to? If the existence of the Empyrean had been enough to get her ancestors exiled to another galaxy, what would people do when they found out she'd resurrected it within herself? She settled on something close to the truth instead. 'It knew I used to be empyrric. It didn't want anything to do with me, so it just... died.'

A thought occurred to her. She took a few deep breaths to calm down – she was out of practice, and she didn't know if her ability would affect the other samples somehow. The last thing she wanted was to melt half the lab or destroy the samples they'd taken care to collect.

When the light had vanished from her skin, she focused on the Empyrean again. In the sample tubes, the parasites danced. She reached out, regret tingeing her mood, and drew one of those lights towards her. It flickered out in an instant.

'Another of the samples has died,' the AI said. 'Allow me to confirm none of those pathogens we generated has contaminated the tubes.'

Palia didn't stop it, but she did ask it to let her out first. Then she lay rubbing her sore wrists as the bed moved out from under the scanner. Blinking at the bright lights, she massaged her ankles with her eyes shut before swinging her legs over the edge of the bed and standing up.

That aching hunger still suffused her body, try as she might to ignore it. It formed a grasping ribbon from her belly to her throat. She had never felt this kind of hunger for the Empyrean before. *We killed so many people in our galaxy just to get rid of it. I've undone all that. I've made it all pointless.*

Taking a deep breath, she squeezed her eyes tight shut. *Focus on the positive.*

'The samples are clear.' The AI turned its attention to her, cocking its head both on the robot and sidelong on the wall screen. 'Do you have an explanation for this?'

'Maybe it was old, or stressed.' Palia shrugged, trying to keep her heart rate level in case the AI could detect a lie. Beyond the sample tubes, she could make out the sparks of other life on the station. The hunger urged her to look further. She ignored it, hoping the feeling would fade with time.

She crossed to the sample tubes and knelt in front of them, eyeing her distorted reflection in their metal sides. If the other parasite wouldn't talk to her, maybe one of these would – or all of them, as a collective. So she made a conscious effort to push her awareness towards them. To her surprise, the push was easier than she remembered, and it felt... different in a way she couldn't quite put her finger on.

The parasites sank back in the sample tubes as she approached, like fish away from an ocean predator. When they reached the far walls, they couldn't go any further, and her awareness came to encompass them. In her mind, they shifted into a storm cloud like the parasite that had infected her had appeared, though she could still see them as individual points. If she squinted, little filaments connected each of them to her. *Not to each other, though.*

Feeling dirty at the contact, Palia tried to think at them the same way she had with the other parasite – not that she'd been able to tell if it had heard her.

Hello, she thought. *I want to talk.*

Hatred slithered from them and settled on her skin like a whisper, raising the hairs on her arms and neck. They said nothing. Palia shivered.

She pushed on. *You can feel again, can't you? You can communicate the way you used to. I could fix you all like that, and we could end this war between us.*

Nemesis, the whisper came. *You who broke us would see us whole? Untrusted, unwanted, exile out of exile. Leave us be.*

I didn't break you. Palia bit down a rising tide of frustration. Too late – the parasites had already seen it, responding in kind with a curl of contempt. *No one alive today broke you. Look at my memories. See what I mean.*

They threw their next words at her with the force of a thunderclap. *LEAVE US BE.*

Reeling, Palia staggered back onto her feet and blinked at the sample tubes. She had withdrawn her awareness, but still those threads connected her to them. *Well, that's a load of zash.*

The AI made her jump a second time. 'Did you detect any problems with the samples?'

'No.' She shook her head, and noted with some concern that ripples of her shock had run through the collective psyche of the parasites. Emotional communication – that's what the Empyrean had begun as, and that's what she had brought it back to. 'But I need to talk to Ruslan, if I'm allowed to leave the room.'

Because she wasn't about to explain what she'd done to the AI, but she would explain it to Ruslan. She had to – the Empyrean was now the best weapon at their disposal. *Again.*

CHAPTER THIRTY-THREE

SHAHIDA COULDN'T BRING HERSELF to relax until the *Inzekir* exited the last jump station on their route, completing their journey away from Tilukettia.

Even then, it was difficult. The scanner had moved to this system after the attack, afloat only by the grace of some kluqetik privateers who had seen off the hive mind's forces. She watched it on the screen now, wallowing in the black, great gashes and craters marking its sides. In places, she could see clear through to its centre. Without a reference point, its size and the fact something so large had been so easily gutted didn't have as much impact as it should. The news readers were probably saying something to big it up, but she had them muted.

All Shahida's attention just then lay on the largest section of the big screen in the centre of the plaza. Everyone else – clustered in enclosed booths on the floor and at tables with food, drinks, work they'd brought with them – had the same focus. Shahida had met up with some of her friends from her peer group when joining the *Inzekir* for this. They chattered, but it formed background noise.

On the screen, the council fled. A group of heavily armoured Reach Guards held a seething crowd back from the steps of Alliance Dome. No news reader narrated the scene – they just left the microphones running on their cameras. Above everything else, the trumpeting roar of angry rahtuan rocked Tilukettia with its sheer volume. Each camera angle shook. Kluqetik clung to every surface they could – walls, flagpoles, balustrades – and made a solid wall of shifting colours with their paddles. Humans projected slogans and artwork and, having never fallen far from the primate tree, threw things at the steps of the Dome.

The grand door, shining with materials from each allied species' homeworld, swung open. Above the crowd, someone attempted to dart in on a gravicycle, but a forcefield drove them back and they drifted to the ground, engine dead, angry fist pumping the air.

From out of the doorway, a black sphere emerged, supported by eight spiderlike legs. Another came behind it, and another, until the last of the council members had left the Dome – although they were a few short. More than just the council member that had contacted her must have gone into hiding from their infected colleagues.

'They can't keep going after this,' one of Shahida's friends said, nudging her with an elbow. 'Look at that crowd! You did that.'

Shahida winced. She'd already had to suffer a round of back clapping and fistbumps for her part in that broadcast. She had hoped that something more interesting – like the council running from the galactic capital with their tails between their legs – would distract them from the actions that had triggered it.

'It's happening all across the galaxy, too,' her friend continued. 'They're kicking all the tuk-a-wa out of government positions. They've started combing through the Speaker's memories and publishing the juicy bits. It's—'

'It's a little sad, actually,' another of her friends added. 'I always understood what the Speaker had been through, at a basic level, but this? Experiencing it?' He shook his head, and the little jewels embedded in spiral patterns on his helmet glittered. 'I had to take a moment. There have been... Some people have killed themselves over it. They found it too hopeless.'

Curling a finger in the helmeted sign for a raised eyebrow, Shahida said, 'Perhaps that's because it *is* hopeless.'

Her friends leaned back from the table with melodramatic sighs. A grin curled on the lips of one of them who had removed her helmet to drink a cup of tea. 'You never fail to spoil the mood, Shahi.'

Shahida inclined her head to the screen. 'Look at those crowds. They're protesting the hardest on worlds where we know for sure that the tuk-a-wa have been spreading without permission or record. What do you notice?'

The grin soured. 'None wearing protection.'

'Well,' another said, 'there are a few…'

'A few is not enough,' Shahida said, 'and their protection is inadequate. Facemasks. Goggles. The tuk-a-wa can infect through a scratch – through the air at close enough range. We all know this. They don't.'

Her friend with the spiral-jewelled helmet gave a mirthless chuckle. 'Maybe you should have included some personal safety instructions in your speech, Shahi.'

'Maybe.' She tried to say it with more of a laugh, but couldn't help it coming out blunt. He was right. Her goal had been to get people up in arms about the tuk-a-wa, about their involvement in the council, about their treatment of the exiles. Of course that would mean getting out in the open and exposing themselves to harm. The fact she hadn't thought of it sank like a stone in the back of her mind, dragging her mood down with it.

'Can you send out another one now?'

She shrugged. 'I don't think it would achieve much, but I guess we could publish some of our curriculum. How many planetsiders have an environment suit lying around, though? By the time enough of them managed to secure a supply, it would be too late.'

'But it would give them a chance to try. Isn't that what this is all about? Chances? A chance to free the exiles, a chance to clean up the council, a chance to overthrow the tuk-a-wa completely?'

As the view on the screen changed to show the council's escape shuttle blasting off the surface of Tilukettia, Shahida snorted. 'Chances. We haven't waited thousands of years to risk it all on chances.'

'No, we waited thousands of years for the gate to open. Now it has, and everything's happening at once, and if we miss the chances we have now, we'll never get them again.'

Shahida rested her faceplate on thumb and forefinger, directing the air jets inside her helmet to massage the bridge of her nose. She'd come here hoping to find relief in the broadcast. Instead she'd realised how many little things she'd messed up and how much messing up she might still have to come.

When she reunited with the rest of the fleet, she would have to ask Palia for coping advice. The woman had the look of someone who had messed up several times and still come out the other side. But then, there was the question: How many had been with her at the beginning who weren't here now?

They floated by the side of the scanner with several other ships, like fish clinging to the side of a whale, and watched the slow progress of its repairs inch along day by day as the galaxy lay in uproar around them. On the ninth day since the *Inzekir*'s arrival, the remainder of the fleet joined them in the system they had chosen as a muster point, streaming in through the jump station from Sol in a long train of generational homes. Kluqetik ships – far more than just Kaktek's – swarmed around as their escort. The ships burned for the outgoing jump station without slowing or unfolding their sails, and the *Inzekir* burned to join them.

None of their casual pace now: they burned for Warden Station with all haste.

When the *Inzekir* pulled alongside the rest, still a few hours from the outgoing jump station, a shuttle flew from Kaktek's ship to dock with it. Shahida waited just outside the hangar, tapping her feet, idly twisting strands of tall grass between her fingers. They didn't have long before the deceleration burn began to bring them below the speed limit and they had to find couches again, but it was long enough for reunions.

The hangar door hissed. Shahida jumped to her feet, accidentally snatching a handful of grass in the process.

'Shahi!' Ruslan came bounding out of the doorway and took hold of her shoulders, touching his faceplate against hers with a light *donk*.

'You're a sight for sore eyes. Now I know what my cousin was nattering on about when he told me about getting on the wrong shuttle on his holiday – ended up nowhere he wanted to go, realised just after the thing launched and had to stare at the shuttle he was *meant* to go on...' He cleared his throat. 'Anyway, what I mean to say is: I didn't plan on being away for so long. Let's not do that again.' Then with half a backwards bounce, he gestured to her handful of grass. 'After all, I leave you alone for a few days and you start depriving the *Inzekir* of its foliage.'

Shahida chuckled, partly at his joke, mostly at this thousand-words-a-minute firecracker leaping back into her life. 'And depriving the galaxy of its council. Let's not forget that.'

'Pah. Plants are more important than politicians.'

While they had been talking, Palia had also emerged from the hangar. Shahida refocused her attention on the woman now. She seemed... different. Mixed expressions of discomfort and hunger warred on her face. Perhaps she just missed her friends. Shahida had never been good enough at reading people to work it out.

Instead, she asked, 'How's Kaktek? I heard about what they had to do with the hatchlings. He can't be happy about it.'

Ruslan shrugged. 'He seemed the most eager to vent them. I don't think he cared that much. Maybe he would have cared more if they were his hatchlings.'

Behind him, Palia opened her mouth, reconsidered, then got distracted by something off in the distance. After a moment, she blinked and turned back to Shahida with her full attention. 'I found something that I think could help you. I've already explained it to Ruslan. If we can find somewhere private to talk, maybe?'

Shahida shot Ruslan a questioning glance, and he gave a nervous chuckle. 'It's *wild*,' he said.

'Okay,' Shahida said. 'What have you got for me?'

Palia's gaze swept the room. Shahida had suggested the Speaker's chambers at first, since she would no doubt want to hear of anything that could help them, but Palia had shot the idea down. Ruslan had just grimaced. None of that made Shahida feel particularly positive about whatever Palia was about to tell her, but at least she could hear it sitting on her own cushions. Ruslan, impatient to see Spartak again, had gone to pick him up from school.

That just left her and Palia.

'Before I tell you this,' said Palia, 'I just want to point out that I haven't triggered any of the scanners I've been through between Earth's moon and this ship.'

Oh, stars, that isn't a good start. She motioned for Palia to carry on and she did so, her voice faltering a little.

'I wanted to see if I could make a weapon to fight the parasites. So I did. I made a virus, but it wasn't good enough.' Palia chewed at her lip. 'Then I realised no one had ever scanned...'

Over the course of the next few minutes, Palia outlined the incomprehensibly stupid risks she had taken for the sake of research and Shahida bit her tongue. Instinct, honed by a lifetime of training, screamed at her to throw this idiot out of the nearest airlock before she could somehow endanger everyone aboard the *Inzekir*. Palia wasn't quite an idiot, she could see that – but she did wonder what sort of operating procedures they *taught* xenobiologists over in her galaxy for her to be comfortable acting like this. Shahida could barely even bring herself to look at the recordings the woman was sharing.

'...and then it killed itself.' A pause followed Palia's last words, and she looked to Shahida with almost pleading eyes.

Though Shahida's curiosity spiked, she tried not to show it. 'This is the part where you tell me why.'

'It could tell I was empyrric. It didn't want anything to do with me. It called me "nemesis". I tried to talk to it, but it just... died.' Palia seemed disappointed – a feeling Shahida couldn't share.

'Unfortunately, we can't inject every tuk-a-wa in the galaxy into your bloodstream to kill them off.'

'No, that's not it.' Shaking her head, Palia shifted on the pillows, legs bunching underneath her like she wanted to get up and pace. 'That's not what's going to help us. What's going to help us is what let me communicate with it in the first place: the Empyrean. The same thing they used to communicate with before it was taken from them.'

'That was something else. The Empyrean was just created to destroy it.'

'Well, it felt the same as the Empyrean.'

'Wait.' The meaning of Palia's words condensed into a tight ball in Shahida's chest. 'Do you mean the Empyrean came back *completely*? On this side of the gate?' A jolt of panic rushed through her. 'What did you do? Did you fix them? Can they communicate across the galaxy again?'

'No.' Palia gave a firm shake of her head. 'Not unless I give them the ability to. I...' She reconsidered whatever she had been about to say, instead saying, 'The parasite, alive or dead, acts as a miniature Prime Nexus. That's what was the source of the Empyrean in my galaxy, and what turned into the gate at Warden Station. And, well, that's what I think has happened, anyway. Whatever I had that made me empyrric, some dormant spark of it reawakened the parasite's old abilities.

'I am my own walking source of the Empyrean. I can sense the parasites, I can talk to them, I can kill them. If that's not the best chance we have right now, I don't know what is.'

Understanding dawned in Shahida's eyes and bloomed as thick bands of fierce hope in the Empyrean. Palia should have known that framing the Empyrean as a weapon would be a terrible idea – even if it was true, and had always been true. Even if they really did need to use it as one. She knew it now, from that look in Shahida's eyes. Palia would have to use it to kill again. She might be asked to repeat the very crime for which her ancestors had been exiled. They might want to make more people empyrric, if they could find a way.

They might undo everything she and Ferrash had fought for.

'We need to see what you can do,' Shahida said. 'This could turn the tide for us. The sooner we find out by how much, the better. We need to get you in a fast ship and take you to the enemy.'

CHAPTER THIRTY-FOUR

WITH THE SPEAKER'S BLESSING, Palia and Shahida hurried back into the shuttle Palia had arrived in and over to Kaktek's ship – all without remembering to warn Kaktek. His surprise lasted a long kluqetik millisecond, but he approved to using his ship for testing. Eagerness and fear flashed across his paddles in a near-indistinguishable tangle.

Now they just needed to find a target.

In a change of direction executed as swiftly as Kaktek's surprise, his ship left the fleet. At its speed, they could jump systems, carry out their experiment and return in time to join the fleet's jump to Warden Station. They had their destination: the ship that had evacuated the council from Tilukettia. All those aboard that ship should be considered hosts. And that meant they should also be considered targets.

Now Palia sat in the same musical amphitheatre she had been in with Ruslan before, her hands bunched into fists and pressed against her mouth, her insides churning with nerves. Passing kluqetik gave her quizzical looks as the green light of the Empyrean washed over her skin, interpreting it as one emotion or another before dismissing it as noise. She had it at a manageable level. She wasn't about to set fire to anything.

She might be about to kill a bunch of people, that was all.

Not like I haven't done that *before.* In the centre of the amphitheatre, above a kluqetik who rattled away on something between cymbals and drums, hung another hologram. Part of the coreworld fleet hung in apparent stillness, forming a protective sphere around the ship containing the council evacuees.

Palia caught Shahida's voice from further around the amphitheatre where she stood in consultation with Kaktek and another two kluqetik. 'Can we sway any of them?'

She missed part of Kaktek's reply with his paddles hidden behind Shahida, but he shifted a fraction towards the end. <—one-off event. We can't count on it happening again. As it is, we can't get through them. I don't think this will work.>

After a brief shake of her head that set the tags on her headdress jangling, Shahida glanced over at Palia. 'The Empyrean,' she said. The drummer set off a harsh rattle. 'How does it work, exactly?'

Palia wished she could remember all the explanations Ferrash had probably given her when she'd first become empyrric, but... well, she couldn't. Lilesh's later training had been too practical to furnish her with any good replacements. So she just listed off what she did remember. 'I can see life and emotions – though it's not always easy to make sense of them. I can take that energy away and throw it back out again to hurt people – and depending on the amount of energy I take away, I can just kill people outright or strip their memories. It's very unstable, though. I've stripped my own memories twice and... I've killed a lot of people I didn't mean to.'

Throughout Palia's listing, Shahida had remained motionless, only nodding once at the end – presumably not approving of her killing people, but she couldn't be entirely sure.

Now, Shahida gestured to the hologram of the fleet and said, 'Can you get us through that?'

Palia looked to the hologram, then back at Shahida, her brows knotting together. 'Do we need to get through?'

'I don't know. You tell me. It's certainly easier if we don't have to.'

In a two-second flash, Kaktek said, <I would add that it is impossible. My ship is fast and can fire in many directions at once, but there are fast kluqetik ships in that fleet as well, and in any case we would not withstand the numbers.>

Closing her eyes, Palia let the hunger take her. Her awareness washed out over the ship and its crew, the flitting sparks of the kluqetik zipping all over the spinning inner cylinder. It washed out further into the void, spreading through unfeeling emptiness, and then... Snatches of something. Light smeared at the edge of her vision, spinning, spinning. Palia felt herself spinning in response. She tried to reach for the light, but every time she turned towards it, it was gone.

Something struck her shoulder and she reeled, legs going limp underneath her. She opened her eyes and flailed about with her arms, grabbing onto soft robes and brushing the impression of solid armour beneath.

Shahida gently pulled her upright. 'Are you *sure* you have regained all your abilities?'

Cradling her forehead in one hand, Palia grunted assent. 'We're spinning, so everything in here is fine, but everything outside is spinning and I can't get a handle on it. We'll have to stop spinning.'

<You could sense them?> Kaktek clicked.

'I think so.'

Wonder bloomed on his paddles. <We will have to stop spinning to burn, anyway. Sink into place. I'll have the process start now, then we can be ready to go.>

With any luck, they wouldn't have to go anywhere. Palia dropped down to the ground on still-shaking legs so the floor could swallow her up like it had last time.

She hoped she wouldn't be joined by her own vomit on this occasion.

Gravity slipped away over the span of several heartbeats, the change so gradual and her enmeshment in the crystalline gel so complete that Palia barely noticed it. When she thought it might be over, she closed her eyes again and reached out with her awareness. There were the kluqetik again, and a few bright lights just beyond the hull...

She snapped her eyes open, heart pounding. 'Do we have an escort?' she asked Kaktek.

<No.>

Anxiety tingled along Palia's nerves. 'So there shouldn't be anyone close to the outside of this ship?'

<There are a few crews returning from quick maintenance. We didn't manage to fix all the last battle's scars at Sol.>

'Okay, that's good, then. I can sense them.' For a moment she had been worried they had unwanted visitors. She breathed a sigh of relief, closed her eyes, and settled back into her awareness. She looked further and further, but her psyche felt like an elastic band stretched too tight. She couldn't see beyond. An ache in her gut urged her onwards, but she couldn't answer the call.

Opening her eyes, Palia shook her head. 'There's a limit to how far I can see that I didn't have before.' Back in her galaxy, she had had a Prime Nexus so big that no one had ever mapped it to draw upon. Here, she had the dead remains of the parasite she had injected wrapped around her brain somewhere. But that was academic. They didn't need to know the details. 'We'll have to get closer.'

<How much closer?>

'I don't know.'

Shahida, as usual, was an unreadable statue – this time because the gel held her sideways and still. But now Palia could see the undercurrent of emotions confined within the scope of her body. She had them on a tight leash – a continuous current strained by tension, no individual emotion distinguishable from the mass.

'If we get too close,' Shahida said, 'we'll need to fight our way in. And that defeats the point of trying to use this against them.'

Hackles rising, Palia twisted in her helmet to face her. 'Weapons have ranges. This one happens to be close. And it's a lot more effective than any long- or close-range weapons you can throw at them today. And selective, too, in the right circumstances.' Realising how fast she had been to leap to the Empyrean's defence, a knot of guilty fear twisted in Palia's gut. *Look at me, with all the collateral damage I've caused, claiming it's selective.*

Shahida said, 'Well then, when we get close enough, what exactly will it do? Say we had no weapons at all beyond yours – could you stop us getting vented?'

'At long range, I could try to shield us, but...' The last time she had shielded a machine she stood inside, it had been a much smaller mech on Munab, Lilesh had been managing most of the shield, and they had still lost the mech. Could she confuse the people on the ships they passed? She should be able to wipe memories to make them functionally invisible, but she couldn't remember how and that would hardly protect them from anyone outside her range. 'The most effective thing I could do is kill everyone on the ships we pass, but I'd rather not.'

<Isn't that exactly what we're here to do?>

Palia shook her head. *Negotiate first. They might be more willing to listen than the samples were.* 'We're here to hurt the tuk-a-wa. Not their hosts. I think I should be able to isolate the parasites and kill them, but I'm guessing not everyone on those ships is a host. If they're aligned with the tuk-a-wa, they'll keep shooting at us.'

'It wouldn't surprise me if they were all hosts.' Shahida snorted from her position in the gel. 'If they've been so bold as to infect the council without permission, they wouldn't stop at a ship's crew or two. They wouldn't stop at anything.' She turned to Kaktek. 'Are you happy to try this?'

The precise emotion Kaktek felt flashed across his paddles in far more detail than Palia ever could have obtained by examining the riot she could see within him in the Empyrean: fear of the infamous Empyrean, fear of being surrounded by ships of a coordinated hivemind, excitement and hope at perhaps being able to deal them a true blow, better than slow and messy political change. No happiness, though. He would be happy if they succeeded.

<We'll go now, as fast as we can, through their perimeter, straight past the council's ship and out the other side. Do what you need to do quickly, or the chance will be gone. My ship is faster and more manoeuvrable than most they have. As long as we don't take too much damage, we'll be out and gone in plenty of time. If this works, we can pull the same trick at Warden Station.>

She nodded, not that he would be able to see her do so, and sank into deep focus for the task to come.

As if sensing her need for focus, some of the kluqetik in the amphitheatre – somehow still able to play within the confines of the gel – buzzed into the strains of a slow lullaby. Faster tunes flashed along within the greater whole, so fast to her ears that they may as well have been continuous notes. The hologram sparkled like the dreams of a projecting night light, and the ships within it grew larger.

The maintenance crews slipped back inside the ship. Palia kept her awareness as wide as she could without straining, watching the range marker on the hologram tick down and down.

As the distance decreased yet further, she asked Kaktek, 'Does this ship have cloaking or something? Surely they should have noticed us by now?'

Kaktek's clicks carried through the gel as vibrations. <We have some cloaking, but it won't stop them detecting our burn. They will have seen it. Remember to account for light delay.>

Of course. She was so used to getting images relayed to her near instantaneously by nexite buoys and drones. Here, without the Empyrean, even a closer drone would have a speed limit to obey. Her heart beat faster at the thought she might not know what was happening until it was too late. At least the closer they got, the less a problem that would be... or the less time she would have to worry before dying, anyway.

Seconds slipped by. A bead of sweat trickled down the back of her neck.

'Anything?' Shahida asked.

'Not yet.'

All at once, the sphere of the council escort burst into motion. Every other ship broke free of it and burned hard towards them, with the rest of the sphere shrinking closer around their charge.

Her mouth dry, Palia pushed at the edge of her awareness. *Show me something. Anything. I can't be this blind. Please.*

Then she felt it: life, so, so distant in her mind, but so alive, and speeding fast towards her. Just like the missiles the lead ships had just fired.

<We're running out of time, exile!>

'I have them!' Palia shouted, exhilaration and fear pounding through her veins. Riding a wave of déjà vu, she filtered out the big minds from the small – the hosts, she hoped, from the parasites. In the instant her mind touched theirs, their voice glared like sunshine over snow.

What is this? they thundered. The missiles exploded far from her ship's hull as the kluqetik shot them down, but more came burning towards them.

Trying to imbue her words with all the acceptance she could muster, Palia sent, *Divert your missiles. Ceasefire. I want to negotiate, but if you keep firing I will be forced to fight.*

The missiles stayed on course. Palia counted one heartbeat, two.

We will not negotiate with the aggressor. With their words came the impression of hopeless odds, of a great stormcloud consuming her little speck of a ship.

<Exile...>

With a frustrated growl, Palia snatched at the parasites' souls, drawing them towards her like dust. She didn't dare touch the larger souls. She knew she wouldn't be able to control what she did to them. Not at this distance. Not at this speed.

One by one, the sparks of the parasites hissed out into nothingness. One by one, they died. Cold gripped Palia's chest. Killing them was so *easy*, like swatting flies. For her ancestors to have only gone as far as they did suddenly seemed a mercy.

Then the distance became nothing, and the attacking ships blurred past them. Snatches of confusion tugged on Palia's attention from the newly freed.

'I've done it,' Palia said. 'I've freed the hosts on those ships.'

<All of them?>

'Just the ones that went past us.' As she said it, a shudder ran through the gel. Something groaned on the ship's hull. Two more ships detached from the protective sphere to come after them.

\<We've lost two spurs. I'm altering course to take us out early. We'll still have to deal with these two and any of the earlier ships that decide to attack. Are you close enough to free the council?\>

Palia stretched until her brain felt like it might snap, but she couldn't sense anyone on the other ships anymore. She'd sense more soon enough, but she wouldn't be able to reach the council. *Zash.* She had to get her message to them, or this would all be for nothing. And what if she was going about this all wrong? One parasite was no more important than any other, unless they *did* have a queen. If they had all rejected her offer so far, surely they would continue to do so.

At the very least, she should free them. But unless she could free every host on every ship in this fleet, they would no doubt be reinfected the moment she left.

'I won't be able to do it,' she said with a waver in her voice. 'I'm sorry. They're too far away.'

\<That's okay. If what you said you've done is the truth, we can still use it.\>

A jarring change of momentum pressed her hard into the gel. Palia's vision blurred. When it cleared, the hologram had changed its orientation. The cloud of ships that had previously attacked them drifted at odd angles, some of them consolidating into a new formation, others staying in place.

Kaktek's ship rocketed towards them, aiming for the open maw of the jump station that lay behind.

While she had her eyes open, her translator tried to make sense of the colours travelling through the crystal again. In the midst of dozens of status reports, she got the impression that their two new attackers were catching up.

She closed her eyes, took a breath, and waited. When the previous attackers came through, they came in bright patches of confusion. Filtering out the bigger patches showed only darkness – she'd been thorough in ridding them of parasites, it seemed – so she ignored them. And if they weren't attacking, she didn't need to hurt them.

Seconds more ticked by, then the dim lights of consciousness appeared at the edge of her awareness. She waited until the whole ship caught up and she could see all of its occupants.

Then she sent her message: *I am empyrric. I did not choose to be, and I did not choose to be your enemy. I destroyed the Empyrean in my galaxy, but I have accidentally brought it back here. I don't want to use it against you – I want to use it to help you. Relay this proposal amongst yourselves. I can restore your emotion and long-range communication to you, and you should feel the truth of this now. In return, cease all hostilities, withdraw from the council and let my people return to our galaxy as their own selves.*

Let us know your answer a week from now and please, let us not be enemies as our ancestors were.

Palia withdrew before the wave of hatred she sensed could reach her, and they barrelled through the jump station. To safety, and then to Warden Station.

CHAPTER THIRTY-FIVE

THE SAILS HAVE ATTACKED the council. They're on the way to Warden Station. Those words, hammered home into the parasite's unknowable psyche, dragged Ferrash out from the recesses of his own mind. He existed, shapeless, aimless, for an eternity. Then he became aware again, and the knowledge of having been in that brief *forever* filled his entire world with fear.

He had missed a lot this time, he was sure. The parasite's psyche roiled with new information. It was as if Ferrash had gone to sleep in a quiet room and woken to find himself in the middle of a busy street. He caught impressions of a child's face amidst a burning sea of hate, got the sense of memories more ancient than imagining. *Speaker*, it called her, mocking the name. Then he felt the touch of Palia's mind on his, as he had felt within the Prime Nexus as they destroyed the Empyrean. But the instant the sensation appeared, the parasite threw a wall in front of the feeling, and the wall said *nemesis*. This wasn't hatred. This was denial. But of what? Ferrash didn't know.

The hosts of Warden Station formed a chandelier of minds around him. They occupied so much of his awareness that he couldn't even process what his eyes were seeing. The minds clustered, each a host like him, part of a sprawling family that granted him a sense of relaxing reassurance. It felt like home here, like the hollow cold of Hesperex, its grey-faced people shuffling through the life proscribed to them in their multi-coloured shells, no emotion staining the air but fear, no freedom straining his nerves but the freedom to do what the Keepers and the Proctor dictated.

A peculiar smugness settled over him. He had found his freedom before. He would find it again.

Candles began to detach in groups from the edge of the chandelier and Ferrash forced himself to reconsider his perspective. They were ships, detaching from the booms of Warden Station. The moment they got slightly too far from the next nearest host, they disappeared from the network of minds. The network felt each loss, however temporary. Not with any particular emotion he could put a name to – and he could put a name to most of them – but it felt it. Nevertheless, a particular energy permeated the hive: a buzzing activity, reacting to an outside threat.

As the networked hosts diminished, Ferrash's vision returned. His attention caught on the flashes of light thrown up by tap water washing over his hands. *Well at least the parasite's keeping up with basic hygiene.*

His hands rushed through the motions. Ferrash mustn't have taken long to wake since the news came through. Everything had just happened so fast. Minds and ships could respond almost instantly. Flesh and blood took longer. Add to that resistance aboard the station, and... Wait, how did he know about any resistance? There must have been some for the ships to have been sabotaged. That had happened last time he had been awake, hadn't it?

The parasite took him along a corridor, and Ferrash realised where the news must have come from: the station in general buzzed with an angry tension. He had only registered it subconsciously, and the distance between his subconscious and the rest of him made it slower to parse. Shouting echoed from further in the station. Who was it? Residents or prisoners? Had they done to everyone else the same as they had done to him?

Wary of being discovered, Ferrash approached the sense of the parasite in his mind. He tried to hold it in the same picture as the rest of the network, but one or the other kept threatening to slip from between his fingers.

When he finally got the two in some sort of balance, the sense of *knowing* each host in the most superficial physical detail made his mind reel. He began picking through them, one by one. Then, with an ease born of decades of processing reams of intelligence, he sifted through en masse.

He didn't recognise any of them. Good.

Motion tugged at his legs. He recognised the length of one of the docking booms sliding past beside him, the travelator bearing him along it.

Panic punched bullets through the fabric of his mind. He sank deeper again, then clawed his way back up. The parasite's awareness shifted around him, like a beast within the clouds, swirling in its search for prey. Ferrash flowed with it. He mimicked what he could sense of its thought patterns, trying to fool it into disregarding him. How long had he not been himself this time? Who had the Sails lost in their attack? Was Palia still alive? Was Bek still freezing in a hole on Hesperex?

To stop his thoughts scattering, Ferrash refocused on his surroundings. They came to the end of the travelator, where five other hosts stood in networked silence and identical sky-blue jumpsuits.

Was this normal? For all he knew, he could have been doing this every day since he last lost awareness. The hosts gave no outward indication that anything was amiss. In the presence of other hosts, they need not give outward indication of anything. That left him little to work with beyond their ever-present minds – and as much as he wished he could escape those, he couldn't. Maybe this was how Palia had felt, never being able to switch off from the Empyrean. But at least the Empyrean hadn't taken all autonomy from her. Not exactly.

Saying nothing, the five hosts turned as one to face Ferrash's left. Ferrash turned left in front of them, towards one of the docking hatches, and they fell into formation: two to either side of him, one behind. Their presence would have itched at his spine in normal times but now, with the cumulonimbus weight of their minds constantly pressing in on him, it was suffocating. His body tensed with an adrenaline-spiking fight-or-flight response that slipped through the parasite's control, his heart racing, his throat so tight he could barely breathe. A memory of the operating table flashed through his mind: the converted shuttle bay, the sorrowful presence of Shahida, the needle in Ilhan's hand, a blunt pain in his leg, the efficiency with which the Sails pulled him clear, pulled him to the airlock, let him vent himself out into—

A leaden weight crashed down upon his conscious mind. As it fell, it tore away all that beautiful adrenaline, every sensation in his limbs, the simple control over his own breathing. He cried out, or tried to, but his grasp on reality faded. His escort took his shoulders and marched him along in a dreamlike haze. Weariness tugged at him. He sank towards sleep.

As he drifted, he swam within the network – and the network dreamed of the gate.

Ferrash clutched at the last dregs of his awareness. The gate. The *gate.* He forced himself to repeat it, each time remembering its importance a little more. *Why are they thinking about the gate?*

He relaxed into the flow of communication between network nodes, between one parasite and the next. They all knew their part of the plan. Whenever they were in contact with another node, they repeated their purpose, their findings, their current condition, their optimal uses. It flowed like a song with a thousand voices singing the same tune with different words.

When he eventually managed to pick out the song of those around him, a chill gripped his soul.

We will spread the Great Convergence. We will make the exiles anew, free from their crimes, their violent ways. We will spread the Great Convergence, and we will not be held back by the aggressors. This has been long in the making. Long, long, long, the entire hive mind echoed, *and we will spread for longer still, until all is within us, and we encompass everything, and everything is one.*

They were bringing him to the gate as a façade, as a friendly face to convince everyone on the other side that more from this galaxy could come through. More hosts. More parasites. He would be Patient Zero. He would be the one to infect his galaxy, and there was nothing he could do to stop it.

CHAPTER THIRTY-SIX

THE RESISTANCE FLEET HAD begun its journey to Warden Station not long after Palia returned from her test of the Empyrean aboard Kaktek's ship. The fleet travelled between the final two jump stations now, but no matter how strongly Palia willed the transit to go faster, this galaxy's technology was more consistent than the nexuses back home had been: consistently slow.

It would be a full week before they arrived at Warden Station. A full week before she could try to save Ferrash.

At least while they waited, they could plan. She sat now aboard the *Inzekir* with Kaktek, Shahida and the Speaker in a meeting room full of bright art installations and hanging vines. Palia thought she even spotted a few of the kind of metal panels Shahida tended to wear on her robes.

Kaktek's legs twitched with an amplification of Palia's own nervous energy. They – her translator flagged they were no longer male – seemed duller than usual. How much of that was down to their reverting to sexless colouration now the mating season was over, Palia didn't know. They rested on a sculpted couch to her left around a circular table, paddles flashing with curses at the slow pace of interstellar travel, fiddling with a multifaceted crystal. Palia couldn't look at it for too long without straining her eyes.

Shahida sat between Kaktek and Palia, her arms folded across her chest, her foot tapping against the floor. They were all frustrated. They couldn't get much news about the galaxy while they were in transit, and all they wanted to do was fight, but this galaxy's technology couldn't get them to it any faster.

The Speaker was the only one of them who came across as nonchalant. Palia supposed it was easy to be patient when you were that old.

As the girl popped another sweet in her mouth, the airlock door opened and the captain came in with his colleagues trailing behind. 'Sorry I'm late,' he said. He flopped down into the seat opposite Kaktek with a sigh. 'We've just come off a call with the other captains. It overran a little. We're not used to having more in the conversation than just Sails.'

The administrator, taking a seat to his right, raised her eyebrow. 'You would think the galaxy had universal standards of inventory management, but no, apparently not.'

'Yes, well.' The captain cleared his throat and tugged at his moustache. 'That's all sorted now. We know what we have and, thanks to Kaktek' – he gave a nod of thanks to the kluqetik – 'we know what's arrayed against us, too.'

Kaktek held their paddles out so all around the table could see. <The tuk-a-wa haven't been able to send many reinforcements to Warden Station. Only a handful of extra ships have arrived since we left, and many of those still present were damaged by my saboteurs. Security has been stepped up and they haven't managed any further action, but they may be able to help us from within the station during the fight if needed.>

The speed of translation formed a dull ache in Palia's head, but she kept her attention on the interplay of colours.

<We have numerical superiority, purely looking at numbers. But your Sails' fleet is primarily defence-focused. You are more suited to acting as an aid fleet in the other galaxy once the fighting is done than you are to combat in this one. Let us not mention the massive potential for civilian casualties. You have limited munitions. Even with additional resistance vessels, we will need to make them count.>

The Speaker swallowed her sweet loudly and said, 'Expect the tuk-a-wa's ships to be well coordinated. They won't be as efficient as they once were, thanks to the exiles, but I expect they will have a handful of operators virtually networked on each ship, and each will maintain close enough proximity with the other operators on their ship that anything they learn that way will be instantly relayed.'

<How coordinated?> Kaktek's paddles gave an indignant pink flash, and emotions prickled around their insides.

'About a match for your people, I would say. If they keep their ships at distances anyone else would deem suicidal, then possibly better. But I doubt the tuk-a-wa could get a connection even if their ships' hulls were touching, and that would mean standing still or docking. I wouldn't worry about that.'

'So what's the plan?' Shahida asked.

The captain leaned forwards and clasped his hands over the table. 'Our number-one priority is the gate. We have to get through it and blockade the other side. If they follow us, fine: you wanted to try luring your friend through anyway. If they don't, we can prepare a defence by the gate and assess the situation over there for any way we can help.'

Palia tried to keep her hopes down, but the thought of going home set her nerves alight. 'So we just get there and fly straight through?'

'We punch a hole. And you' – the captain fixed Palia with a stare, and her mouth went dry – 'will be helping us keep the way clear.'

A week after their meeting, with the fleet's exit at the jump station imminent, Palia followed directions to the *Inzekir*'s central zero-G hangar. When she saw the fighter lying in wait, she swallowed. It looked like a shard of crystal, easily shattered.

At least when Palia had last been expected to wield the Empyrean against parasites from inside a ship, the ship had been more substantial. This time the captain wanted her in something smaller, faster, more suitable to working its way into tight gaps and widening them for others to follow. So for the entirety of the battle, she would be relying on the skill of her kluqetik pilot, the integrity of their tiny fighter's hull, and her own newly reawakened ability with the Empyrean to keep her alive.

She didn't have much choice. The pilot was already in there. Palia floated into the kluqetik fighter head first, trying to follow the pilot's rapid instructions, and cracked her knee against a sharp-edged bit of metal.

'Zash!' She bit her lip, took a deep breath and wriggled further in, ignoring the pain stabbing through her knee. The *Inzekir* groaned again – a deep-throated peal it apparently only made when they were about to exit a jump station far past the speed limit. The noise set her teeth on edge. She had to keep taking deliberately slow breaths to stop worrying about what that meant: they would soon arrive at Warden Station, and she would have to perform miracles.

If I can get inside this zashen ship first.

<Please hurry,> the crystal that made up the fighter flashed at her, relaying the pilot's words within its structure. <We will need to launch as soon as we clear the jump station.>

'I know, I'm sorry, I'm trying.' Palia twisted through a tight section, scraping her spine along a knobbly protrusion. 'I can't fit in as tight spaces as you can.'

<Humans often accompany us in these ships.>

'Then they must have to diet for it,' she said, though she had picked up on a purple note of exaggeration in the pilot's speech.

At last, she half fell inside the crew compartment, keeping her hands clasped close to her so she didn't inadvertently trigger any of the controls. Crystal pressed against her on all sides, and the pressure shifted as the fighter moved, presumably into its waiting launch tube. It was all she could do not to back right out again when gel oozed in to fill the space around her.

If this is all made of that stupid crystal, why couldn't it have just reshaped to let me in easier? She was about to dive into that line of thinking, but the *Inzekir* groaned again and she thought better of it. She needed a clear mind for this.

She closed her eyes. 'How long until—?'

The groan shifted into a musical squeal. Then, like a whale breaching the surface of the ocean, the *Inzekir* passed through the jump station. Palia felt it – a dark wave that chilled her skin for a fraction of a second and left bright afterimages floating in her eyes. The groaning stopped. The next second, acceleration kicked her in the chest and the gel squeezed tight around her. She gasped for a breath that wouldn't come.

<Do you need visuals?>

Palia wanted to ask the pilot what they were on about, but she couldn't squeeze any sound out of her throat.

<Tch, humans fainting in their own launch tube acceleration. Uncontained flesh. Whoever thought that was a good idea? Fainting and fainting, every time. I will give visuals. Might need reminding space exists when they come round.>

The crystal around her became transparent, then filled with a hologram of space. At the same moment, the acceleration dropped away and Palia gasped before falling into a bout of coughing.

'I was awake,' she croaked when she was done.

<Good. You can use your manipulators to transform the projection.>

Guessing they meant her fingers, Palia tried wriggling them. Through a quick round of experimentation, she worked out how to control her view, then set it to look at the way ahead.

'Ancestors save us,' she whispered. Either Kaktek's estimates had been wrong or his definition of 'not many' ships didn't match hers.

A hurricane of lights swirled in the dark before them. She couldn't even make out Warden Station. The swarm of the hive mind's ships was too dense and they were too numerous. The only thing immediately behind them that they didn't obscure was the gate, enormous as it was. Palia's breath caught in her throat at seeing it again. If only they hadn't been so close to it when they had destroyed the Empyrean. If only they hadn't fallen through. It wouldn't have got rid of the problem, but it might have made it someone else's. For a while.

<Are you ready?> the pilot asked.

Palia bit her lip so hard she tasted blood. 'Is punching a hole still the plan?'

<I haven't been told otherwise.>

'Even with so many of them? If we dive right into the middle of that, I don't think I can deal with so many.'

<There are as many as we expected. Many are drones.> Their words carried a measure of frustration, and some sub-chatter about the slowness of humans. <Prepare.>

A sickening coil of fear wove around her gut. Palia turned her attention to their own forces. The fighter she was in clung close to the side of one of the Sails' ships – they had come too far since launching for it to be the *Inzekir*, she thought. In front of it and to Palia's right, spiky kluqetik ships formed a protective shell, tapering to a point somewhere in front of her. That spear was like the living embodiment of her anticipation: sharp, looking straight at the enemy and the gate, but from any other angle like a rope pulled too taut. Every second she expected fighting to erupt, but the hurricane kept swirling, and they edged closer.

<Contact in ten seconds.>

So soon? She'd never get used to how little distances made sense in space. As the long spear of the resistance's ships began to rotate along its axis and little bursts of fire bloomed from missile launches like a million little fireworks, she closed her eyes.

The Empyrean opened up before her, the nearest of her allies spinning alongside her, the Sails a fixed point in the centre. She could only just sense them, and the whirlpool of their souls made her dizzy. The same would be true of their enemies. Chaos, velocity, aggression. Somehow she had to work with that.

Ferrash might be one of them. A shudder ran through her at the thought. She dug her nails tight into her palm against the resistance of the gel.

<Three.>

She pushed the thought from her mind, her heart aching. She couldn't afford to think like that. Instead, she blocked out the spinning core of the spear as best she could and focused outwards.

<Two.>

Palia filled her lungs. At this speed, with this strategy, they might as well be a bullet. It could be over in a heartbeat.

<One.>

She opened her eyes. The hurricane rushed at her, all light and chaff and movement. Warden Station spun round, and round, and...

Contact. Light flared in her awareness. She clawed at it, trying to filter parasites from hosts where she could, but not stopping to make sure. She clawed at it, and life guttered and failed at her touch. In the crystal display, an emerald filigree stretched like a web between Palia and the nearest enemy ships. It followed the spin of the spear, wrapping tighter and tighter, never quite strengthening as much as Palia thought it would. But the parasites were only small. She was being selective. Controlled.

Took me long enough to work that out. No accidental explosions this time. But she couldn't shake a chill at how easy this was, how many hundreds or thousands she might be killing in the space of a heartbeat. The parasites didn't overload her the way a human soul did, or would take much longer to do so.

The pilot took them on a weaving path that ducked under and over enemy drones, sometimes flying in formation with allied drones, sometimes splitting off, always following the rough direction of their rotation. Fire spilled over their hull. An indicator in the display showed their lasers firing constantly, cycling their activity so none of them overheated, but she couldn't see them out in space.

Where Palia had attacked, the hive mind's ships grew erratic and got in the way of the others. If she kept this up, they might just make it. She stared at the light of the gate behind the battle, filled with a hunger not for the Empyrean, but for *home.*

Then a formation of ships dropped from the void in front of them, burning to match their rotation. Palia couldn't sense them in the

Empyrean. If she could, with similar velocities, they would have been easy to deal with.

'Those are drones,' she said. 'I can't do anything about them.'

<Noted.>

They were coming closer to Warden Station, she realised. With each rotation, it grew larger in the crystal, the ragged damage from recent sabotage more obvious, the gun emplacements at the end of each boom more threatening. *They're pushing us into range.* The tip of their spear no longer lined up with the gate. If they couldn't get back on target, they would all die here, crushed against the station's hull.

Something crashed against their fighter with a piercing screech. Palia cried out and tensed in a futile effort to brace herself amidst the already-bracing gel. They darted through a gap between two of the attacking drones, firing as they passed in a blur.

The station rotated into view again. It shone brightly in her awareness for a moment. A brief sensation of shock jolted through Palia before it went out of range. She shook it off, though a tugging sensation remained. If she could take out the gun operators, if they weren't automated, then...

That sensation again. It flared on the next rotation and Palia recognised it for what it was: another empyrric, their shock masking the all-consuming black hole their presence formed in the fabric of the Empyrean. Palia's heart hammered in her chest. *Lilesh!* She was still alive on Warden Station.

<Lilesh,> Palia sent. <Lilesh, are you getting this?>

In the next moment, her elation turned to horror. Her implants told her they couldn't find a connection, a bridge opened up between her and Lilesh in the Empyrean, and the speck that must be Lilesh flared into brilliant incandescence.

CHAPTER THIRTY-SEVEN

FERRASH RODE A SICKENING current between one level of consciousness and the next, one moment smothered beneath the weight of the parasite's control, the next so acutely aware of his own bodily sensations that the simple touch of fabric on his skin sent shockwaves of disgust through him. The nebulous clouds of the five nearby hosts beckoned across the ocean. A harness strap dug into his right shoulder and made his shirt scrape across his collarbone. Communication flickered between the nodes of the network. Something in the shuttle squeaked, and he felt the movement of each cilium along his ear canal.

By fixating on one sensation – on the light of the gate in their forwards viewscreen – he managed to pull himself together. By the looks of the measurements it displayed, they would reach it inside ten minutes. That tallied with the sense he got from the parasite.

I have ten minutes to stop this happening. But he couldn't just throw himself out the airlock – the five other hosts would go on to infect his galaxy without him. He was only here for leverage. If he could figure out a way to get the airlock open or breach that hull, that would at least delay them until they sent the next ship... But none of that accounted for the fact his mind was locked down tight. As much as he oscillated between different levels of consciousness, he could sense the prison of the parasite's control firmer than before, like a glass barrier between him and his body's controls.

Ferrash tried, as much as he was able, to think quietly about his auxiliary AI. He didn't want the parasite finding out about it, if it hadn't already. Its one thread was still ticking quietly away, unnoticed.

One thread, one copy of his mind. It could launch dozens more at a moment's notice. He might not even need that many to wrest back control of his body. If he triggered it, just one could give him the edge he needed to get out of here.

He hesitated. That way meant death. And death wasn't really freedom; it was a deeper oblivion than even this. He wasn't about to throw his life away for a delay that was a blink of the hive mind's eye.

What if that delay is all it takes for someone else to be able to finish the job?

Before the chill of his thoughts could grip him completely, his gaze shifted to the rear viewscreen. He couldn't stop the thrill of excitement that coursed through his mind. *That would be the someone else.*

A spearhead of ships stabbed into the night behind him, the ships of Warden Station swirling around it like a school of fish. The resistance had reached the system less than a minute earlier, and the bulk of the battle lay far behind Ferrash's shuttle. Missiles and flak met and flashed like lightning between the fleets. The tip of it sheered from right to left, away from the gate, pushed by weight of fire from the hive mind's fleet.

He paid closer attention to the spear. There, just back from the tip... a shimmer of green, a faint filigree, turning and twisting from where it attached to one of the attacking ships. *No.* Dread and the attention of the parasite scattered his thoughts for a moment. *It can't be. We destroyed it.* But there, clear as day, was Empyrean fire. Ferrash couldn't sense the network – it was too far away. Nor could the parasite, but a sharp flare of recognition ricocheted between it and the other hosts. The host piloting the shuttle, connected to the wider network by more mechanical means, sent query after query and redistributed the responses to the others.

Nodes were falling out of the network. Parasites were dying.

Nemesis. The word fell like a raindrop from one host's mind, to be joined by another and another, until all the hosts shouted the word in a ceaseless torrent.

Palia, Ferrash thought, and bitter relief washed through him. It had to be her, somehow. He wanted to shout for her in his mind, with all his strength, in the vain hope that the shout might reach her and she could catch him in time. But that would attract the attention of the parasite, and then he would be suppressed, and he would be blind.

The parasite began to turn his gaze from the offending viewscreen, but then the green wave changed. The next time the fighter reached the closest point in its rotation, the Empyrean fire attached to it billowed towards Warden Station – just for a moment, then it returned to normal. Then a blinding beam of light tore through the hull of the station, so bright it was almost white. He winced. Through the shade of his lashes, the beam shifted and jumped. Flickers of it glinted from windows along the rotating habitation circle. Something exploded partway around the ring.

For a moment, nothing happened. Information flooded between the parasites – queries, hypotheses, *nemeses*.

Before he could even start on his own theories, the station exploded. Lashing green tendrils melted the ring free from its central hub and parts of the structure flew in separate directions. One of the docking booms came loose and punched a hole through the nearby ships, scattering debris across the void, taking several other ships out in the aftermath. The parasite seemed to latch onto his shock. It couldn't experience the emotion itself, so it dived deeper and borrowed his.

Seeing an opportunity, Ferrash tried to insert one of his own thoughts into the swirling mass of the parasite's mind. *We should stay and deal with this. They need all the help we can give.*

The parasite's grip tightened, then retreated. *Do not think to influence us, child of our enemy.*

So much for that, then. As if in response to Ferrash's impertinence, the shuttle's engines burned again, kicking him back into his seat. He remained pressed there for two seconds before it eased up. After that, the fact he still couldn't move his own muscles was entirely down to the parasite.

The last wash of green faded from the faces of the other hosts. In the darkness of the shuttle, their faces blurred into one amorphous face: no defining characteristics, no little quirks of personality, no subtle motions to indicate the background processes of a human mind. The bodies differed, the height differed, but it may well have been the same cloned head transplanted onto separate bodies. And now, with the only source of illumination the blue-tinged glow of the approaching gate in the viewscreen, those same features gained stark outlines.

Ferrash fixated on the ripples of the gate surface. Ten minutes had turned into ten seconds. It didn't look that close. It didn't look that far, either, and nothing about it changed as they moved closer. He willed something through the gap from the other side – a ship, a piece of debris, anything on a collision course that would stop them going through.

Five seconds to go. The gate shuddered. Above them on the viewscreen opposite Ferrash, a dozen spheres punched through from the other side of the gate, trailing blue streamers of light behind them as they broke the membrane. He'd never seen anything like them.

Three seconds to go. From the same spot as the spheres, the blunt nose of a ship that could have fit all dozen spheres within its cross-section bulged from the membrane. Ferrash stared up at it, then at the name printed on its hull: *Explorator Four*. The name was in his galactic standard language. The font was Rythian.

But Rythe hadn't had any ships in the Hesperex system when they had destroyed the Empyrean. How...?

One second to go. By the time the number on the display registered in Ferrash's brain, the *Explorator* had passed them, and their shuttle's nose had slipped through the membrane. By the time he blinked, they were through. To his own galaxy. To home. To where the *Explorator* had just come from.

Then his mind exploded with noise, every muscle in his body spasmed, and he smashed the back of his skull against the headrest.

CHAPTER THIRTY-EIGHT

BLOOD FLOODED FERRASH'S MOUTH. The iron-rich tang of it lingered, but the burning pain where he had bitten his tongue darted towards and away from him like a fish trying to escape a hook.

He couldn't do anything about it. Nothing existed in his mind but screaming. The blinding light of the gate's ring flooded his vision, spinning as the shuttle turned to decelerate. Trembling seized hold of his right arm and wouldn't let go. Waves tossed the surface of the ocean in his mind, and he tumbled through their troughs and valleys, flailing in desperation for the way up, the way out. Vision came in snatches. The other hosts moved in freeze frames, millimetre by millimetre, and time became a viscous mass.

What's happening? Was the parasite dying? Could it not survive this far from the rest of the hive?

Grasping onto the train of coherent thought, Ferrash surfaced. Impulse shot across the fabric of his mind like lightning, and every impulse wracked another muscle. He cast about for the other hosts and counted five. *No, six.* The sixth roiled so close to his parasite that he hadn't been able to distinguish them at first. It was the reason for the lightning. It fought for control with his parasite, back and forth, pummelling it with impulse after jagged impulse.

For a moment, his consciousness jerked fully back into his body. He gasped a ragged, bloody breath, then plunged back under. The two thunderheads collided. They pressed lower towards him and the force of their collision almost pushed him back beneath the waves, but he clung on. They tore at the ocean, ripping parts of it away, into themselves, throwing Ferrash's awareness in fragments into their own grasps.

He tried to hold himself together amidst the barrage of thoughts. *How dare... mote of the ancient... recompense... sundering of our souls... foe lost to... NEMESIS... judge yourself to take...* Half-glimpsed images flashed before his eyes. Memories came to his mind that he realised weren't his only as they were snatched away.

There are two parasites inside you. Ferrash stamped the thought out in cold, hard words. *They are fighting. Use this moment.*

Riding the peak of the next wave, he lunged for the mental command to activate his auxiliary AI. He only just managed it. As he fell back down towards oblivion, the sharp clarity of the AI reached for him. Its thought processes spread through his mind faster than he could keep up with without being fully connected, faster than either of the parasites. For the first time, separated from them, he felt the full scale of it: the threads of a thousand virtual minds crowding out the sky. The processes weren't just running in the back of his mind anymore. They were all of it.

When the AI connected, it pulled him back into control of his body with a jolt. He gagged, the sensations too much, too sudden. Around him, the other hosts turned in their seats. One had risen halfway out of their harness.

Ferrash twisted his harness free, a growl of pent-up frustration escaping past his bared teeth. The AI fed him actions and he carried them out. With a sharp blow to the head of the host nearest him, he splattered drops of blood through the gravity-free air. The host that had risen tugged free from their harness and launched themselves across the room at Ferrash. Ferrash grabbed hold of the unconscious host's hair and used the grip to flip himself upside down, twisting to avoid his enemy.

In such a small shuttle, he didn't have room to manoeuvre. The host grabbed Ferrash's belt on the way past and their momentum cancelled out. As soon as his toes touched the ceiling, Ferrash bunched his legs and pushed off, hauling the host's body in front of his shoulder and tucking his chin against his chest. They collided with another host as they were rising and a sharp *crack* resounded through the shuttle.

Something grabbed hold of Ferrash's legs. His consciousness dipped, and for a moment the churning landscape of the ocean crept into the waking world. Nausea churned in his stomach.

Their deceleration burn kicked Ferrash in the chest. He went flying towards the rear hull, only saved from a blow that would have knocked him out by the restraint of the host's hold on his legs. How many now? Two to go. No, three. The host he had used as a shield rounded on him, clinging tight to a chair, spitting blood. Ferrash could feel blood congealing on his face – the droplets he'd made earlier had flown back with him during the burn.

Teeth chattering, the engine's vibration juddering through his body, Ferrash tried to peel himself from the hull. He barely managed to raise his chest from it. The burn was too strong. One of the parasites was getting the upper hand in his mind. He had to finish this before they took full control.

With a glint in their eyes that Ferrash was probably imagining, the host clinging onto the chair drew a knife from their belt and held it out in one shaking hand.

Scatz.

In the instant the host let go of the knife, the burn stopped. Ferrash pushed off and sideways with as much force as he could muster. The knife flashed towards him like it had been fired from a gun. A line of cold fire burned down the side of Ferrash's hip. He yelled, the air in his lungs jostling the blood that sprayed to clump in the air before him, set into a spin by the impact of the knife.

He clung to the pain, the crutch that kept him conscious. He grabbed the knife as it sailed past him, rebounded from the corner and powered towards the two hosts left in the transport compartment with him. Splinters of pain screamed across his hip and down his left leg.

The host that had dropped the knife on him scrambled for the handhold they had lost. They weren't fast enough. Without thinking his target through, Ferrash jabbed at the host's throat. The knife punched through the side of their neck. Arterial crimson jetted out of the gash, splattering across Ferrash's face, getting in his eyes. He kicked back blindly, trying to rub them clear. A boot caught him in the face. He flew to the back of the hull again, but this time grabbed a handhold on the ceiling to steady himself.

When he managed to clear his vision, he saw the host's body tumbling end over end, bouncing from one side of the shuttle to the other, propelled by its own exsanguination. A pressure built in Ferrash's skull. Whatever the parasites were doing in there, it was coming to an end. The waves of his subconscious kept tugging him back. His legs trembled, setting the lower half of his body into a light spin.

I don't need this. Not now. Gritting his teeth, he judged an angle to the last host in the compartment as they hooked their dead companion through a harness strap and bunched their muscles for an attack. He gripped the knife tight.

Then his head cleared. He fell into the familiar sensations of his own body, the weight of something *other* dissipating from the folds of his brain. Ferrash breathed into the freedom, and a warm voice of many layered whispers floated to him from the back of his mind. *You have control. We wish you luck in ending this.*

Ferrash lunged, filled with vicious delight for newfound freedom and the blood pumping through his veins.

The host rushed to meet him. They collided in the centre of the shuttle, the host grabbing hold of Ferrash's knife arm to halt his attack. They pushed off the wall and thrust Ferrash towards the hull. Before he hit it, Ferrash reached out with his free hand and grabbed the trailing foot of the harnessed corpse to swing clear.

When the host tried to grab for the knife, Ferrash brought his elbow down in a sharp blow to the host's temple. Their head lolled back. He stabbed them through the heart to make sure and kicked them back when he drew the knife free so the blood wouldn't litter his end of the shuttle for a while.

Something clicked behind him. Ferrash tucked into a ball and kicked towards the back of the hull, throwing the knife towards the noise in the same moment. It thudded into flesh, but Ferrash didn't see where it had landed until he uncurled at the far end.

The pilot stood in the doorway between compartments, the knife sticking out of their shoulder. As Ferrash watched, they yanked it free and kicked off the doorframe to advance. Ferrash flew to meet them, angling so his feet began to flip to face the far end of the room. Their paths crossed when they were perpendicular to each other. Ferrash reached an arm around the host's neck and grabbed their knife arm at the same time as pinning the other against the host's chest in a tight hug.

The ceiling tapped against Ferrash's shoulder and they rebounded at a crawl into the centre of the space. The host's wriggling made their movement unpredictable. Ferrash couldn't let go of either of their arms for fear of a free one using the knife, so he wrapped both his legs around the host's torso and knifeless hand, then snatched the knife free and plunged it into the side of the host's neck.

He left the knife in, this time. Any more blood and the shuttle would be more bath than atmosphere.

When the host's body stilled and Ferrash could be sure they were dead, he disentangled himself from it and navigated the floating bodies until he reached the pilot's compartment. His hip was really starting to burn now, and he winced as he pulled himself through the door to get to the controls.

Before he could assess the controls, though, his gaze caught upon the view.

Hundreds of ships surrounded him, almost all of them the same smooth spheres he had just passed on the other side of the gate. Those nearest to the shuttle had what looked like weapons trained on him, but they didn't appear in any rush to attack.

Just as well, or that fight would have been over much faster.

If he squinted, he could make out another ship the size of the one that had followed the spheres through the gate. Beyond that, nestled within the dark of the void, the icy glare of Hesperex formed a bright pinprick. A lump formed in his throat. His life on that planet hadn't been easy, but between that, the Munabi Wilds and the ship he'd recently blown up, he didn't have many places he could call home.

With a shake of his head, he found the broadcast controls and pulled himself into position by the mic. He stared out at the strange spheres and their distant overseer.

'Rythe,' he said, 'this is Ferrash Progmannae. I think we have some catching up to do.'

CHAPTER THIRTY-NINE

LADY CHARANTE STOOD IN the control room aboard *Explorator Two*, frowning at the little shuttle in the projection before her. Across the display, the captain cast her gaze around the crew, a bemused expression plastered over her ordinarily calm features.

'Do we know a Progmannae?' the captain asked. 'It's a Protectorate name, so I guess it's no one new, but...'

The name sounded familiar, but Lady Charante couldn't put her finger on it. That it was familiar at all was ridiculous – she had never left Rythe before now, had no reason to recognise anyone in the Protectorate... Ah, but she knew someone who did. With any luck, her husband was awake and not too high on painkillers. When the Empyrean died and the fighting Hegemony and Protectorate fleets had shredded themselves at high speeds, debris had severed his legs. The Rythian fleet had rescued him.

<Fabien,> she sent, <what's the name of that Protectorate lad you know?>

The reply came two seconds later as the captain began to shrug and reach for the microphone controls. <Ferrash. Why?>

<Ferrash Progmannae?> She remembered him now. He'd turned up at her wedding under a different name, and Fabien had only told her about him later. Later, minus his legs, as he explained how the Empyrean had died and who had been responsible.

<Yes?>

<Rightio.> She nodded and raised a hand to forestall the captain. 'I know who he is.'

The captain's other eyebrow shot up to match the first. 'Enlighten me, please. Or better yet...' she gestured to the controls.

'Oh. Well.' Lady Charante looked back and forth between the captain and the controls, then shrugged. 'If you insist.' She walked over to the display screen and touched it to toggle the mic. 'Ferrash, this is *Explorator Two*.' A dozen questions tried to jump off her tongue all at once, but she shook them off. 'Do you need us to come and pick you up?'

His voice came again, crackling as if through interference. 'Please. Might need some medical assistance, too.' The line crackled again before she could reply. 'Oh, and I've a few bodies in here with me. Watch out for them. You'll want to assume everything's contaminated, too.'

She rolled her eyes. 'I'd ask if you always arrive in this state, but from what I've heard about you, I think I know the answer. Anyway,' she said as the captain opened her mouth to interrupt, 'we'll come get you. Hold tight.'

The captain locked the microphone controls and gave Lady Charante a level stare.

'What? If you didn't want me making any promises, you'd have spoken to him yourself. Tch. We're hardly going to leave him there, are we?'

'We don't know what's happened to him over there.' The captain leaned over the display, her chest intersecting some of the projected drones. 'You've heard what the reconnaissance drones have managed to feed back through the gate. A civil war, a hive mind controlling people. That's not to mention any regular pathogens the man's picked up that we haven't encountered.'

'So? He told us to expect contamination. We quarantine him. Don't you go telling me we've got space travel down pat without investing in any sensible quarantine protocols.'

Sighing, the captain ran a hand over her face. 'Okay, fine. We can manage it. But he'd better not try anything. Who is he, anyway?'

Lady Charante grinned. 'Oh, he's just the idiot who got us all in this mess to begin with.'

By the time the crew had sealed off and prepared a section of the ship for quarantine – which wasn't long at all, as they completed the task with alarming efficiency – Ferrash was waiting in the airlock where his shuttle had docked. Lady Charante spotted him peering through the small rectangular window as the last of the crew hurried out of the room. An environment-suited medic waited for him with a small trolley of equipment to treat the injury he'd described on the way in.

A series of offbeat footsteps and heavy taps approached from the corridor. With a hiss, the door to Lady Charante's right opened and Fabien hobbled in, leaning heavily on his two crutches, concentration leaving deep furrows in his pale brow. Metal flashed from between the bottom of his trousers and the top of his slippers where his legs had been replaced with temporary prosthetics from the thighs down.

He glanced into the quarantine area. 'Is it just him? No one else?'

'No one else,' she said.

Fabien sighed and came to a halt beside her. 'Has he said anything about what's happening over there? Besides what we already know?'

'He hasn't had time yet.' Lady Charante slipped an arm around Fabien's back to support him. 'We got his medical details, he asked what the *Explorator Four* went through the gate for and, the captain being a paranoid little sot, she refused to tell him.'

'Well, I'll know if he's him. Once we have a chance to talk, I should be able to put her fears about parasites to rest.'

Lady Charante shrugged. 'I'd rather say it depends how good the parasites are. I'm sure you'll know him, dear, but you don't know xenobiology, and we don't know exactly what these parasites can do. So maybe err on the side of caution?'

Fabien just made a non-committal noise and leaned against her arm. On the far side of the quarantine area, the airlock door buzzed. The medic pulled it open for Ferrash to exit. He emerged coated in blood from head to toe, his hair dripping with it, his footsteps leaving a trail on the floor. Blood spattered the walls of the airlock behind him.

'Oof.' Lady Charante winced. 'Unless that's all his, I don't think he was joking about the bodies.'

After a brief argument with the medic, Ferrash went to be hosed down. When he reemerged and the medic started working on him behind a privacy screen, Fabien turned the sound transmission on between their two rooms. Ferrash had asked as much on his way here – he hadn't wanted to waste any time.

'Ferrash, it's Fabien. It's good to see you come back.' An unspoken 'but' rode the end of his sentence.

When Ferrash spoke, his voice was strained and urgent. 'I need you to send every ship you have through the gate. There's fighting over there. They need your help. They're trying to break through.'

Lady Charante gave Fabien a worried glance. 'They' was a vague description, and its owners might not be people they wanted showing up this side of the gate.

The grimace on Fabien's face suggested he shared her concern. 'Who exactly would we be helping?'

Ferrash gave a pained grunt and the medic whispered an apology. 'Complicated. But Palia's with them. They're fighting against the... Against people we can't let through the gate at any cost. They're infected with parasites.'

The captain's voice rang out through the speakers and Lady Charante jumped. She'd forgotten the woman could listen in. 'We already have that scenario covered. We sent the *Explorator Four* and its drones through to defend the gate and warn that travelling through it would meet with resistance.'

A muted protest from the medic suggested some reaction on Ferrash's part. 'No,' he said. 'No, don't stop all of them coming through.

I think Palia's group is trying to get here. They're clean, or at least fighting on the right side. They'll all die if you force them to stay there. You have to help them through. Now. Look for the ships making a long line towards the gate.'

'I'm sorry, but we can't risk—'

'Damn what you can or can't risk.' A growl underscored his words. 'The station fleet is *scatz* compared to yours. If any of theirs come through, quarantine them like you've quarantined me and they won't be able to do a thing about it.'

The captain remained silent.

Fabien tilted his head towards the speakers. 'Captain, please do as he says. If nothing else, this gate is here to stay. If we help one faction, we have a baseline for diplomacy.'

'Just have to hope it's the *right* faction,' Lady Charante said, though Fabien's wince suggested she hadn't helped his argument.

The captain's sigh came through the speakers as white noise. 'Fine. But I want that man run against every test we have for parasites. Invent some more if you have to.'

Ferrash limped out from behind the partition, looking smaller than he had when he entered in a flimsy medical gown. 'I can give you a head start on that,' he said with a grimace. 'You'll find two parasites in me. One of them's dead. I think the one that's alive is technically the good one.' He caught Fabien and Lady Charante's gazes on the other side of the partition and shrugged. 'Long story.'

CHAPTER FORTY

PALIA LAY COCOONED IN the crystal gel of her fighter, numb with shock, her vision filled with the tumbling wreckage of Warden Station. The pilot's messages only registered after... well, she didn't know how long it had been, but probably ages for a kluqetik.

<Human! Human! Have you lost grasp on your brain functions again? Soft flesh, I have been flying gentle for many seconds now. You should be fine.>

Fine? Lilesh was dead. Lilesh – that woman who could control the chaos of her empyrric energy so completely – had tasted it for the first time since losing it, drawn too deep, and lost control. Palia had got too close. Lilesh had come within range of the nexus formed by the dead parasite in Palia's brain, and she had regained access to the Empyrean. The remains of Warden Station were her grave and her legacy. Lilesh had done that. She must have been trying to escape with her refound power and had gone too far, had killed herself, her fellow captives, her jailors. Everyone on the station. Gone.

Palia swallowed. 'I'm fine,' she said.

<Was that your doing?>

'No.' She closed her eyes against his anger, crimson in the crystal, green as the Empyrean ever was in her awareness. 'Not directly. Someone else used... *me* to do that.'

<Look how we let all the shiverlings loose to trip us up.> The translator made him mutter it like a curse. <Someone used you. Could they use you again? I will fly us—>

'No. She was the only one. We're rare, and I would sense if there were more.' Sensing his doubt, she added, 'And the parasites hate us so much that they'd rather kill themselves than share a mind with us. So we're safe.'

The pilot paused for half a second. Palia tried to get her mind back into the combat, but she couldn't pick out what was going on in the wheeling display of ships, let alone tap into her awareness.

<'Safe' is a dangerous word.> An indicator flashed in the display before her. <Our ships are off course, trailing sideways. Can you correct us?>

'Only if you fly us right to the front,' she said without really thinking it through. Being at the front of the spear of ships would expose them to the most danger. And if she still couldn't get things straight in her head by the time they got there, there wouldn't be any point. But it was too late. Acceleration made the gel press against her. Ships blurred past — Sails ships, kluqetik ships, enemy ships.

I need to keep my mouth shut next time. Palia closed her eyes to try getting a grasp on the Empyrean again. It came easier this time, and it wasn't like Lilesh existed to tug at her energy anymore.

<Approaching the front.>

Palia opened her eyes. They flew through the centre of a rotating cone of kluqetik fighters and drones. This formed the tip of the spear that had been pushed away from its target of the gate, and the fire of their flak screen made it seem as if Palia flew inside a tube of light. Ahead of them, it tapered to a point. Discounting all the spinning sparks in her awareness, Palia could just about make out their enemies beyond the flak. How long until her allies couldn't keep up the flak screen anymore?

Then, before she had time to blink, they passed through the tip of the spear. Space opened up before them, filled with the angry swarm of Warden Station's ships. As if immediately sensing the gap in the flak screen, the nearest launched missiles. At this close range, the fighter's displays barely had time to highlight them.

Her pilot gunned the thrusters and they pirouetted around the missiles, further from the tip, marking the way for the rest of the spear to follow.

Well, if it's the gate we need to get to... Palia sought out the nearest enemy ships and drained the life from the parasites aboard, shaping their essence into the twirling ouroboros Lilesh had mastered, but around the fighter instead of within her. The energy tugged at her, so she kept the tether moving – an ouroboros connecting an ouroboros. She wouldn't slip up. She wouldn't lose more memories to the Empyrean.

What she *would* do was fight.

She fired a jet of the Empyrean from the fighter outwards in the direction of the gate. She would make their little ship a beacon for everyone behind them. And if anyone got between them and her galaxy, she'd carve them in two.

As the jet melted through the hull of a ship that turned too late, an orange note of surprise came through from her pilot.

'Don't worry,' she said. 'It's—'

<I am unconcerned by your light show, human. We have company. It has come from your galaxy. Can you identify it?>

A section of the display zoomed in. Palia hesitated before dropping most of the jet to squint at the image. A small ship floated near the gate, unmoving. She didn't recognise its design at all – not sleek enough for Hegemony, not blocky enough for Protectorate. It could be anyone else, but if she narrowed it down to parties who had been involved in the war... Could it be Rythe?

'It's not ringing any bells...'

<Why would that matter? We wouldn't hear bells from here. That would be a terrible method of communication.>

Palia lost her focus and the remnants of the jet skittered off into the void, scoring across the plates of enemy hulls. 'I mean I don't recognise it, but then I don't know what everyone's ships look like. Are they–?'

Before she could finish her question, the surface of the gate began to oscillate and shimmer. Then spheres – drones? – began shooting out of it in no particular formation, at speeds so fast they formed streaks in Palia's vision. She tried to pan her camera angle to follow them but lost herself in the chaos around them.

'Where–?'

<Your eyes are too slow and things are too close. They swarm like a hive. Perhaps we are too late.>

'They're small, aren't–?'

<–they? Yes. Small. Might be drones. See their pattern and it might not be too fast for you. Be aware: they have begun transmitting a message of alliance. I hope this is not a trap.>

Without Palia's prompting, the crystal before her switched to a near-static view of the battle. There was their spear, looking fragile within the churning mass of the enemy fleet, tip diverted from the gate. And there... there was something else. The spherical drones swarmed through the gate, cutting straight between the ships of Warden Station and the ships of the resistance, like a long glove pulling itself down an arm. On the inside: the bones of the Grey Sails' ships and the flesh of their armed allies. Bright explosions marked where incoming fire picked off dozens of the new drones, but more just raced to fill the gap.

Palia sucked in a deep breath. 'They're giving us a chance to get through. Go. Go!' But before she reached the first 'go', her kluqetik pilot had already lined the nose of their fighter up with the clear path to the gate and gunned the thrusters. The breath she had drawn in rushed out in a gut punch of acceleration.

A vivid, fierce joy welled up both in the crystal and the Empyrean, like a grin written in colours. <To stars unknown, to species unmet, to depths unexplored, unsoared, to adventure's reward. Fly, swift shiverling, fly!>

They breached the gate, and the world filled with light, and Palia's heart leapt for the sight of home.

CHAPTER FORTY-ONE

THE STANDARD DESIGN OF a Grey Sails ship, unaltered for thousands of years, had never been geared towards combat. They had basic defences, yes, and the design had to account for thousands of years of use, wear and tear, and the hazards of long-haul space travel. Shahida had always imagined that, besides the lack of fresh air and real gravity, the feel of living on the *Inzekir* wasn't far off what someone living on a planet might feel. It felt solid: the carrier of countless lives, the witness to generation after generation, sailing through the black with its bulk still intact.

Fragility didn't seem to apply to it. Not until she had to go to the reinforced emergency shelter with her husband, her son, and every other soul aboard. Well, besides the bridge crew, given the bridge was just as secure as the shelter. She had tried to stay as calm as possible, holding Spartak's hand both to reassure him and stop him running off. But as more people crowded the corridors, as the effects of gravity slipped away and they began to float, as they came to the rows upon rows of padded seats... she found she gripped his little hand tighter and tighter.

'Mum...' he said, high-pitched and quiet.

She looked down. The whites of his wide eyes shone in the bright light. 'Sorry love.'

Letting go of his hand, she pulled him closer to her in zero-G and wrapped an arm around his waist. He immediately wrapped his legs and arms around her and pressed his head against her shoulder. Warmth washed away the edges of her nerves. She shared a small smile with Ruslan, then went to their allocated seats.

After they had each strapped in and settled against the gel couches, it only took ten minutes for the rest of the shelter to fill. They had regular drills, but where people would usually chatter between themselves, today they remained silent – besides the old man three rows back who liked to sing nursery rhymes as people settled in. She wanted to find his voice reassuring, but the tune sounded off-key and sinister.

Darkness might have been better. They kept the lights up bright to make people think everything was normal and operational, but it had the sterile starkness of an operating room. And she rarely went into one of those if something was going *right*.

Ruslan started pestering Spartak about his next school project. Shahida tried to join in, but the first jolt of acceleration made her lose her focus. She imagined the maelstrom they were leaping into: into the jaws of Warden Station's fleet, into the jaws of the hive mind and, if they were lucky, into another galaxy before those jaws could close. All that would separate their home from the enemy was a determined but small group of fighters and one crazy lady with an ancient and terrible weapon.

Shahida closed her eyes. *I wish I hadn't been at that briefing.*

The *Inzekir*'s tannoy woke Shahida up.

'You may now unfasten your harnesses and exit the shelter. Please wait until your assigned warden invites your row to leave to minimise congestion at the doors.'

She blinked around her, head fogged with sleep. Ruslan smirked at her.

'What happened?' she asked.

'You slept through the whole thing, that's what.' His voice was as chipper as usual, but once her vision cleared, she could see the tense glint of stress behind his eyes.

Unfastening her harness, Shahida looked around the shelter as if she would be able to see anything outside. They didn't have viewscreens in here. Some of the lights had gone out further down the shelter, but she couldn't tell from this far away if that was just because everyone had left that section.

'But what—' she started, but a warden appeared at the end of their row and motioned for them to leave. Ruslan picked Spartak up this time, and Shahida had to continue her question as they navigated along the guide rope to the exit. 'What actually *happened*? Out there.'

'Well, you were snoring when they made the announcement, so I don't think you heard.' Ruslan made an expansive gesture with one arm, forgetting he was holding Ruslan and sending the two of them floating around the rope. Spartak cackled, and Shahida hoped he wouldn't turn green and throw up like he had in one of the drills. Regardless, her husband grinned. 'Welcome to a whole new galaxy, Shahi. We're through.'

Shahida let out a sigh of relief. The motion pushed her back ever so slightly. They were through. They weren't dead.

Then another thought struck her: Here they were in a whole new galaxy untouched by the tuk-a-wa. A galaxy where it was safe to set foot on a planet unprotected, where you could breathe fresh air, feel the touch of terrestrial life upon your skin. She looked at Spartak, giggling and spinning, his cheeks rosy and dimpled, and her heart filled to bursting.

While Shahida hadn't had anything to do or watch during the battle of Warden Station, she still wished she hadn't fallen asleep. How many announcements had she missed? There was so much to take in. Warden Station had been destroyed. Ferrash was alive and tuk-a-wa free. He had already made contact with the rest of the exiles – who were apparently the reason the resistance had made it through the gate without more casualties. And there had been many of those amongst the fighters.

Now she needed to catch up and find out what happened next. They all did. So they met on the bridge of the *Inzekir* – Shahida, the Speaker, the officers, Kaktek and the representatives from this galaxy. Palia hadn't returned from her task alongside the kluqetik yet, but Kaktek reassured her the woman was alive, so Shahida didn't let herself worry about it.

After a round of handshakes and introductions – the representatives seemed perturbed by their introduction to the Speaker, having already shaken hands with her – they each took a place around the table. The captain poured tea for everyone, his moustache and every line of his face drooping, but his eyes bright.

At last, the captain took his seat, cleared his throat and glanced at the three representatives who had boarded from one of the ships – the *Explorator Two* – guarding this side of the gate. 'I know there are urgent issues affecting your galaxy, but we must deal with the threat of the tuk-a-wa first. I understand you have people in need of rescue and planets in need of relief. We can't give that help fully without leaving the gate unguarded, and that would be tantamount to an invitation.'

'Ferrash explained some of what's going on,' said Fabien, a short-haired blond man in the middle of the three newcomers. He leaned on the table as if he needed its support, his face pale. 'But I don't think he knew the full situation. How bad is it? What do you have to deal with?'

The woman to his left, Lady Charante, her hair a tangle of fiery red, kept casting concerned glances his way. In stark contrast, the man on his right lounged in his seat, and the dark skin of his chest formed a triangle where he wore his shirt half open. He had arrived after the other two, having been summoned from elsewhere. He had introduced himself as the Steward of Rythe, so Shahida supposed he must be important.

It was this man who spoke before anyone could answer. 'In addition, is there any aid we can provide?'

The bridge staff glanced between each other, then the captain spoke. 'We're beyond the point where any of us could change things in our galaxy. Just going back through the gate would be suicide now they're expecting us. And after that... well, it's a big galaxy with a few jump stations serving as choke points. I can't imagine navigating or fighting that, and I shouldn't have to. We are, after all, a civilian vessel.' Weariness dripped from his words.

The steward raised an eyebrow. 'What if you had ships that didn't have to stick to those routes?'

'How many ships? How strong? How fast? What happens if the combat moves planet-side? What happens if the enemy replicates your technology?' The captain shrugged. 'In my unprofessional opinion, continuing to fight will only subject people to a longer, protracted war. That's if we could even stay alive for long enough to begin with.'

Breaking the silence that followed his words, the Speaker said, 'The fate of our galaxy is now in the hands of its current occupants, for better or worse, and we can only influence from the sidelines. We need to know how their fight fares to understand how we may proceed. You still have drones on the other side of the gate, don't you? What have they picked up since we left?'

'They're either lying or we have more to be worried about,' Fabien said. 'One of your... exiled council members? He sent out a demand for the tuk-a-wa to attend peace talks, threatening to use the Empyrean on them if they didn't. But Ferrash told us your galaxy didn't have the Empyrean, so...'

'So he was right until around a few weeks ago, and then he was wrong, and now perhaps he's right again because the Empyrean is back to being your problem.' The Speaker waved a hand. She had painted the nails bright orange, and the flash of colour was off-putting. 'In any case, I suspect they're bluffing, but the tuk-a-wa don't know that. Have they responded?'

'They're refusing to talk until they've been able to punish... They're a bit incoherent about who they want to punish, but that's the gist of it.'

Lady Charante hopped in on the end of his sentence. 'And your planets over there are splitting down lines. That council member has his little posse, the hive mind has theirs, and you have a lovely little civil war cooking up.'

'There have been enough of those lately,' Fabien muttered.

The captain leaned back in his chair, rapping the table with the fingers of one hand. 'We made sure to distribute all those instructions for making handheld scanners before we left, didn't we?'

Shahida nodded. She'd suggested that herself, given she had made the mistake of not doing so earlier.

'So the tuk-a-wa are running out of options,' said the captain. 'They overplayed their hand early and the galaxy's turned against them. Their only two options are fighting at home and pushing through to this galaxy.'

Her voice darker than her young vocal chords could quite manage, the Speaker said, 'They will view the return of the Empyrean as an existential threat. Fighting at home will expose them to it, as far as they know. So their only option is here. If they can't find their way here, they will do everything they can to remain in power in our galaxy from a distance. While they will select targets to infect with great care, they will meet any potential threat with swift and indiscriminate violence.'

'We have to find a way to beat them once and for all,' Shahida said. 'If they won't stop, we have to stop them. If Palia could reactivate more of the Empyrean in your galaxy—'

'If Palia could *what*?' Fabien sat up abruptly, his face even paler but with a red flush breaking through the former greyness.

'She—'

The Speaker waved her down. 'That is a longer story than we have time for, and I...' For once, she seemed at a loss for words. 'I don't believe confrontation is the path we should be following here.'

Shahida turned to her, the breath catching in her throat. 'The tuk-a-wa chose a path of open aggression when the exiles came through the gate. They cemented it when they attacked the scanner and they've shown they can't be trusted time and time again, not least by infiltrating the council. There may have been thousands of years of peace, but that's nothing for them. They've always been this way. They fought us before. They almost wiped out your entire—'

'I am aware,' the Speaker said, 'of the damage they have done. Do not think for a moment that I have forgotten.'

Embarrassed, Shahida inclined her head. But of all the people to decide against confrontation...

'Our galaxy still stubbornly clings to the notion that wiping a living thing out entirely is abhorrent. Humans look at the abandoned Earth and are held back by guilt. Kluqetik look back at first contact and wonder if they could have done better. Rahtuan care too greatly about ancient laws, whether they are fit or not. Even confronted with the psychecide, many times complete, of thousands of species over hundreds of thousands of years, they quail from the solution.' The Speaker wrinkled her nose and shook her head. 'Don't mistake me as agreeing with them. My point is that the will of the majority of our galaxy would be against any... *exterminative* action. If we pushed for it, they would demonise us, and we would not gain as much ground as we could.

'No, the exiled Council have provided us with an opportunity, unbeknownst to them. If the only reason the tuk-a-wa won't accept their offer for peace talks is that they want to break through into this galaxy first, why don't we humour them? I say we should invite one representative from each major faction to peace talks *here* and we strike an agreement on how things work going forwards.'

'I should hope,' the steward said, 'you don't expect us to go parcelling off sections of our galaxy to hand over to them.'

'Of course not. They're looking to stay alive. Any deal we strike should have them back to at least where they were before the gate opened. We should push to have them abandon all hosts of Allied species. We should confine them to a single planet, or a guarded station.'

The steward raised an eyebrow. 'Why can't you just treat them the way you treated our progenitors? Make a gate to another galaxy, send them through, and this time close the gate forever. Or destroy it. Either way, they wouldn't bother us then.'

'And if that galaxy held life? No, no,' the Speaker shook her head. 'We're not dumping them on someone else just to get them off our backs. Besides which, they're patient enough to find a way back to us eventually.'

The thought of the hive mind creeping towards them through the darkness between galaxies was almost worse than the thought of them being beside and amongst them.

'Any objections to that plan?'

Around the table, people considered, then shook their heads. Even Shahida, though she itched to strike back at them.

The captain considered the speaker's proposal, his face screwed up in thought. At last, he said, 'Yes, only...'

'What?'

'Does this have to be on *my* ship?'

CHAPTER FORTY-TWO

Palia wriggled her way out of the gel, feeling a lot like a very inflexible eel and trying to ignore the mirthful pinks and yellows that dashed through the crystal around her. When she at last flopped free of the fighter, she landed on the floor of the *Explorator Two*'s airlock docking tube. This was a Rythian ship. Fabien was on it. Ferrash was on it. Both were alive. Out of all the ships newly crowding her galaxy's side of the gate, of course she had asked to be dropped off on this one.

Standing, she brushed herself down. She still felt the cling of the gel even though none of it had stuck to her.

<Will you be okay in there?> the pilot asked. With their words transmitted through the crystal, it felt more like the ship was talking to her.

'As long as you're not about to fly away now, sure. I'm not through the airlock yet.'

<Very slow.>

'You can only pump air so fast.'

<Air isn't such a big issue. Kluqetik can survive many minutes without it.>

Palia bit back her first reply, noting the humour in their words' patterns, and sighed instead.

<You are also slow to get jokes. I won't fly away yet. Don't worry. Besides, the strange door has no handle. I am interested to see how you will open it.>

'Thanks. And it's a door membrane. It just... opens.' As she said it, the airlock chimed and the membrane turned green, so she stuck her arm through and made it disintegrate in demonstration.

<Strange door. Anyway, good luck. I will go once you step through.>

Good luck. Their parting words kicked up nerves like silt from the bottom of Palia's gut and brought her thoughts back to the reason she was here. She stepped through the membrane. Through a small window in the next door – a physical one, this time – she caught sight of a clean medical room. Quarantine, to be precise.

Decontamination spray blasted over Palia and she fingered the scanner clipped to her belt. All they had was Ferrash's word for the fact he was no longer part of the hive mind – not the *bad* hive mind, no, because having a good parasite shacked up in your brain was so much better. The Speaker's plan might have worked. Her parasite might have overpowered the other, or it might have gone the other way. Even if it had won, in what state did that leave Ferrash?

As if the thought had summoned him, Ferrash appeared in the window and went to lean against a medical bed facing the airlock. His emotions shone and rippled with a calm sturdiness, healthier than she had ever seen them, unsuppressed. He gave her a quick smile, and she couldn't help but smile back. She had so many butterflies in her stomach she might as well invite a survey team to categorise them all. To see him *here*, alive...

Palia paced the airlock, tapping her fingers against the grip of the scanner. The decontamination spray had finished ages ago. It must be almost—

The airlock chimed. Palia bounded over to it and shoved it open with her shoulder, then rushed towards Ferrash. She forced herself to stop just out from the edge of the room, still about three metres from him.

'Just a moment.' She unhooked the scanner from her belt and held it out in front of her, gripping it tight enough that her knuckles went white. *Come on, come on...* <Negative.> *Yes!*

A grin plastered itself over her face, tugging at her cheeks, and she ran the rest of the way to Ferrash, who had stood from the bed. Palia dropped the scanner onto it, then wrapped her arms around Ferrash's waist and buried her face in his neck. Ferrash hugged her back, his hands warm on her back, and gave the top of her head a light kiss.

'Palia,' he said, voice barely above a whisper, 'I'm still... I got rid of one parasite and gained another. It's saying it won't do anything, but I don't know if you should be in here.'

'I know. I don't care.'

'Don't you?' He drew back to regard her, one eyebrow raised. 'You're a xenobiologist. You should be in a hazard suit or standing on the other side of that window right now.' He inclined his head to a full-height window separating this room from the next.

'Or dissecting you.' She chuckled.

'Please don't.'

Their eyes locked, and Palia experienced a momentary sensation of distance even pressed right up against him. How would she *know*, really? How would anyone know who held the reins inside someone's head? Did the Speaker never act like a young girl because the young girl was never in control of her own body, or had she simply been exposed to too great a weight of memories to act like that anymore? Was Ferrash acting like himself because the parasite from the Speaker's species had given him full control, or because it was a good mimic? She had never seen him under the influence of the last parasite – perhaps she would have found him just the same then.

Ferrash's eyes softened during the silence of her thoughts. 'It says I don't have to host it forever, you know.'

Palia blinked and brought her mind back to the present. 'It speaks to you?'

'It—' His breath caught in his throat and he glanced away, eyes shining. 'Yes. It speaks. And it... it remembers everyone it ever was. Not like the Convergence.'

'The what?'

'The Great Convergence.' As if speaking the name had taken the wind from his sails, Ferrash slumped back against the side of the bed. 'It's what the tuk-a-wa called themselves.' He gave a bitter laugh. 'A million voices, subsumed and converging into one great sameness.'

Palia took his hand in hers and rested beside him, trying to imagine what Ferrash's mind must have been subjected to these past few... weeks? Had it really been that long since they'd opened the gate? She leaned her head against his shoulder, exhausted. In that moment, her bones felt so heavy with weariness that they might just sink plain through her flesh and reduce her to a puddle of lumpy goop on the floor.

After a few moments with neither of them talking, Palia asked, 'If you don't have to host it forever, who does? It can't just leave your brain without killing itself, right?'

Ferrash didn't reply for a few moments. Then he said, 'I have two options, really. I could transfer it back to the Speaker whenever I want, no questions asked. Or I could keep it with me and try to find a place for it.'

'A new host, you mean.'

'No. It...' He stared up at the ceiling, through the ceiling, as if every star in the galaxy shone through it for his eyes alone. 'Apparently some of the mind's hosts were exiled here along with us, ages ago. They were the ones responsible for building the gate, for creating the Empyrean, and they've been lost to the rest of the mind ever since. They've always been like the tuk-a-wa are now – they can't properly connect unless they're close. So it wants to reunite, and it hopes they're still out there, somewhere.'

Palia eyed him sidelong, trying to strangle an unwelcome strand of jealousy at this connection he seemed to have found within the hive mind. 'I think we'd have noticed if we had a hive mind running loose.'

'They don't run loose. They're not like the Convergence. They don't reach out and try to consume everything they touch – that's why they didn't come out on top on their home planet. They'll just be sitting quietly somewhere, trying not to cause trouble.'

'So the complete opposite of us, then?'

Ferrash laughed. 'Yeah, we don't really do "sitting quietly", do we?' He fell silent then, and a contemplative look came over his face. 'It would be nice to, though, once all this is sorted out.' Wistfulness wound as a band of green around his core.

She loved the sound of it. She would happily kick back for the rest of her days and never get up to anything dangerous again, or have to kill anyone again. And yet... 'You won't be able to find them if we're sitting quietly in one place and they're sitting quietly in another.'

He shrugged. 'I more meant metaphorically. We can travel, help people out, see what we find. Like an extended cruise.' After a pause, he added, 'We'll need a new ship, though. I blew ours up. In any case, our first stop should be Hesperex.' Now his emotions wound tighter and his brows bunched together. 'I made a mess there, and Bek's right in the middle of it. At least, I hope he's still there.' He didn't say 'Still alive', but the implied words hung in the air between them.

A chill crept through Palia at the thought of Hesperex and the thousands of empyrric keepers it had housed. Some of them would surely have been killed in the revolution, but if even one of them remained alive... The last images of Warden Station glared at her from her memories. If Lilesh could do so much damage piggybacking off Palia's new internal nexus, what would a handful of keepers be able to do? What if there were hundreds left?

She closed her eyes. 'I can't come with you.'

'What? Why?'

'I...' Chewing at her lip, she tried to think of the best way to phrase it. 'I did something that turned out to be both stupid and not stupid.' Then she described her desperation to do something useful, her fruitless experimentation on the parasite samples, her decision to inject herself with one and everything that had come after. 'So if I went down to Hesperex, I'd undo everything we worked for.'

Ferrash inclined his head, a faint smile not quite managing to break through his concerned expression. 'Well, you wouldn't undo the galaxy-wide crash we caused.'

'No, but we weren't working *towards* that—'

'It was just an accidental side-effect. I know.' He sighed, then turned his head to look her in the eyes. 'Are you okay? You never asked to be empyrric. You wanted it gone. And now you've gone and got it again.'

His words made her insides twist. She didn't want to examine how she felt about the Empyrean. She didn't want to give it any more of her time. But her emotions sat there, glowing in the awareness she hadn't wanted back, and she couldn't help but see them. She denied them names, though. She kept them as a churning sea of light and motion.

'I'll manage,' she said. 'And I don't think it's permanent. You go down there without me and find Bek. Give him a hug for me. While you do that, I'll see if the Grey Sails can help me out. The parasite's body is wrapped around my brain. If their surgery's about as good as ours' – or better, she supposed, since their technological advancement hadn't been impacted by exile to another galaxy or relied on the Empyrean – 'and if it was just the body that made me like this, then maybe removing it will remove the Empyrean too.'

'Sounds like a plan,' he said, then squeezed her against his side. 'As long as we don't end up spending the rest of our lives trying to kill this thing just for it to keep coming back, okay?'

Palia tried to laugh, but it came out as more of a nervous squeak. 'Please don't tempt fate.'

'Wouldn't dream of it.'

CHAPTER FORTY-THREE

FERRASH FELT STRANGELY VALIDATED by the fact that Rythe had found a way around the speed of light that didn't need a jump station or a nexus. They had always come across a little too smug, a little too knowledgeable, a little too secure in their position as a solitary planet in the middle of two often-warring nations. He had suspected they had something up their sleeve. He had been right.

'You could make a fortune selling these, you know,' he said to the pilot as the familiar storm-clad ball of Hesperex grew to fill the canopy.

The pilot snorted. 'They're not for sale.'

'Figured as much.' No one had ever been able to travel so far so fast at all, let alone without any infrastructure tying departure to destination. With these ships, you could get to food faster, help faster, launch attacks faster. The latter was likely what made Rythe reluctant to sell. But with everything Ferrash had broken, he doubted anyone had much of an economy to throw at new ships, anyway.

The thought soured his mood. An instant later, something different about the view of Hesperex caught his attention. Where normally the whole sphere would have been beset by roiling clouds, now patches of the surface showed through – and not just the strings of light that escaped through little slivers in the cloud at nightfall. No, whole city grids peered through the gaps. It was as if with the Empyrean gone and the Keepers with it, they had finally had chance to pull aside the curtain.

The last time Ferrash had been on Hesperex, it had been in the fiery grip of a revolution he had started. Bek had been captured and used against him, but Ferrash hadn't been able to free him. He'd had to send his mother instead. So he was relieved to see those city grids, but he would be more relieved to see his old friend again.

If he still lived.

They plunged beneath the cloud line, largely unmolested by turbulence, into a mild snowfall. It shrouded the way ahead of them. The jagged spurs of rock that marked the approach to Five-Fifty-Four's spaceport didn't look so threatening anymore, covered in soft white. Ferrash craned his neck around the cockpit, yearning for the familiar landmarks of a city he had mostly hated.

'You're going the wrong way,' he told the pilot. They had veered left at the last spur rather than carrying straight on. It wouldn't surprise him if the automatic descent system had given up the ghost – or if a Rythian system just couldn't connect to it.

Shaking his head, the pilot said, 'The spaceport's out of action. They're trying to fix it up, but I imagine it'll take them a while. It wouldn't surprise me if they made it smaller and opted for an orbital station instead. I've heard they're considering a space lift.'

Ferrash lay back, too stunned to reply. The fact that the people of Hesperex were still coherent enough to be called a 'they' was surprising enough. 'They' implied a unified entity: one voice, making decisions for the planet, or at least this one part of the city. That they had things well enough in hand that they could consider an engineering project so big...

They left the sea behind and moved over the city, the uniform blocks of grey rooves peering out of the snow like stepping stones. The pilot brought them down on top of one of this level's many pastehouses. A forcefield covered the roof, shielding it from the snow.

Stepping out of the ship with a bag of supplies slung over his shoulder, Ferrash breathed his first breath of Hesperex air in weeks. The cold wasn't as biting or heavy as it had been then, but it carried a tinge of smoke to it.

'Get in touch when you need a ride back,' the pilot called, and sent him a frequency he could use to contact one of the blink drones in orbit. 'How long do you expect you'll be?'

Ferrash grimaced and surveyed what little of Five-Fifty-Four he could see from this vantage. 'I could be here for years and not find who I'm looking for.' If Bek was still alive. If no one here bore a grudge against Ferrash for something he had – or hadn't – done before and decided to take revenge, like they had on Warden Station.

'You can contact me as well, right?' Ferrash wanted to make sure Palia had a way to join him when she recovered from her surgery.

'Yes. It won't be a problem.'

'Okay. Thanks.' A group of figures in patchwork had gathered by the door to the stairwell. They watched the landing pad like a group of colourful scavengers. Ferrash stood out from the vatborn like a sore thumb in the purple coat he'd borrowed from a Rythian, having gone through the gate with nothing but Warden Station's casual uniform.

Resisting the urge to grip the Rythian pistol he had also borrowed, Ferrash headed towards his welcoming committee. Behind him, the ship whirred back into life for departure checks.

When he got within a couple of metres of the group, a short woman with a white diamond of fabric sewn to her sleeve jerked her chin at him. 'Hold arms out sideways.'

He did as he was told, then stayed still as she patted him down.

She stepped back without confiscating his pistol and instead gestured to the bag of supplies. 'Take that off. We will check.'

Ferrash hesitated, but he couldn't exactly say no. Each of the group had a pistol holstered at their side and even though he might be able to come out on top if he fought back, they could well be allied to billions of other people on Hesperex who could take him out before he could achieve anything else. So he shrugged the bag off his shoulder and handed it to the woman, who retreated a few paces to inspect its contents.

The man in the group eyed the scars on the side of Ferrash's face, but said nothing. It was the last person in the group who spoke next.

'What is the purpose of your visit?' they asked. They enunciated the words with such slow care that it sounded like they had only learned the language recently, though their 'th's still had a hard edge to them.

'I'm looking for someone,' Ferrash said. 'My friend, Bek. He was being held—'

'Captive, yes.' The vatter's face lit up at the mention of Bek's name.

Ferrash blinked. 'I can... send his genetic identifier if you need it? There are a lot of Beks—'

'Saralbek Julius Nossar?'

Hope and perplexity wound around his heart. 'Yes. But he never used those names on Hesperex. How–?'

With a genuine smile, the vatter leaned forwards and patted Ferrash on the shoulder, momentarily forgetting their grammar and enunciation. 'You come with us! We will take you to him. He is alive and well, and has spoken of you, and will be happy to see you.'

If Hesperex kept being so unlike itself, Ferrash might have to go and lie down somewhere to get his head around it. Was everyone so open now the Keepers couldn't monitor and feed off their emotions? Whether Palia might have reawakened their abilities or not, perhaps she would have been swamped by the change. His surprise must have shown, because the vatter chuckled.

'It has been a long time since you have been to Triff, no?' They used the lowspeak name for Five-Fifty-Four. 'It has gone through many changes, as have we who live in it. Bek taught us many of these things to change. He is a good man.'

'He is.' The breath of Ferrash's words mingled visibly into the cold air. He retrieved his bag from the woman notably lighter than it had been before. She'd removed everything edible – a week's supply to be exact. Oh well. There had to be food for people still to be alive here, so he guessed the pastehouses were still in active use. Who knew, maybe they'd even learned to make it taste nice and look less... well, like paste.

The woman hurried back into the building and the vatter gestured for Ferrash to follow them into the stairwell, leaving the man standing watch over the landing pad.

'Does Rythe send you supplies?' Ferrash asked as he followed the vatter down the stairs. They could hardly be expecting anyone else to come visiting if not Rythe. No one else had blink ships. Or, for that matter, intact ships.

Below him, they tilted their head from side to side. 'Some. Not enough.'

'People going hungry?'

As they descended, a hubbub of chatter and noise rose up the stairwell to meet them. Ferrash frowned, curious. When they reached the ground level, they passed an open door to the pastehouse and his curiosity deepened. Crowds of people filled the benches in there. A few still huddled over their paste and brew, not talking, just like the Hesperex Ferrash had left behind. But most laughed and joked with each other between mouthfuls, smiles on their suspiciously rosy faces. Were they *drunk*?

Oblivious to Ferrash's astonishment, the vatter continued onto the street, saying, 'We can't feed everyone. It isn't the capability to produce food that's the problem – enough paste growers are still active that we could do that. It's the logistics.' They turned towards the Tower of Voices, which seemed shorter than Ferrash remembered it, though it was hard to tell if it just disappeared into the clouds. 'We need people to operate the growers, people to maintain them, people to transport the paste from grower to house. The pipes don't all work after the fighting, so transport is manual. Then there's the logistics of how much to transport where. The population isn't uniform. We don't know where everyone is. People move.'

It was exactly the sort of problem Ferrash could absorb the data for and set his auxiliary AI to finding a solution, but it sounded like things might be broken enough that they didn't even *have* the data.

'Is the net down?' he asked. He hadn't detected it since arriving.

The vatter eyed him over their shoulder through the falling snow. 'Less level heads than mine destroyed it.'

'Why?' Just for the sake of destruction? Maybe that shouldn't surprise him too much, given the violence that had erupted before his departure. But it was a stupid move; the net was a system linking and organising everything on Hesperex. It should have been able to handle any logistics they threw at it.

They passed beneath the shadow of a sky bridge. The vatter said, 'The breeding programme was all hooked up in those systems. The progs wanted it gone. They made it gone.'

Ferrash stayed quiet for the next few steps, but as they rounded a corner, he couldn't help himself. 'It wasn't. The Keepers kept their systems separate. The breeding programme was on there.'

'Well.' The vatter clicked their tongue. 'They didn't know that. Wish they had.'

Not for the first time, Ferrash realised he really should have organised the revolution a little better. Much better. Then again, the speed at which everything had happened had proved all his planning useless anyway. He gritted his teeth at the frustration of it. All this destruction because of him. All this death and suffering because of his plan for a bloodless revolution...

'We're here.'

Ferrash blinked and refocused his attention on the building in front of them. Its outwards appearance didn't belie its purpose, but the faint chemical smell lingering by the door did. It was a vathouse, one of many.

'He's still in a vat?' Ferrash asked. That wouldn't be so bad, to miss most of the fighting in a slow-aging sleep, but that couldn't have happened, or Bek wouldn't have been able to teach them what he knew.

The vatter laughed, shook their head and pushed the door open. 'No. This is home. For us, and for the new administration on Triff.'

'New administration? A government, or...?'

'Or.'

They didn't elaborate, and as they moved into the foyer, Ferrash didn't press the point. As pungent as the chemical smell was, it didn't turn his stomach as much as it would have if the vats were in use. Still, dozens of people crowded the space. They had to push through them to get to the stairs at the far side of the room.

Ferrash peered over people's shoulders and around elbows as he passed. Each group clustered around one of several tables, datascreens in their hands, either waiting their turn or deep in discussion with the person staffing their table. So, 'or'. Organised enough to be called an administration, not enough to be called a government. Or perhaps just too local to earn that designation.

On reaching the stairs, a man and woman in patchwork straightened from their conversation and assumed a casual resemblance to guards.

'Who t'is, Senet?' the woman asked, sweeping Ferrash with a wary gaze. That was more the Hesperex he remembered.

'Friend of Bek's,' the vatter replied.

'Could just be sayin' so. Lyin'.'

'*The* friend of Bek's.'

She raised an eyebrow. 'So so? On, t'en.'

At her gesture to proceed, they started up the stairs. Ferrash waited until they rounded the first landing to ask the vatter, '"The" friend?'

'Bek has spoken of you. A lot.'

Unsure whether to be flattered or concerned, Ferrash eyed the way ahead. A door blocked his view of whatever lay beyond. Someone had painted the dull grey walls in bright, crude patterns that swirled in tightening spirals the higher they climbed. While the noise of the lower floor had already receded, he could still hear voices. If he could bring himself to believe everyone he had met so far, Bek was behind that door. A lump formed in his throat.

The vatter reached the top of the stairs and pushed the door open, holding it for Ferrash once he had stepped through. But Ferrash couldn't move from his spot by the window. Glare from the snow outside and the lights inside blocked his view of the room. What if he stepped forwards and Bek wasn't in there?

While he hesitated, the voices in the room made themselves clearer. A couple of people spoke over each other, trying to get a point across. There must be a meeting or discussion of some kind going on inside.

Then Bek's voice cut across them.

Ferrash leapt up the remaining stairs and into the room. Snowglare from the room's windows outlined the curves of Bek's face as he turned from a map he had been examining on the table.

For a moment, neither of them said anything. Then Bek's face split into a grin. 'Ash? Took your time.'

Not wanting to waste words, Ferrash stepped forwards and pulled him into a hug. Tears chilled Ferrash's cheeks by the time he pulled back. They held each other by the arms.

'Where have you been?' Bek asked, eyes glistening, his voice a little choked.

Ferrash laughed. 'Another galaxy, believe it or not.'

Rustling reminded him of the other people in the room. They straightened around the table, eyeing each other with confused frowns. The same confusion grew in Bek's eyes and he raised an eyebrow.

'Come on, Ash, be serious.'

'I am.' He drew a deep breath to get his voice under control. 'You haven't heard? Rythe hasn't said anything?'

'We've been too busy to ask anything but when they can get us supplies. They said it's difficult with the nexuses being out, which I'd guess is because the Empyrean's gone.' He winced. 'Well, didn't take much guessing. The effects were pretty immediate.'

A quick glance around the table showed everyone leaning forwards, keen to hear news about the wider galaxy – and perhaps the wider universe they hadn't known about before. So, after a moment's hesitation, Ferrash obliged them. He tried to start at the beginning, as near as he could remember it, and he found the seylenon in his head volunteered facts he hadn't known before.

He told them about the tuk-a-wa, about the civil war that spanned the known galaxy, about how their ancestors made the Empyrean to fight against the hive mind. They listened, rapt. Their whole lives, they had been slaves to the Empyrean's shadow. If not the Keepers, the Kept. They might have been sannots, progs, Kept themselves. Their whole lives, they had gone without an explanation. Maybe they hadn't even realised they needed one.

With some reluctance, Ferrash moved on to events within his lifetime: How he had started the revolution, badly. How he had destroyed the Empyrean, badly. How all those bad decisions had led to the conditions of their ancestors' exile being satisfied and opened the way to the galaxy they once called home. He skimmed over most of what had happened afterwards. They would find out soon enough, and Ferrash would be more comfortable telling Bek in private.

Bek considered the story for a while after Ferrash had finished speaking. Ferrash watched the little movements of his face muscles, trapped in the fearful worry that in these few weeks away, in leaving Bek in captivity on Hesperex, a new distance had grown between them. The people around the table began chatting amongst themselves in low voices.

After a while, Bek brought his gaze back to Ferrash and smiled. 'You never did do things by half measures, did you?'

'Never.' He let his relief flood into his own smile. 'But what about you? I...' The skin around Bek's eyes crinkled. 'I couldn't get to you. I had to send—'

'Your mother. Have to say, I never expected that. She got me out, hooked me up with some of the rebels, but... She died, Ash. I'm sorry?' His confusion turned the last sentence into a question. Bek knew a lot of what she had done to him growing up.

'It's okay,' he said, but somehow a pang of sadness touched his heart. 'She did what I needed her to do. How did she—?' How did she—?' No, that didn't matter. Ferrash shook his head. He could well imagine how a high-ranking keeper might meet their fate when the Empyrean died and an angry, keeper-suppressed mob noticed. 'What happened after?'

Bek let out a breath that was half laugh. 'That's lots of ground to cover, Ash. Lots happened.'

'Hey, I told you about my lots of things happening. You can tell me about yours.'

He rolled his eyes. 'Well somehow despite mine not involving hive minds and other galaxies and big space battles, I'd still say it's more complicated. Lots of moving parts.' He tilted his head to one side, eyes suddenly sharp. 'You know how Hesperex is.'

Pretty much all the parts on Hesperex had been set in motion by Ferrash's hands, and Bek had found that out the hard way. Ferrash grimaced.

'Anyway,' Bek said, 'I haven't even made introductions yet! This is who I've been living with all this time.'

He gestured at the others around the table then, before Ferrash could get a word in edgeways, began introducing them one by one. He almost bounded from one to the other, leaving Ferrash taking faltering steps to catch up in his wake. At first he thought there were so many because these were who Bek shared a nearby hive house with, but it turned out they all slept in a huddle on the floor in another room on this level. Men, women, vatters, and all shared an easy familiarity with Bek that made Ferrash feel like he was looking at all this from the end of a long tunnel.

Ferrash would outlive Bek. Born from the vats, Bek's remaining days were limited to the artificial lifespan the Protectorate had imposed. Ferrash had always wondered if the pace of their lives evolved to match that. And here was Bek, with more lines and blemishes on his face, with a new family, with a new life that didn't include him.

The seylenon tried to console him. It nudged him with the family it brought with its thousands of willing voices. But Ferrash didn't want them. He wanted Bek.

CHAPTER FORTY-FOUR

Two weeks had passed since the fight at Warden Station, and Shahida was warily enjoying the relative peace on this side of the gate. She sat on the spongey moss of one the *Inzekir*'s parks, contemplating the message that had just come through on her implants. Palia kneeled on the other side of the picnic blanket, telling Spartak about some of the animals in her galaxy with a series of animated gestures. A slight hesitation slowed her every move and made her smile seem tense, but Shahida couldn't tell if it was a continued reluctance to be around children or just discomfort following her brain surgery the other week. It had been an easy operation, all things considered. If only the parasites stayed that still while they were alive. She would happily fry them out of people's skulls every day until all their hosts were free.

There were enough of them that she'd be dead before then, of course.

The thought brought her attention back to the message. <The last of the representatives has arrived. We're making preparations to begin talks tomorrow. If you want the seat reserved for you, you'll want to transfer to the *Mediator* tonight.>

Since the fight, everyone had been preparing for peace talks. The resistance – comprising the entire Grey Sails' fleet and its allies – and Rythe maintained a close blockade of the gate, letting no one through. On the other side, the tuk-a-wa and the remnants of the council had gathered.

The peace talks were ready to begin, and they had reserved a seat for her. *Her.* A nobody but for the fact that she had once had a chance to be Speaker. She wanted to go – a speaker with a lowercase 's' if nothing else. The tuk-a-wa had to be put in their place to stop them consuming anyone they pleased, and she would argue that until she was blue in the face. But that was the problem: she would argue. She wasn't a diplomat. She wasn't a politician. The problems she needed to fix were problems she could tackle by poking around in someone's brain, not by talking. Not by debating.

Knowing a problem shared was a problem halved, Shahida turned to Ruslan and shared the message. 'Should I go? I don't know if I'll just make things worse.'

Ruslan gave her that irritating, unconcerned smile he liked to wear when she was worrying over nothing. 'You can always sit there quietly.' He couldn't help chuckling a little as he said it. 'You're not made to be a fly on the wall, Shahi, whether you're in the room or not. If you don't go, and you don't get what you want, you'll curse yourself for not being there. If you do get what you want, you'll wish you were there to see the look on their representative's face.'

Shahida laughed and couldn't help picturing Ilhan with his too-wide smile. Would his disappointment have been as comical? 'Am I always that easy to read?'

He shrugged. 'To me, yes, most of the time.'

'Well, then, I bow to your superior wisdom. I'll go.' She made a mock bow for good measure, but a little tingle of nerves danced in her gut.

'Of course you will.' With a grin, he added, 'Besides, now I get bragging rights for my wife being part of history.'

She fake-punched his shoulder. 'Stop it, you.'

The *Mediator* was a single, unoccupied habitation ring detached from one of the newer Grey Sails ships and pushed out into space far from the gate, with a wide cordon past which no unauthorised ships should travel. A Rythian blink ship took Shahida to it from the *Inzekir* in a heartbeat. One moment she couldn't even see it, the next it was right there in front of her, spinning through the black. The pilot clearly hadn't got bored of her passengers' surprise yet, and her laughter followed Shahida out into the shuttle bay.

'I'm glad to see you're joining us.' The Speaker's voice made Shahida near jump out of her skin. Somehow the massive headdress that made up for the girl's shortness wasn't enough to make Shahida notice her.

Shahida looked up and down the corridor. It was completely empty. A few hundred metres away to either side, bare metal bulkheads had been put in place to seal this section off from the rest of the ring.

'Where is everyone?' she asked.

'Locked away,' the Speaker said with a cherubic smile. Before Shahida could ask for clarification, she began walking along the corridor and continued. 'Each delegation has its own suite. The doors are set up so only one delegation can be in the corridor at any time.'

'Taking precautions, then.' She would have been livid if they hadn't. 'What about the talks? Are we doing them from our rooms?'

The Speaker shook her head. They came to a bare door with the words 'Sails Delegation' marked on its surface. This ring must be very new – Shahida hadn't seen a single bit of greenery so far.

'We will speak in the same room to minimise any risk of outside interference or interception, but we'll all be behind glass.' The Speaker opened the door and gestured for Shahida to enter the airlock first. 'We've thought it through, Shahida. Don't worry.'

If I don't have to worry about anything, is there any point me being here? But Ruslan's words came back to her. She had to be here to worry, or she might miss the one thing they'd overlooked.

Once the airlock finished its scan, it opened onto a deserted reception room, the thick sofas empty but dented as if recently sat in. Given it was just past midnight, Sails time, Shahida wasn't surprised. Then again, given how important tomorrow's talks would be, she would have expected at least one of the captain's staff to have chosen late-night cramming over a good night's sleep.

'Is there anything I need to know before tomorrow?' Shahida asked, turning to face the Speaker. 'Anything you might be holding back from me?'

The girl stepped over the threshold and closed the door behind her, her expression unreadable. Perhaps some things were just too complicated to sit on a face so young.

'I understand that you're still upset about my withholding information from you when making the exile a host,' she said. 'I have apologised for this already, but I apologise again. The tuk-a-wa may not be interested in human behaviour, but they have infected enough of you to be particularly adept at reading expressions. If you seemed anything but fearful at what you were pretending to do, they would have suspected something.'

'I trusted you,' was all Shahida said. She realised she had dug her fingers into the back of the sofa.

'Did my lie hurt you? No. Were my actions something you would have opposed? No.'

'Yes.' A fire rose in Shahida's belly, and she took a step forwards. 'You only ever take willing hosts. You make a point of that. Millennia after millennia, you have chosen not to spread but to decant from one host to the next. No doubt you could have found at least a few willing hosts each year, but you didn't. Or did you?' The fire, for a moment, flared into fear. 'How do I know there isn't a dormant parasite of yours inside each of our brains? How do I know you won't just activate us all at once when there are enough of us and the tuk-a-wa are no longer a threat?'

The Speaker's face had paled a fraction. She pressed her lips into a thin line. 'If I had done so, scanners would have picked it up.'

'We calibrate our scanners to the tuk-a-wa, not you.'

'Not at the beginning.' The Speaker's voice took on a sad note. 'At the beginning, nobody trusted me. I was always under watch, always scanned. My chambers and the bridge are monitored to this day – a formality, really. They never had need to modify them. There was a time after that when I was so revered, I was carried on a litter every-where I went, almost worshipped. Do you see my hordes of faithful now? Had I intended to dominate, would I not surround myself with them still?'

Shahida tried to keep any relief her words might bring at arm's length. 'So if I'm to believe all that, make me believe this: You won't stay in this exile's mind now that you have him. You won't influence his will to keep you.'

'He will make his own decision. But he has *touched* my mind, my voices. I can't deny that may influence him indirectly.'

They stared at each other for several seconds, knowing in that moment that things would never be the same between them. It didn't matter what the Speaker said. It didn't matter how much Shahida wanted to believe it. If the Speaker – if the seylenon – had taken full advantage of the opportunities it had had to infiltrate the galaxy, she would believe anything. She would be conditioned to.

At what point does a parasitic organism become the next mitochon-dria? How much would either the seylenon or the tuk-a-wa have had to adapt to become part of their host species' genome?

'Get some sleep,' the Speaker said softly. 'I'll see you tomorrow.' Then she headed into the next part of the suite and disappeared from view.

Shahida sighed, contemplated calling out to ask where her room was, then settled down on the sofa to take her suit off. Perhaps there was a diplomatic way she could ask for seylenon to be included in standard scans. Or perhaps she'd just blunder into it like she always did.

She earned some odd looks from the bridge crew when they came into the reception room. She glared at them bleary-eyed and still not quite awake from the sofa. She had never been a morning person. Sails time, it was six a.m. At least they treated her to breakfast.

Two hours later, after a thorough briefing over their meals and several cups of coffee, a chime announced their corridor slot. They all filed into the airlock, then into the corridor and along it, following a glowing line on the floor. That brought them to their own booth in the conference room: not the first group to arrive, but not the last – either might make the tuk-a-wa suspect a trap.

Three other groups eventually joined them: the exiles, with human representatives from the Hegemony, Rythe, the Protectorate and several planets within the Confederated Outer Reach; the uninfected council members from the Allied Reach in Shahida's galaxy; and the tuk-a-wa, with a bulky, chitinous species she had never seen before standing beside two humans and a kluqetik.

Shahida pulled a seat back from the glass and sat down, a voice in the back of her head telling her this would all take a lot longer than she thought.

'Who gets to start?' she muttered in the administrator's ear. She didn't know if their microphones were on or not, assuming the booth had them.

The administrator shrugged. 'Hard to find a neutral party to chair it.'

That was true. She was so used to the Sails being a neutral faction in galactic politics that she forgot that wasn't the case anymore. Not where the tuk-a-wa were involved. And anyone in *this* galaxy had a vested interest in not letting the hive mind near them. Anyone in Shahida's galaxy theoretically fell on one side or another depending on whether they were a host or not. That left no one, unless another galaxy decided to pop in for a visit.

To Shahida's surprise, the versor who had recited Modjo's Law took to the central podium. Hardly neutral. A hesitant stirring of hope rose within her.

'People of the galaxies both ancestral and exiled,' he began, 'you are invited to this place to discuss peace, to speak of the events that led to conflict, to put in place agreements by which such conflict may not be repeated. I, Sunardi ibn Tirto al-Retrien al-Inzekir, stand here as witness and record for posterity. I will hear and recount the decisions made here today for generations to come, and when I am gone my memories will become record.'

He looked around at them all, his spiked headdress gleaming and glistening under the bright overhead lights. 'Let us begin.'

CHAPTER FORTY-FIVE

By THE FIFTH DAY of the peace talks, Shahida found herself wishing more people on the *Inzekir* would develop a need for brain surgery so she could be called back from holiday and excuse herself from the delegation. Days on the *Mediator* stretched longer than she was used to, filled with bitter argument, and she couldn't even sleep in her own bed or be with her family. Her head ached with the medley of angry alien tongues and their translations.

At six that morning, she stumbled into the lounge area of their suite with a mug of the strongest coffee she could stomach. The captain of the *Inzekir* and two other captains – a rahtuan and a kluqetik – from the Sails fleet huddled on the floor around the coffee table, flicking through transcripts and newsfeeds. They had been that way when Shahida had gone to sleep at one o'clock, although they had at least been talking then.

Avoiding the sofa where the *Inzekir*'s administrator lay snoring, Shahida settled down in an armchair. She sipped at her coffee. It always made her nauseous if she drank too fast on too little sleep and an empty stomach.

'What's the plan for today?' she asked when she had got through half the mug. A headache was starting to come on behind her left eye.

The rahtuan captain replied, 'We think something's happened. Not sure what.' She didn't look up from her screens.

Shahida leaned forwards. 'What do you mean?' She tried to catch some details from the screens, but the captain had customised the views so much she didn't know what she was looking at.

'There's some suggestion among the public and a few smaller news stations that known tuk-a-wa hosts have been distancing themselves from each other across our galaxy.'

'Aiming for maximum spread?' Each host could contain multiple parasites, could infect multiple people, could start a chain reaction of the same.

She nodded. 'That's my guess.'

The *Inzekir*'s captain massaged his temples with his thumb. 'If we can get something official, if we can find proof of them infecting people, we can use it against them. We've got three hours. If you want to help, you can search the feeds with us.'

Shahida nodded. Anything she could do to help, she would, but this wasn't going to help her headache.

'The proper process was not followed!' the tuk-a-wa's chitinous representative roared – truly roared, like Shahida imagined a dragon would. 'The traitorous commander of Warden—'

<We have covered this point each day since these talks began,> Councillor Rusuressen said from within his tank. <You had infected much of the council by then. Our permission was by your hand. You locked those you hadn't infected out of the decision. It was not the proper process to begin with. May we move onto more constructive topics?>

'I fear that may be impossible.' The rahtuan captain's trumpeting echoed around their booth and rivalled the tuk-a-wa's earlier roar. 'It is quite clear that the tuk-a-wa have no real intent to negotiate. In the early hours of this morning, we received reports that they had begun preparing for mass infections. Their hosts have spread out across inhabited space, and contagion models indicate they are optimising for a fast assimilation of native populations.' She turned her broad head to regard the host. 'With their ships gathering at jump stations, they obviously intend to take our galaxy while our backs are turned and while we are keeping them from this one. What, then, is the point of these negotiations if all that lies ahead is war?'

Rusuressen's tank bubbled. <We know about their ship movements and have been shadowing as much as possible, but their other movements... Do you have evidence of this??

'I have just sent it to all representatives.'

Shahida watched the tuk-a-wa's host. Parts of its face armour moved, but it remained silent. Unlike the other delegations, theirs didn't have to speak to each other to confer.

At last, Rusuressen spoke again. <You are right. The exiles' ancestors were right. We should unleash the Empyrean on them again, if there is no hope of their ever being peaceable.>

The host's armour twitched. 'There is no need for such drastic measures.'

<Indeed, enacting psychecide on a whole galaxy is drastic, large enough that we would need to coin another word for it so we had sufficient label to pin on your corpse.> The translator made Rusuressen's words drip with contempt.

'We were merely removing ourselves from harm's way,' said one of the human hosts, a large woman with the same slick smile as Ilhan. 'Thanks to the Sails' propaganda' – the Speaker snorted, and the woman's smile faltered for a moment – 'we feared hate-fuelled attacks from those around us. When primitives march a formation into battle, do they not spread out to minimise the casualties of localised attacks?'

Behind Shahida, voices whispered. Some of the media team had sequestered themselves back there with all their screens, conducting live sentiment analysis and working out the best angles of attack. One of them leaned forwards, tapped the Speaker on the shoulder and whispered something in her ear.

The Speaker stood up. 'If you are so fearful, it is no wonder you shrink from negotiations. I'm sure you would prefer the council not to get their violent way, wouldn't you? You wouldn't want to face the

Empyrean again, yes? Then I think it is time for a gift to entice you into these talks properly, and to put the council's mind at ease. Do you remember a world with seas of steaming grey and endless mud flats, with dirty yellow skies and a pitiful sun?'

In the tuk-a-wa's pod, the hosts all straightened.

'You do, yes.' The Speaker's lips curled into a smile. 'The planet we shared together: let it be my gift to you. I relinquish my claim. Have it. Have it all, for perpetuity! But take your ships, pick up your hosts from where you have spread them, and take them there. The council, I'm sure, will be magnanimous enough to hold the Empyrean at bay for you. And on your part, you will no longer threaten the galaxy with your contagion. A fair trade, yes?'

For a moment, silence reigned. Every armoured plate on the foremost host seemed to bristle and rise from its skin. The tuk-a-wa clearly weren't fans of having what they had held as their own territory for millennia offered up to them.

The stream of vitriol that exploded from them a moment later confirmed that.

'You shouldn't have provoked them,' said the man from the media team. In his consternation, he seemed to have forgotten that the Speaker was several tens of thousands of years older than twelve, and his voice had taken on a patronising edge. 'You didn't need to spin the offer like that.'

The Speaker leaned into her girlish side, folding her arms with a pout. 'It's my own planet I'm giving away. I'll spin it how I like.'

The rahtuan captain rumbled from where she was lying on the floor. 'We should be able to get them back on track. They're on the back foot.'

Shahida said, 'I think it'll take more than that.' She kneaded the back of her neck, trying to work out a kink from too long spent staring at various screens. 'If they think they can get away acting faster than the Empyrean can attack, if they find out that...' She didn't voice her worry. The Empyrean once again did not exist. They could probably bring it back easily enough if they needed to, but right now, with Palia's parasite excised, they didn't have it to hand. Palia insisted it wasn't as powerful as it had once been, in any case. It wouldn't have been as great a threat as Rusuressen implied. The tuk-a-wa couldn't find that out. And with how far they'd distanced themselves... Shahida shuddered to think of the galaxy becoming theirs in a heartbeat.

It was the Inzekir's captain who spoke next. 'Even if we have what it takes, what then?' Every face in the room turned to look at him as he stood staring at the feeds on a wall-mounted screen. The room temperature dropped a fraction. 'Speaker, you said it yourself some time ago: The tuk-a-wa have the patience to wait as long as they need to achieve their aims, and from what we see, their aims have never wavered from total incorporation. They are functionally immortal. Their mind goes on regardless of what happens to individuals. They are too numerous and elusive to wipe out completely – not without enormous cost.

'So what if we do come out of these peace talks successful? Picture a full victory: They relinquish their hosts from member species. They retreat to their homeworld.' He shook his head, eyes still fixed, unseeing, to the screen. 'Hundreds of thousands of years from then, will they just have crept back into the same position as they're in now? If they see the galaxy cycle through a weak era, will they strike? It's not today's problem, but it is our problem. We may be the only ones to be in a position to resolve it.'

No one spoke. An uneasy feeling settled in Shahida's gut. He was right, of course. The tuk-a-wa had had millennia to change their stripes.

The media man licked his lips. 'Your words imply that the only true solution is complete xenocide.'

'It's them or us. I hate to reduce it to that, but it's the truth.'

'What do you suggest, then? We can't strike now. For the stakes we're talking about, it wouldn't even matter if we were ostracised as badly as the exiles, but that's not the problem. Right now, they'd spread faster than we could kill them.'

The captain turned to Shahida. 'When your exile friend experimented on the tuk-a-wa, she created a virus, didn't she?'

A kernel of hope flared in Shahida's chest. 'Yes, though it wasn't fit for purpose.'

'It doesn't matter.' He waved a hand dismissively. 'We can make it fit for purpose. We can make *something* fit for purpose. I said the tuk-a-wa are functionally immortal. In a sense, so are we. We can work on this, generation after generation, independent mind after independent mind. The tuk-a-wa won't know what's coming for them.' He grinned. 'They sit around spreading their stagnant spores, growing in size but nothing else.' He punctuated his next sentence with a pointed finger. 'We innovate through *difference*. They want to play the long game? Then let them. We'll win.'

Shahida doodled on her tablet to occupy her mind as she waited in their booth for the other delegations to show up, the quiet hum of conversation surrounding her. None of the tuk-a-wa had arrived yet. This was unusual – the parasites didn't distinguish themselves between early birds and night owls. They got up when they needed to get up. They slept only to maintain body functionality.

Hope clung to her like a warm blanket. Since the captain's speech, some of the Grey Sails' best scientists had shipped off to Rythe with the records of Palia's experiments. They didn't have any samples to work on – that would have to wait until it was safe to retrieve Palia's remaining parasites from the moon and bring them through the gate – but they could begin preparations.

No matter what state the tuk-a-wa walked out of these talks in, the resistance would find a way to end them. It was only a matter of time.

The chatter around her stopped. Shahida looked up to see the chitinous tuk-a-wa taking its position behind the glass. Its kluqetik and human companions hung back in the shadows.

'You join us at last.' Over in the exiles' booth, the lounging Steward of Rythe lifted his head from where he had been resting it on his knuckles and said, 'I do hope your commitment to these talks isn't so low that you'll just stop coming one day. It wouldn't do to have to send a wake-up call.'

The host's nostrils flared, but its tone was measured. 'We are committed. We are withdrawing hosts to ships as we speak.' It glowered at the Sails' booth – straight at the Speaker, Shahida imagined. 'The Grey Sails' *interference* has resulted in violence against our units, and greater civil unrest. To remove our units from harm, and as a gesture to their usual homes, they are leaving. We are ready to talk.'

Shahida gave a grim smile. She was hardly an expert on the body language of a species no one had seen before, but its plates shifted in much the same way they had when it had been shouting at them in the first week. It wasn't happy with what it was saying. Or, devoid of real emotion as it was, its words contradicted its true goals, and it wished to display an artificial discomfort.

<Then know this,> said Rusuressen. <None here seek to destroy you. As psychecide is outlawed and abhorred, so too is xenocide. We merely seek to set clear boundaries in a manner such that you, untrustworthy as you have continually proven to be, will not and cannot breach them.>

'We are... understanding of this. Name your terms.'

The councillor invited their booth to speak, and the rahtuan captain stood, her voice booming. 'First, every host you have not yet moved aboard a ship, you must move. Any non-host must be allowed to leave those ships. You must do this by the end of this week and report where travel time has made it impossible to do so. We will be shadowing your ships and your hosts to ensure you do this.

'Second, you must move all your hosts to your home system, gifted generously in full to you by our Speaker.' Both human hosts scoffed at this. 'You must do this by the end of this month, again communicating where it is impossible.

'Third, you must disembark all your hosts onto the planets of your system. You will return the ships to their owners or systems of origin on autopilot. If you retain any ships of your own system, you will destroy them.'

'You would strand us,' the host said.

'We would unmake you as a threat to others.'

The host shook its heavy head. 'Our planets cannot support so many. Our atmospheres, where we have them, will kill most.'

'There's a simple solution to that,' Shahida said. She paused a moment, almost surprised she had spoken as everyone turned to face her. 'Many of those hosts weren't willing to begin with. Release them as hosts and ask them after a week of freedom if they are willing to return. Those who consent can stay in...' She searched the others' face for ideas. 'A ship, stripped of engines, as a temporary measure.'

'Temporary would imply we would lose them.'

Shahida shrugged. 'Well, some of us *do* die of old age.'

The host shifted on its feet and stared at each of the other booths in turn. 'You would diminish us.'

The Steward of Rythe waved a hand. 'When a warlord is defeated, provided their demesne has not collapsed, their land is returned to its original borders. This is just how it goes.'

Shahida suspected the steward was taking a bit of creative liberty in his statement – not that she knew what a *demesne* was – but it seemed to mollify the host. The conversation went round the booths for several minutes, but the tuk-a-wa's remained silent.

At length, the host broke into a gap in the discussion. 'We will accept these requirements in exchange for one favour.'

The room went deathly silent.

'As we were evacuating the council from Tilukettia,' it said, 'our nemesis contacted us.'

'Your nemesis?' a red-haired lady in the exiles' booth asked.

'An exile possessed of the Empyrean.'

Palia. Oh, stars above, what had that woman told them?

The host waded further into the silence. 'She offered our emotions back in exchange for peace. She wanted to return us to how we were, before she... before her ancestors stripped us of who we were. You see us as untrustworthy. Perhaps emotion and empathy would have encouraged us to gain trust for reasons other than advancement. We recall it was once easier to be trusted. We recall there was such... beauty, in exploration, in expansion. Now we merely emptily hunger for a feeling we may no longer grasp. Let us feel this once more. Let us feel. That is all we ask. We wish we had considered it when it was offered. We have considered it now.'

Beside Shahida, the Speaker held a hand to her mouth. Her face had gone pale. From an uneducated perspective, giving the tuk-a-wa their emotion back was just and almost noble. Yet in their booth, they knew full well that this would also return their long-range communication. A tuk-a-wa confined to a single planet was still a heavy threat when they could coordinate across seemingly any distance at the speed of thought, wasn't it?

In any case, the real problem was obvious. Shahida had only recently excised the dead parasite that had brought the last remnants of the Empyrean back.

'The Empyrean is gone,' said the Steward of Rythe, a smug smile plastered over his face.

Smug? Why was he smug? Shahida swore under her breath. He'd just revealed that the council's greatest threat was a lie. Had he even known about Palia?

'This cannot be.' Each of the tuk-a-wa hosts whipped their gazes around the room as if their controlling mind wished to scan everyone's expressions in an instant. 'We felt her. We felt it through her. We felt again in a way we hadn't for so long, and then it was gone. We saw it used again in the fight for the gate. Where has it gone?'

Somewhere in a hazardous waste disposal unit, then an incinerator. But Shahida didn't tell them that. Still, no one else spoke and the captains were looking at her, so she licked her lips and said, 'She wanted it removed. She didn't want to be empyrric.'

A low rumble came from the host's throat. 'She did say she didn't choose it. Are there no others?'

'No.' And Shahida wasn't about to tell them the way Palia had found to make more. 'It's gone for good.'

The hosts stared as one into empty space, their faces impassive. If Shahida hadn't known they couldn't experience the emotion, she would have called them forlorn. At least they didn't seem triumphant. None of them had twigged that the threat hanging over their heads was gone now – or enough of the council's ships were now shadowing their movements that one fake threat had been replaced by a very real one. Hope had been dangled before them, and now everything it represented was gone.

Just when Shahida was itching to break the silence, the chitinous host raised its head and said, 'This is all, then. All there is, forever.' Its plates shuddered. 'We will withdraw. We will follow your instructions. We see from the ongoing riots that there is no room for us to return.

'We accept your terms.'

CHAPTER FORTY-SIX

FERRASH SAT BY THE edge of the landing pad, staring up at the light of Palia's shuttle entering atmosphere. A clear sky ruled over Hesperex, the first he had ever seen in his lifetime, and a multicoloured throng crowded the streets. Despite the cold, local pastehouses had started sending food out to groups in the street. They huddled together on the floor and chatted over food. Somewhere in the direction of the Tower of Voices – the top of which had indeed been blown up during the revolution – a haphazardly tuneful band began to play.

On paper, Palia was coming here to deliver news. In reality, any news she brought with her would be out of date, already relayed by the larger blink ship that had brought her here. But she'd cut the parasite out of her head and wanted to see Bek – and set foot on planetary ground again – so here she was.

When her shuttle settled down on the pad in front of him, it melted the crust of the ice and snow that had claimed its place there during the snowfall. Palia stepped out supported by Shahida. Still in her environment suit, Shahida turned her hooded head this way and that to take in the undisturbed skyline. She made a point of staring down at the ground. Her gait was unsteady. Two other figures stepped down behind them, one about the same height as Shahida, the other – a child – only coming up to her waist.

'I hear you sorted everything out,' Ferrash said.

Palia smiled at him and stepped free of Shahida's support. A few strands of white hair fluttered free from her hood. 'No dead parasite rotting in my head, no parasites allowed this side of the gate, ever. I think it's as sorted as it'll get for a while.'

Beside her, Shahida took a step in the direction of the tower of voices and reached towards her helmet. She removed the faceplate and tilted her head up to the sky, taking a deep breath and closing her eyes. A thick band of freckles stretched across the copper skin of her nose.

On opening her eyes again, Shahida scowled at the sky, glanced briefly at the ground, then fixed her attention on Ferrash. 'It isn't as much as we should have achieved, but it's a start.'

The taller of the two figures who had disembarked behind Shahida removed his visor too, revealing a handsome face, slightly lighter than hers with a moustache impressive enough to have been wasted under a helmet. He turned to the child and set about removing their helmet, too, though he met with some protestation.

Ferrash raised an eyebrow. 'It might be free of the hive mind this side of the gate' – one of them, anyway – 'but you picked a bad planet for a family holiday.'

Shahida leaned over the half-wall that edged the rooftop. 'If they're having street parties, it can't be that bad. Anyway, I've never been down to a planet before. Few of us have. The closest most of us ever come is the Moon, and even then we're not supposed to go there. So if nothing else, we're staying here long enough to drop Palia off and find out if you want to hitch a lift somewhere else or stay here.'

'Fair enough.' Ferrash shrugged. 'Just be careful. Don't go wandering off. Wasn't long ago that Hesperex's idea of a street party involved a few more guns and explosions.'

'Noted.'

Catching Palia's eye, Ferrash inclined his head towards the stairwell. 'Bek's not far. Come on.'

He led the group down the stairs the same way he had come upon his arrival. Even with all the celebration in the street, Bek still hadn't left his post. Ferrash found him leaning back in his chair, a datascreen in one hand, the other massaging his temples. Bags hung under his eyes. He wondered if this was how *he* had looked for most of the time

Bek had known him, with his head full of plans and the logistics of an interplanetary empire that wasn't strictly his to play with.

Bek glanced at the door when Ferrash entered and put the data-screen aside a moment later. He unfolded his tall body from the chair and cleared the room in three bounds.

'Palia!' He wrapped her in a hug, then held her at arm's length. 'How are you?'

She chuckled. 'Woozy, but happy to see you. The last time I saw you, you had a hole in your head and most of your blood was on the floor.' Try as she might to keep a laugh in her tone, Palia visibly paled.

'Well,' Bek said, 'I'm glad I was luckier than my clone, then. And who's this?'

A small crowd had gathered by the door where Shahida stood with her family, most of their attention fixed on her son, much to Shahida's obvious discomfort. Palia introduced the three of them and their home within the Grey Sails.

'Ah, you are our new go-betweens, then?' one of the vatters asked.

Shifting on her feet to keep her son a little more behind her, Shahida tilted her head. 'Collectively, yes.' Since the agreement, the Grey Sails were now the only faction permitted to travel through the gate.

Ferrash cleared his throat and tried to put Shahida at ease before she got any more disturbed. 'You don't need to worry. Most of the people in this room are vatborn. They're not used to seeing children.'

'Least this one doesn't scream like the little ones,' said a woman towards the back of the room. 'Some of those about, now.'

'So,' Bek said, 'you're all set to start helping Rythe with the relief efforts, right?'

This time, Shahida nodded. 'I know they've started organising it. I'm not involved in the talks anymore, but it's underway.'

'Good. I don't envy the logistics.' He cast his gaze between Palia and Ferrash, then looked back to Shahida. 'Will you all be alright here for a bit? I'd have someone give you a guided tour, but every building looks the same here, and it's buildings as far as you can walk.'

'We'll be fine.' Shahida's hand drifted closer to her knife, but she seemed a little more relaxed than earlier. Her husband had already lost interest and wandered to a window to watch the crowds below.

At a gesture from Bek, Ferrash followed him into a more private room, Palia close beside him.

'Something wrong?' Ferrash asked. A *thunk* sounded behind him as Palia shut the door.

'No, no, nothing wrong.' Bek flopped down onto one of several mounds of pillows and gestured for them to do the same. 'Just didn't want to bore everyone with our chatter. They've got lots of work to do, after all. Can't go distracting them.'

Ferrash took the invitation and sat down on the nearest pile of cushions, wincing as various injuries – old and new – sent pain stabbing into his side.

'And speaking of there being work to do...' Bek eyed Palia as she sat down, the need to focus on movement rather than make eye contact betraying his nerves. 'I could always use extra hands here. Ash, you know this place like the back of your hand. You know all the systems, the people—'

'They'll have changed fast over the rebellion.' Ferrash kept his voice soft. 'They won't be the same systems I knew. I can clone my AI for you to set to work, but you'll need to feed it new input.'

'I can't feed you that input?'

Squinting out through the glare of a nearby window, he said, 'I can't spend any more time on Hesperex.' He felt it in his bones, in the subtle dread that lingered no matter how superficially happy the world appeared on its surface. Even the fact that he assumed superficiality – it didn't matter what Hesperex turned into. Nothing he did would matter. It would always be a concept full of bile and blood.

He shuddered at the memory of burying his daughter's bloody corpse. 'I'm sorry, Bek.'

For a moment, Bek looked like he wanted to argue, but then the hope drained out of his eyes. He tried to mask it with a smile. 'So if you're not staying here, where next? What are you going to do?'

Ferrash glanced at Palia, who shrugged.

'It's not like we'll be short of opportunities to help people,' she said. 'It would be our own mess we're fixing, after all.'

With a sighing laugh, Ferrash nodded. 'We'll see if Rythe needs a hand, or just... hitch a ride with them. Hop from one planet to another, explore a bit while we're there, stay just long enough to make sure people will last until we're back.'

'If we even go back. There are a lot of planets. And you'll want to hunt for whatever happened to the seylenon, won't you?'

Glad he had told Bek about his benevolent parasite in private a couple of days before Palia arrived, Ferrash leaned back in his nest of cushions and considered. Sure, everything was a mess. But this wouldn't be so bad. The thought of helping people without turning to violence or schemes for a change left his heart almost weightless. They didn't have to travel forever, not if they didn't want to. And they could always visit Hesperex from time to time.

'So that's what we'll do, then,' he said. 'A grand sightseeing tour of the galaxy, just you and me.' He turned to Bek, knowing he shouldn't float the possibility but unable to stop himself. 'There's always room for one more.'

Bek's smile was more genuine this time, but he didn't try to hide the sadness in it. 'My family's here, now.'

The words drove a spear through Ferrash's chest. Bek hadn't meant them to hurt, but they did. Maybe this was how parents felt when their children flew the nest.

'Well,' Ferrash said, 'you always complained I never took you to any parties. How about we have one big going-away party, right here. Say goodbye in style?'

'Ash!' Bek grinned. 'I thought you'd never ask.'

EPILOGUE

THIRTY-THREE YEARS LATER:

THERE WAS AN ANCIENT saying in the Hegemony: All roads lead to Viken's Garden. It had long since fallen out of popularity. The Hegemony encompassed so many worlds now that of course not everyone's ashes could be buried on Viken's Garden. The planet could only take so many trees.

And yet Palia found herself drawn back there again.

She sat in the cockpit of her and Ferrash's private blink ship, staring at the vivid green orb that seemed identical to the memory of what felt like a lifetime ago. Ferrash sat in the seat next to her, one hand holding hers, another holding the canister of Bek's ashes close to his chest. His eyes were out of focus, and the grey that made up most of his hair now gleamed in the cabin light.

'You okay?' she asked, not that she needed to. A few decades travelling the galaxy together and she didn't need the Empyrean to know what he felt.

He blinked, nodded. 'Yeah. It's just... Last week on Hesperex made it all sink in. *Scatz*, he had a bloody long life for a vatborn, but I could never really bring myself to believe I'd be around when he died.'

Not until Hesperex, when they had arrived just in time to catch Bek's final days. Ferrash had watched the life slip out of his old friend's eyes and then they had watched the people of Five-Fifty-Four burn him. Thousands had lined the streets. Palia suspected it was the thought of just how many souls Bek's life had touched that affected Ferrash the most, but she kept her theory to herself.

'Stupid thing is,' he said, 'and this isn't even the seylenon talking...' He drew in a deep breath and stared at the stars through the top of the canopy. 'I can't help thinking he could have lived if only he'd become a host. If only I'd mentioned it. His body would die, but his soul would still be there with all the rest.'

Palia checked that the automated landing system had them on course for the orbital platform. 'I didn't think you believed in souls?'

He shrugged. 'I don't know. Some questions are too big to ask and too big to answer. But the memories of people' – he tapped his forehead – 'in here, they feel alive. Quieter than a living mind. Content, almost. But alive.' For a long moment he was silent, and the shadow of the platform's hangar fell over them. 'A lot of the questions I want answers to are so big I know I won't be alive to answer them.'

She squeezed his hand, watching him out of the corner of her eye as the ship moved towards its designated landing spot. In all those decades of exploration, trekking across planets to help those who needed it, sightseeing whenever need dried up, Ferrash had never once found a remnant of the seylenon. He had multitudes inside his head but even then, the void outside disturbed him. His fragment was one member of a larger choir. In company, he experienced isolation. And now with Bek gone... All he had was her and the voices in his head.

They left the ship together and made their way towards the shuttles that would take them to the surface. They hadn't changed much since Palia's last visit, besides a fresh coat of paint. She winced at the memory of that last visit. It had been Derren's funeral – the child her mother had forced on her. The child she had lost to the Empyrean, when all this began. She had refused to speak to her mother, had lost her temper when her mother tried to talk to her. Things would never be easy between them, but at least they could hold a conversation now without being at each other's throats.

With some reluctance, Ferrash deposited Bek's canister in a secure slot towards the front of the first available shuttle. He hovered over it for a second or two more before turning and strapping himself into a seat beside Palia.

'It's not a long flight,' she said. 'And there's a good view.'

He nodded, then a moment later when the engine kicked in, he asked, 'What happens when there's no more space for trees?'

So on the journey down, Palia acted as his tour guide. She told him the little they knew of the history of Viken's Garden, listed the species that called its vibrant ecosystem home, explained how managing it had worked over the millennia. No doubt he already knew most of it. Spying on the Hegemony, he would have had to know things like this. Everyone knew about Viken's Garden, even if their own personal road didn't lead there.

In any case, listening put Ferrash more at ease. He stared out across the sunlit cloud layer, then across the silver-green canopy of the garden. As they grew closer to the ground, his gaze grew more distant, the muscles of his face more slack. A light appeared in his eyes. It felt so at odds with her meaningless patter that Palia trailed off. Ferrash didn't notice.

She followed his gaze beyond the shuttle's viewscreen and met nothing but the mottled shades of emerald within the canopy. Light filtered through the leaves, adding brilliant flashes of white and gold.

At length, he said, 'I can hear them.'

The shuttle reached the landing pad and settled onto its legs with a hiss. Palia leaned forwards. 'Hear who?'

'The seylenon. The remnants. All of it.'

She unbuckled her harness and turned around in her seat, taking in the endless sea of trees around them. 'Where?'

'In the trees, in the birds, in the lizards. In everything living, besides humans.'

Palia refrained from pointing out that *he* was human and tied to the seylenon, but she couldn't help being reluctant about stepping foot outside. It was a stupid reluctance, really. In all the decades they had been together since his infection, with everything they had shared, the parasite was one thing they hadn't.

'Why *here*, though?' she asked. 'Why Viken's Garden?'

'Viken was one of its hosts. One of the scientists who created the Empyrean. He settled here when it was still a dustball and refused to move on when the rest of the fleet found better systems to settle. It was where he came to die. A self-imposed exile. The other hosts didn't want to be separated, so they stayed with him. And...' Here, Ferrash frowned. 'It's arguing with itself over this bit, but I think it wanted to exile itself, too. Restrict its mind to one planet and never encroach elsewhere.' Just like they had forced the tuk-a-wa to do.

So this world had always been a world of the dead. Or not. The hive mind was very much a living thing threaded through its ecosystem, and if it had told Ferrash all that, then it had been here since the beginning. The Speaker had said she only took willing hosts. Ferrash, apparently, had been the exception. But perhaps the motto had also been unique to that individual. How could a lizard or a tree consent to such symbiosis?

The shuttle beeped at them to leave, so Ferrash unbuckled himself as well and they stepped out into the brightness of day together. Warm air brushed against their backs as it took off for its next passengers.

'So this is it, then?' Palia asked, taking Ferrash's hand in hers. They began walking towards the designated planting site. 'The remnants only ever settled here. They're nowhere else in our galaxy?'

Ferrash laughed. 'To think of all the time we spent looking for them...'

'To think of all the time we spent *exploring*.' Just like they'd wanted to. 'What will you do now?'

He blinked. 'I don't know.' A leaf landed on his head and tumbled down his hair, alternating silver and green. 'It's been part of me for so long now, I think my head would be too quiet without it. Perhaps I should lay it to rest here with the rest of its memories, but I don't know.'

'Well, there's plenty of time to make a decision. We can talk it over later, or tomorrow. Whenever.' They had booked a lodge for the next couple of weeks. Staying places a day or two at a time didn't have much appeal for them these days.

They made it to the planting spot just before midday, when Bek's funeral was scheduled. Fabien greeted them there with his sympathetic smile, flanked by Lady Charante and their two children. Palia hadn't seen them in years, and the sheer amount they had grown hammered the weight of time into her more than Ferrash's grey hairs. A host more people she didn't recognise had turned up, too. Speaking to a few of them, she learned these were all people Bek had spent time with during missions in the Protectorate. The ripples of his short life had spread from one side of their galaxy to the other. She brushed away a tear.

No one from Hesperex had joined them – even Bek's children. It was less a matter of crossing borders, more that they had already had their celebration and didn't need another from a culture that wasn't theirs. Most of Bek's ashes had been scattered from the very top of the Tower of Voices. Some had been mixed into jewellery for his children in the Hegemony fashion – they had apparently inherited his love for everything foreign – and the rest was in the little canister Ferrash had just handed with some reluctance to the elderly curator.

Palia took Ferrash's arm and steered him towards another group of people so he wouldn't keep staring forlornly after the curator. She left him chatting to the Rythian spymaster, who he had struck up a fast friendship with during their initial years in the Rythian aid effort. Most of that friendship had been founded upon how funny Ferrash found the amount of intelligence Rythe had on him back in his spying days. He hadn't seemed to find it embarrassing at all.

When the curator returned, the sun shone directly overhead, spearing through the gap in the trees in a golden column of light that picked out the darting forms of every insect flying through it.

'Everything is ready for you,' the curator said.

They all gathered in a circle around the pre-dug hole, their chatter fading into nothing. The curator took them through the standard speech, then began to play a slow, mournful tune at low enough a volume that they could still speak over it without raising their voices.

Palia frowned. The track sounded familiar, or perhaps just the voice... She leaned close to Ferrash. 'Is that...?'

He nodded, a smile settling across his face. 'Think so. When I filled the form in, it asked if he had any favourite music. I didn't pay enough attention for sure, but I knew he liked Austela.'

'We all did.' The woman might still be alive now if she hadn't chosen to help the three of them against the then-Magister. So many friends, dead, and not even ashes to show for it. At least Bek had lived to die a natural death.

Around the circle, those who chose to offered their stories of Bek. Those from the Hegemite transitors were the funniest – and bawdiest. Ferrash even audibly groaned when he found out what Bek had got up to on one important mission. Palia remembered him telling her, long ago, that he never complained because Bek always managed to get some information from his escapades. Perhaps he might have changed his mind if he'd known just what those escapades were.

At last, though, the time came for the planting. The curator passed the silver-green sapling into Ferrash's hands. Palia shivered at a vivid sense memory of Derren's funeral – the same warm-earth smell, the same wind whispering through the trees. Her heart ached for a moment, to know the man he might have become if things hadn't turned out like this, if the Magister had never charted that course, if Palia had never hidden, if... If, if, if. No matter how long she spent trying to ignore that word, it always came back.

Ferrash knelt in the dirt before them and placed Bek's sapling into the hole. Its limbs waved in the air, as sprightly and energetic as Bek had been in life.

If the Protectorate hadn't artificially limited the vatborn's lifespans, Bek would still be with them now. But that was a stupid 'if' to contemplate. He had known how long he had. He had lived that time to the fullest. He had thrived, hopeful, even in the grip of a terrifying regime, and he had survived to see its downfall. Few enough died of old age in such times, no matter how you defined 'old'.

'I'll remember him,' Ferrash said, quiet enough that Palia had to strain to hear him over the wind. 'I'll remember him, and no matter what happens, my memories will go on past my death, and he and I and... and everyone I know... we'll go on existing until the universe ends, or this world crumbles to dust.'

He gave the soil a last firming pat, then stood up and wrapped Palia in a warm embrace. When he pulled back, the tension had drained from his eyes and a genuine grin lit up his face. 'Come on,' he said. 'Let's throw a party that would make Bek jealous. And when it's over' – he glanced up at the shifting canopy of leaves – 'let's get in touch with the Sails. I'm sure the Speaker wants to know where the rest of her memories have gone.'

THE END

ENJOYED THIS BOOK?

This may be the end of the Galaxy of Exiles trilogy, but it's not necessarily the end of the universe. If you want to find out what Bek was getting up to on Hesperex while all this was happening, watch this space. I have plans for him.

If you want to find out what those plans are, you can do so by subscribing to my newsletter (FranklyWrites.com/newsletter). I send out updates once a month, and it's the best place to hear about new releases.

I also maintain a wiki with more information about the Galaxy of Exiles series. If you're interested, go ahead and check it out at www.FranklyWrites.com/lore.

As ever, if you enjoyed this book, I would love it if you left a review on the store where you bought it, or wherever you prefer to review your books. It not only helps other readers find my books, but can also let them know what to expect and judge whether it will be their cup of tea.

ACKNOWLEDGEMENTS

As those who have been following my newsletter will know, this book comes out of a pretty turbulent time in my life. Physical health issues with a generous side-serving of mental health crisis delayed its release past my original estimate. This was incredibly frustrating, of course. I'd written the first draft. I just needed to edit it, then handle all the little bits left over for publication. And it was the last book in the trilogy, dammit! I wanted it out there.

Unfortunately, when you rely on your eyes for editing and it's your eyes that pack up, things get very slow very fast.

I would like to thank everyone who supported me through this time, foremost of whom is of course my husband. He's seen me through my lowest moments on multiple occasions and continues to be great to bounce book ideas off (even if he does keep trying to persuade me to use third-person omniscient). Thanks go to the rest of my family, too, for being sympathetic to my situation and putting up with several fed-up rants.

Of course, it would be terribly remiss of me not to thank you, the reader. If you've got this far, it likely means you've read the rest of the trilogy, and you might have had to wait longer than expected for this instalment. I'm so happy you stuck with me long enough that we could draw this story to a close together, and I hope I can take your imagination on many more adventures to come.

With any luck, at least one of those adventures will involve dinosaurs.

My writing group probably has the impression I never write by now. A side effect of writing my first drafts in a big burst of a few months is that when I write one, I suddenly end up with far too many words to have people read every other week! But they have, as ever, been incredibly helpful with the odd chapter and blurb I've thrown their way, and they're always nice company. Particular thanks go to John and Lee for being my convention buddies at Eastercon. One day I'll shift my social anxiety enough that going solo won't be so intimidating. But for now (and, well, forever), the moral support is very welcome.

Finally, massive thanks to Kate at Nerd Girl Edits, for assessing all three manuscripts in this trilogy, and Rebecca and Andrew at Design for Writers, for doing the covers and formatting to go with them. All three were incredibly understanding this year when I had to delay work due to my eye problems, and all three have done an incredible job throughout the series. As of the time of writing, I haven't seen the cover for Out of Exile yet, but I'm certain it will be an excellent accompaniment to this finale.

ABOUT THE AUTHOR

Katherine Franklin spends far more of her days than is healthy glued to a screen, writing stories when she's not writing code, but she manages to venture outside once in a while as well. She loves science, but didn't love her physics degree enough to do anything about it. Fiction was always her first love.

Katherine lives in Yorkshire with her husband and a horse-sized dog, where she practices martial arts, oil painting and far too many little hobbies to count in her spare time.

You can find her on Twitter and Instagram (@FranklyWrites), Mastodon (@FranklyWrites@wandering.shop), Facebook (@KatherineFranklinAuthor) or through her personal website (www.FranklyWrites.com).

Milton Keynes UK
Ingram Content Group UK Ltd.
UKHW030041261024
450168UK00006B/63